ENDORSEMENTS

Not often, but sometimes a book will haunt you after reading it. **THE PARDON** is that kind of book. Not only is it a great story (once I started it, I couldn't put it down), it is one I will probably think about for the rest of my life. If you just like an incredible story, read **THE PARDON.** You'll love it and the skill with which it is written. But if you want to know what's really important in life, this book is a double gift.

Steve Brown

Key Life — broadcaster, seminary professor, author

A masterful blend of fact, fiction, and faith — of history and a lesson for younger people of what Cuba's "paradise" and the true nature of Communism looks like.

Cal Thomas

Syndicated Columnist

THE PARDON is a real "page-turner," complete with twists and turns in the plot that makes it a rollicking good read! Rodney Powell has written a novel that tells a compelling story … and unashamedly draws its inspiration from the Greatest Story ever shared with mankind.

J.D. Hayworth
Member of Congress, 1995-2007

A powerful and timely lesson from an unfortunate history that we ignore at our peril. Strong writing and deep research yield a fast-paced narrative and a ringing call to recognize and nurture our freedoms, before it's too late.

Stanley K. Ridgley, PhD
Author of BRUTAL MINDS | Drexel University - Prof of Business

A nation fighting for its soul. Our answer — Christ Jesus. This novel offers a window into life in Castro's Cuba. Meanwhile, a dangerous movement is remaking the United States into a Marxist-Socialist society. If they have their way, what will life in America be like? Read THE PARDON, and you will find out!

Neil Frank, Phd
Fmr Dir — Natl Hurricane Ctr & Chief Meteorologist KHOU-TV

So vivid are the Cuban places and persons, that you might mistake Rodney Powell for having been there to witness the tumultuous events of the Castro takeover and tragic aftermath. That Powell is able to use the moment to offer the grace of God in such a poignant tale is a tribute to his mastery of plot and prose.

Dave Courvoisier
Fmr Anchor - KNTV Channel 13 Action News, Las Vegas

Rodney Powell has crafted a grounded tale teeming with history and political intrigue. Interweaved into this character drama are themes of economics, clashing ideologies, envy, strife, and the redemption found through Christ Jesus. THE PARDON is a visceral, poignant read that demands to be shared with others!

Andres Segovia
Host - The Andres Segovia Show, Anaheim CA

THE PARDON

RODNEY POWELL

Published by RealMedia.US | 20831 Rosehill Church Rd, Tomball, TX 77377

Library of Congress Cataloging-in-Publication Data

POWELL, Rodney S.

The Pardon | Rodney POWELL

Summary: "A Soviet officer in Cuba during the Cold War. A crash strands him in America. A former ally turns his worst enemy. Can he survive and find a way home?" — Provided by publisher.

Subjects: Christianity — Cuba — Cold War — Fiction | Christian Fiction | Historical Fiction

Hardback: 979-8-9876233-0-5
Paperback: 979-8-9876233-1-2
eBook: 979-8-9876233-2-9

Printed in the United States of America

Dedicated to My Beloved Bride

Gayla Powell

who has trusted me
because she trusts the Lord first

PROLOGUE

——◆——

April 16th, 1995

CUBA — the largest island in the Caribbean. It's a natural paradise of idyllic beauty that contradicts the island's bedeviled history. Its warm, crystalline waters wash onto some of the most exquisite sun-drenched beaches on the planet. And its temperate climate is merely a part of the tranquil atmosphere that permeates the island, at least serene from the perspective of an outside observer.

From the outside looking in, Cuba portrays an easygoing quality — cigars, salsa, rhythm, and rum — a place almost suspended in time. And who can forget the classic cars that cruise the streets of Havana? Well, there's truth in all of this. But it is also true that Cuba's enchantments are a deceptive veil for the island's more unsavory underbelly.

To set the stage for this story, we should understand how Fidel Castro came to rule Cuba in 1959. An excellent place to begin is with Fulgencio Batista, the villain of pre-Castro Cuba. One in a series of dictators, Batista controlled Cuba twice and came to power through a coup both times.

Batista emerged amidst a power vacuum after the overthrow of a previous strongman, General Gerardo Machado. The collapse of the despotic government headed by Machado in 1933 gave rise to the young and charismatic military sergeant, Batista. He took over and remained in power until 1944 during his first term in charge of Cuba. Corrupt, Batista enriched himself, but his rule was otherwise benign. Two other leaders succeeded Batista, both from a center-left populist party.

Watching from Washington as Cuba's political developments played out, the American government was displeased with the trends they were observing. The Spanish-American War in 1898 had established the United States as the dominant power in the Caribbean region, further bolstered by the completion of the Panama Canal in 1914. As a result, the United States had the strength to intervene in the political affairs of many Caribbean island nations, including Cuba. A variety of corporate lobbyists interested in Cuba's natural resources, along with Batista's own funding, led to his comeback. Batista returned to power for the second time in a 1952 American-backed coup.

The Batista era was a golden age of tourism in Cuba. Americans, Mexicans, and Canadians flocked to the island for play and relaxation at renowned hotels and casinos, where celebrities like Ginger Rogers and Frank Sinatra performed to adoring crowds. Batista ushered in major gambling enterprises and orchestrated the arrangement so that he and his cronies could harvest Cuba's newfound riches. The mafia had an active presence in Havana, and Batista gained much of his wealth by taking bribes and payoffs. He and his inner circle also pocketed a sizable share of all casino revenues and amassed a fortune.

Let's not mince words — the greedy and unscrupulous Batista had lost touch with his people. Outside of Havana, most Cubans experienced an austere existence. They felt little benefit from the increased tourism in their capital's ritzy resorts. Public unrest grew. Then, to make himself appear to be the legitimate president of Cuba in 1954, Batista held a charade election with no lawful rival candidates.

Young firebrand lawyer Fidel Castro sought to force Batista to court to answer for the illegal takeover in 1952, but Castro was thwarted. He decided that the legal processes to take out Batista wouldn't work. So he gathered a group of socialist revolutionaries and armed up.

In 1953, the Castro brothers, Fidel and Raúl, along with a handful of rebels, raided the army barracks at Moncada. The attack failed, and Fidel and Raúl Castro were captured, which put them in the media spotlight and brought them considerable attention. The truth is that Fidel and Raúl were lucky — many revolutionary insurgents were executed on the spot, which generated a swell of negative press for the Batista government. These events and the media coverage surrounding them ignited the first sparks of the Cuban Revolution.

The Castro brothers weren't done yet. In exile, they regrouped and planned another attack. In 1956, they sailed from Veracruz, Mexico, on board the sixty-foot cabin cruiser yacht, *Granma*. Accompanied by a group of eighty fighters, they landed on the southeastern coast of Cuba, where Batista's army was waiting in ambush to kill or capture the majority of the insurgent force.

The Castro brothers and Argentinian guerilla Ernesto "Che" Guevara were among the fewer than twenty fighters who escaped Batista's bloodbath. This small cadre of revolutionaries then encamped in the Sierra Maestra mountains, where they began a slow and relentless guerrilla campaign against the Batista government and its forces.

Castro's guerrilla fighters raided remote army garrisons in the countryside for munitions. They also seized control of land and redistributed it among the peasants. In return, the peasants supported Castro's guerrillas against Batista's army, and some even enlisted in Castro's ranks.

Consequently, the war didn't die down as Batista hoped. Instead, its small size just made it harder to extinguish. The conflict smoldered until it spread like a wildfire among the peasants. This made it almost impossible to distinguish supporters from uninvolved commoners.

Castro's unrestrained ambition manifested in bloodthirsty butchery. Pro-Castro rebels arrested, tortured, and executed Cubans as the insurgency spread. By mid-1959, revolutionary courts had executed hundreds who had ties to the Batista government.

Cuban support for Castro's revolution expanded in the late 1950s, fueled by the Batista regime's escalating corruption, avarice, brutality, and inefficiency. Confronted with armed opposition, Batista's heavy-handed regime turned tyrannical. His notorious secret police and security forces resorted to torture and murder to root out the rebellion. Batista also suspended constitutional rights and imposed heavy censorship controls on what the media reported.

As a result, the United States severed relations with Batista and imposed an embargo that prohibited the acquisition of more American arms. In the end, Batista's regime collapsed under the weight of its own corruption. He commandeered three air force planes around midnight on December 31, 1958, and fled to the Dominican Republic.

Thus, Castro's once small revolutionary movement had grown from a flickering flame to a raging inferno that toppled the Batista government and consumed the entire nation.

Batista's legacy would be the totalitarian communist Castro regime, which supplanted Batista's dictatorial rule with its own version of tyranny. Most Cubans agreed that Batista needed to go—there was little dispute on that point. Even so, the Cuban Revolution had been less the result of Batista's cruelty, corruption, and indifference than of Fidel Castro's charisma, nationalist rhetoric, and ambition. Batista was just in the way of Castro's plans, so he deposed him.

Against the backdrop of Batista's excesses, Fidel ascended to power with pledges that were nothing more than a smokescreen. Plenty of Cubans hailed Fidel and his rebels as they vanquished Batista, but the real revolution occurred as Castro rolled out communism for the Cuban people.

Overnight, everything changed for us. When Fidel Castro took power in Cuba, most of us thought life would be better. With Batista gone, we had high hopes to share profits from tourism, oil production, sugar cane, and cigars. We knew Castro worked with the communists, but most of us knew little about communism. Many struggled to accept the dangerous things they heard about Marxist ideologies. We remained hopeful that such fears were unfounded and that this would not be so damaging for our own families — "hopeful" being the operative word.

So many of us put confidence in Fidel, never assuming he could be associated with something so outrageous. But we were dead wrong. We had replaced one dictator with another. The bravery and sacrifice of so many on Fidel's behalf had been meaningless. Castro had duped our people, convinced them to fight, and used them for his own ends.

Once entrenched in power, he tightened his grip. The government confiscated private property, enacted land takeovers, and nationalized foreign assets in Cuba, which transferred privately held means of production to government control. Castro formed a full police state coupled with a judicial system gone mad. This resulted in political imprisonments and overt killings. Many opponents of Castro just disappeared.

It didn't take long for the promised Cuban dream to turn into a waking nightmare. Instead of helping the people, Castro was obsessed with silencing anyone who dared to portray him as either illegitimate or excessive. *Granma*, the official newspaper of the Communist Party of Cuba, depicted Cuba as an egalitarian utopia run by a government that could do no wrong. Meanwhile, ordinary Cubans lived under fear of pervasive state surveillance that they could feel following their every movement.

The United States had been among the first to recognize the legitimacy of Castro's government following the ousting of Batista, but those ties deteriorated when Castro nationalized parts of the economy, including American oil refineries and sugar mills. Washington's smile soon turned to a frown as they realized this new leader was even worse than the old.

By early 1960, United States President Dwight Eisenhower had already begun to plan concrete measures to remove Castro from power. He held meetings about this matter at the White House with President-elect John F. Kennedy. The plan that emerged was the Bay of Pigs Invasion. Under covert direction by the United States government, the 1961 amphibious landing of CIA-trained Cuban counter-revolutionaries on the southwestern coast of Cuba lasted only three days and was a disastrous rout. Its humiliating failure led to serious shakeups and tensions in international relations among Cuba, the United States, and the Soviet Union. As a result, Fidel Castro gained a formal alliance with the Soviet Union and benefitted from their military and economic aid.

The stage had been set, and the die cast. What came next could have escalated into a nuclear holocaust, for the tensions and conflicts that arose out of the Bay of Pigs Invasion culminated in the Cuban Missile Crisis, also known as the October Crisis of 1962. Leaders of the United States and the Soviet Union faced off in an ominous political and military showdown over the installation of Soviet nuclear missiles on Cuba, a mere ninety miles from the Florida peninsula. On the brink of nuclear war, the confrontation was defused when Soviet leader Nikita Khrushchev agreed to withdraw the Soviet missiles from Cuba, and the United States promised not to invade Cuba.

These events shook the world and formed the backdrop of my life and the story that follows.

In the early summer of 1961, we were first acquainted with Soviet Lt. Col. Vladislav "Vladi" Gavrilov. I say we — at first, he and my brother, Marco Rivera, worked together. Let me explain.

The USSR dispatched a contingent of "advisors" to Havana during those early days of the Castro regime. As a young attorney fresh out of law school, Marco was appointed to collaborate with the Soviets alongside his routine duties as a prosecutor for the Castro government. That's how he met Vladi.

I wouldn't say Marco and Vladi were close friends, but they knew each other as much as any of us Cubans knew the Soviets. Everyone was ambitious and passionate about grand ideologies, and everyone had their self-interests. The Soviets wanted to impose their ideas on Cuban society, while Fidel and Raúl took what they could get from the Kremlin and did whatever they wanted anyway. We were struggling to sort out what we believed, and the harsh lessons of life hit fast and hard.

These two men, Marco and Vladi, differed on many things. But to put it bluntly, what they shared in common — besides their sharp minds fueled by ambition — was that they were both communist God-haters. They wouldn't blush at that statement, either. No, they were proud of that description. They were not ignorant — at least not always.

They were intelligent men. In fact, Marco and Vladi would think themselves brilliant by the world's standards, and I assume most would agree with their self-appraisal. That said, they were met with the truth — and, time and time again, it was rejected. I daresay they consequently paid an enormous price.

Little did any of us foresee how our lives, particularly those of Marco and Vladi, would be braided together over the next three decades. Looking back, I see how the sovereign hand of our Lord directed the course of our lives. This is their story. And part of it is my story, too.

Julio Rivera, MD.
Lakeland, Florida, USA

PART I

A FISH OUT OF WATER

IMPOSING PARADISE

"*Perdóname!*" exclaimed Vladi, using the basic Spanish he'd learned during his brief time on the island. His remark asked Marco to forgive him, but his eyes and the tone of his voice betrayed no apology. It wasn't his thick Russian accent that made him seem disingenuous. It was his feigned sensitivity.

"You really enjoy arguing with me, don't you, Marco? You cannot win this argument, comrade. Not only are you not equal to my intelligence, I am in the right. Plus, you are a little bit ugly and no match for my handsomeness." Vladi could not help but throw that last friendly barb. He knew full well that Marco was playfully provoking him.

Whether it was his intimidating presence or a justifiable terror of his military authority, no one dared challenge Vladi. No one except Marco. Not that their ideologies were completely different — they both believed in the advantages of communism, even if it were not for the same reasons. But Marco enjoyed goading the rugged Soviet Lieutenant Colonel, and he played devil's advocate to question the veracity of his claims.

The small, windowless tavern where a small cohort of Soviet military men and their Cuban liaisons gathered had a musty smell and felt stifling. In the summer of 1961, it was one of the few places where they could get a decent meal. The midday heat and humidity seeped into and around everything, making the prospect of doing anything other than relaxing an arduous task. The muggy air of Havana soaked their clothes, and a persistent sheen of perspiration gave the patrons a faint glisten.

"Then are you saying there is no corruption within a socialist society?" Marco persisted. "I think that to say that capitalism is a corrupt system, but not see the corruption of our own government, belies a certain naïvety. I expect more from an intelligent, worldly soldier like you."

Though Marco smiled as he spoke the last sentence, Vladi was fixated on the word "corruption." He bristled to hear someone say that the ideals he had dedicated his life to were corrupt. *So typical of Comrade Marco.* Vladi tried hard not to roll his eyes and sigh.

Their spirited conversation was fueled by freshly-brewed *cafecitos*. Insanely sweet, creamy, and espresso-like, the Cuban "small coffees" were served in tiny porcelain cups any time of the day or night. The caffeine coursing through their veins helped to enliven the discourse between the two men.

"You compare our system to that of the Americans?" Vladi scoffed. "Come now, that is an insult to everyone here. It is an insult to your own country — a country that provides equal benefits to all citizens and promotes economic equality."

Marco puffed out a laugh. "Equality, yes. You are correct. Everyone here is equally poor," he said as he gestured around the room. "The only opportunity anyone has is the one they are given — the one chosen for them. There are no choices based on talents or passions. But capitalism — that's all about the freedom of choice, the freedom to not live in poverty, is it not? What's so bad about that?"

"Well, not everyone here is poor now are they, Inquisitor?" Vladi gave a pointed retort. "Plenty of people benefit from this so-called 'corrupt' regime, do they not, Comrade Marco?" A smug grin spread across Vladi's face, referring to the fact that Marco and his family were well connected to the Castro government. They didn't suffer the extent of poverty that Marco pretended to know and care so much about.

Marco brushed the snide remarks aside, but Vladi persisted.

"Comrade, I know full well you have seen and enjoy the benefits of association with the Communist Party of Cuba. Not only that, you cannot tell me it is a system not based on fairness."

Vladi had found Marco's statements about the "poor" laughable in their hypocrisy, and he pointed it out to expose Marco to ridicule. But it was more than that. He couldn't find a counter to Marco's point. The best he could do was try to diminish the credibility of the feisty Cuban's adopted position.

"Is this corruption you speak about another of your ridiculous conspiracies, Comrade Marco?" Vladi continued striking at other beliefs he knew the man held close. "Have we not heard enough of your paranoid ideas?" He gave a short laugh and turned to make eye contact with the small crowd of a dozen amused listeners, searching for support that he would not get. Still, he persisted. He failed to discern that when he criticized Marco's positions, he also assaulted the beliefs of others in the room. At that moment, it didn't matter to him.

"I know, of course, you also believe exaggerated tales of the Triángulo del Diablo — the Devil's Triangle." Vladi threw this red herring into the exchange, well aware that superstitious Cubans sensationalized the mysterious disappearances of ships and aircraft in the area and attributed them to something paranormal — their spirits in the sky.

Vladi held these rumors, as well as the people who believed them, in contempt. To him, the simple-minded Cuban people lacked cultural and intellectual sophistication. They had a poor understanding of natural law and were conditioned by their Roman Catholic religion to accept many illogical beliefs that arose from either naïvety or fear. Vladi knew there were logical and scientific explanations for their superstitions but felt that the people were too ignorant and primitive in their thinking to understand the truth.

Pivoting back to Marco's point, he continued, "Likewise, the things you spout about government corruption are misconceptions — sensationalist fairy tales spread by ignorant and rebellious morons."

Determined not to be redirected, Marco didn't even acknowledge Vladi's attempts to knock him off-kilter. He picked up right where he left off: "What incentive does a communist system give the people to work, hmm? When they're not working for themselves, there's no reason to work harder — there's no greater benefit. That is just human nature, my friend."

Vladi huffed, "And so that is to say that capitalism encourages people to work hard, you think? I do not. It encourages greed, Comrade Marco, for people to think of what to do for themselves and not how they can contribute to the greater good of all their country."

"Is not fostering economic growth through creating one's own business something for the greater good? Yes, it's a personal gain, but there are also broader benefits," Marco countered. "A richer country leads to more opportunities for everyone." For all anyone knew, Marco may have been even less a fan of capitalism than Vladi, but he knew how to make it sound idyllic. He folded his arms and leaned back, satisfied with his rebuttal.

"You will never convince me that a system based on greed has broader benefits for anyone," Vladi maintained. "You see that greed at Cuba's doorstep right now, don't you, Comrade Marco? American greed allows them to think they have the right to take what they want at the tip of a nuclear missile. It is the reason I stand here, Comrade Marco. But have no worries, comrade. We are here," he gestured toward his Soviet comrades, "to ensure everything proceeds according to plan. I am confident that is how it will be. You can rest on my word."

"Well, we may disagree about capitalism," Marco answered with a small laugh, "but the one thing we can agree on is how we feel about imperialist American aggression. Let's find something else to disagree on another day. I have important matters to attend to, and I'm sure you do too." And with that, Marco put an end to another one of their regular "spirited conversations." He held out his hand, which Vladi took in his bear-like grip and shook firmly.

As the argumentative type, Marco could be critical to a fault. He had a contrarian streak, and he wasn't one to back down from a fight. He often liked to stake out the most controversial position on a subject of ethics that invited contention.

To be fair, Marco may have had a point in many of those arguments. But for him, it was about more than just being right. He gained satisfaction from ensuring everyone knew that he could exercise his ability to dominate in almost any debate. He thought highly of his skill, which, along with family connections, was what had brought him up through the party ranks to his present status as a budding prosecutor. On days like today, when he felt like his arguments weren't getting anywhere with Vladi, he at least made sure to have the final word before they ended their discussion.

The whole conversation that day seemed to be an academic exercise, but it revealed the degree of underlying commitment each man had to his ideologies and how they applied in the context of this island nation's communist revolution.

Vladi was staunchly dedicated, obligated by honor to hold the party line. Marco felt conflicted over his beliefs, but he didn't want to admit it outright. What he considered an inherent sense of justice caused him to feel personal reservations about the system to which they were both so connected. These ideas weighed more and more on Marco as he witnessed the brutal activities of Castro's pro-communist revolutionaries.

The contention he started with Vladi that day was more than just Marco's usual sport with his idealistic Russian friend — these supposedly theoretical arguments were a test.

A TALE OF TWO MEN

Marco RIVERA

The year 1961 marked the height of executions performed at the hands of Castro's regime. By some estimates, almost four thousand Cubans, some of whom had not even reached adulthood, were summarily slaughtered in extrajudicial assassinations. There were so many executions and disappearances that no one could pinpoint the exact number of lives this terror had extinguished. The official cause of death was often recorded as "heart attack" — a description as misleading as saying they died because they "stopped breathing."

Except for the most well-connected, many Cuban families also endured both political oppression and economic hardships. This compelled many to risk their lives to traverse the Florida strait on makeshift rafts. They braved this danger in hopes of making it to the U.S. coast as refugees.

Marco Rivera, a first-born son, now in his mid-twenties, belonged to one of those well-connected families. Like many young Cubans, he had assimilated into the Communist Party early on, not so much because of ideological affinity but motivated by pragmatism. Belonging to the Communist Party of Cuba brought advantages and opened doors — party loyalty conferred power and privilege.

As fortune would have it, Marco's situation allowed him to study law at the Universidad de La Habana. That's not to suggest he didn't deserve admission into the institution — Marco's distinguished scores in the Jesuit high school he attended reflected his keen intelligence.

Marco was an eager learner. Like generations of Cuban schoolchildren before the revolution, Marco was taught his native colloquial Spanish and the fundamentals of English. He read every book he could get in his hands, although censorship under the new regime limited what was available to him.

The legal profession suited an ambitious and pragmatic young idealist with a strong interest in justice and debate. Because of family connections within the Communist Party of Cuba, Marco was well positioned to have an official post in the future. He aspired to be a judge in Havana, an appointment he believed would suit his abilities.

For the present, Marco served as an Inquisitor for the Ministry of the Interior, a heady office for a know-it-all postgraduate law student. He had just started his new work but already felt at ease with its responsibilities. That would change with time. For now, the assignment required Marco to extract confessions and prosecute political prisoners, sometimes regardless of whether their representations were founded in reality. Marco relished his newfound authority — maybe too much.

Marco had been selected by the Cuban government to serve as a temporary liaison to a Soviet task force that supported their increased political detentions. His assignment was to codify any new policies recommended and approved during meetings with the Soviets. In reality, the exercise was nothing but a formality that lent a veneer of legitimacy to Castro's extralegal machinations. Marco's position also gave him the privilege of accompanying "Che" Guevara to meetings as an aide, a role in which Marco found no small degree of pride.

Despite the title of Inquisitor, in person, Marco failed to garner respect from his Soviet advisors. Because of his brazen assertiveness, the Soviets mocked him as "Marshal Marco," a reference to American sheriffs. Marco merely feigned offense at the derogatory characterization. In actuality, the comparison to a "cowboy" lawman indulged his ego and perhaps added even more swagger to his step. Marco took it as good-humored ridicule. He had a serious countenance and didn't notice that they were mocking him. He had no notion that the Soviets' true opinion of him was even less flattering.

"There goes Comrade Inquisitor, strutting like the hot-headed bantam rooster that he is," would be their inside joke. "I wonder who he will peck to death today?" The Soviets laughed even more when one tucked his arms like chicken wings and ran around pretending to peck furiously at his comrades.

Whatever anyone saw as his faults, Marco had an inquisitive intellect. That, however, could be a double-edged sword. His curiosity and desire to learn sometimes led him to risky new worlds. During law school, he came into possession of a contraband copy of the book *Democracy in America* by Alexis de Tocqueville. Curiosity overcame his conscience and compelled him to taste the forbidden fruit — he read the prohibited manuscript in secret. Given his penchant for debate, Marco expected it would be easy to dismiss its precepts. Instead, de Tocqueville opened Marco's eyes and left him confronted with new moral dilemmas about human nature, faith, and community.

Marco had heard rumors about life in America and struggled to reconcile those anecdotal reports with inconsistencies in the state propaganda that emanated from approved information sources like Cuban radio and *Granma*, the official newspaper of the Communist Party of Cuba. *We are told the United States is a land of injustice, violence, and hate, Marco ruminated. But then we hear reports from others who have been there, that America has pleasures of its own and is a land of opportunity. Well, which is it?*

Many young devotees of Cuba's communist revolution looked up to the USSR as the archetype to which they aspired. They romanticized the USSR as a dream come true — a tangible product of real social upheaval, one that reshaped the fundamental rules of society and power. But the reality was that Cuba had its own flavor of communism distinct from the Soviet Union — some referred to it as "Castroism." Indeed, Havana took money from Moscow, loads of it, but Fidel seldom took orders from the Kremlin. In the end, Cuba was run according to the personal ideologies of Fidel Castro and his family.

Marco would never admit it, but he struggled to sort out his core beliefs. He absorbed knowledge like a sponge, but his ability to formulate many disparate ideas into a coherent worldview eluded him. Meanwhile, he found himself caught up in the currents of his environment.

Vladi GAVRILOV

Ten years older than Marco, Lt. Col. Vladislav "Vladi" Gavrilov was born in Kavkaz in southern Russia, on the coastal plain between the Caucasus Mountains that bordered Georgia and the Caspian Sea. He was born on October 29, 1929 — the same infamous date the Yankees called "Black Tuesday," when America's insatiable Wall Street crashed, and the Great Depression unfolded.

Vladi exemplified the ideal Soviet child, a paragon of political conformity from the start. He accepted the traditions of Vladimir Lenin from early childhood and continued them throughout his formative years. Leading up to admission to the Communist Party of the Soviet Union, Vladi had been a member of the Little Octobrists, next the Young Pioneers, and then the *Komsomol*, the All-Union Leninist Young Communist League.

He embodied the ideal Communist youth and lived correctly — none of the smoking, drinking, religion, or sexual promiscuity that characterized the Soviet view of Western entertainment culture. Throughout his youth, he was taught that the party was the soul of the people, and Vladi worked hard to ensure he did his duty for all party organizations. Always the first to volunteer for the menial tasks allotted to youth who aspired to party membership, he believed this to be the only path to success or even comfort in the Soviet Union.

Prepared and eager to enter the Red Army as soon as possible, Vladi's rise through the ranks was meteoric. At thirty-one years of age in 1961, Vladi was prodigiously young to have achieved the rank of a Lieutenant Colonel, a field grade officer in the USSR.

Vladi tackled whatever situation the military threw at him with confidence — his fearless determination was unrivaled. His superiors took note and made use of him. "Someday, he will be a great hero for the *rodina*," his commanding officers would say, always confident he would make the motherland proud.

To this point, much of Vladi's service had been in the elite *Spetsiálnogo Naznachéniya*, known also as SPETSNAZ. He completed extensive training as a reconnaissance officer, already a veteran of far-reaching assignments and rich combat experience. He participated in clandestine operations in the Indochina War that supported the emergence of North Vietnam. And although undocumented operations were thought to have "never happened" in Lithuania, they did suppress guerilla factions of Balkan nationalists who were enemies of the rodina.

During Vladi's military career, SPETSNAZ evolved into the Special Purpose forces. Soviet civilians knew little about their country's special forces. They operated under the main intelligence directorate established by KGB head, Yuri Andropov. The choice of the command staff received special consideration in the formation of Special Purpose units. Their tasks were often direct orders assigned by commanders of the districts.

Vladi was deployed to Cuba in May of 1961, within weeks of the failed U.S. invasion at Playa Girón, on the east bank of the Bay of Pigs. This debacle was already the talk of the barracks when Vladi arrived. The running jokes mocked the Yankees and their imperialist ambitions, including satirical wordplay about "imperialist American pigs slaughtered in Bay of Pigs" and references to the "Bay of Yankee Pigs."

The Soviets could already recite the account: American political leaders had sought to bring in CIA-trained forces to subvert and overthrow the Castro regime. Their attempted landing along the Bay of Pigs' jagged coral shoreline was thwarted by the forewarned Cuban Army, positioned to guard the shore when they arrived. As a covert operation, the mission was executed without the air support needed to ensure its success. Furthermore, the surrounding jungle thicket and the vast crocodile-infested mangrove swamps of Zapata proved impenetrable.

In the end, it was all for naught, as Castro had intelligence about the invasion in advance, and his forces were ready. This was upheld as a humiliating rout for

U.S. forces at the hands of the Cuban Army. Moreover, America's failed military operation had caused Castro to lurch into the waiting arms of Kremlin allies.

Vladi was a true believer in the mission to support the Castro-led government in this tropical outpost. He was confident that a Soviet presence was essential to protect the families of both Cuba and the Soviet Union as a deterrent against an unconstrained aggressor — namely, the formerly-allied United States, which now seemed to be on the brink of pulling the nuclear trigger.

Vladi's assignment in Cuba was simple and brutal: coordinate the development of facilities that managed various "undesirable elements" of Cuban society — conscientious objectors, religious proselytizers, or others deemed political enemies of the revolution. This included a variety of programs, from re-education in forced labor concentration camps and incarceration in filthy rat-infested political prisons, to El Paredón, or "the wall" — to face execution by a firing squad.

As commander of the Soviet task force advising the Cuban government on procedures to process and manage political detainees, Vladi and his staff participated in high-level meetings with Ernesto "Che" Guevara. Che was a young Argentinian-born doctor and a co-revolutionary with the Castro brothers. He had been granted Cuban citizenship, which enabled him to hold a government position bearing legal authority. Che directed courts-martial and had oversight responsibility for prisons.

Vladi was always a first choice for any assignment — affable, polite, and winsome — yet fearless, almost to a fault. He had the nerves of a Siberian bear and never cowered in the face of adversity. Ambitious and idealistic, Vladi had been indoctrinated in Marxist ideology and taught that capitalism fostered greed, degeneracy, and exploitation, among other evils. He also considered himself a scientific atheist and, therefore, a pragmatic thinker. His actions were justified because they were in the service of logic, which is what he reminded himself if ever a shadow of doubt crept in.

Vladi was also prideful and self-righteous without being aware of it. As a rigid humanist who followed rules and laws to the letter, he judged himself virtuous by his own standards.

As for the Cubans? He would not say so outright, but Vladi viewed himself and his Soviet comrades as superior to the Cuban people. That included the officials he advised. Vladi had no doubts that he was the beneficiary of unparalleled training and the product of a culture far nobler and more refined than that of Cuba.

Clean-cut, rugged, and handsome, his presence was hard to ignore when he walked into a room. With Vladi's dark features, he would not stand out against the Cuban population were it not for his height, which was accentuated by his lean-muscled swimmer's physique. Swimming and deep sea fishing were the two favorite aspects of his assignment in Cuba. In fact, despite infrequent opportunities to swim in Russia's cold climate, Vladi was a natural swimmer.

Despite all the attractions and beauty of Cuba, Vladi missed his wife, Irina. When they first met, he had shown little interest in young Irina. Vladi felt he was more mature than her in the beginning, but with time he grew to appreciate her charm. Together, they had a wonderful young family — three girls and, upon his deployment, Irina was expecting again. This one he just hoped would be a boy. *Finally, a son!* he thought.

Sadly, Vladi would not be there when his progeny entered the world, as the requirements of an up-and-coming military officer demanded gut-wrenching sacrifices. Now, as a devoted husband and father, Vladi more than anything wanted to be back with his family.

A DANGEROUS DISTRACTION

In mid-October of 1961, Vladi received his orders to return to Russia, along with a long-awaited leave of absence. He hadn't been able to be home for the birth of his and Irina's fourth child, but now Vladi would soon meet his newborn and spend time with his young family. He was consumed with wondering whether he now had another daughter or a son, as he'd long wanted. The thought made him happy every time.

When Vladi had deployed, Irina had been early in her pregnancy. All communications with home from Cuba had been cut off due to the nature of the Soviet mission. He never received word about Irina's delivery or the gender of their newborn. The answer would have to wait until his family met him at the train station on his return home to Kavkaz.

By the time Vladi's departure date rolled around, tensions had escalated between Cuba and the United States. This gave Vladi mixed emotions about leaving. Despite his complete dedication to his assigned responsibilities, the post had been both physically and mentally exhausting. Vladi awoke every morning with a sticky sheen of sweat and went to bed on his creaky military cot in exactly the same condition. The tropical heat had not relented, and he was more than ready for a break from military life after six months on near-constant high alert.

Most of his comrades back in the USSR would have coveted the opportunity to spend six months or more on a warm, exotic island. True, Vladi enjoyed his tropical assignment for the most part, and he'd have some stories to tell back home. Swimming in the aquamarine blue waters of the Caribbean, feeling the sultry humid air, acquiring a taste for Latin foods, and even the sport of verbal sparring with Marco had made his time there tolerable, in fact — dare he say — somewhat enjoyable. But at heart, Vladi was a family man and eager to be with those he loved. The six months away from his family had felt like six years. He also longed to be back in the familiar environs of his home country.

Being on an island in the Caribbean meant braving occasional, but severe, tropical storms. It was late in the season, and Cuba had been spared the onslaught of Hurricane Carla in the Gulf of Mexico just one month earlier. But now, a tropical depression south of Jamaica had developed into Tropical Storm Gerda. Just as Vladi was preparing to leave, it bore down on Cuba as heavily as homesickness did on his heart.

Vladi weighed his options for returning home to Russia: *Do I take a long two-week voyage aboard a dirty supply ship or catch a military hop on an airplane? The airplane will be faster. I do not want to delay returning home more than necessary.* Even by air, it was a long stretch across the Atlantic to the port city of Conakry, Guinea, along the west coast of the African continent.

The Tupolev Tu-114 was a four-engine turboprop airliner, the fastest aircraft of its class capable of transatlantic flight. It had a wing that was swept like the Americans' Boeing 707. The Tu-114 could fly as high and as long and nearly as fast as its jet counterparts. A long-range variation, the Tu-114D, was used by the Soviet military. The number of passengers and cargo volume were reduced in favor of additional fuel tanks. It played a vital logistical role in transporting Soviet personnel around the globe.

The long flight on a military hop wasn't luxury travel. But it was undeniably more expedient than crossing the Atlantic by ship. Even with the stopover in

Guinea, a flight would shorten Vladi's trip from weeks to days. *I will get to spend my thirty-second birthday with my family,* he thought, smiling to himself. His presence for anyone's birthday, his own included, was reason enough for celebration.

Besides the volatile weather ahead, a transatlantic flight came with its own perils. The Tu-114 was a reliable aircraft. Vladi only hoped the maintenance crews were conscientious in attending to their duties. There were stories of mechanics with vodka hangovers who failed to tighten bolts on critical components — the sort of thing that would be impossible to rectify mid-flight over the Atlantic Ocean.

Eager to head home, Vladi hoped this weather system wouldn't delay his departure. Anxiety robbed him of sleep. On the cusp of this long-awaited return, any delay felt like an eternity. He kept checking his pocket watch, completely unaware of the frequency with which he did so.

The pocket watch was a vintage timepiece emblazoned with the state emblem of the Soviet Union. It was one of the few possessions Vladi carried as a memento of his connection to home. When Vladi had reached the age of sixteen, his father had given it to him as a gift, and he had treasured it ever since. He sometimes lay awake during the hot, sleepless Cuban nights and thought about the moment he would give the keepsake to his own potential son as a coming-of-age gift. If it turned out he had a son, of course. Otherwise, perhaps he could give it to his —

"Gavrilov! *Vstavat pora!*"

His thoughts were snapped off by his commanding officer's shout. Other outgoing personnel rolled out of their cots. Tuesday morning, 0403 hours.

We are leaving now? It is an unexpected change, Vladi thought as he dressed and pulled together his belongings to ship out. *It must be the safest time to travel to get ahead of the storm.* Sooner is better than later, he supposed, although it wasn't the Wednesday 1750 departure time he had planned.

Hoisting his gear on his shoulder, Vladi reminded himself this was the fastest way to travel. Despite the improbable perils of a long flight across the vast Atlantic Ocean, soon he'd be back home. He focused on that joyful return.

Come now, there is always weather in the Caribbean, and the airplanes are fine, Vladi reassured himself. *The storm is not that bad yet. Plus, the pilot can fly over or around the worst of it,* Vladi reasoned. *There will be turbulence, but it is to be expected. We will fly out of the Devil's Triangle before this storm hits hard.* Vladi enjoyed his own final sarcastic dig on Cuban lore and gave it a short laugh. *A Soviet officer entertaining the insensible fables of these naïve islanders? Ha!*

Eight long hours passed — it was now well beyond noon. *Why did they need to call us before daybreak? Hurry up and wait — it is the standard operating procedure for the Soviet military,* Vladi sighed. He could have spent days camped out at an airport if he had been waiting for anything other than a flight home. Now, the afternoon heat exacerbated Vladi's impatience. He noted other passing aircraft. Observed birds flying over. Watched clouds soaring past. More hours crept by.

The airport operations officer on duty when they arrived earlier had already left for the day. His replacement stopped by and notified them they would board in about a half hour. But a half hour came and went, and then another, and another.

Since when does thirty minutes mean three hours? Vladi brooded. *Always in Cuba.*

"They are still preparing the aircraft," the airport operations officer informed the waiting passengers.

Why? What is taking so long? Vladi kept wondering. *Talk about a creeping delay — none of us are getting younger! Perhaps I should have taken the slow boat home instead,* he mused.

At long last, the afternoon airport operations officer showed up in the late afternoon to escort them to the aircraft.

I've been looking forward to this all day, Vladi stewed. Well, it turned out it was not quite go time — they were only moved out from the shade and left to wait again on the hot tarmac.

Vladi picked and tossed shells and pebbles on the tarmac while he sat on his duffel bag and looked at the tall Tu-114 aircraft standing on its spindly landing gear. Nearby, the flight engineer awaited weather updates while Vladi watched him methodically work through preflight checks.

It was the flight engineer's responsibility to inspect the aircraft before every flight, including control surfaces, engines, and propellers. The condition of the counter-rotating propellers was crucial, as they would often get nicked. A close inspection was always important because the runways and taxiways of airports in Soviet territories were notoriously unimproved surfaces. Gravel, dirt, and sand debris were often ingested into the engine intakes and hit by the props.

As the props were counter-rotating, the prop in the back was often obscured by the forward prop. A flight engineer was supposed to pull the forward prop through to get a better view of the prop behind. If a nick was discovered, it needed to be filed smooth to avoid stress cracks.

Vladi was observant and interested in what this crew member was doing. He seized the moment to amble over to the flight engineer and engage him in conversation.

"*Privet*, comrade."

The flight engineer looked at Vladi and nodded in acknowledgment. Without saying a word, he continued his duties.

"Have you heard these Cubans' strange tales of the so-called Devil's Triangle?" asked Vladi, making sure to accentuate a tone of derision and mockery. "What do you think of such stories? Entire ships and aircraft are rumored to have disappeared under mysterious circumstances. Such foolishness, right?"

Vladi had often overheard superstitious Cubans sensationalize these disappearances by attributing them to paranormal activity. He viewed this with the same disdain he held for the local fables of dolphins protecting a lone swimmer from marauding, blood-thirsty sharks. "Ridiculous and childish," he would always mutter as he shook his head.

Trying to impress his fellow officer, Vladi hadn't even listened for the flight engineer to reply. Instead, he offered his own logical explanations for the Devil's Triangle legend, something for which he had waited to find the right person to tell. He launched into his rationale for the unusual phenomenon, oblivious to this crew member's knowledge and experience of flying in the area.

"Like always, science has an explanation, not superstitious folklore. I am sure you know that there are seasons of unstable weather conditions in the Caribbean region due to tropical storm systems that pop up. During these storms, cold air high in the atmosphere gets pushed down in violent bursts and hits the ocean like a sort of bomb."

Vladi animated his impassioned explanation with expressive hand movements.

"The force explodes outward and creates a giant squall line of wind and water. Powerful forces like that would capsize any boat or shred an airplane at its seams, hurling it into the sea. That is all — you think? Any expert would agree, no?"

The flight engineer never looked up from performing his preflight check. Vladi sensed he may not be listening closely enough and continued even more emphatically, as though doing so would convince the man of his hypothesis.

"Once a seagoing vessel is disabled, Gulf Stream currents would carry it away from the reported location. Searchers looking for the vessel lost at sea would have difficulties due to the vast search area. Although the disappearance may have seemed mysterious, that does not make it paranormal or unexplainable." In Vladi's ever-pragmatic mind, these dubious legends arose from a combination of unverified details and flawed logic.

With a walk-around inspection of the forward prop areas, the flight engineer was satisfied that there were no nicks or cracks on any of the eight propellers. He wasn't acclimated to the Caribbean heat, and he was eager to get through this perfunctory ritual and back into the shade. Without bothering to get up on a ladder, he neglected to notice the stress crack on the back propeller of the #3 engine. He was just trying to get through his routine preflight checks, and tune Vladi out so he could focus.

He discerned that Vladi was talking for his own benefit. "There are many misconceptions," he stated simply. He didn't specify whether the false assumptions were those of which Vladi opined or the Cuban stories. Despite his intentional ambiguity, the flight engineer continued, "We are here to ensure that everything happens in an orderly manner. I am confident that is how it will be. You can rest on my assurance, comrade."

STORM CLOUDS RISING

At last, sixty souls boarded the aircraft: fifty-one passengers and nine crew members, including the cockpit and inflight crew. Vladi was among the first to ascend the twenty-five steps of the airstairs and board the plane. In true Soviet military form, the interior was spartan gray, with not a ruble wasted on human comfort. Vladi took his choice seat toward the aft of the fuselage, just behind an exit door on the port side. That row provided a few extra inches of precious space for his long legs. Moreover, Vladi was confident that in the rare event of an emergency, he could man the exit to assist in evacuating the aircraft.

The Tu-114 was a large and heavy aircraft requiring an airfield with plenty of runway. This was especially true for Havana, where the warm air had low pressure density. Loaded with passengers, cargo, and fuel at its maximum gross weight, the captain set maximum power for takeoff. The four powerful NK-12 engines surged with a thunderous rumble, and the forward momentum gently pushed everyone back in their seats. The nose of the aircraft rose, and Vladi felt its smooth, steady lift. Up front, the crew breathed a sigh of relief when the Tu-114 lifted off after using almost all of the runway.

"Cutting it close there, Captain," the first officer remarked with a nervous laugh.

Vladi rechecked his watch. *Wheels up 1613.* He made a mental note, then tucked the timepiece away in the front pocket of his trousers. Vladi prepared to settle in for a while — their next stop would be the west coast of Africa.

As they climbed out, they could see they were coming closer than they anticipated to the storms they had observed off in the distance while taxiing. Vladi and his fellow passengers swayed in their seats as winds aloft buffeted the plane. It was to be expected as they ascended into the teeth of Tropical Storm Gerda, he reassured himself as he closed his eyes and thought through the logistics of the flight to occupy his mind. They would take a northeast course into the night and arc to the east to avoid hostile United States airspace before making their way to the African continent.

Once the plane climbed to ten thousand feet toward its cruising altitude of twenty-six thousand feet, Vladi felt himself relax just a little. He adjusted himself in his seat to find a comfortable position and prepared for the long flight ahead.

That's when the trouble began.

The lightning and sounds of thunder intensified as they knew they were getting too close to the line of thunderstorms. Stress on the airframe was the captain's gravest concern, as the storm cells could cause severe damage to the aircraft. Anticipating severe turbulence, the captain made an announcement that grabbed Vladi's attention.

"Comrades, this is the captain. We will be passing through an area near some intense storm activity for a while. We are encountering some turbulence that is heavier than usual. All inflight crew and passengers must take their seats and strap in immediately. Please remain seated until we notify otherwise."

Before long, they were engulfed in the dark, swirling clouds of the tropical storm. Vladi felt his stomach drop as gusts emanating from the tempest whipped the aircraft violently. Seatbelts and teeth rattled. Carry-on luggage stowed overhead on flimsy open netted shelves fell onto the passengers and into the aisle. Sudden short drops in altitude caused by changes in air pressure and downdrafts made everything that was not completely secured bounce around the cabin.

Lightning flashed around them with blinding brilliance as the forces of nature tossed the aircraft about as if it were a toy miles above the ground. *I do not think even the pilots expected it to be this bad.* Vladi gripped his seat, partly to keep from being flung out of it and partly out of raw fear, although he would never admit to the latter.

Every passing minute felt like an eternity. "How long will this go on?" A nearby passenger echoed his exact sentiments.

"This is a fast aircraft. We may be out soon. I am sure our pilots do not want to stay in this storm any more than we do," Vladi reassured the man, as much as he was reassuring himself.

About an hour out from Havana, Vladi overheard the crew radio their coordinates, which put them somewhere near latitude 27° N.

Assuming the navigator's bearings are accurate, we have already flown beyond Grand Bahama Island. Our pilots sound calm over the radio. We should not worry until they do, Vladi concluded as he looked out the round window, almost desperate to see the cloud-obscured island. After passing over this last sliver of land, they would soon be arcing out over the vast, open Atlantic Ocean.

As the captain navigated his way between storm cells, another brilliant flash burst outside the windows, accompanied by an ear-splitting crack. This was no ordinary thunder, and that flash was not a harmless streak through the air.

"It was just a lightning strike," the first officer remarked.

The captain did not disagree.

"Wait . . . no, it is not," the flight engineer contested. "There is erratic fluctuation in the RPM on the #3 engine."

The NK-12 powerplant, a nearly fifteen-thousand-horsepower monster, caused the whole aircraft to shudder hard and with increasing intensity. An aft propeller blade had broken off the #3 engine. The combination of centrifugal force and the aircraft's dropping and rising in the storm turbulence added stress to a hairline fracture at the root of the blade, causing the blade to break free. The blade struck the aircraft, making a hole two feet in circumference in the lower mid-cabin fuselage in the forward cargo hold beneath the passengers.

Without warning, the aircraft began to depressurize, and a thin mist filled the cabin. This was accompanied by a sudden temperature drop. The loss of cabin pressure happened so rapidly that Vladi could only gasp as the situation turned critical. His head snapped toward the window, and his hands flew up to protect his popping ears. Sensing air rushing from his lungs, he immediately reached for an oxygen mask, knowing he and the other passengers would lose consciousness in seconds without supplemental oxygen.

"Need . . . shut down the #3 engine," came the flight engineer's recommendation.

"Ahh! No," the captain objected. "We are too heavy for such severe downdrafts from the storms. Losing thrust in an overweight aircraft puts us at risk."

Instead, the captain pulled the #3 engine power level to idle, hoping that would reduce the severe vibration. It seemed to work. The vibration subsided. The cockpit crew sank back in relief. But their respite wasn't to last.

As the damage threw the #3 engine out of balance, the same engine blew and catapulted more fragments into the fuselage. Other parts of the disintegrating engine hit the #4 engine, causing a loss of thrust and an instant fire indication bell. Orange flames shot out from under the wing. Realizing both engines were completely lost, the crew immediately exercised their memory items to shut down the #3 and #4 engines. The fuel shutoff valve was actuated with the fire suppression sequence. To their relief, they were able to get the fire out on the #4 engine.

As the crew ran the remainder of the shutdown checklists, the autopilot disconnected. With the #1 and #2 engines still at maximum continuous power, the aircraft immediately began to roll to the right. The captain struggled to regain control of the aircraft by feeding all the left rudder he had.

"The #2 system lights are on . . . lost hydraulics . . . must be leaking fluid somehow," the flight engineer called out to the rest of the crew.

The Tu-114 could maintain flight for some time with the failure of two engines, but the captain knew they didn't have enough hydraulic pressure to control the plane's roll with the #1 and #2 engines set at high power. He reduced power so that he could roll the wings level again.

The crew understood that the best they could do with two engines throttled back and the loss of a primary hydraulic system was to make a controlled descent and ditch at sea.

"All inflight crew and passengers prepare for impact!" came the rushed announcement over the PA.

The words sounded surreal to Vladi's ears. *We can't be . . .*

The captain had learned by heart that the safest way to ditch an aircraft was to reduce to the slowest possible speed, at a minimum descent rate, and maintain wings level to the horizon. He had trained many times for this emergency scenario.

Adrenaline coursed through Vladi's veins. His breathing quickened along with his pulse. *Remember your training. Do not panic. Your head must remain clear.* These rote phrases entered his thoughts effortlessly. He tightened his seatbelt and tried to keep steady as he donned a dusty military-issue life vest. His strong hands were tense as he cinched it around himself. *Perhaps I am being overcautious. Military comrades would say it is "womanly" fear,* he supposed. But this wasn't the time to worry about who would notice his justified sense of uneasiness.

He took a deep breath to steady his nerves and gave himself an internal pep talk. *You are a Soviet officer cut from courage itself!* Then he occupied his mind by studying the aircraft's interior configuration. He examined the orientation of the release mechanism of the adjacent door and estimated the number of paces to alternative exits.

Being a military man at heart, Vladi turned his attention to the other passengers present and checked to make sure they were all properly secured. As he took inventory of the men around him, he studied their faces.

Then the cabin went dark.

In the pitch black, the deep roar of the remaining engines filled Vladi's head with noise and his heart with dread.

Up in the cockpit, the first officer read off the descent rate and altitude to the captain as they descended through one thousand feet above sea level. The captain carefully reduced speed as they got lower. Hoping to reduce their descent rate as they dropped below one hundred feet, he began to pull back on the yoke. Airspeed started to bleed off. To their advantage, the turboprop engines could handle a low-speed approach not possible in the more modern jet aircraft. He reduced to 180 knots . . . 170 knots . . . 160 knots — their descent rate also began to slow. The captain strained at the control wheel, which felt unresponsive. Suddenly, the aircraft rolled right again as they lost sufficient hydraulic power to counter the thrust on the #1 and #2 engines.

It was too late to correct.

The Tu-114 was wing down. The right wing contacted the water below and cartwheeled the aircraft, breaking it apart. The nose slammed into the water, rupturing the sealed cockpit and ripping it open like a can of sardines, instantly killing the captain, first officer, radio operator, and navigator. The flight engineer, seated toward the back of the cockpit, was ejected by the force of the impact.

The aft one-third of the fuselage, with the empennage, separated from the aircraft as the remaining mid-section with fuel-laden wings and long-range auxiliary tanks exploded into a fireball.

Like they were in the belly of a tempest, Vladi could feel uncontrollable vertigo. The last thing he remembered was feeling extremely nauseated. A chill overtook his body, and a contrasting sensation of intense heat crept up his neck just before everything went black.

BLOOD IN THE WATER

Vladi's hearing returned first. The instant he became conscious of his surroundings, he detected sounds around him. The tail of the aircraft floated. In pitch blackness, he could hear and feel the cabin rapidly filling with seawater. He immediately took action. The military had drilled water evacuations with him blindfolded until it came as second nature for Vladi.

Vladi plunged into the bone-chilling ocean water and felt his lungs seizing up. Every Soviet military man knew the dangers of cold-water shock. The human body's instantaneous natural response to sudden immersion in frigid water could be fatal. The shock could trigger an unprepared person to involuntarily gasp for air. Had he been submerged at that instant, he might have inhaled seawater and the leaking jet fuel instead. These first moments were critical.

Without panicking, he exited the sinking aircraft in mere seconds. He emerged from the water with a deep, rasping heave.

Waves washed over him relentlessly, and the taste of saltwater filled his mouth and nostrils and stung his eyes. Dark clouds blotted out the stars. Vladi quickly realized he would have to spend the night in the ocean, buoyed only by the life preserver he wore. As if the terror of nighttime adrift on the open, black ocean were not enough, temperatures on the October sea were chilling.

Survival would be a race against hypothermia. Being in excellent physical shape increased his odds of survival, but Vladi knew even he could reach his limits if left in the water too long.

The storm thundered like a colossal monster in the pitch-black darkness, fragmented only by flashes of lightning. The wind howled across the ocean. Most pieces of the wreckage that didn't sink right away to unfathomable depths beneath the swells were soon dispersed by ferocious waves. He scanned the rolling water-line for any other survivors. He thought he saw a head rise above the undulating swells now and then, but all he could hear was the howling of the wind.

Vladi sighted one larger piece of the aircraft debris that had remained afloat. He labored to swim over to it and dragged his torso on top to allow his vital organs to stay out of the water. And there he clung for life.

Maybe an hour had passed since the crash — it was hard to judge time — when Vladi had brief contact with another crew member. It was the flight engineer he had spoken with before they departed Havana. He was splayed out like a scarecrow, his back at an unnatural angle. Vladi guessed that the man suffered a broken spine. Vladi estimated they were within thirty to sixty feet of one another, although constant bobbing in the storm swell made it difficult to gauge distance.

Is this man still living? Vladi wondered as the waves rocked him back and forth. Vladi couldn't determine if he was making voluntary movements or just being moved like a rag doll afloat on the water.

"*Vi zhivi?* Comrade! Can you hear me?" Vladi shouted with all he could muster. No reply. "Comrade, are you still with me?" He choked on the salt in his throat, and it caused his voice to crack.

The pilot answered this time. "Comrade," he called to Vladi weakly, Comrade, I cannot move."

Oro, what can I do? Vladi wondered. He attempted in vain to paddle his way toward the injured pilot, unsure what he might do even if he could reach him.

Vladi found solace in the sight of another person, though in his condition, he didn't know how long the pilot could endure. *I am sorry, comrade.* Vladi pitied the helpless man. *I cannot help you. I hope you sleep in peace.*

The ocean became calmer as the long hours of endless night wore on. Vladi's consciousness drifted in and out. He was beginning to fade again when — thump! Vladi's eyes flew open. Something had bumped against his leg. He looked into the inky water, but in the dark, it was impossible to see. Soon enough though, beneath flashes of lightning, Vladi observed the ominous black fins of predators breaching the water.

"Oh no!" Vladi's hoarse voice scarcely rose above a whisper.

To his horror, he watched a surreal scene unfold. The sharks had detected blood from the pilot's wounds and encircled the helpless crew member. Like sea wolves on the hunt, they stalked the injured man. Unable to swim, the pilot made an easy target.

"Comrade! Comrade!" Vladi could only muster a squeak. "Sharks! Sharks! Swim away!" It would be pointless anyway, and he knew it. His words were futile, and any splashing around would encourage the sharks to strike faster. But he felt helpless, and all he could do in his despair was try to shout a warning.

Like an echo from a horrible nightmare, Vladi heard the pilot make a muffled cry for help. "*Pomogite!*" His faint plea was stifled.

Then, as if the water had become electrified, Vladi could hear thrashing, shrieks of pain and terror interspersed with gruesome gurgles. A red cloud of blood blossomed around the doomed crew member as sharks devoured the man in a merciless demonic frenzy. Whirling and snapping like mad dogs, hideous flat snouts came out of the water and closed on the pilot's floating carcass, biting off body parts with terrible snuffling grunts.

I think I am going to be sick, Vladi retched.

He had no time to be sick, for he also faced mortal danger. The sharks circled, and the bloody water attracted more to the area. Even in the dark, Vladi knew those hyenas of the deep were there. They bumped against him some-times, whether by accident or to get a feel for their next meal he did not know. He tried as much as he could to remain calm, to float without disturbing the water in hopes that the sharks would ignore him.

The Cubans believed many things that Vladi did not, such as stories of swim-mers being surrounded and defended by a pod of dolphins in shark-infested wa-ters. Vladi had never been convinced of its truth. As some would say, there were no atheists in foxholes, nor doubters in shark waters. Given his circumstances, Vladi decided to reserve judgment when he spotted a set of curved fins breach the surface.

These distinctive fins dipped and circled with force. Fins, friendly and hos-tile, appeared and disappeared beneath the water's surface with tails thrashing about. The sporadic illumination of far-off lightning flashes allowed him to catch glimpses of this watery drama unfolding. After several minutes the com-motion stopped, and as far as Vladi could tell in the inky darkness, the fins had all gone back below the surface.

All returned to calm, save for the wind. Vladi let his cheek rest on the piece of wreckage with a small thump — he was sapped. To his amazement and relief, he couldn't avoid an overwhelming feeling that he'd somehow witnessed the kind of remarkable experience the Cuban peasants talked about.

Could those curved fins have been dolphins? Could the sharks have been fended off by — ? Hmm. He scoffed at the thought, but it lingered.

As far as he could tell, he was alone again in the dark ocean, even if he wasn't aware of the truth. The God whom Vladi insisted did not exist was merciful that night, and Vladi passed the rest of it undisturbed by anything that lurked in the deep.

The long-awaited daybreak came as a tremendous relief. Vladi turned to look in each direction and searched for land. As the sun peeked over the horizon, he could make out a coastline to the west. Despite his exhaustion, the sight brought him hope and revitalized his energy. He began a paced swim in that direction.

At times he stopped to rest and get some full breaths. The fatigue that came with just staying alert while afloat was catching up with Vladi. As he scanned the horizon around him, his burning eyes watched ships pass far in the distance. They were mere specks in an ocean that went on forever. Though he could see them, he was invisible to distant vessels. He conserved his strength and wasted no energy calling out or waving his arms.

His energy waned, but he tried at least to move in the direction of land. However, no matter how much effort he made to swim, Vladi was at the mercy of the currents that carried him along. Powerless to make any measurable headway toward land, Vladi felt discouragement set in.

How much longer can I continue in the open water? Certainly not another night. What are the chances anyone will ever find me? It could be hours, or days, or . . . The thought was too unbearable to ponder.

Daytime brought different problems. Vladi remained exposed in the ocean for hours, bobbing like a cork, with nowhere to find relief from the scorching sun as it reached its zenith. His thirst had become almost unbearable. He felt a thousand reflections on the surface of the water magnified onto his exposed face, intensifying the burn. Beyond exhausted now, he entered into a kind of delirium, drifting in a state between consciousness and blackness.

If only those dolphins would arrive now and we would swim to shore, he mused.

Between the sun, salt, and thirst, Vladi knew that dehydration was depleting his energies. His mind began to meander. Most troubling among a jumble of disjointed thoughts was the unsettling realization that he would never see his wife, Irina, nor their children again. *I will never hold my newborn — never see him — or her. Is it a son or a daughter? Did anyone ever tell me? I can't remember now. Irina? Irina? Iri...*

Vladi snapped back, having spotted something moving in the distance. *Is it a boat? I think it is a boat —* but he couldn't trust his fatigued mind. As it drew closer to his location, he held up his hand and waved. Vladi hoped it wasn't a mirage — this was worth a shot. As it got closer, he could tell for sure that it was a boat.

The *Reel Secrets*, a forty-foot Chris Craft Sport Fisherman with an enclosed bridge, slowed its twin V8 550 horsepower engines and changed course in Vladi's direction. On his way back to port from a deep sea fishing excursion, a local recreational boater had spotted him. Vladi stopped wondering whether it was a hallucination or reality as the boat drew nearer. He was being rescued — he hoped.

In a moment of lucid thought, Vladi's mind rehearsed scenarios of how the encounter might unfold. He didn't know his location and which nation's mariners might trawl these waters.

Who is on this boat? I cannot be sure if this will be a rescue or capture. I could be a political prisoner — maybe never be found.

Vladi knew that if he were turned over to U.S. officials, he would endure interrogation at the hands of the CIA. He imagined that this would involve the use of torture, a matter in which he was an expert down to the most brutal details.

His position in the Soviet military would be of value to the United States. Gary Powers, an American U-2 pilot, had been captured by the Soviet Union a little over a year prior. Powers was tried and convicted of espionage. Vladi knew about the spectacle the Soviet Union had made out of the spy they were holding. The capture of a Lieutenant Colonel of the USSR involved in Cuban operations would result in him being used as a political pawn in the dangerous game that was playing out at that moment.

If I survive, how could I face the Soviet leadership after the embarrassment of allowing myself to be taken captive? They might not trust that I did not compromise security under interrogation. At the least, my career in the military is finished. Then what would they do to me? Worse, what fate could befall my family? Oh, Irina.

The boat was getting closer. He needed to think fast, but he struggled to think at all. If Vladi said even a word, his undisguisable accent would reveal his country of origin, even if he offered no other information. However, he had a more immediate problem — his military uniform. He considered wriggling out of his ripped and waterlogged military dress shirt. That turned out to be more complicated than he imagined because he would first need to take off his life preserver. He had the vest halfway off when he gave an exhausted gasp.

There was another unsolvable predicament. *Achhh, my tattoo!* Ever loyal to his communist ideals, Vladi had a hammer-and-sickle tattooed over his heart. If he jettisoned the uniform, it would reveal his allegiances in the starkest fashion. Either way, his Soviet identity would be almost impossible to conceal. He wriggled back into the vest. *Forget it.*

It was too late to evade the rescue. Besides, he had nowhere else to go. He couldn't outswim the boat, and he couldn't stay in the water not knowing what other vessels might or might not pick him up. It was either certain death or this boat. He chose the boat.

Vladi, ever the warrior, determined it was necessary to be taken. He would await the opportunity to escape or neutralize his rescue party should they be hostile.

With how many men will I need to contend? He squinted into the sun and tried to see on board. *I do not even have the strength to fight anyone. I could not even defend myself against an old woman right now.*

He had been trained to kill if necessary to survive, but now Vladi was so weak that he could barely get aboard the boat, even with assistance.

Impossible. The word echoed in his weary mind. *Impossible. Dolphins had not saved him. That would be like a miracle. Any intelligent man would realize it is impossible — ne mozhet bit. Now this boat, out of nowhere, far away from land? Ne mozhet bit.* All these thoughts floated through his delirious mind. The rapid approach of the engines jolted him back into the moment, then he drifted into unconsciousness. So much for fighting anyone off.

A thick sun-kissed hand reached toward the water and pulled the ailing soldier onto the deck. Vladi pitched forward and sprawled over on his side like a beached whale, his lips cracked and his eyes rolling back in his head.

The skipper shook his head. The crow's feet around his kindly eyes crinkled as he swung his weathered face to look back out to where the man had come from. This man was in grave trouble — on the verge of death. The captain hardly noticed the uniform and didn't think much about it. He saw a dying man in need of help. He swung the boat around and gunned the engines, cutting through the choppy waters and heading home.

The skipper knew these waters as well as anyone. Only ten minutes before, he'd been heading back to shore without anything to show from this outing. The sea was rough, and fishing was off because of the storm. He hadn't anticipated that the biggest catch on this outing would be pulling in a man overboard.

THE ONE THAT GOT AWAY

"Well, look at what the captain dragged in," Dan laughed, making a play on a common saying. The English colloquialism went over Vladi's head. Despite his inability to understand, Vladi was in no frame of mind for any lighthearted conversation, even if the man doing the talking was saving his life. He gave the skipper a hard stare.

Dan didn't seem to be bothered by it in the least. His kind, merry eyes hinted at mischief. The deep tan of his skin and wrinkled forehead were telltale signs that the man had spent long hours under the sun, and Vladi wondered if the skipper's brain might have also gotten a little baked as a result.

Dan, poised in a captain-y stance, continued in a genial tone, "Hey, buddy, what happened to ya? How'd ya get out here?"

Besides the fact that Vladi understood almost no English, he was determined to remain silent. He didn't want to give away any information that might identify him or compromise his beloved country. At the same time, he was so exhausted that he could barely keep his eyes open.

Typically an easy-going character, Dan tried not to show alarm, but Vladi's appearance troubled him to the core. It was clear there was something awry with the guy he'd just fished out of the open water.

"Heeey," he said in a feigned tone of suspicion. The tall skipper bent to-wards Vladi as he dried out on the deck. "You're not one of those pilots who got lost in the Triangle, are you?" he queried as he squinted at Vladi. "You didn't travel through time or another dimension, did ya?" Dan laughed again, his mouth open wide. He was close to Vladi's face, a bit too close, which only made the Russian more uneasy. Vladi could see Dan's teeth were in desperate need of dental work — an off-putting sight that caused him to cringe and recoil.

Despite Dan's jovial demeanor, he was no stranger to being in a troubled spot. He could sense the man's distress, and it wasn't just from having been afloat at sea. Dan's empathetic nature refused to compound Vladi's unspoken problems, whatever they may have been. He maintained his pleasant demeanor and decided not to press the subject, at least for the moment. "I'll let ya catch your breath, friend," he said as he gave Vladi an easy tap on his shoulder and returned to the bridge, leaving Vladi alone on the deck.

Vladi was exhausted and suffering from the extremes of exposure. He'd endured everything from the cold night in the ocean to the sun's inescapable midday heat. He didn't even know how long he'd been in the water. Normally collected, his emotional state bounced between hysteria and despair as delusions from dehydration and near-hypothermia wracked his battered mind. He was hungry – no, he was starved – and thirstier than he'd ever been in his life. The skipper seemed like an alright fellow — he might give him some water if he knew how to ask. But Vladi's sun-chapped lips didn't have the strength to open and call out. Even if he did, he resisted using the few English words he knew to request help.

As if he could read Vladi's mind, Dan popped out from the bridge again. The knit cap covering his head seemed at odds with the short sleeves of his shirt and the heat of the sun.

"Had to go in and make sure this big old gal stays her course," Dan laughed as he smacked the side of his boat with a good-natured slap. He could see that Vladi was unwell, and his tone softened. By the looks of the man's salt-parched lips, he was dehydrated.

With weariness, Vladi tried to watch Dan as he ducked his head and disappeared back into the cabin. Dan's cheery whistle faded as he wandered farther back into the cabin and then grew louder as he again popped out of the door. He stretched out his hand and offered Vladi a salt-corroded metal cup filled with cool water.

"Here, friend, you need this water," he said in a soft voice. "I wish I could offer you something to eat, but me and my girl here were just taking a quick spin around the pond, as my mates in the U.K. would say."

Vladi at least recognized the word "water," and sitting up, he grabbed the cup. He sucked up the refreshment like a sponge. When finished, he stared into the cup with longing, desperately searching for more drops of life-restoring fresh water.

Dan noticed and poured Vladi more water from the jug he had brought out with him. It was all the potable water he had on board, but Dan could see this man needed it far more than he did.

Grateful, Vladi drank the second cupful with more deliberation and kept his eyes fixed on the unusual skipper.

"The storm doubtless stirred up some tasty finnys," Dan said wistfully, using a slang term for fish that he'd made up. "But the brine is still pretty angry from Gerda, and it's not the kinda risky venture I want to be takin' today." Dan pressed on despite the lack of response. "I love fishing though, don't you?" he prodded with a grand smile.

Though his strange guest hadn't uttered a word since Dan had pulled him in, Dan believed that the man understood what he said. "It keeps me sane in this crazy world," he grinned, amused at his own secret joke.

Vladi, though, still had no idea what the skipper was talking about. Even so, Dan's easy tone had a calming effect on him, lulling Vladi in his exhausted state.

Dan had only provisioned for a short solo excursion, so he had no food stocks onboard to offer his unexpected and starved passenger. As they tracked along the coast near the Loxahatchee River, Dan spotted something afloat in the water. With a long-handle landing net used for retrieving game fish, Dan bent over the edge and scooped up an orange. Taking it out, he placed the fruit in Vladi's hand. It was early in the season for oranges. Perhaps it had been blown down from the storm. And since no citrus trees grew along the beach, it must have floated down the chilly spring waters of the Loxahatchee.

"Guess it's your lucky day after all," he told Vladi with a wry smile. "Someone up there must be watching over you." It was a small gesture, all Dan could offer him. But in his moment of need, to Vladi, this was everything.

Vladi clawed at the peel with desperate fingers and devoured it ravenously. This orange was unlike any fruit Vladi had ever tasted before. Of course, there were seasonal tangerines back in Kavkaz, and he'd enjoyed Cuban oranges, but they were pale and had a sharp flavor by comparison. The meat of this fruit was a vibrant orange color, more sweet than tart. Vladi would have inspected it longer had he not been in such a desperate state of hunger. Juices dripping to his chin, it tasted as fresh as if it had just left the tree, and its nourishment provided Vladi with the sustenance he so desperately needed at that moment.

As the sweet fruit revived his senses, Vladi took a closer look at the surrounding landscape. *Where is this? This skipper is perhaps an American. Is it Florida?*

Beyond Miami and the Keys, Vladi had given little attention to Florida's geography. Though he'd never seen Florida up close except in black and white photographs, he rightly deduced that this was the place, but he couldn't ask the skipper for confirmation. If anyone discovered that he was a Soviet officer amid the tensions of the developing Caribbean Crisis, he could be arrested as a possible spy.

If Americans treat political prisoners as the Soviets do, my family will never see me again. As he tried to fend off worrisome thoughts, the acidic fruit churned in his empty stomach.

On the outside, Dan seemed happy and unassuming. He sang joyously off-key as if he didn't have a single care in the world. Far from naïve, Dan had seen his share of hard realities. Perhaps because of his own difficult past, he believed that everyone deserved the benefit of the doubt. Dan sensed something unusual about Vladi, and it wasn't just the tattered uniform, which he couldn't quite place. He cast a discreet glance at the man he'd picked up while keeping one eye on his course through the water.

Vladi remained silent, but he didn't appear to be a threat. And if he were, Dan had a fishing harpoon with a light patina of rust that he dubbed "Captain Hook." It stood ready and waiting for just such an occasion.

What possible explanation might there be for this man to be floating in the Atlantic Ocean? Dan wondered. *I wish he would say something, anything.* His passenger refused to utter a word — did he even know his own identity? Had a boating accident caused amnesia or traumatic muteness? Had he fled Cuba as a political dissident? Both were plausible, but another thought kicked around in the back of his mind.

Dan's superstitious side couldn't help but wonder, *Is this one of those weird Devil's Triangle incidents?* As cracked as some people thought it was, he'd seen too many inexplicable things on the water. There was something strange and unusual about that area. And to prove the point, one of those strange things was at present eating an orange and sun drying on the back of his boat.

Vladi's mind also turned as he tried to figure out just what this skipper was all about. The fishing gear on deck and the few English words he recognized told him that the man was a fisherman, yet the *Reel Secrets* was quite luxurious for a fishing vessel. *It is not like any fishing boat there is in Cuba.*

Aside from its powerful gasoline engines, the boat's hull was constructed of solid Philippine mahogany, and its side and stern decks were made of Burma teak, both expensive species of wood. Maybe this was an example of the obscene American capitalism he had heard so much about.

Do all Americans have such extravagant boats? he wondered. Yet Vladi's keen senses told him there was more to the jolly skipper than met the eye. Something in the way the man carried himself and interacted with him hinted that there was more to his story.

Dan noticed how Vladi stared hard at him and tried to keep the mood light by pointing out some native species that floated and grazed near the shore. "Look, lad! Mermaids," Dan gestured and chuckled. "Just joshin'. Those are manatees — 'bout the gentlest creatures God put on this earth. Ever seen one before?"

Vladi didn't give it a glance.

Undeterred, Dan continued with a story. "One time, coming back here after a day of fishing, I lost my balance and fell off the boat. In a matter of seconds, I found myself surrounded by these fat sea cows — sorta scary. In the water, they're bigger than they seem. I didn't want to make no sudden movements and spook 'em, ya know. So I stayed real still. You'll never guess what happened. They came up to me and ever so gently nibbled my hands and feet, then they kissed me on the head! I thought to myself, if the ol' mariners could see me now," he snickered, "they'd be mighty jealous of all them mermaid kisses!"

Still, Vladi showed no emotion, not even the hint of a smile on his rugged sunburned face. Dan had concerns about the fellow. His mermaid story always, without fail, at least garnered a smile. But Vladi's continued stoicism had Dan bewildered. The charming fisherman's upbeat attitude and wit usually won people over right away.

Of course, Dan was accustomed to having a rapt audience of fishermen at the marina. He could command the room and get big laughs from his hilarious stories. Other fishermen never cared that most of his stories were made-up and exaggerated. They loved to hear his endless tales of crazy escapades and amusing one-liners. His wacky character and comical eccentricities had earned him the good-humored nickname "Daffy Dan." But from this man — nothing, not even the hint of a smile.

Dan could tell that the fellow had some unspoken troubles. He didn't want to add to the man's misery by alerting authorities that he had picked up a mysterious stranger who appeared out of nowhere. Instead, he radioed ahead to the marina to arrange help for his passenger discreetly. Dan was concerned that this man needed medical attention right away no matter how he came to be bobbing around in the ocean.

Vladi heard Captain Dan make the call. He couldn't understand the skipper's words. He surmised by the tone of the conversation that Dan was arranging some sort of assistance, but he couldn't be sure what kind. *He is contacting the authorities, no? Perhaps he needs help for me or for himself. I cannot know. I do not like this either way.*

Vladi again started to feel uneasy. *When we arrive at shore, what options do I have to avoid capture?* Even if the skipper had refrained from making intrusive inquiries, medical personnel certainly would. *I need to take immediate action. I do not even want to contend with the possibility of being taken prisoner.*

Dan noticed Vladi eyeing the speargun that hung just inside the cabin door. The "hip loader" was three feet long, compact for a speargun, but its dense teak wood handle and stainless steel mechanism that held multiple loaded bands made it far more lethal than it looked. Whether a testy shark or the rare specter of pirates that might cross his path, Dan was ready for the fight. But now, with the possibility of a threat right outside his cabin door, it would be a matter of which man could reach the weapon first.

Vladi calculated the risks in his sun-drenched mind. *There is no question I could take this man in hand-to-hand combat if I were not so weak. Even if he reached the speargun first, I could take it from him. But right now, it is risky. He does look somewhat strong. I do not have confidence that I would prevail.*

Vladi saw the skipper look at him as he spoke over the radio, but the second Dan's eyes flicked away to check the mouth of the port, Vladi's intuition took over. *NOW!*

He lunged for the speargun, but to his surprise, Dan's reflexes were faster. In an instant, Dan yanked the ship's wheel and the boat listed to starboard. The sharp, unexpected move sent Vladi off his feet and sprawling back onto the deck.

The men locked eyes in a tense moment, and Dan detected a hint of fear in Vladi's. Mindful that the man was distressed and irrational, Dan had given him some leeway — a warning instead of a steel hook in his torso.

Vladi, however, saw that Dan was unfazed, and it unnerved him. The good-natured skipper had sent him an unspoken message, and his tacit warning worked to discourage Vladi from trying that again.

The skipper whistled a tune and carried on as if nothing had happened, much to Vladi's surprise. He was sure that his aggressive attempt would have been met with an equally violent response. But the easy-going Dan had responded in a way that was stern, yet maybe the kindest defense possible. He could not believe that he wasn't staring at the sharp point of the fishing spear at that moment.

Dan reasoned it was possible that his unusual passenger had mistaken his benevolent call to shore as some kind of danger to himself. *What would make him reach for that speargun? Is he afraid? Or maybe his noodle is just garbled from being baked in the sun and he's not in his right mind. How can I let him know that I'm just trying to help him? I don't want this fellow to hurt either of us if he's actin' crazy like that.*

With almost exaggerated caution, Dan approached the man with hands raised chest high and knelt on one knee in front of him. Dan made sure to remain just beyond the reach of the man's long arms. He attempted to use the tone of his voice and hand gestures to convey that he was not a threat, but a friend who would help him.

"I'm here to help. Help. Friend. I'm a friend, okay?" he said, pointing to himself. Vladi continued to stare, but Dan detected that some of his alarm fading.

Maybe something got through to him. Dan relaxed a bit. *I'd still like to know what's goin' through his head.*

Although he no longer considered violence against the skipper, Vladi remained aware of the ominous possibilities ahead of him, not the least of which were interrogation and torture.

Perhaps this skipper is trustworthy, but who knows about other Americans who will be waiting for us? he reasoned. *I must not fall into the clutches of the U.S. government.*

With deliberate slowness, Dan rose to his feet and walked backward to the controls. Being so close to the marina, he had no choice but to turn his eyes to where his boat was heading. Vladi once again took the opportunity to act.

Pulling himself onto his feet, Vladi sprung from the *Reel Secrets*' bow and dove into the warm water. He resurfaced a good distance from the stern. He could see Dan scurry around to the bow then attempt to steer back to the area near where Vladi went overboard. After repeatedly circling the area, Dan scratched his head, perplexed. There was no trace of his mystery passenger. He had vanished almost as suddenly as he had appeared.

Sure hope that poor fella will be alright. Dan lifted his cap and scratched his head, then chuckled. Ever the fisherman, he couldn't wait to tell a story of the "big one" that had gotten away. *Nobody will believe it,* he thought.

HOPE OF SAFETY

Swimming underwater, Vladi remained near the rocks to avoid vessels approaching the marina. He came up for a big gulp of air, then submerged out of Dan's sight. The darkened waters allowed him to continue undetected as he made his way between two boats docked in a low-traffic area of the marina.

He needed somewhere to rest and regain his strength without attracting attention. He climbed onto one of the docked boats, slipped beneath a protective canvas cover, and collapsed, overwhelmed with exhaustion. In almost no time, he drifted into unconsciousness.

Vladi awoke to a pitch-black sky. His damp clothes clung to him in the humid night. It took a moment for his groggy mind to get oriented. *Where do I go from here?* he asked himself. *I am maybe safe for a short time, but perhaps men are looking for me now if the skipper has reported that he found me.*

He may have escaped for now, but he was nowhere near safe. Stranded in the territory of his nation's arch nemesis, who would come looking for him? Presumably, no one knew he was there, except for the skipper. No one even knew he was still alive. And the worst part was, given the current political situation, there didn't appear to be any way home. He had to be the one to save himself.

Under the cover of darkness, Vladi slipped out of the boat and back into the water. He waded through the thick tangle of red mangroves along the shoreline, which further exhausted his already spent energy reserves. Each careful step through the intertwined branches felt like one of the twelve labors of Hercules. Vladi emerged after considerable time and effort working past the spider-like mangroves, pausing for a moment to breathe. He took stock of his surroundings and saw the lights of a town to the west. He oriented himself in that direction and began to hike inland from the coast.

Except for a few miles, the area was sparsely populated. Small rodents that ran across the road in crisscross patterns were the sole signs of nocturnal activity. Well, Vladi did catch sight of a nutria here and there — giant invasive water rats that propagated in the pine glades of the southern coastlands. Canals paralleled the corridor on either side for miles like stagnant weed-strangled ditches against a backdrop of slash pines and cabbage palms. Bald cypress trees with Spanish moss draped from their limbs stood ominously like ghostly sentinels foretelling doom to those who entered. Whatever life existed within this marshy area — snapping turtles, gars, and water moccasins — remained mostly hidden beneath the black water's surface.

Vladi found it easier to remain undiscovered in this almost uninhabited area. Yet he didn't stay as concealed as he had hoped, because the swampy sawgrass posed its own unique threat — alligators.

In the light of a bright rising moon, Vladi noticed the reflective glow of silent eyes that lurked in the tall water grasses protruding from marshy areas. The blackish gator resembled a living submarine that put its eyes out above the water to watch while suspending its treacherous mass beneath the surface to feel the vibrations of its prey.

Vladi was nearly on top of one gator before he spotted it. At first, it looked like an algae-covered log bobbing in the stale water. Then it moved. Up close, the dinosaur-like predator turned out to be considerably larger than Vladi had ever imagined. Its slight movement stirred the stench of a muddy swamp — a fishlike odor. When the reptile opened its long mouth, Vladi was near enough to catch its breath that smelled of death — like rotten meat.

The bull gator made his ominous presence known. He oscillated between a deep guttural hiss and a low throaty rumble to intimidate and establish his territory. It exhibited no fear of anything!

Without warning, the colossal gator emerged, its massive tail thrashing as if it were a tree trunk. It would have been powerful enough to break a man's leg with ease.

This exhibition of dominance from the gator guarding its territory worked well. It sent Vladi into a scramble for the safety of the road. The waterways alongside the road were so filled with alligators that he could have been walking across them this whole time.

I would rather take my chances on the asphalt.

As the hours passed, Vladi became ever more tired — bone-tired. There was no respite from the non-stop buzzing and biting of ravenous swarms of salt marsh mosquitoes. The relentless assault of a million blood-hungry bugs prevented him from stopping anywhere to rest. Despite his fatigue, Vladi kept moving inland, scouting for water, food, and an out-of-the-way place to rest. He trudged miles through the night, moving toward higher ground.

Vladi's effort paid off. Farther inland he found more oranges, and he devoured several with great satisfaction. Peering through the darkness, he saw that they were coming from the vast citrus groves that now lined the sides of the road for miles. A handful of the fruit was not much, but enough to revive his strength and enable him to continue moving.

As daylight cast a shadow from behind, Vladi encountered a patrol of turkey buzzards overhead, looking for the cadavers of mammals that the alligators had not found first.

Some miles later, he made first contact with two-legged creatures — a group of men walked along the road in his direction. Out of instinctive caution, Vladi leaped into the grove of orange trees and hid behind one of the more substantial trunks. Vladi was too big to hide, and a passerby might have been amused at his silly attempt to conceal himself.

The men were laborers on their way to work. They proceeded on foot, unaware of or at least unconcerned about his presence. But as they came closer, he noticed something striking about them. *They are Cuban!* The Cuban dialect of their Spanish was unmistakable.

For the first time in days, Vladi felt a sense of brightness. *Ukh ty! Here, in America, there are people that I can approach.*

He felt some security in the fact that Cuban politics were aligned with those of the Soviet Union. He surmised there was minimal risk of being handed over to authorities even if they suspected something mysterious or unusual about his presence. He assumed these would be his political and ideological brethren.

Despite the hardships that had befallen the Cuban people, it always amazed Vladi how amiable and obliging most Cubans he met were. Even if he judged them to be lacking in overall sophistication and believed that many of their traditions were backward, he couldn't deny that they were gracious and generous.

They were gregarious people — Cubans would talk to just about anyone and seemed to spend much of their days in the company of others, for their lives were tightly interwoven with one another. Walking along any avenue back in Havana, Vladi often noticed people out and about, socializing, playing baseball and dominoes, eating, and enjoying themselves. They sat outside their homes and talked with neighbors, engaging with one another and the community around them. They valued relationships with family and friends above almost everything else.

What's more, they were warm to foreigners. Until now, Vladi had taken this for granted, but in these circumstances it mattered and might save his life. He began to reconsider his preconceptions.

Among the diaspora of Cuban refugees in the United States were households already in exile from the regime of Batista, the dictator who preceded Castro. Others were among the politically aware minority who perceived the red tone of Castro's revolution and got out early. They understood right away that the classless society Fidel had promised was a mirage. It was more of a pretext for Castro's inner circle to plunder land and resources than an actual recalibration of society.

The Cuban refugees had risked everything — their own lives and their families — for the hope of a better life in America. Thousands fled to Florida and erected shacks or set up housing in whatever location they could find. The Cubans had an innate and incomparable ability to survive and thrive under hardship.

It was perhaps the Cubans' most remarkable asset — their own indomitable adaptability and bottomless capacity to improvise. Some had left areas of Cuba where they dealt with unpaved roads, where people depended on illegal cable hookups for electric power from utility lines, and where running water was an occasional luxury. They just had a different outlook from other, more conventional societies. With ever-present adversity, survival became a process of adjustment. They made do. And Vladi admired that.

Perhaps residing on an island occasionally battered by hurricanes compelled the Cubans to develop this aspect of their character. After all, nothing averted a hurricane or prevented the destruction it caused. Their only option was to disentangle and pick up what they could salvage, then figure out how to reuse the pieces.

Vladi walked back out to the road. He held up one hand and called out to the men. *"Amigos!"*

The men whipped around to see who called. Their faces betrayed a hint of bewilderment as Vladi approached them.

These men knew almost everyone in the community of Cuban refugees, but they didn't recognize this person. He could communicate with them, speaking basic Spanish, albeit with a thick accent. The Cubans spoke little English anyway, so at least they shared a common language.

At first, they were wary of this man in tattered clothes and wondered if he might be a Soviet plant attempting to infiltrate their American settlements. They overcame their initial reticence after seeing that he clearly needed aid.

These Cuban refugees and others Vladi later encountered were warm-hearted, friendly, and free of preconceived notions or opinions. The men recognized Vladi was in trouble and waved for him to follow along, pointing the way down a road toward a small white ranch house.

A kind woman greeted them at the door, broom in hand. After a short explanation from the men who brought him, she gave Vladi an empathetic smile as she ushered him inside.

Alongside their own families, they provided him with food and shelter in one of their homes. They did so without hesitation, even though they were of humble means themselves. The rundown house had a front yard of shell and dirt patches that sprouted crabgrass here and there. Even though their small home was already crowded, it beat the alternative of being outside with the rain, mosquitoes, and alligators.

Vladi was grateful, happy to accept their assistance for a brief time until he could figure out his next move.

FAMILY MATTERS

Vladi ended up living with the Cubans for longer than expected, and he soon fell into their way of life. Strong familial ties were a hallmark of the Cuban refugees. It was not uncommon to find multiple generations living together. Two and sometimes three generations of Cuban families stuffed themselves into tiny living spaces. Elderly parents were cared for by their children, and small children enjoyed the wisdom, joy, and love of their grandparents all in one home.

Vladi often found himself thinking about his own children as he watched the Cuban fathers play with their sons. Although Vladi's military responsibilities demanded that he be deployed away from home for long tours of duty, he always tried to make up for it whenever he could be home.

Even though Vladi hated being away from them, returning home was the best feeling in the world. When he walked through the door, his girls would run to him, arms wide, and shout, "Papa! Papa!" With his huge arms, Vladi would wrap them all in one big bear hug as Irina looked on with a contented smile. He hated that he would ever have to let them go and leave again at some point.

Vladi spent his days home playing with the children. Outside in the Russian winter, they built snow forts. The girls would chase him through the snow until he allowed them to catch him, laughing and jumping on top of him. When their little noses were red and runny from the cold, they would go inside and warm up with hot cider and warm baths. He would put them to bed, and even though their little eyes were sleepy from their fun in the bitter cold, they would insist that Papa read them a story.

Vladi obliged with pleasure, although often they would be asleep before he could finish. He would kiss their little heads and linger a moment to look at their sweet cherubic forms as they slept. He wished he could hold onto them like this forever.

Before he had children, Vladi had never realized how much they would become his world and consume his thoughts, even when he was thousands of miles away from them. Over these long periods apart, he imagined them as they grew older. He wondered what they were doing, what they looked like, and if they even remembered their Papa or if he was just a hazy figment that lingered in the back of their minds. Another part of Vladi disliked whenever these memories bubbled up. They led to an unyielding ache in his heart that he had no way of soothing.

Watching how these Cuban families interacted and cared for each other every day evoked sentimental memories for Vladi in another respect as well. They reminded him of the family of his own childhood. A first-born, Vladi had a close relationship with his younger brother and sister.

Vladi and his brother Erik shared a special bond growing up. They were almost the same age, with Vladi being only two years older. The younger boy was full of mischief, which could be fun but often got him into trouble — trouble Vladi was always there to try to help bail him out of.

Both boys had a natural love of the open air and were avid outdoorsmen. They enjoyed close proximity to the Sulla-Chubutla River and a small nearby lake where they could cast a line and catch whatever was biting. Erik was a superb angler and could be found fishing during every spare moment. He had such innate skill at fishing that it seemed like he could coax the fish onto a bare hook! Even Vladi could not help but be impressed at the abilities of his younger brother. It made the days spent fishing together happy times, now both fond and poignant memories for Vladi.

The boys were equally skilled hunters. Their wild hog hunts were the most thrilling experience of their youth. The Russian boars were tremendous in size, some more than four hundred pounds! The wild boars were alert, wary, and dangerous up close, which gave the hunt an added element of risk and challenge that they relished.

Their hog hunting adventures got started almost by accident — before then, they had never given thought to hunting the tusked beasts. It happened one season as autumn gave way to winter, the year Vladi turned seventeen. Erik went out hunting for deer. An unexpected encounter with a wild boar grunting and snuffling its way along the trail caught Erik off guard. The brute charged Erik. With a split second to react, he leveled his weapon and fired. He knocked it over, but Erik was startled to see it remained very much alive. The massive boar's tough hide was like armor plating, and the gunshot only enraged the beast. Erik's adrenaline surged as the boar shook off the hit and stood back on its feet to resume the charge, angrier and fiercer than ever. Erik's eyes widened, and his chest tightened as his legs leaped into a sprint. The wound had slowed the boar just enough to afford Erik time to shinny up a tree to safety until it eventually moved along.

When he met back up with his brother, Erik described the encounter to Vladi with fantastic excitement. "You would not believe. This boar was practically invincible. Brother, it was this huge!" Erik exclaimed. Eyes wide with charged passion, he stretched his hands demonstrating its enormous size. "I shot it! I know I did. I knocked it over, but it had the armor of a tank. It charged even after I shot it." He made charging motions with his hands to add effect. "It hardly slowed down from the bullet. I thought it was dead when it toppled, but then it got back on its feet and came again! This time, mad as ever!"

Vladi tipped his head, intrigued and amused. He coaxed his feverishly excited kid brother to tell him more. "How did it look?"

"So angry — snorting and making a horrible grunting-squealing noise. Dark bristled hair that stood up on its back."

To tease him, Vladi imitated his wide-eyed expression and gestured for him to continue.

"Those things move fast, even through thick brush. I ran, but it was bearing down on me! I hurried to load another round, but the rifle jammed. I clambered up a tree to get away from that monster!" Erik continued his expressive gestures to emphasize the danger, demonstrating with his hands and legs exactly what he had done.

"I have to say, it smelled awful – maybe the worst thing my nose has ever smelled in my life. It was so strong I could smell it up in the tree. That repulsive musky odor, it still assaults my nostrils." Erik wrinkled his nose in disgust and feigned gagging.

Vladi smiled as he listened to his brother's wild story and observed the accompanying hand motions. It was so typical of Erik. Vladi couldn't hide his skepticism though. He loved his little brother, but he'd grown up with the kid and knew that Erik's stories had a tendency to stretch credulity. It could be difficult sometimes to discern when to believe all or part of his fanciful accounts.

"You have such wild tales, brother," Vladi said, lifting his brow and trying unsuccessfully to conceal a smirk. "If true, why have I never encountered a monster pig in all my years of hunting?"

Erik lifted his shoulder with an emphatic shrug. He had no idea why they had never come across the wild hogs before. But he insisted that he told the full truth. "If you do not believe, then we will go back hunting together next time, and you will see for yourself," he suggested.

True to his offer, Erik insisted that Vladi come along for a hunt the next time he went out. "We will search for what you say are nonexistent 'grunters,' but you will see I have not just made up wild stories."

Vladi sighed. *He has gone further than usual with this farce.* But he agreed nonetheless. "Let us go," he told Erik with exasperation. "Show me this mysterious tusked beast laden with armor."

Despite his sardonic tone, the woods were beckoning, and Vladi was eager to accompany Erik into the forest. At least they would spend time together, and that was always enjoyable regardless of what the activity may be. Plus, *if Erik's wild story proves to be true, Vladi reasoned, it is a good idea to be with my little brother to ensure that no "grunters" harm him.*

Both superb marksmen, the young men were outfitted with 7.62 Russian caliber hunting rifles with standard five-round magazines. Vladi had a 1938 model SVT-40 semi-automatic, fitted with a small but functional scope. Erik carried an old Mosin-Nagant, a bolt action rifle that soldiers and snipers alike relied on through the Great Patriotic War. He was a crack shot using a sling, even with just iron sights.

As they had done many times before, they crossed over the crystal clear Sulla-Chubutla River. Sunlight danced like an explosion of diamonds on the bubbling cold waters that tumbled beneath the bridge. They picked their way through the weathered grass of the meadow beyond, already sighting tracks left by various creatures that had emerged from the forest in the early morning.

The young men climbed the ridge, their breath trailing behind them like a cloud. With light steps, they eased into the alpine forest, woodlands they knew as well as men knew their own backyards. These were their woods — they'd grown up in them. All around were the familiar sights and fragrances of nature they had known their whole lives. It felt like home.

Before long, the boys were deep into the forest. They moved almost without sound despite the deep mulch of pine needles and autumn leaves on the ground.

Once situated in their favorite blind, the place Erik had chosen, their bodies stilled and faded into the surrounding scenery. This was the location they always knew would be most likely to yield fresh meat for the kitchen table — a spot in the woods they knew as well as their places at that old rough-hewn oaken table.

A chilly breeze stirred from the north. Silent and unmoving, they enjoyed a deliciously peaceful moment. But after hours in the cold woods, no hogs were seen. The temperature continued to plunge, and the boys' cold-numbed faces glowed pink. Again, Vladi teased Erik for making up the story of a "ghost boar."

"Come now, did you just make up all this to impress your older brother?" Vladi asked him half-jokingly. He laughed before Erik could answer and playfully told him, "There is no need to make up stories to impress me — as the older brother, I will always be superior, no matter what." He ruffled his brother's fuzzy head in mock roughness, but Erik was not amused, nor was he dissuaded. He needed more than ever to prove that he was telling the truth. Yet, this day would not be that day.

Another week passed. Erik suggested they try again. Vladi rolled his eyes, realizing his brother would not give up on this. Once more, he agreed to go out. Unbeknownst to him, Erik had baited a spot in the woods.

Days earlier, Erik had dug a hole and filled it with a mash of grain and vodka, allowing it time to ferment. It was like he'd rung the dinner bell for wild hogs. Sure enough, when they reached the baited spot, the area had been trampled and rooted up. It looked as though a tractor had plowed through the undergrowth. Clearly, something had been there and partaken of the odorous bait. Erik was confident that whatever it was would be tempted to return for more of his savory mash.

The afternoon that the boys returned to the forest was cold and damp. A frozen mist hugged the ground. Overhead, raw winds blew the remaining leaves from the deciduous trees as winter settled in with cold, gray days. The leaves that didn't fall clung as dreary remnants, defying rain, wind, and snow.

After a few hours of waiting in silence, Vladi grew impatient with his brother's boar hunting endeavors. The only "hog" they had seen was a clumsy hedgehog that picked up a snack as it waddled its way through the underbrush.

Vladi reclined against a tree, his eyes closed in boredom. He suddenly sat up straight and looked over at his brother. Erik's astonished expression showed that he had also heard it. Straining to see through the dense thicket, they couldn't identify what caused the commotion. They could see the smaller trees swaying, however, like a dinosaur was tearing its way through the woods and coming their way.

Vladi's eyes grew larger as the creature that shook the trees came into view. A monster boar that surpassed their combined imaginations crashed its way through the brush and into an opening about sixty feet away.

After exchanging an incredulous glance, the brothers eased down flat to the forest floor so as not to be seen. Each aimed his rifle in silence and, on signal, fired in unison. One shot hit the boar's left flank while the other hit its neck. Even with its armor hide, the boar could not withstand the simultaneous shots. This time, it dropped instantly. With a surge of adrenaline, the brothers jumped up and whooped in victory, patting each other on the back.

Erik let out a yell, "I told you! I told you!"

Remembering what had happened last time, Erik eyed the slain pig with suspicion. He approached it with care to make sure it was dead. Vladi watched as Erik crouched with his rifle barrel extended and neared the animal. He poked it and jumped back, both brothers ready to run if a resurrection occurred.

To their relief, it was indeed dead this time. They felt a bit sheepish and laughed before they turned to talk of the smoked pork they couldn't wait to devour. While their stomachs rumbled, their jubilation faded as they realized something they had not anticipated before — how were they to hike out of the woods carrying the dead weight of a boar nearly the size of a bear?

From then on, the challenge became somewhat of an obsession, and the boys were always planning their next wild boar hunt. Vladi hadn't known it at the time, but this turned out to be one of the character-shaping activities of his youth. As he gained experience hunting the wild boars, Vladi transitioned from using a rifle to hunting with nothing but an eight-inch double-edged knife.

In time, Vladi and Erik got several Caucasian Ovcharka dogs to take on their hunts. With their keen noses, the dogs could locate and surround a boar. This allowed Vladi a brave opportunity to dive onto the agitated boar and stick the beast in the heart from the underside, all while evading the boar's sharp tusks.

Any man who could handle the hunt with that approach needed the courage of a lion, and Vladi proved fearless!

Though a killer in the hunt, in contrast, Vladi was a protector when it came to his loved ones. He vigilantly guarded his younger siblings in every respect. Knowing this, they always felt it was better to be with Vladi than apart from him.

As with Erik, Vladi shared a close and loving bond with their sister, Olga. She was the kindest person in their lives, always giving and sacrificing her own well-being to care for the needs of others — and doing it all without complaint.

Olga committed much of her time and resources to caring for the many abandoned children in the region. Widespread alcoholism proved to be a vice that devastated families and had a wasting effect on the community. It manifested in so many ways. Women gave birth, only to abandon their newborns. Orphanages were filled to capacity with forgotten children. Babies were born with severe physical and mental damage because of their mothers' alcohol abuse during pregnancy. The alcohol poisoning left many of these children with physical disfigurement, learning disabilities, seizures, and a life of isolation filled with emotional complications. Those who survived infancy had a hard life ahead of them, one which no amount of love could make whole.

With all of her heart, Olga poured herself into caring for the many children who were housed in the orphanages. She volunteered her time to give them each as much individual attention as possible. Olga let them know that there was someone in this world who cared for them. She understood how Marxism was an unfeeling god that would never tend to their souls. In denying a man's soul, it stripped away the foundation of human dignity and individual value. So she prayed with the children and told them about God's love. Olga felt deeply for their plight, something her own tender conscience would never allow her to neglect or ignore.

The dynamic of Vladi's relationship with his soft-hearted sister suffered one seemingly insurmountable barrier. To Vladi's embarrassment, when Olga was a teenager, she confessed to him her belief in and commitment to Christianity. More than just embarrassed, Vladi was mortified by what she told him. She was not pledged to the government-sanctioned Russian Orthodox Church. Even Stalin himself once promoted it for the good of the state. Instead, she was devoted to a rogue form of Christianity. She believed everything about the God she read about in a contraband Bible and claimed this was the true faith of Jesus' first-century disciples. This was a dangerous stance, one which Vladi could not protect her from.

Nonetheless, Olga had inherited the same courage Vladi had — she was as fearless about her claims concerning God as Vladi had ever been facing a wild boar. After she divulged her secret to her brother, Olga seemed much freer. She became more open and outspoken about her faith as she got older, always praying and talking about the Bible. Few other people seemed to know as much about what Vladi thought of as a contrived collection of archaic writings.

Partly out of fear for her welfare and partly out of contempt for the beliefs she held, Vladi would lodge insults and jabs at her faith at every opportunity. Though he now regretted them all, one exchange continued to sadden him even years later.

"Why do you keep embarrassing yourself and us, believing a farce?" Vladi demanded when he saw Olga in prayer yet again. "One must not risk her own safety for something that does not exist." He knew he could never win this argument with his sister over her religion, but perhaps he could appeal to her self-preservation.

Olga, being selfless, did not respond to his provocation. She knew her brother well and what he was trying to do. She gave a gentle answer, going back to the heart of the matter. "Just because you do not believe He exists does not make it untrue. There is evidence all around us, dear brother, even in the fact that God still provides for you even when you do not believe in Him."

"I do not need whatever is in your imagination," came Vladi's scornful retort. "Let me ask you this — if your supposed God is so loving, why would He allow all those children to be abandoned and orphaned in the first place, then leave an impossible, tragic mess for you to take care of?"

"How do you know that God does not intend to use me to care for them in other ways? Would this not be His goodness?" Olga asked, maintaining her composure.

"Nonsense!" Vladi scoffed, exasperated by his sister's brainwashed thinking. "You help them because you are good, of course. No deity comes down and asks you to do it."

As mild and kind as she was, Olga found Vladi's abrasiveness on the subject trying. Olga turned her face away and closed her eyes for a moment in silence. She prayed for grace and considered how to respond to his caustic remarks with love and gentleness in a manner that pleased God.

She answered in a way that she hoped would help her brother understand that her trust in God made her who she was and motivated her to care for others. "You do not know what you are saying, brother," answered Olga. "Although it is true that heaven does not speak to me directly, I am who I am because Christ Jesus is my King, and He has chosen for me to follow Him. Even if I were wrong about my Master, and I am not, I would not have one regret about living a virtuous life to help these children. My soul would not have it otherwise."

It was hard to argue with that. Vladi knew that it would not be right to try to dissuade her from doing good. But he did worry about the consequences she might face for being so outspoken about her beliefs. It was a sort of battle that went on for many years. However, he would not speak about it to anyone else, both out of shame and concern for her safety.

Yet Olga was never dissuaded, and she continued to try to appeal to her unbelieving brother. How could she try to help others but abandon trying to help her own flesh and blood to come to know the Savior? She would continue to challenge him and his beliefs just as much as he challenged hers.

In his arguments, Vladi often referred to the example of their country's leaders — above all, Peter the Great. "If an enlightened hero such as Tsar Peter saw no value in the church, why should I? Are we now more enlightened than one of the greatest men to ever lead our country?" he would argue.

And whatever he thought of the Bolsheviks, Vladi felt that they also had it right in their contempt for religion. The priests and bishops who had brainwashed the people with their religious myths and legends had done the country a disservice and, in his opinion, had rightly been removed after the 1917 revolution.

He would also point out that it was unlawful to follow anything outside of the official Russian Orthodox Church — and, as a Christian, Olga should abide by the law.

Vladi admonished his sister, "You recognize how precarious it is to express such views plainly. It is well known that even Orthodox priests are treacherous — they betray their own parishioners. There are whispers, which I take as fact on reliable authority, that they cooperate to keep favor with the KGB."

She sighed as he continued, gazing out the window of the small family home into the snowy, gray dusk.

"What I am saying is that you should trust no one, sister. You know men who are fathers, husbands, and brothers, imprisoned under harsh conditions for the same beliefs as you. If it is discovered you talk about such foolishness, anyone could denounce you, and then officials will surely come after you!"

Olga would smile and quote the apostles, responding that, like them, she was obligated to "obey God as ruler rather than men." It was often infuriating how she had an answer for everything. For Vladi, unity of the Communist Party, the people, and the nation was the holy trinity of the Soviet Union. He wanted nothing to do with Olga's religious ideas, which seemed to influence everything she thought, and he wished that sometimes what she said didn't make so much sense.

Despite their differences in beliefs, Vladi cherished his sister. He respected the person she was, even if she considered her character and values as nothing more than the product of her faith.

As for Olga, her admiration for her oldest brother never wavered. Short of forsaking Christ Jesus, she would give anything for her brother's good. To that end, she always prayed for Vladi, even when he neither knew nor cared. It was the best way she knew to help him.

When he came of age, Vladi dutifully entered the military. Military service was compulsory for young men, but not all of them relished the opportunity. Still, it was no surprise to anyone when Vladi rose to the top and excelled in any and every responsibility assigned to him. His ever-faithful sister prayed for him every day of every year that Vladi was away on duty — and she would never cease in prayer for him, even after he went missing.

ADAPT AND OVERCOME

s a Soviet officer, Vladi had a plan for everything, but military manuals offered no guidance for his current situation. Given the circumstances, it would be difficult for anyone to remain optimistic.

Over the next four days, Vladi recovered in the little rundown house where he stayed with a Cuban family. The clangs of kitchen pots and loudly spoken Spanish lilted in and out of his days and nights. The stiff knots he felt in his stomach had nothing to do with the food. The simple home-cooked stew served in tin bowls was delicious.

What will happen next? he asked himself over and over, but no answer came. His constant source of anxiety was this lack of direction. For now, he relied on the warmth of these kind people, but it couldn't last forever. He needed a plan for the next move forward.

When he realized that he might never go back home to his family, he felt so much pain that it manifested itself physically in his upset stomach and deep in his chest. During these despondent moments, he reached for the precious pocket watch his father had given him and held it. His bear-like grip clutched the old watch as if it contained his entire existence.

Since his plunge into the Atlantic, the watch had been at a standstill. Rendered inoperable, perhaps it was beyond repair, but it didn't matter. He would never get rid of this — it meant too much to him. The fact that it had been through the same rigors and had remained with him seemed almost like a miracle.

I should not say it is a miracle — that is foolishness. That is the effect of Olga's God talk rubbing off on me. I will just say it is a fantastic coincidence.

He had received the pocket watch from his father, who said that Vladi's grandfather had passed it down to him. The old watch was a vintage timepiece, one of the first produced after the Great War. It was adorned with the proud insignia of the USSR.

I can never lose this watch from my father and grandfather. It is all I have in the world that has meaning. It is the proud symbol of the rodina. When Irina and I have a son, one day I will pass it on to him.

As a loyal Soviet patriot, being alive far from his home was more torment than languishing in a gulag. He spent those initial days in despair. Vladi couldn't stop thinking about how he could return to Russia and his beloved family. But now, the two nations were on the brink of war, and he was in the land of the enemy. At this point, he didn't know of any Soviet embassy where he could seek asylum.

Even if he could fake an accent and pretend to be an American, any attempt to "defect" to the USSR from the United States would raise suspicions and alarm. He also had reason to fear his own government. If he got caught, they wouldn't care how or why — he would be compromised.

Despair drifted into desperation, and Vladi's daydreamed schemes of how to get home became wilder and less plausible. He fantasized that he could hijack an airliner and force the pilots to fly to Russia, but he soon returned to his senses.

Come now, what am I thinking? How could my conscience ever justify endangering innocent people just for me to return home? One must know the chances that such a scheme would enable me to walk back onto Russian soil and into the waiting arms of my own family

— *they don't exist.* No, he needed to remain a free man if he ever wanted a chance to see his sweet Irina and children again.

I have no way home, he determined. *I must find a way to survive for now and wait for an opportunity. It will come.*

Even though the refugee families shared food, shelter, and clothing with him, Vladi knew he would need to find a way to look after himself. Still, Vladi felt safest within the Cuban community, where he partially blended in. For the time being, he resolved to remain there until he could find a way home.

Immersed in the Spanish constantly being spoken through his daily interactions with the Cubans, Vladi's Spanish skills gradually gained a level of fluency. The refugees also helped Vladi learn some basic English they knew. This wasn't much, but it was a start.

His newfound friends were also kind enough to help him find a job in the citrus groves where they worked. *It is not much, this work, but it is what I need right now.* He earned dollars in cash, enough to pay for essential needs. It also helped to occupy his mind. And beyond just his physical needs, the Cuban refugees gave him something he needed even more — their genuine friendship.

Weeks turned to months in the citrus groves alongside the Cuban labor hands. The work evoked Vladi's memories of Russian summers. His birthplace, Kavkaz, was in southern Russia along the coastal plain between the Caucasus Mountains that bordered Georgia and the Caspian Sea. They had all four seasons in Russia, and they were beautiful. The summers were hot, and the winters were freezing. Winter brought constant snow, so they worked in the garden through the warm months tilling the soil and planting a garden to prepare for harsh weather. Summer was for planting, weeding, and canning. It also created opportunities to make extra rubles selling garden produce. City people loved the *babushki* from the villages. They were the grandmas of the community and always had the best, freshest food.

In time, Vladi learned how Cuban defectors made the journey to what they called the "free world," having arrived with great expectations only to find that life in America brought its own difficulties. These were just different from the troubles they experienced in Cuba.

Every day was consumed with struggles to get past the latest series of problems. Their daily life depended on the resourcefulness and ingenuity of people who relied on their imaginations to get through each ordeal. Cubans had developed survival skills that were different from those taught to Vladi in the Soviet special forces. Still, they were equally valuable competencies that enabled the refugee families to make the best of any hardship.

Perhaps for the first time, Vladi could relate to the Cuban exiles' plight, and he grew to respect their fortitude. He recalled the tribulations of his own family during his childhood in Russia. Every year, there was a big celebration on May 9th to commemorate Victory Day, the surrender of The Great German Reich in 1945. But even after World War II, life remained difficult for ordinary families in Russia. The Soviet Union had strong autocratic leaders, and the common people were kept poor. Families did their best to enjoy life any way they could under these circumstances, but their constant focus was always survival, ensuring they could put food on the table from one day to the next.

Vladi worked shoulder-to-shoulder with the Cuban men day upon day, followed by relaxed evenings spent together as his fellow workers drank cervezas and sang traditional folk songs. They sometimes asked why Vladi didn't partake, but he'd just shake his head and hold up his hands for "no" without explaining. With time, Vladi developed trusted relationships and began to let down his guard and tell them more about himself.

The Cubans hardly batted an eye when they heard Vladi's harrowing tale. Many of them had also endured dangers and great difficulties in their own passage across the Florida Strait. Instead of a shocked reaction upon learning his identity, the Cubans understood his predicament better than most people would have. His relatable struggles endeared him to them. They playfully called him *Moisés*, a name meaning "saved from the water."

Vladi had little familiarity with biblical figures, so he didn't understand the reference at first. When the Cubans told him the Bible's account of Moses, he didn't like it, as he found being compared to a religious figure offensive. After they explained that Moses hadn't just been saved from the water as a helpless baby, but how he became a respected leader throughout all of time and history, Vladi found satisfaction in being identified with this revered ancient character. He eventually accepted the name, little realizing how fitting it would become.

UNWITTING CAPITALIST

Season upon season, as Vladi labored alongside the Cuban refugees, he learned how to cultivate citrus trees. He enjoyed springtime the most. When the groves were in bloom, delectably sweet orange blossoms filled the warm air with nature's perfume. Vladi periodically stopped for moments to inhale and savor the rich fragrance, one of the small joys he found in his new life.

The seasons turned into years. Years he spent away from his home, his family, and his country. Years he spent hidden in what he had been conditioned to think of as a hostile nation. By now, the USSR had long since listed him as missing in action and presumed he had perished.

Vladi grew more depressed with each year that passed. *Why could there not be some "underground railroad" to Russia, like from Cuba to the United States?* he sometimes wondered. He was powerless to resolve the inconsolable desire in his heart but, with time, he began to accept his fate.

On sleepless nights — and there were many — he would lie awake passing his fingers over his old pocket watch. It was the only tangible connection he had with home — the sole reminder that he had once existed in another place and time before this one.

I wonder what my family is doing right now? The middle of the night for him would be the beginning of another day for them in Russia. *It is morning there — what are they doing today?* He imagined his children asking what happened to Papa, and he could envision Irina crying over those questions for which there were no answers.

Despite his sadness inside, Vladi used his time wisely and made the best of his situation. He'd become fluent in Spanish and conversed easily with the Cubans. He spent so much time with them that the rudimentary Spanish he had struggled with back in Havana now flowed as smoothly as a clear brook. He learned English too, though it required a more concentrated effort because he had minimal communication with anyone outside of the Cuban community in Florida.

Sometimes overly anxious, he had a persistent concern that someone would notice that he was a Soviet officer. He thought of himself that way so, naturally, that's how he assumed the rest of the world saw him. Then one day, a simple encounter resolved this matter of identity in his mind.

At a convenience store, there was a grizzled man in a trucker hat. Vladi and the gentleman both walked up to the counter at the same time, making it impossible to dodge him. The old fellow courteously gestured for Vladi to go ahead of him. Vladi paid for a jug of milk and a chocolate bar before giving an appreciative wave as he stepped away from the cashier.

The man didn't seem to notice anything strange about Vladi. He had simply said, "Howdy," and grinned. Vladi realized for the first time that he blended in with American society. He gradually began interacting more with Americans whenever he felt comfortable enough that his Russian accent would not raise questions.

In time, Vladi excelled as a labor hand in the citrus groves. His work ethic and performance were so sterling that none of the bosses cared about his background. They didn't ask, and he didn't tell.

Above all, Vladi was astute and observant. Despite his humble work as a labor hand in the citrus groves, he soon began to develop a working knowledge of the business aspects of citrus farming. He worked as hard as two men and, more importantly, he worked smart. He asked intelligent questions and took every opportunity to learn from the foremen and anyone else with more experience.

Despite his relative success doing field work in the citrus groves, Vladi became unsatisfied with being a mere labor hand. He was a natural leader, and the urge to apply himself and excel couldn't be suppressed. The big question that occupied his thoughts was, how? How could he do more with his life beyond physical labor in the citrus groves? How could he use his intellect to overcome any constraints holding him back? Vladi owned no land, and regardless of how hard he worked, he had no prospects of possessing the resources to acquire his own orchard properties.

Frustration resulted from the mismatch between his understanding of how things functioned and the realities in front of him. The way everything worked back in the Soviet Union was so different from the way things were for him now.

If I were back home, he thought wistfully, *the state would provide everything to operate the business. Of course, the state would own it for the good of all, but no one would be concerned about how to find money and land out of thin air to make a farm.*

Ultimately, Vladi understood that discouragement wouldn't take him to his goals — specific, deliberate action would be needed. In time, the Russian realized that opportunities would not just be handed to him, and that he would need to create them. *Am I standing by for someone to hand me everything, no?* Vladi reminded himself. *Is this not the land of opportunity? Then I must consider options and take hold of them. How can I take what I have to make what I want?*

This was a departure from the precepts of communist thought instilled from his youth. But he needed to adjust his mindset, and he understood as much. His existence and future were at stake, not some intransigent dogma. Vladi told himself he didn't even have to agree with it, but if he wanted any opportunity within the American capitalist system, it would be necessary to understand it and adapt in a pragmatic sense.

Vladi found this difficult to reconcile at first. *But this is not the same place. Here, the rules are different. It is merely a matter of survival,* he reasoned. *I do not need to approve of their ways — but what is there to prevent me from exploiting an opponent's weaknesses to my own advantage?*

In Vladi's mind, he was still in hostile territory, and the soldier within persisted in his deployment of what he considered to be survival tactics. Still, no matter how many times Vladi repeated that rationale in his head, *it is about survival* became almost a mantra he had to force on himself. The changes in his ingrained worldview were not easy at first. Deep within himself, Vladi felt like this betrayed everything he stood for. Nevertheless, over time, he allowed his mindset to adjust and acclimate to his contrary environment.

Ever resourceful, Vladi realized that many of the things he had already learned about citrus production could be helpful to him. Still, that was not enough — he needed to observe more to understand how capitalist businesses operated.

Profitability is the driver behind many decisions owners make, he noted to himself. He also noticed competition with other citrus producers. It led them to make the most of labor, supplies, processes, and operating efficiencies. It intrigued Vladi that businesses were allowed to compete with one another and that they even tried to be competitive. Vladi liked that. This marked a fundamental departure from the precepts of communism ingrained in his thinking.

He observed how employment worked under this system — the relationship and distinctions between wages and profits — and how they worked together. *I guess owners do not keep all the money they make,* he began to realize. *They need to use some of their money to pay workers and buy equipment and fertilizer. Hmm — to juggle finances and resources on a large scale could get complicated,* he judged correctly.

On occasion, Vladi would strike up conversations with the workers and bosses from nearby orchards, gauging the sentiments and needs of the local growers. A sense of competitiveness driven by self-interest for their own operations led to occasional less-than-friendly interactions, particularly between the bosses. Vladi made a personal effort to maintain relationships with competing growers throughout that area, discerning that he could gather information from the ways other organizations were run and how their workers were treated.

He could see many shortcomings in the system and, therefore, opportunities to change things for the better. He could excel if he relied on his own abilities and capitalized on his strengths.

If nothing else, his Soviet military training taught Vladi about organizing personnel and assets. He noticed the growers labored and lived under the thumb of middlemen — the shippers and citrus agents who took an ever-growing share of their profits. Middlemen bought the fruit at meager prices and charged exorbitant rates for the fruit packaging. Furthermore, they took ten percent of all gross sales as their commissions.

Free enterprise permitted this. *I imagine growers resent losing much of their profits under compulsion,* Vladi deduced. In his mind, an embryonic business strategy of his own began to take shape. Now he understood that capitalism and opportunity could be about identifying needs and coming up with solutions that no one else had.

Vladi organized a meeting with other local growers to discuss ideas for how to eliminate the shippers and agents that siphoned off so much of their profits. "I cannot imagine you are happy with how you must run things. You lose profit to middlemen who do not add value to what you have broken your backs to produce," he told them, striking at the heart of the matter. The assembled group answered his words with nods and murmurs of agreement.

"But what can we do about it?" one man asked, mopping sweat from his brow with an old rag.

"They have tied our hands because they know we need their services," another grower added.

"That is why I hoped to speak with you all — to seek a solution," Vladi declared. "I have watched and thought for a long while. I may have a partial solution, but I am also here to ask for your experienced input on the matter. If we put our heads together, we can figure this out."

His confidence inspired those who attended. They had just accepted the way things were, but now, a rank-and-file labor hand had come along who would tell them how they could retain more profit. They didn't care where he was born

— all that mattered was that he knew the business and he was bringing them solutions.

After much productive discussion among the men, each with their unique perspectives, they realized that by doing their own packaging, shipping, and even some of the selling, they could retain a greater share of the revenue from a season of work. There was no practical way to eliminate all the middlemen, true, but there were ways they could take on some of that role themselves.

That modest initial meeting produced a viable solution, and something more unexpected emerged. A cooperative, or co-op, came together, orchestrated by Vladi. They had not anticipated on that day how impactful that meeting would be, but it would soon transform the marketing and distribution of Florida citrus throughout the state and across the country. It allowed for extensive growth in the industry as thousands more acres of citrus were planted throughout the state. The citrus co-op began to pack its own oranges with boxes that carried the name of each grower's product and branding.

Now producers now had options to sell through multiple channels: to distributors, directly to consumers, and some at auction. Vladi's "revolution" did more than just help local growers and change the way things had been done for years — it also helped him ingratiate himself within the local business community. His reputation as an entrepreneur with a sharp business mind — "a man who takes decisive action to get things done" — spread. *Think of the irony, he sometimes mused, a Soviet capitalist!*

As a result, Señor Vladi, now becoming known as "Moisés" to others within the broader community of citrus farmers, became a trusted consultant to the local growers. One-third of the nation's citrus came from central Florida — this was big business. They handsomely rewarded him with a share of the profits he helped them realize. After all, it had been his clever distribution model that increased their own profitability.

With a foot in the door of the capitalist system, it now became easier for Vladi to slip right in. Not only had the door of business success opened for him, but he hadn't realized that his ideas also gradually slipped through the doorways between his long-held perspectives and convictions.

I may have started as a labor hand, but there is no law in America that says I must be one forever, he mused as his new way of thinking took hold.

Old conversations with Marco Rivera echoed in his mind. *Marco may not have believed a word of his pro-capitalist rambling, but he seemed to have a point to his arguments. Here is a chance to choose my own life.* Before coming to America, Vladi never had such opportunities, and it took him years to understand that they had been there in front of him all along.

Had he endeavored to run such a venture back home, he would never have had his own profits to reinvest to grow his business — it wouldn't have even belonged to him. The state would have controlled everything — the labor, his wages, and his hours. And now, the formerly avowed anti-capitalist had a goal of land ownership.

He eventually reached a point in his mind where he gave up deliberating about land ownership in terms of political and economic ideologies. He simply accepted it as a logical next step. He knew that having his own land for growing citrus was the path to long-term stability within the agriculture industry and long-term financial security. The workers and even the bosses were hired hands and could be replaced like the equipment they used. Vladi wasn't greedy, but he was smart, and he knew that to remain a labor hand or even a consultant was not the strategic way to move forward.

Vladi also rationalized that by owning his land, he would be in a better position to help the Cuban community that had taken him in and become something like a family to him. *In many ways, I owe them my life,* he thought. He had genuine gratitude for the help that had been given to him. *Now I know a way to help in return, making use of these resources. Nothing is wrong with being resourceful, especially for the good of others.*

Thinking in terms of the benefits his success would have for the community helped to settle the matter in his mind. He still rejected the idea that profit was his driving motive. Vladi needed to see things through the lens of the greater good — a concept for which he felt proud and one he had valued his whole life. If the profits were making life better for everyone, then the profits were, by defi-nition, good.

Inherently competitive, the industry's competition did not deter Vladi in the least, nor did it bring out a savage streak in his character. Vladi was driven by the challenge to outsmart his business rivals, and he could do it fairly within the system already in place. In the process, he became tremendously wealthy.

A NEW LIFE . . .
A NEW IDENTITY

As Vladi accumulated the money to buy his own land, concerns arose about some of the legal aspects. So far, he had concealed his real identity from anyone who might turn it against him. Up to this point, he could answer to a nickname, "Moisés." However, that didn't make his alias legitimate within the American system, including the State of Florida. For him to take title to land, he needed a legal identity; so he returned to his Cuban companions, who had become his confidants over the years.

As Vladi shared about his predicament, they laughed. A new identity? That was no problem. Refugees in the Cuban community faked them all the time. In fact, they knew just where to find a person who specialized in producing counterfeit documents for illegal residents at a reasonable cost.

Within a week, Vladi's friends led him to a place they called *la oficina*, "the office," some miles away. It was little more than a shed, not unlike some of the removed places where Vladi's men would have interrogated sequestered captives during his time in the military.

I am not so sure about this. What do we know about this person? he thought, looking around with a wary eye. He didn't like that they had come to a complete stranger, about whom he had reasonable reservations and misgivings, in a little out-of-the-way place that would make anyone pause with concern.

My friends would not lead me into danger, he concluded. Still, he hesitated for a moment in the doorway. *What am I really walking into here?*

Within an hour, they were done. He could smell the ink, still wet, on his documents as he walked outside, looking down at the paper in his hands. It was official — sort of. He could conduct business as Moses Moskowitz in America. He fixed his intense gaze on the written characters on the paper. It seemed strange to see it in print. This surreal life he was experiencing became a bit more . . . real. He felt as if a little something within him had been lost.

Vladi took a deep breath and reminded himself that it was a necessary exchange. He rationalized, *There is always some sacrifice to reach a worthwhile goal. Perhaps it is a small yet compulsory compromise. There is a new life to begin.*

Over the next five years, Vladi used his new identity to acquire land as he planned. He took the vital knowledge and skills he had learned as a labor hand and consultant and worked to develop his own efficient citrus growing operations. He established a brand for his company and its produce: Red Star Citrus. The name was a tribute to the red star in the Soviet insignia, but only he would know that. He offered both reliability and reasonable pricing to cooperative middlemen who had formerly caused such headaches for the growers. Everyone trusted him, from the bosses to the field hands, because they remembered him from his days laboring alongside them.

Vladi experimented with cultivating a particularly sweet variety of citrus of Mediterranean origin — the Moro blood orange. He had to risk a portion of his resources for the research, but his experimentation met with prodigious success. The burgundy-fleshed fruit had a distinctive aftertaste, similar to a raspberry or strawberry. As an early adopter of this unique and desirable strain, Red Star Citrus had a corner on the local market.

His wealth grew commensurately and conspicuously. Vladi had never been around anyone who had become as affluent as himself, so he had no role models for managing his sudden wealth. *What will I do with all this money?* he often asked himself, staring at his ledger.

By the mid-1970s, the co-op that began under Vladi's guidance represented almost half of all Florida citrus growers. Despite his prosperity, he still felt an insatiable emptiness. He had accumulated wealth that most Americans only dreamed of, but it couldn't replace his family. And, the fact that he had no family around — at least not his wife and children — to share his achievement with simply added to his misery. He was surrounded by warm Cuban families, but they always gazed at him with a hint of sadness in their eyes. They knew his story and sympathized with this man so many admired — a man who was ever-lonely, isolated from his own family.

Vladi never stopped despairing of this unintended estrangement from his family — from Irina, his daughters, and the one child he had never seen. If they somehow knew about the plane crash, they could have inferred that he had perished years before. He imagined his sweet Irina, believing herself widowed, remarried after his years of absence, her new husband taking Vladi's place as his children's father. Did they call him Papa? Would they compare their new father with the one they lost, or would their young memories cause him to fade into just an ethereal impression in their minds? Was that worse than his children never knowing him at all? If they walked past each other on the street, there would be no recognition by either.

Vladi's thoughts created an inner torment from which he found no escape. They grew increasingly bitter with time, and it took its toll on him. His friends could see his youthful vigor and energy fade, even beyond the natural course of aging.

If he could not work to help his family, Vladi felt that at least he could fulfill his mission of helping others around him. Not only did he help the citrus growers, but he also established himself as a resource for Cuban refugees. Familiar with the inner workings of Castro's Cuba and possessing the financial resources to get things done, Vladi could provide a haven for refugees in and around his citrus groves. Word got around that "Moisés" could help their family members, enabling them to make safe passage across the sea from Cuba to America.

Whether purposeful or incidental, over the years Vladi had indeed become a capitalist in America. What would that idealistic Soviet officer who left Cuba years ago think of him now? Vladi not only lived and worked among the arch-foes he had vowed to vanquish as a young Russian soldier, but he had now become one of them.

As a Soviet officer, Vladi had been naïve and ignorant about the workings of the capitalist system that he opposed. But during his time exposed to the freedom of the American economic system, Vladi grew to understand capitalism better than most Soviets or Cubans — perhaps even better than many Americans.

More remarkable, the success Vladi realized had all happened in a relative vacuum. Beyond the activities directly related to his business, Vladi had limited experiences participating in this new society, one not centrally controlled. As a result, there were ways in which he was still maladjusted. There were blind spots in his comprehension. In his mind, for example, labor always represented something people were coerced into. Even though he understood how to run a profitable business, Vladi hadn't come to fully grasp other facets of freedom in an empirical way.

Though successful by the world's standards, he led a life under a different name that he didn't feel was his own. Florida never felt like "home." Vladi could admit, if only to himself, that America could be enticing to someone used to a relatively gray life in the Soviet Union. And, sure, he had achieved some measure of status among his peers in the community of citrus growers, but who were these people who surrounded him? They weren't his wife and children, so did it even matter?

PART II

- THE FREE WORLD -

SHADOWS OF DOUBT

When Fidel Castro first rode into Havana with his rebel army of anti-Batista guerrillas, he was hailed as a Cuban Robin Hood — a messiah, a savior, the man who would return Cuba to freedom, prosperity, and happiness. Families wanted to believe in the hopes of a new socialist utopia, and that Fidel would solve all the problems that plagued their lives. But by the mid-1970s, the revolution sagged under more than a decade of grand promises — some realized, many still a dream. Fidel himself couldn't avoid his need to address the copious failures of a multitude of disastrous economic policies. Ordinary Cubans spent every day just finding ways around oppressive laws and burdensome restrictions. Many grew weary of waiting on the revolution to fulfill its bold claims.

Marco Rivera had moved up in the ranks of the Communist Party of Cuba, but he found it less fulfilling than he had anticipated earlier in his legal career. He wasn't so blinded by ambition that he couldn't see what was happening around him — to his country, his people, his community. His performance and commendations as an Inquisitor were overshadowed by the growing discontent he felt with Fidel Castro's government and its heavy-handed tactics and political persecutions. Of course, Marco kept such judgments to himself. He would be in jeopardy if those thoughts were ever uttered or known to others. There were consequences for any suspected opposition.

Still, Marco knew he wasn't alone in his sentiments. The revolution had not produced the socialist utopia Cubans were led to believe would result from Castro's rule. In many respects, it felt much the opposite. Without a doubt, the revolution that toppled the corrupt U.S.-backed dictator Fulgencio Batista had its merits. But under Castro, Cuba had devolved from somewhat of an island paradise to a more depressed and insular society.

At the dawn of the Castro era, many families assumed there were advantages to embracing the Castro regime, but their support faded as the government encroached ever further into their lives. For the Cuban people, home was no longer a haven. Instead, it had become a place of inescapable terror. Many who once supported Castro's rebels became disillusioned as Castro revealed the red tint of his revolution.

Castro remade Cuba's political, economic, and social frameworks. The state was in charge of everything and above everyone but him. As a result, the Castro dictatorship was a thousand times more vicious than the one they had ousted. The Cubans had given over their lives to a political ideology that turned out to be hollow and dangerous.

The Castro government maintained academic and labor files on each citizen with official records of statements or activities that could bear on that person's loyalty to the regime. Before one advanced to a new school or position, the individual's record had to be deemed acceptable. The inverse was also true. The Communist Party kept track of individuals with the right aptitude and proper attitude to handle more responsibility and promoted them up the ladder.

Young Cuban men who grew their hair too long or wore their pants too tight were suspected of being either pro-Yankee or homosexual, and Castro's government jailed both. Castro described homosexuality as "a bourgeois perversion," maintaining that such abhorrent behavior constituted a menace to society. To speak one's mind to the contrary about such "tendencies" could result in being sentenced to a labor camp for rehabilitation. Communism was also intolerant of religion and similarly severe toward anyone or anything deemed to be "undesirable elements" of society.

Cubans who dared to express an independent thought were exposed to their dreaded neighborhood Committee for the Defense of the Revolution (CDR). The CDRs were the lowest Communist Party apparatus in the hierarchy, and they were insidious informants. They were organized by city blocks. The president of each local CDR was the individual to whom neighborhood snitches reported. They passed along information to Castro's feared Stasi- and KGB-trained Ministry of the Interior. A CDR president had the power to execute with a finger simply by identifying and denouncing anyone suspected of counter-revolutionary activities.

This surveillance network was so omnipresent that Cubans were afraid to vocalize any complaints. Any neighbor who was a *bembelequero*, a gossip, could bring trouble. Even in their own homes, they avoided speaking the names "Fidel" or "Raúl" in any way that could be interpreted as negative for fear that prying ears might hear. Instead, they used codes.

To touch invisible epaulets on the shoulder connoted Raúl and his generals. When anyone dared to criticize El Comandante, they stroked an imaginary beard to represent Fidel. Should someone ever venture to whisper anything more explicit, they might do it where they believed the crackling static of an old RCA Victor radio or the whoosh of a fan pushing thick Caribbean air around a small room would drown out their words.

In the wake of the revolution, the course of one's life could only take one of three pathways. They could follow the masses and submit to Castro's dictates regardless of whether they approved or not. They could take the bold path and resist, even though they knew it would be suicidal. Only the bravest or most desperate risked everything to side with a handful of outspoken dissidents that the government stalked, harassed, and imprisoned. The last option was to flee.

As a result, many Cubans defected to America, their neighbors to the north that they were told were an enemy. However, defection wasn't an easy feat. The government effectively limited exit visas to diplomatic missions and other official business. Cuban citizens could get them on different premises, but if people sought permission to leave the country of their own volition, they were dealt with thereafter as traitors to the revolution. Consequently, if they were employed, they would be immediately fired from their job. Many people were relocated away from home and family to isolated corners of the island to do agricultural labor or work in the quarries, sometimes for as long as two or three years.

In their disillusionment and growing desperation, America now seemed to offer a better life for many Cubans despite the perils of the journey there. Stories began to surface among the Cuban population about a Señor Moisés in America who came to the aid of defectors. As talk of this heroic man circulated, tales of his generosity became legendary, if not somewhat exaggerated and distorted. These reports tended to take on a life of their own, and were enticing more Cubans to risk traversing the Florida strait to America.

Marco kept his ears tuned to what Cubans called the *bola*, the word on the street. These rumors had reached Marco's attention, although at first he dismissed the existence of any real Señor Moisés. Intuitively, his first inclination was to be skeptical.

The supposedly heroic Señor Moisés seems too good to be true — likely the invention of some desperate malcontents with fertile imaginations, he reasoned with himself. Yet what he heard had a believable quality that he could not quite put his finger on. He became more curious as stories continued to swirl. *Could any of this be true?* he began to wonder.

It was dangerous to independently appear too interested in a man rumored to aid Cubans in illegal defection to their northern enemy. But the more Marco heard, the more intrigued he became. He found it difficult to suppress the pervasive questions he had about this Señor Moisés. Every rumor Marco heard added fuel to the fire of his curiosity. Questions about the man's identity and activities burned within him until he couldn't stand it anymore.

Who is this man? What are his motives? Where does his money come from? How could he be smuggling defectors without getting caught? Risk or no risk, Marco had to have the answers.

Marco tried to be casual with his questions, subtly digging for more information on this Señor Moisés. *Did he truly exist? Who knew him? How could* the stories be trusted? If this was a myth, could it be some form of propaganda ploy by the Americans to spur dissent among Cubans? Even worse, could the Señor Moisés legend be a decoy, bait by communist hardliners within Marco's own government used to catch dissenters?

Marco's inquiries into this mysterious individual were fruitless. In fact, he could find no one around Havana who had first-hand knowledge of Señor Moisés. But they were convinced that he existed and that the fantastic accounts of his benevolent deeds were true. Still, Marco told himself it was smart and in his best interest to remain skeptical. After all, many such tales of dubious credibility circulated among the Cuban people.

But then something happened that overturned everything he thought he knew.

Marco was walking alone early one evening along the Avenida de Maceo, familiar to locals as the Malecón seawall. Once a venue for the Cuban Grand Prix, the seawall's roadway and broad esplanade stretched over four miles along the rocky northern coast, from the mouth of Havana Harbor, along the north side of the boroughs of Centro Habana and El Vedado, to the Almendares River. Marco was not alone in his appreciation of the tranquility here. Cubans had nicknamed the Malecón seawall "the world's longest sofa."

Marco let his mind wander, carried along by the ambiance of Havana that permeated the soupy island air. Crackly old RCA Victor radios and light, rhythmic music from guitars and brass wafted across courtyards and cobblestone alleyways. The varied sounds deflected off the crumbling walls of art deco buildings before mingling with the mechanical growl of old model Studebakers and Chevy Bel Airs that chugged their way through Havana.

Marco watched the waves lap in a soothing perpetual pattern as the sun made its western retreat. After work, he sometimes lingered along its promenade to take in the golden-orange hue of the horizon, in no rush to get anywhere. The setting was conducive to introspection. It always helped him relax, especially after a difficult day of work.

There were many difficult days, so Marco went to this spot often. It felt like these days brought new pressures, and he welcomed this momentary refuge now more than ever before. He hummed a random set of notes, something to calm and distract his mind.

In his role as Inquisitor, Marco had been given responsibility for investigations into two high-profile figures. One was a discordant ringleader, Francisco Díaz, who had recently defected to the neighboring island of Jamaica and put himself just beyond the reach of Cuban officials. As a principal actor behind the counter-revolutionary movement, Díaz was an agitator who persistently stirred up trouble wherever he went.

The other individual the Cuban government had its eyes on was an international lawyer and businessman, Miguelito Cervera. Cervera had a U.S. education and ties to prominent figures within the former government of Cuba, notably Fulgencio Batista himself. He wasn't a troublemaker, but his travels and questionable business relationships beyond Cuba made him a suspicious character who warranted being carefully watched.

The now blood-orange sun receded as Marco stared out across the sea and fell into deep thought. In all his days as a Cuban prosecutor, he had affected so many lives, and he remembered each one he had effectively ruined. For most, their only crime had been disagreeing with the government.

One case was distinctly seared into Marco's mind and left an indelible scar on his conscience. He had interrogated and prosecuted a husband and father for the simple possession of a Bible. In the process, he had ruined an entire family. A three-man tribunal sentenced the accused to a decade in prison, where he was beaten and suffered deprivation that made death seem a preferable alternative. It made Marco think of his own religious brother, Julio. *How easily it could have been his life that was destroyed.*

Even now, as he stood at the water's edge, that case still tormented Marco. He wished the waves could wash away the all too vivid memories of that man's family looking on as the verdict was rendered against the hapless defendant. It made him take a hard look at his own life choices. How could he justify what he had done as right or even necessary? He enjoyed prestige and power, and his personal compensation was considerably better than what more ordinary Cubans might receive. *But was this all worth it?*

Furthermore, even as a professed atheist, some vague sense of God was realized in Marco's conscience — a conscience that had begun to trouble him more often than he would have liked.

Marco looked up to the star-filled sky. *If you are there, God, make yourself known to me!* As Marco turned away from the vast sea, the wonder of which he had reflected on many times, he knew deep within himself that there was no denial of the existence of a God who had created such magnificent wonders. And if that were the case, someone may have also seen everything he had done. *If there is a God out there, I truly hope He is as merciful as Julio claims.*

On his way home, Marco walked along the street he took nearly every day. He took that path so often that he knew every crack in the pavement, every stoop and who he would find on it, and every car that parked along there, which were not many.

But tonight, something was different. Although dusk had dimmed the light, Marco noticed that difference the moment he turned the corner. An old model Plymouth, one he had never seen before, was parked about fifty feet ahead of him. Marco slowed his pace while he tried to get a sense of the situation. This was one of the rattling scenarios he feared in his mind. His nerve endings shot tingling electrical jolts through his arms and torso.

Despite his caution in probing the existence of Señor Moisés, Marco feared that his inquiries had not escaped the eyes and ears of the island's political police, those he most hoped would never notice. He had already found peculiar things happening around him, though nothing overt.

One particular matter bothered Marco — he had started to find small personal items around his office placed in different locations. His office door was supposed to remain locked unless he was present. Even when he was there, the only regular visitors to Marco's office were his assistant, his supervisors, and junior military staff who couriered correspondence to and from the Ministry of the Interior. Something that would normally seem innocuous now became deeply unsettling. Was it a warning sign that he was being watched? His paranoia deepened, and Marco began to feel he was being followed and watched more closely.

It was a common axiom, "Not a leaf falls in Havana without a Castro knowing it." Cuba's foremost authoritarian institution was its spies. Given his own position, Marco knew this as well as anyone. One needed to practice discernment about whom he met or talked with. Trust was at a premium, for not everyone was who he said he was.

Informants came from anywhere — they were part of everyday life. Cuba's insidious "inform on your neighbor" policies meant anyone could spy on anyone. Eyes were everywhere, always on the watch for hints of dissent. Distrust and suspicion became woven into the fabric of society. Just the slightest chance that someone could be observing and listening seemed enough to keep people's mouths shut and opinions to themselves. Consequently, it was only natural that some paranoia crept into otherwise pedestrian thinking.

Marco eyed the Plymouth — he could see a man's face in the side mirror of the car, but it was a face he did not recognize in a car that did not belong there. His heart rate spiked. *Someone must have discovered I have been asking about Señor Moisés. Is this man following me? Is he waiting in ambush? I don't see anyone else. Is he alone, or are others hidden?* Dozens more thoughts raced through his mind as the distance closed. Feeling vulnerable, Marco had a critical decision to make. *Do I run or defend myself?*

Marco crossed over to the other side of the narrow street and quickened his pace just a bit. He hoped to pass without any kind of interaction, keeping a close eye on the man the entire time. Marco was especially nervous about what might happen once he passed the vehicle and his back would be to the stranger, leaving him vulnerable.

He had nearly gotten beyond the car when the stranger spoke. Marco's muscles sprung tight, his legs involuntarily stopped in mid-motion. "Would you wish to receive the kindness of Señor Moisés?" the man calmly asked.

Is this a trap? Marco knew for a fact that government operatives used such tactics to catch dissidents — he was well-versed in these methods. Up to this point, he had concerns — now the fears he had all along were substantiated. *What if I am now the subject of a Cuban investigation? I have done nothing, but a corrupt tribunal won't care.* Even the most dauntless man would be shaken by the prospect.

If this isn't a set-up, though, this man is either foolish or brave — it is a bold — no, an insane — act to utter the name of Señor Moisés so openly on the street. Whatever the case, clearly someone was watching and listening. *Why else would a stranger ask me this out of nowhere?*

Marco turned to get a better look at the mystery man who casually sat in the driver's seat, his head barely turned in the direction of Marco. The man wore a brimmed hat that further cast shadows on his face, making it almost impossible to distinguish his features, especially from Marco's distance.

I don't like this. Should I answer or keep walking? What if I can uncover the answers I've been searching for? No, have you lost your mind? Don't be a fool! It isn't worth the risk! his brain shouted back at him, yet something tugged at Marco's insides and kept his feet planted.

Marco pulled himself together and took a cautious approach. Feigning ignorance, he put on his most innocent voice and asked, "Who is Señor Moisés?" ensuring the inflection in his voice conveyed some surprise at being asked such a question. This would hopefully solidify his façade.

The shadowed man, however, was not fooled by his attempt. "You do want to know more. I overheard you inquire about him," insisted the obscured voice. Marco's nervousness shot towards panic, and for a moment, his thoughts scattered from his brain in a million directions. He had indeed been found out. But by whom?

He leaned against a pole, hoping to look relaxed. In reality, he needed it more to support his weakened legs. After a dramatic pause to compose himself and steady his voice, he challenged the stranger, "Step out and show me your face!" Marco hoped to project confidence that belied his alarm. "Who are you?" Marco demanded of the man, but a hint of anxiety seeped out now.

The man answered without hesitation, "I am Acheros."

"And what exactly is your business with me, Acheros?" Marco asked through slightly clenched teeth. He emphasized the man's name with a tone of sarcasm. He wouldn't fall for a fake name, and he wanted the man to know it.

No matter how sharp his senses were, nothing could have prepared Marco for what the man had to tell him in the next few minutes, and in no scenario had he been ready to believe it.

After he left, he felt shaken and unsettled by what he had heard. He needed to talk with his brother, Julio, as quickly as possible.

GOD PROTECT US

The younger of the two Rivera brothers, Julio, was a doctor in his mid-twenties. He had the more mild-mannered, thoughtful, and compassionate nature of the two siblings. Like his older brother, Julio was intelligent and did well in school. But beyond sterling academic scores, Julio had something about him that Marco seemed to lack — Julio felt an innate calling to care for others. The course of his life centered not on personal ambition but on helping the less fortunate around him who experienced hardships and needed competent medical care.

As a child, Julio imagined he would become a priest, to serve in a way he felt he would do the most good for his people. However, the evolving political realities and his family's eventual affiliation with the Communist Party of Cuba made it impossible.

Despite over ninety percent of the Cuban population being Roman Catholic, Castro banned all religion. Even the observance of Christmas could result in severe consequences. Castro subscribed to the belief of Karl Marx that "religion is the opiate of the people," and he made atheism the official creed of Cuba.

The state sought to stamp out all religious influence. The government confiscated church property and expelled religious workers, particularly those who represented any opposition to Castro. Few were spared. Hundreds more were deemed "malcontents," the *desafectos a la Revolución*, and sent to forced labor concentration camps alongside vagrants, homosexuals, and others whom authorities deemed undesirable.

But religion had been more than just banned — those who practiced were viewed by the government with utter contempt, and the faithful were characterized as "social scum" by Fidel himself. Anyone connected to his dictatorial regime had no choice but to view religion and its believers in the same way.

By divine providence, Julio got accepted to ELAM, the Latin American School of Medical Sciences, before the revolution. Had it been any later, he would have been asked in his medical school admission interviews, "Do you believe in God?" Julio would not have denied God, but to answer yes would have marked him as someone out of step with the revolution, and there would have been repercussions. In sum, they would have withheld any education and the opportunity to become a physician. It would have altered the course of his life to contradict the dictate of Castro that prohibited belief in God. Julio would have been an exile in his own country.

Despite how high up into the Party organization the Rivera family's connections extended, Julio remained sensitive about spiritual matters. He believed that God was calling him, and the government could not ban God from his heart. He tried to live a morally pure life as much as he knew how. He prayed and was ever-conscious of sin in his own life. He watched and listened for signs from God, but whatever his soul lacked seemed to remain elusive.

He tried to make himself right by pouring his life into helping other people. He hoped that his efforts to serve would earn God's approval. On the surface, Julio's heart may have been temporarily calmed, but deep inside, his soul was still far from being at peace. Julio had a strong conviction that God would want him to use his life to serve others, and he believed God had given him a desire to work as a physician. And there was no doubt that the neighborhood assigned to his care by the state was in desperate need of a doctor just like him.

Dr. Julio Rivera's office was on the ground floor of a concrete building that was in a state of slow, crumbling deterioration. Terra cotta stucco chipped away in flakes beside a wilted flower that Julio meant to replace whenever he had a chance. Anyone who needed to see Dr. Julio could walk in — the door was always open.

Those under his care were familiar with Dr. Julio. He had dark hair, contrasted against a white coat worn over his medium build. Everyone knew that there would be a smile sure to greet them as they came through the door. As patients sat on the stainless steel exam table, shards of Caribbean sunlight peeking through the metal shutters onto the drab green wall, Julio would listen, sympathize, encourage, and console the injured and ailing.

Basic medical supplies and medicines were often scarce. The residents of his community almost always lacked the comprehensive care they needed. There were times Julio couldn't give his patients something as simple and basic as bandages or aspirin to help their pain — his scarce medical supplies sometimes dwindled to almost nonexistent. Julio was powerless to get more. Insofar as he could afford it, he would have paid for things out of his own pocket, even if being a doctor in Cuba did not pay as well as in other parts of the world. Even so, Julio could give them what he did have in abundance — compassion and empathy.

Despite his professional standing as a doctor, Julio struggled to acquire a pair of quality eyeglasses for himself. He had needed eyeglasses from a young age, but none were available for children. A fifth-grade teacher once noticed him sitting on the front row in the classroom with his neck craned forward, squinting. Upon enrolling in medical school, he obtained a donated pair. He couldn't have done all the required reading without his eyeglasses, even though they weren't quite ideal for his eyesight. He only ever had that one pair. Nothing but frustration came from his futile efforts to get new eyeglasses. People's lives could have been improved in big ways by such small things — but then, this was Cuba. So Julio worked with what he had.

Julio had come to know each of the almost four hundred families that he served — who they were, what they did, their education level, their family dynamics, their hobbies, and even their vices. He believed one of the best things he could do was listen to each of them. By knowing them, he might better help them according to their individual needs rather than treat people as if they were just another sad figure coming through in an endless stream of broken humanity that needed to be fixed and pushed out the door to make way for the next infirm person.

Though he gave everyone extraordinary care, Julio was most watchful of those who needed a little bit of extra looking after — the elderly, pregnant women, and those with chronic ailments. He kept a close eye on their condition and well-being. The fruits of this extra labor were evident. His section had the lowest infant mortality rates in all of Cuba — in fact, the lowest mortality rates in general.

On the day the mysterious stranger approached Marco, Julio had just made house calls at the apartment building across the street from his office. He finished checking on two women in the late stages of their pregnancies before he called on an older couple in the building, unofficially his favorite patients.

"Señora Medina," he said in a firm yet gentle voice that he would have used with a small, naughty child, "You haven't been keeping your swollen ankles up, have you? Are you doing too much?" Both knew her edema belied a heart condition, but she turned her head to avoid looking him in the eye.

She sighed. "You know *mi esposo* needs to have his food. Who else is going to make it for him?"

"I know," Julio expressed his sympathy, "it's hard to stay off your feet. But you need to take the time to keep them up to help the swelling." He then added with a mischievous smile, "As for your *marido*, you have been allowing him to smoke, haven't you?"

Mrs. Medina gave an equally mischievous smirk in return. "Who says? Did he tell you that, that weasel?"

Julio was humored. "No, he hasn't ratted you out, but the empty cigarette boxes did. How do you suppose he got those, hmm?"

The elderly woman grinned. "Nothing gets by you, Señor Doctor. You've caught us, your naughty *pacientes*, sneaking around when you aren't looking. What are you going to do about it?" she asked with playful mock defiance.

Julio gave a wink in turn. In a way, they, as well as the others he treated, were almost like children to him, even those old enough to be his grandparents. "I am going to check on you every day for the rest of this week to make sure you both behave yourselves. I want to see your feet up and him taking daily walks," he told her as he stood up to leave.

The old woman grabbed his arm and pulled him back towards her face. "*Tirano*," she said as she kissed his cheek and shooed him out the door.

He walked out with a broad smile, almost laughing as he stepped onto the street and closed the door behind him. He knew she didn't think him a tyrant. His smile quickly faded, though, when he looked across the road to see the ashen face of his brother, who stood outside the door to his office.

"You do not look well. Are you feeling sick?" Julio asked, his dark brows knitted with concern. Without a word, Marco turned and walked toward Julio's apartment. Confused and a little alarmed, Julio followed.

When Marco felt they could talk in the safety of the apartment, he answered Julio's question — he recounted an almost unbelievable story about a man who had approached him and offered to take him to America.

Both men knew that defection from Cuba presented a tremendous risk and could have severe consequences. "I think it may be a trap," Marco concluded after he told Julio the story. He hoped his brother could help him assess the inherent risk that came with this bold proposition. Julio was more level-headed and calmer than he.

"I understand your excessive caution given your position, but maybe it isn't a trap. Maybe it's a doorway. Perhaps, after all my prayers, this is how God provides you a way out," Julio countered after some consideration.

"With all the suffering we see every day, you still think there is a God in this hellish place?" Marco scoffed, forgetting his budding feelings about God just hours earlier. "And if this is your God, why would He choose to save me and leave others to suffer their torment and the bane of things beyond their control?"

Julio did not have the answer, but he gave his brother a look that he was free to interpret how he wanted.

Marco took a deep breath. "I mean, I understand why God might try to save you out of this place. You are one of the best men on this earth. But the stranger, Acheros, approached me. Why would God have him approach me? If God is up there watching from heaven, then He well knows that I've been good, but I've also wronged some people in ways that trouble my mind now. Perhaps it would exclude me from such mercy in this life. So why?!" Marco looked distraught. Normally confident to a fault, Marco was now confused.

Even if Marco left God out of the equation, one glaring question remained. Why would this Acheros risk his life to ask Marco, a man with a notorious reputation as a zealous prosecutor, if he wanted to defect? Did the man have a death wish?

Whether he could claim God as his benefactor or the shadowy Señor Moisés, defection from Castro's Cuba was not a decision to be taken lightly. Its repercussions could be deep and long-lasting. He wouldn't let his decision hinge solely on the chance of help from a merciful deity who may or may not turn a blind eye to his transgressions, nor was Marco ready to put his full trust in a rumored legend of a man. Those ideas couldn't be reconciled with Marco's logical way of thinking. They were just too far-fetched.

As usual, Julio saw things in a different light and tried to reassure his brother. "We don't always know the full workings of God, but perhaps He has something planned for you that you have not even conceived. Recognizing that you have done things unworthy of God's kindness is the beginning of a repentant spirit. Who knows, you may come to know Him yet." Julio gave a wry smile. He knew from past experiences to tread lightly when he communicated with Marco on the topic.

"Your God aside, this would still be a dangerous undertaking. Would it be worth the risk?" the ever-pragmatic Marco grasped for guidance.

"The question is, are you willing to give up your connections, your official position, your whole life of work for the uncertain possibility of something else?" Julio asked, allowing Marco to arrive at his own conclusions. "Is it dangerous? Yes. But don't be so quick to rule God out of the picture. He is an integral part of this discussion. If it is indeed His will for you to leave now, He can ensure your safety."

Marco paused for a moment, his eyes fixed in contemplation. *More than most, I am aware of the repercussions of defecting from Cuba. But there is so much wrong, so much that I yearn to leave behind. Am I willing to give up everything for which I've worked so hard and leave this for a life so uncertain? Well, what would I be giving up, really? Life as a government thug?*

That first euphoria of power had waned, and each interrogation, each torture, each imprisonment had stolen another piece of his soul. The conscience that he had pushed aside began to resurface and prick him, but Marco had gotten himself entrenched so deep in this system that he couldn't imagine a way out.

What would abandoning my position and my connections earn me if I walked away from it but stayed in Cuba? He shuddered to think how he would be labeled. *Either way, this is an all-or-nothing decision.*

Beyond his own position and connections, there was Julio to consider. *This decision is not just about me — it could become a life-or-death matter for him as well.* If Marco chose to go, his decision would have consequences on the lives of people he left behind. His innocent brother would be under constant suspicion. He would be followed. He would be harassed, and maybe worse.

What kind of life would that be for him, always looking over his shoulder and making every move with some degree of ever-present fear? It would be a problem for any of their associates, but even more so for an immediate family member. Knowing all this, one would have to act with a certain amount of selfishness to leave.

"You keep saying 'you this, you that,'" Marco told Julio as he came back out of his thoughts. "When I say this is a dangerous decision, you well know I don't mean just for me. You are aware that I can't leave without you. This is an 'us' situation," he pointed out, hoping Julio would understand what he meant. There was only one way he would leave, and it was with his brother by his side.

"You don't need me to go with you. I am a doctor who is needed here — needed by our people. I can't just leave them. I can't," Julio emphasized, emotion catching in his voice. Marco was asking him to abandon those under his care, those he had nursed back to health, those he knew and loved and who depended on him. Marco may not have had any reason to stay, but Julio did. It was too much to ask.

"God will protect me if you leave. And with prayer, He can give you a safe journey as well," Julio assured him. The answer, however, angered Marco.

"Now I think you are just using God as the answer to everything instead of thinking about reality! The consequences of my leaving are well known to you — we've seen this over and over again. Does that mean God has judged the families of other defectors unworthy of protection? Because He knows well what they have gone through. I know what they have gone through because I've put some of them through it!" Julio could see Marco's distress in his eyes as a sheen of sweat formed on his brow. Given the proclivity for unjust payback in Castro's Cuba, Marco knew the persecution of his brother would be a certainty.

Julio winced a bit at his brother's angry allusion to his past doings. He had to admit he had no idea what would happen to him if he stayed. He sighed. "I don't know, Marco. I don't know what will happen to me or other family members. But if you disappeared alone, it would be less conspicuous. It could be made to look like a missing person situation. These things do happen. You would know."

Marco gave a derisive laugh. "Oh, right, 'Your Holiness' will lie to the authorities and say I just accidentally went missing? If we both leave, our extended family members have enough clout behind them to make it through, not to mention they are well-practiced liars. But you, my dear brother, have neither of those things to protect you."

Julio paused for a moment to consider. It was an impossible dilemma, and he did not want the pressure of deciding for Marco. With a calm, resigned voice, he gave his answer, "I think you should leave if that is what you feel called to do in your heart. Please feel that you can go without judgment or worry about my welfare. I'm not convinced that leaving is the right thing for me to do."

"What is your real objection, Julio?" Marco challenged. "You want to stay and help our people? You cannot help them from prison! You cannot help them if you are maimed from torture!" Marco's voice got louder. "Maybe there are others, our people exiled in America now, that need your help. You can pursue whatever you believe to be your true calling there — you can be a man of God without the worry of persecution." Marco couldn't believe those words had come out of his mouth. He had never said that out loud before.

Marco stood with his hands on his hips. He looked at the ground and gathered his thoughts. When he spoke again, his words were measured and low. "You worry about our people, Julio, but what about me, your own brother? Are you not worried for my soul? Because I can tell you what will happen if I stay here and continue as an Inquisitor for our government. If your God is really out there, I will surely meet with His judgment." Marco did not altogether believe in hell or his eternal soul, but he felt the appeal to his brother's beliefs might sway him. He glanced up to see if his words had any effect. Julio did seem more concerned.

"I told the stranger, Acheros, that I would not go without you, and I meant it," Marco refused to waver. "The man told me it would take some extra work and money, but his Señor Moisés, supposing he exists, would help both of us. So are you willing to come with me? If not for your own sake, then for mine?" Marco hoped that Julio's unselfish nature would concede and allow him to make the life-altering sacrifice Marco asked of him for the good of his soul.

"You know if we leave, we can never come back," Julio reminded him. He wanted to ensure Marco thought it through. No matter the decision, there would be sacrifices and consequences that could never be reversed.

"I understand," Marco said in a near whisper. The thought of leaving his homeland forever did tug at him. "Perhaps the political situation will change in the future, and we will have the opportunity to return. But I know that if we don't go now, we may never have another opportunity." Was this Marco's attempt to console his brother? Or himself? He didn't know.

"But as I said, the whole plan hinges on whether you accompany me or not. Either we both go, or neither of us goes. Are we doing this together?" Marco asked and held his breath, awaiting his brother's answer.

Julio sensed the characteristic pragmatism in his brother's argument. To leave would be a chance for Marco to start fresh, to begin a new life that his conscience could live with. Julio anticipated it would also provide him with new freedoms for the good. Though deep down he had trepidation about leaving, Julio also knew he could not fill a certain emptiness that gnawed at him while they remained in Cuba. Maybe this would help him find what he always needed.

He replied with confidence and composure, "Yes, we are doing this together. *Dios nos proteja!*"

DEFECTION ON
THE HIGH SEAS

ven though Marco had been the one who had pushed to leave, fear closed around him as their departure became a reality. Anxiety caused him to doubt his decision. He looked down at his small bag containing the few articles of clothing and essentials that now constituted everything he owned in the world. Beyond that, he and Julio had brought a couple of water jugs. There was no other provision for even the most basic necessities on the trip. It was suddenly frightening to have almost nothing and be headed for an unknown future.

Still staring at his bag, Marco thought, *Having little more than the clothes on our backs could be the least of our worries.* Others had risked everything and fled only to be detained by the Cuban authorities or intercepted by the U.S. Coast Guard. Marco knew that if they were caught by American authorities, they would be sent back to Cuba and straight to prison — or in his case, probably worse. Those who left the island were considered traitors and were guaranteed to be dealt with as such.

Because Cuban authorities guarded the coast against defections, leaving the island was a harrowing experience. Less than a hundred miles separated Cuba and America — less than the width of the Florida peninsula — yet the journey sometimes lasted days. A few days might have seemed short at any other time or to any other travelers, but for the Rivera brothers and those who took the risk with them, it would feel interminable. The brothers' angst grew palpable as the day of departure approached.

"We are in God's care," Julio told his brother. But Marco wondered which of them he was trying most to convince. *Even so, he thought to himself, I wish I had Julio's confidence that his God will be watching over us and protecting us as we go.*

Despite Julio's assurances, Marco couldn't help but think about every worst-case scenario they might encounter. Three months prior, eleven Cubans had starved to death when their homemade boat stalled in the treacherous Caribbean waters. Those who survived drank rainwater rationed using syringes. Could they expect something similar to happen? These terrible possibilities felt endless.

If the man calling himself Acheros was to be believed — and Marco still wasn't entirely sure he could be — their journey had been underwritten by Señor Moisés. Their passage would not cost *un centavo*, although it could cost their lives. They were assured safe passage.

Marco gave little credence to those assurances. *What is the assurance of a shady stranger and a shadowy savior? How can either of those men control what happens once we leave our shores?*

Leaving their home would mean they were committed. Once they set foot on that boat, there would be no turning back. Taking a collective breath, they walked out the door of Julio's apartment on the outskirts of Havana and to their fateful decision. The arranged car pulled up, and they climbed in through the only working door. Without delay, the driver took off, leaving Havana in a westward direction. This was not the nearest departure point for Florida, but the brothers assumed the plan was to take them to a remote area where their getaway would be undetected.

Locals referred to these cars as *almendrón* and *cacharros*, or the old jalopies, similar to the car in which Acheros had waited for Marco a few weeks earlier.

The cars were vestiges of a bygone era, somehow trapped in the present. It was amazing that Cubans could keep them running, Frankensteined together with whatever parts they could make work.

They rode in the 1957 Chevy Bel Air across the beautiful Cuban countryside for several hours. However, the ride felt much longer, due in part to the crumbling, poorly maintained roads but mainly because of their anxiety. Marco frequently looked at his brother to gauge how he felt. He hoped to see a calm Julio, a sight that would ease his own anxieties. He wasn't sure how to feel about what he saw each time – Julio's lips moving in nearly constant prayer.

On this dangerous journey, Marco and Julio traveled with other defectors: a boxer and a Santeria priest, the latter of whom blessed their expedition with a splash of rum and a sprinkle of chicken blood. Marco smiled at the rum, but Julio looked uncomfortable with the ritualistic gesture.

At the water's edge, a Cigarette boat awaited — long and narrow and fast. The slender, lightweight vessel was built for small crews and high speeds, one of the reasons they made excellent "rum runners," perfect for a quick sprint to the United States.

Professional racer Donald Aronow had come up with the "go-fast" design, setting a new standard for the maximum performance of 1960s-era speedboats. Marco and Julio were more fortunate than most to make their run to Florida in such a modern boat. Most people traversed the treacherous waters in small dinghies and rafts that were far from anything that could be considered seaworthy, and they certainly could not outrun Coast Guard vessels.

Aronow's Cigarette boats were legendary, both for breaking speed records and breaking laws in the Florida Keys. Colombian cocaine smugglers ran the speedboats to evade the U.S. Coast Guard and other law enforcement officials. It was a shrewd choice for human smugglers as well.

The men boarded the boat. Marco walked over to Julio and stood so close that he pressed the back of his shoulder. Absorbing the scene around them, it wasn't long before the brothers got a glimpse at the other defectors.

The priest, a quiet and unusual man with an enigmatic air about him, was difficult to read. He made his way to a corner of the boat with hardly a sound and sat down, presumably just trying to keep a low profile, preferring to keep to himself and be left alone. The boxer exemplified the polar opposite. An uncommonly aggressive man with an agitated demeanor, he seemed ripe for confrontation. If no one would give him a fight, he seemed disposed to stir up the trouble himself.

Despite the priest's efforts to remain unnoticed, he looked like an easy target for the bully — someone unlikely to make a fuss. It didn't take long. The boxer strode over to where he was sitting and demanded the man's seat.

"You're sitting in my spot!" he barked.

The priest just looked at him with surprise plastered across his face.

"I said get up! I had my eye on this spot first, and you presumed to run ahead and take it for yourself. Don't make me move you myself," the boxer taunted menacingly.

The priest had no desire to escalate a situation he surely would not win. Collecting his things, he got up to move and was even courteous in his manner. Clutching his bag to his chest, he made a timid attempt to shuffle past the boxer.

It wasn't enough for the bully. As the priest moved towards another seat, the boxer shoved the priest in the back. The sudden, violent push sent the man flying off balance. Julio, who watched the incident with disgust, quickly reached out to catch the poor man before he hit the deck.

Still hanging facedown across Julio's arms, the priest's voice was barely audible. "That was quite unnecessary." Unfortunately for him, the boxer also had a keen set of ears.

"You should have moved the first time I asked you!" the boxer bellowed, getting down near his face. Catching sight of the bag the priest had dropped as he fell, the boxer picked it up. "If I hear any more backtalk from you, your bag is going straight into the water," he threatened, holding the bag towards the rail of the boat to show he meant business. The priest, for his part, had been right — the whole ugly scenario that the boxer had created was totally unnecessary.

Before he could do anything else, the boxer suddenly shrieked and threw the bag away from him. The girl-like screech elicited laughter from the boat's crew. The unexpectedly frightened and bewildered look on the boxer's face provided a humorous contrast to the hard countenance he had portrayed just a moment earlier.

With visible agitation, the boxer tried to explain himself, muttering, "Some . . . something moved inside that bag! There's something in there!"

Incredulous, the crew continued to chuckle as they turned back to their final preparations to make sail. The brothers remained fixated on the situation, unsure of what to make of the whole scene. Seemingly able to decipher the other's thoughts, they turned to look at one another.

"This will be interesting," Julio stated, raising one eyebrow.

Marco nodded knowingly. "Or disturbing," he added.

The priest, infused with a spark of courage, picked up his bag. He extended it to the frightened boxer, "Here, take it!" he said in a soft, calm voice. The boxer backed away, stumbling over the water jugs Julio had set down.

"Hey, isn't this what you wanted? Take it!" the priest insisted. But the boxer, who had previously looked big and intimidating, now seemed small and frightened. Embarrassed, he slinked away to the other side of the boat, as far away from the priest as he could. He occasionally eyed the priest's bag with suspicious terror, as if he expected something horrible to crawl out of it at any moment.

Shortly after the incident, everyone else on the boat took their seats as they shoved off away from the dock. The whine of the twin engines rose, and a sudden burst of speed threw the passengers back into their seats.

As the boat quickly reached its cruising speed, Marco and Julio could not help but feel another fear — one they had not anticipated. It's an odd reality that most Cubans, including Marco and Julio, had never learned to swim, even though no point in Cuba is more than sixty miles from the sea. They had never been on a boat with a motor, let alone traveled across the water at this speed. What they could see of the choppy water in the moonlight seemed to whip by as salty drops that splashed up and encrusted their faces.

To put some distance between them and the shore, the boat's pilot pointed the bow directly into the waves and headed towards the darkened horizon. Hitting the chop at high speed made the boat almost jump over the waves, creating a few centimeters of air between the keel and the water. Even though it didn't lift much, every time the boat came back down it felt as if it were crashing down from the heights. The bouncing action jostled the men in their seats so much that, at times, Marco feared he might fly right over the side of the boat. Watching the bow rise and hop over waves, Marco squeezed his salty eyes shut. He felt sure that it was only a matter of time before the boat flipped over and they were all tossed into the pitch-black deep.

Marco's grip on his seat tightened as he started to sweat despite the cool ocean air. Not being much of an outdoorsy person, he could get motion sickness just rolling around on his desk chair. But this felt like rolling in every direction at once, and his stomach did not like it. When he pried his eyes open to look over at Julio, he could see that his brother had returned to prayer. They were in for the longest night of their lives.

The rough waters also took their toll on the ostensibly tough boxer. His face had turned a pale shade of green, evident even in the moonlight.

The priest noticed this too. He kindly offered the boxer some herbal remedies to quell his seasickness. The boxer's expression turned from one of illness to dread.

"I want no part of your sorcery," was the boxer's brusque response. "I would rather throw up over the side of this boat for hours than take anything from you, you strange little man." It was going to be a long night for everyone.

As the morning sun began to peek over the horizon, the sleep-deprived brothers sensed something amiss, and this time it had nothing to do with the boxer nor the mystery inside the priest's bag. They soon realized the sun was on the wrong side of the boat.

To their surprise, instead of racing straight toward the Florida Keys, the boat had headed west and then south, following a long arc toward the Yucatán Peninsula.

Marco felt instant concern about this apparent "detour." His heartbeat quickened. He sat up straight in his seat and swung his head all around, desperate to gauge the situation. Helpless to gain any further intelligence by nervously checking around him, fear immediately took up residence in his mind once again.

This is it, his anxious mind whirred. *My worst fears — I knew it! We were tricked into a kidnapping and extortion scheme. How could I be so stupid to get on this boat with strangers?* Marco's mind ran toward utter panic.

Marco began to hyperventilate and in his mind cursed mysterious strangers and that ridiculous legend of Señor Moisés. *Of course, no one in Cuba had first-hand knowledge of the man because they met a terrible fate and were silenced forever! Now it all makes sense. Why would some stranger just offer people free passage? How could I have been so taken in by these fairytale promises? I am smarter than this!*

Indeed, the brothers learned along the way that their escorts weren't exactly model citizens. The men who operated the craft, either Mexican nationals or Cuban defectors themselves, belonged to a smuggling ring whose activities ranged from transporting human cargo to bricks of cocaine. At least two men were fugitives — one on the run from a federal indictment in Miami, and another was alleged to have extorted Cubans who traveled this same route.

Shocking. Marco's thoughts were thick with sarcasm. He had good reason to fear the type of characters in whose hands he had entrusted their lives. To make matters worse, these thugs were all in the pocket of *Cártel del Golfo*, the murderous Gulf Cartel of smugglers and other criminals using Mexico as a base. *We have jumped from the frying pan straight into the fire*, Marco postulated sardonically. But in this case, as the brothers had overheard, the "fire" had a name — Isla de Mujeres.

The boxer was the first passenger to verbalize what everyone thought. Belligerently, he demanded of the crew, "Hey! Where are you taking us? This doesn't look like the direction of Miami!"

The only person to answer him was the priest, who spoke their dreaded thoughts in a calm but direct statement, "They may be intending to take us for ransom. You know these things do happen." Somehow, hearing the words aloud made them more frightening. It felt closer to reality than just a possibility in an anxious imagination.

The priest's response roused the ever-present agitation of the boxer. He now got up from his seat on unsteady legs to approach the crew and demand answers right from the source.

"Hey! *Siéntate, cobarde!*" one of the smugglers ordered the boxer when he saw him rise.

"No, I won't sit," the boxer answered with smoldering defiance, staring the man down. How dare the man refer to him as a coward — he had only screamed like a little girl once, and that was because of whatever that weird thing was in the priest's bag! "I demand to know where you are taking us!" the boxer yelled, angry fists clenched at his side.

"I said sit down!" the smuggler repeated through gritted teeth. The other smugglers looked on. They also glared at the boxer. One rested his hand on his Kalashnikov AK-47, daring the boxer to try something.

The boxer, though, remained defiant. He was ready to explode into a fight, even though his meaty fists would be no match for the smugglers' weapons. The other passengers held their breath in dreadful anticipation.

What happened next startled nearly everyone on the boat. The priest came up behind the boxer and, bending slightly to reach out, tugged on the angry man's shirttail. Without a word or hesitation, the boxer sat back down in his seat. They weren't sure whether it was sorcery or plain old good sense, but the brothers were both impressed.

With everyone back in their seats, the boat lurched as the pilot slammed the throttle down. They were now approaching the calm waters that surrounded the island. The steep slant of the rising sun darkened the almost-clear turquoise waters into a deeper hue, and palm trees drew closer into view.

As they neared the shore, the light shone on the brightly-colored buildings that dotted the coast, and a few small, winding streets also became visible. The island was picturesquely charming, and the passengers, who had never seen it before, were captivated by its splendor and allure.

The priest, reluctant to break the enchantment in the air, barely breathed his words, "Isla de Mujeres — sanctuary of Ixchel, Mayan goddess of the moon, love, and fertility."

The curious passengers turned to him, captivated by this witch doctor-turned-tour guide.

Now with a spellbound audience, he continued, "The legends say that the island's inhabitants were the goddess Ixchel herself, her daughters, and her court of women. They built a temple, and ancient Mayan women would make pilgrimages across the water to the island. The journey represented their transition from girlhood to womanhood, so they brought hand-carved figures of women as offerings."

The boxer shifted in his seat. Marco and Julio leaned in closer, fascinated with the tale.

"Many years later, the first men to step on the island came from afar in wooden boats." The priest dropped his voice for dramatic effect. "By that time, though, Francisco Hernández de Córdoba and his *conquistadores* found the island abandoned, but not empty . . . "

The priest paused, enjoying the looks of rapt attention from his audience.

"What did they find?" Julio asked, his voice barely above a murmur, as though afraid of breaking the silence.

The priest's teeth gleamed in a mischievous grin. "Human skulls."

The boxer turned another shade paler. Marco squirmed in his seat, also a tad squeamish, already feeling queasy from the rocking motion of the boat.

"They also found obsidian and jade left behind," the priest continued in his normal tone as he leaned back in his seat. "And there were carved statues of the goddess crafted from silver, gold, and clay. Because of this, the men named this place Isla de Mujeres."

"Island of women," Julio said under his breath.

The romance of the legend had taken the men out of the moment as they gazed on the shores. They tried to envision the ancient women of the island.

Marco suddenly sniffed a sarcastic chuckle, breaking the spell the story had cast over them. Isla de Mujeres sounded like such an exotic and wonderful place to land. He found it ironic that this little slice of paradise might turn out to be their own personal hell.

Once the speedboat navigated the reefs that shielded the three-square-mile island, it puttered into the docks at Laguna Makáx. The Mexican Navy had an outpost nearby, but they were no concern to the smugglers. They only had one slow patrol boat — no match for the Cigarette boat — and that assumed the young men stationed there even cared what the smugglers were up to.

Mexican Navy personnel would make an appearance for roll call each morning. Afterward, they would make their way to various posts around the island where they could throw out a fishing line and wait until it was time to return. They weren't interested in chasing smugglers, and the boat crew never considered them much of a threat.

The boat docked, and the smugglers wasted no time jumping off, not wanting to delay disembarking. "Let's go," they ordered the passengers out of the boat. Marco and Julio looked at each other and shrugged, understanding it was futile to do anything but comply. The boxer, to no one's surprise, resisted.

"I'm not going anywhere with you." He planted his feet defiantly and crossed his arms across his massive chest. "We agreed that you would take me to Florida, not Mexico for who knows what reason. I will not leave this boat until we are on an American beach." The boxer appeared ready to take on anyone who dared to come near him.

One of the smugglers grabbed his Kalashnikov rifle and leveled it straight at the boxer. "We don't have time for this, and we won't suffer your belligerence any longer," the fed-up smuggler warned him. "I will give you ten seconds to get off this boat," he told him in a cold, unfeeling voice.

The boxer, incensed by having been called a coward by the man holding a gun to him, refused to back down. "I said, I'm not going anywhere," he hissed back.

The trigger finger of the angry smuggler twitched as he set his aim. A corpse could easily be tossed overboard without consequence. The only thing that kept him from pulling the trigger was that they only got the rest of their payment when they delivered their passengers alive. A dead man was a valuable loss on a trip like this.

The thick tension abated when the priest rose from his seat and gently brought down the boxer's arms. Once again, to everyone's shock and amazement, the boxer calmly left the boat without another word.

At the Rocamar Hotel on Isla de Mujeres, Marco and Julio's defection seemed to have come to an indefinite halt. One of the island's oldest establishments, the small hotel had a colorful history. Its name meant "rock of the sea," derived from a giant rock at the edge of the water where the Gulf of Mexico and the Caribbean Sea converged.

At low tide, a person could climb onto this huge rock. From that vantage point, one could look across the water and almost see Cuba in the distance. The sight could have made the brothers a bit homesick except for the fact that they were under guard and confined to a corner room at the end of a small courtyard. They could see nothing, only wait and hope. No matter where they were or what they were doing, Cubans were masters at waiting.

The smugglers locked the boxer and the priest in another room, preventing them from communicating with Marco and Julio. Their separation of the passengers left Marco disheartened. If the ordeal turned violent, Marco had put his hope in the boxer's ability to overpower the armed thugs who kept them detained.

Marco's legal mind was racing. "I don't know if you could call it a kidnapping, because we left with them voluntarily. But we also aren't free to leave." It didn't matter how it was legally classified — it looked like trouble no matter what label he applied to the situation.

Julio didn't seem to hear him. He was praying again.

"I hope you are praying that either the boxer can protect us or God supernaturally gives us the strength to fight, should these thugs become violent," Marco told him. Julio opened one eye and gave his brother a look. Marco wished he had half the calmness and confidence that he sensed his brother had.

The brothers found themselves exposed and vulnerable in a human pipeline operated by unsavory characters with a reputation for exploiting Cuban defectors. *What do they want?* From the shadowy Acheros and this Señor Moisés, who supposedly bankrolled their defection from Cuba, to the smugglers who now held them in Mexico, Marco had begun to doubt everyone and everything.

"Did they know I had an official position of high rank and connections and think I can provide a nice ransom? Do they think my connections might give them some type of special leverage? Well, won't they be surprised to find out that a high-ranking defector will do nothing but catch prison and torture, all worse for everyone," Marco sniffed. His last flippant, facetious remark did nothing to lighten the heaviness in the room — it only reinforced the feeling. Hour upon hour, his mind found new and frightening questions and scenarios to contemplate.

HOOKING BACK

everal days passed in a hotel room that, under other circumstances, might have been pleasant. Then things once again changed course without notice. The smugglers gathered the men from their rooms and ordered everyone back onto the Cigarette boat on which they had arrived. Without fanfare, they were once again on their way out to sea.

Marco remained somewhat perplexed by what had happened but soon realized they were now at least heading in the general direction they should be. Although he had feared the worst, he now understood that the detour was just a ruse, winked at from all sides, and one that gave traffickers command over the middle crossing. They had not been in danger, at least not from kidnapping. No, quite the contrary. The smugglers had gone out of their way to avoid potential problems. Still, the full measure of danger had not yet passed. Perhaps the most treacherous part of the journey lay ahead.

Marco had known all along that the journey would be difficult and dangerous, but what had unfolded proved to be more perilous than he had anticipated. The stress of what might happen, and his sense of responsibility for not just his own life but that of his brother, was more than he had bargained for. He wondered, *Was the gamble of getting there, the concessions and perils of leaving Cuba, justifiable?*

Marco tried to turn his mind to other subjects, but what it grasped placated him even less. Though Marco tried to rationalize that he had nothing to fear, the stories he had heard from childhood about people trying to cross the waters lingered in his memory. Cuban lore was replete with terrifying accounts of monstrous storms that capsized boats, and tales of people being dumped into the water and then drowning or being devoured by sharks. He didn't know whether these stories were real or exaggerations meant to scare people from attempting to flee from Cuba.

All those people couldn't be wrong about the perils of the sea, could they? Maybe this is just an area where violent storms take down planes and sink ships. Maybe it is as perilous as the tales claimed — whatever the cause, the danger is real!

When a wall of high, dark clouds gathered on the horizon and lightning flashes menaced through the towering cumulonimbus formation ahead, he couldn't reassure himself any longer. Though the storm was still a long way off, the wind picked up, and the emerald blue waters turned white with choppy waves. Marco had thought the choppy waters were scary before, but he had no idea of the terror a real storm-tossed sea would bring him. The boat's bow rose up and over the crest and then slammed down over each angry wave. Fear-induced adrenaline overtook his body as the entire vessel was buffeted from side to side by the gusting gale.

It's like those grim stories we've always heard of people drowning trying to cross. This is how it happens to them — it's happening to us now! Marco could see no way out of capsizing.

As the air temperature plummeted and lost its tropical warmth, he again began to second-guess their decision to leave Cuba. *We took a gamble, and we're going to lose. I'm sorry I bet Julio's life on this too. What was I thinking? Why didn't he stop me from this foolishness?*

Marco could see the line of rain from the sky to the water, and he soon felt its stings, like small pellets being shot at his face and head. Flashes of lightning became more frequent. He could see fluorescent blue forks touch the waterline on the horizon. The air shook, everything shook, as thunder rumbled through his body and the monster grew nearer. Between the sounds of the fast-approaching storm, Marco could hear the soft voice of Julio mumbling in prayer while, across the boat, the priest chanted low and mysterious words that were indistinguishable to his ears.

For a moment, Marco almost wished he had someone to pray to for rescue, but it would feel ridiculous to pray to a God he wasn't sure he believed existed. Instead, he would have to make do with hanging on to his seat and hoping that the boat's pilot knew how to negotiate swells now approaching eight feet.

Each minute the boat rocked and slammed through the water felt like an eternity, giving him plenty of time to think about his own mortality. *If we don't make it out of the storm, what happens to me?* He found the options unsettling. *If I die, will I just go into the void? Or is there something else, like Julio says? I don't think I've ever hoped for Julio to be right more than at this moment.*

His daydream turned nightmarish as he envisioned an immense, dark, frothy wave swelling up next to the boat, rising higher than the buildings of Havana and looming over the boat before crashing down over them. He imagined the boat pitching up perpendicular to the water, and Marco saw himself tumbling feet-over-head backward into the sea. Bubbles and tempestuous water surrounded him and tossed him, disorienting him so he couldn't determine up from down.

I can't swim, but maybe I can find something to float on until we are rescued, he tried to reassure himself. That placated his nerves for only a moment before another worrisome thought followed behind the last one. *What is under the water anyway? So many creatures with teeth swimming below. I've always heard they are attracted to ship-wrecks.* He imagined the unknown terrors of the deep grabbing him and pulling him down, down, down into the abyss. Marco shuddered — his imagination had gone from bad to worse.

After what felt like days, the boat began to fall back into a steadier rhythm over the water. The rain no longer stung him, and the air itself turned calm and fresh. Sensing the change, Marco opened his eyes, not even realizing they had been squeezed shut for the duration of the storm. He blinked through the glare of the sun and looked around for an indication of where they were. Before he could take in the full scope of his surroundings, he heard a commotion from the smugglers.

One of the men hurried over to the passengers and motioned with his hands for them to get down and lie on the deck of the boat. When the boxer looked like he might protest, the smuggler grasped him by the back of his neck and shoved him to the floor. He attempted to get back to his feet, but a raised eyebrow from the priest stopped him long enough for tarps and canvases to be thrown over him and the rest.

Marco held his face down onto the floor of the rain-soaked boat, breathing in the smells of fuel and the musty canvas rustling over them. Julio was pressed in next to him, still praying, of course. With the tarp obstructing his sight, Marco struggled to make out what was happening. He could only sense the vibrations of motors, and the splashing sound of water against the side of the boat.

Through their excited chatter, Marco could hear the words *policía* and *guardacostas*. From those few words, it was not hard to guess what had put the smugglers in a stir. Given the other perils they had faced, the fear of capture had long faded from the forefront of their minds, but here it confronted them again.

Of course, the Americans would patrol the coast. It was well known that they repelled potential threats to their shores, including defectors. Marco tensed up with dreaded anticipation. He waited to hear a bullhorn blare from an American boat, commanding them to stop and allow the authorities to board. Marco considered that he might have been naïve to think the smugglers had done this before and would know how to avoid these risks.

As it turned out, the smugglers knew exactly what to do when they spotted a U.S. Coast Guard vessel, even if they couldn't predict exactly where those vessels would appear.

Marco could hear and feel the whine of the engines as the speed picked up, and his body shifted on the deck as the boat turned. *I hope that means they're outrunning the Americans and we don't look suspicious. This boat seems fast, but can it outrun and lose the U.S. Coast Guard?*

Marco didn't know anything about boating. He had no way of knowing how fast a Coast Guard vessel was compared to the boat transporting him and Julio. For that matter, he had no idea how near the Coast Guard had come or if they had been detected. He couldn't see nor otherwise tell what was happening, which frustrated him. It left his beleaguered imagination to fill in the gaps once again.

Without warning, Marco felt the air lift in a swoosh, and sunlight flooded onto him. He turned on his elbow and peeked up to see who had lifted the tarp that had concealed him and his fellow passengers. It took a moment to adjust his eyes to the light, but as soon as Marco gained focus, he recognized the silhouette that stood over them as one of the smugglers. He collapsed back down to the deck with relief.

"*Levántate!*" the man told them. "It's safe to get up and see your new home." Marco stood up next to Julio, who was trying to wipe the salty film from his eyeglasses. The brothers looked out toward the Plantation Key shoreline with its sand and turquoise waters. Although they had grown up with similar landscapes in Cuba, this was the most welcoming sight Marco had ever seen.

Marco turned to see his brother's reaction. Julio just had a big grin on his face. Marco turned his eyes back to the landscape. In unison, their lungs expanded spontaneously as if responding to the freedom in the air.

UNEXPECTED REUNION

When their boat approached the Florida coast, Marco felt as green as the beautiful, shallow waters that surrounded the land. The storm they had encountered was just a typical afternoon thunderstorm in Florida, but the seasickness that resulted pushed Marco's limits. He wondered with irritation why Julio, the doctor, hadn't brought fewer prayer beads and more useful medicines for such a situation.

Their boat pilot brought them into the sheltered inlet to Snake Creek on the western point of Plantation Key, then throttled back to an idle. Marco rose to his feet, but as he looked ashore, he saw that they were not alone. Had the Americans found them out already?

He soon learned that they had nothing to fear. The defectors were greeted and assisted to safety by a network of Cuban exiles on American soil. They were loaded in a produce truck and traveled for nearly two hours. As they got closer to Miami, they were astounded to see the city's skyline.

"I've never seen buildings so tall," Marco remarked. Many of the buildings were lined with small balconies. *I wonder if people live way up in the top of those, he thought.*

Julio looked to where Marco referred, but his eyes couldn't quite capture the details as they moved past the buildings at American highway speeds. "If they do, I don't think I would want to be in one of them, perched up on a little balcony like that."

"I think I would like sitting up high, watching all the little people down below me," Marco decided.

Soon they passed beyond the skyscrapers into suburban Miami. They were first brought to a communal-type safe house in Hialeah, a square, white building devoid of any adornment or architectural character. Marco and Julio stood in front of the building for a moment, looking at their first home in their new country. Here, they would be given warm food and temporary shelter.

Julio wiped the sweat from his nose that prevented his ill-fitted glasses from staying in place. "The weather isn't any less humid here than at home," he commented. On an altogether different topic, he mused aloud, "I wonder if they have any sort of medical office on site."

"Are you going to try to be the doctor here as well?" the sweat-soaked Marco asked testily. "We're not settling down here, Julio. Let's take a shower and get some rest."

"I hope there's something to eat around here." Julio rubbed his famished stomach.

The food was simple, the kind of institutional fare Americans might find in a school cafeteria — but it hit the spot. After the ordeal of their journey, Marco and Julio were treated to a delectable feast consisting of sloppy joes and pizza.

In the days that followed, they would be helped with finding work, a place to live, and integration into the community of refugees in Florida. But before that would be the much-anticipated meeting with the mysterious Señor Moisés who, behind the scenes, funded and directed this underground railroad to freedom. Now, though, Marco had little time to contemplate the meeting as sleep took fast hold of his exhausted mind and body.

A few mornings later, Marco and Julio awoke to a commotion. Right away, Marco assumed the worst. *Oh no, a raid!* He scrambled out of his plain white bed sheet and jumped from his cot to the door in one leap. He flattened himself against the wall behind the door of the bunk room. Marco looked around. None of their bunkmates were still in the room. Only the brothers remained.

Marco peeked through the opening between the door and the frame, but he couldn't see anything. He also didn't hear Julio's footsteps as his socked feet walked up behind him, but he could hear the breathy words from his lips. Julio was whispering in prayer again. Marco rolled his eyes in exasperation. Couldn't his brother find a more practical way to help with the situation for once?

"Move over. I can't see anything from here. Go pray on your cot or be useful and go out into the hall and see what is happening," Marco ordered his brother.

Julio glared back at him with narrowed eyes.

Rolling his eyes again, Marco gently pushed Julio out of the way and came out from behind the door, peering down the hall from the door frame. He could see the silhouette of a tall, well-built man who had stepped through the doorway. *Well, at least there is just one, so that is a good sign,* he thought to himself.

To his astonishment, instead of panic, Marco found the atmosphere in the room abuzz with excitement. Many enthusiastic refugees surrounded the man as they thanked him and introduced themselves.

No way that he could be an American authority, Marco concluded.

One of the Cuban handlers noticed half of Marco's face sticking out of the room. "Señor Marco, please come. Bring your brother. We want to introduce you."

Without waiting for his brother, Marco stepped out into the hallway where he could better see the face of the man who had walked in. The man's eyes widened in immediate recognition and surprise. It took Marco a moment, but then memories overwhelmed him — memories from a decade ago. He knew that face. He had debated with it a hundred times. Granted, several years of age were added to his features, but there was no mistaking him. Still, it seemed almost impossible to believe.

"Vladislav?" Marco half-whispered as Julio came up behind him.

Perplexed by the expression of shock on his brother's face, Julio cocked his head in confusion. He wiped his eyeglasses as if it might give him more clarity, but he didn't recognize the man his brother was staring at, even with clean lenses.

"Señor Marco, Señor Julio — this is Señor Moisés, the one who helped you out of Cuba," the proud handler said as he presented the man.

Concealing any look of surprise on his face, Vladi introduced himself for the sake of appearances. "I am Señor Moisés. It is a pleasure to have you here," Vladi said as he walked toward Marco with an outstretched hand.

Marco slowly took his hand and shook it. The look of bewilderment in his countenance said it all.

"I hope I will get a chance to speak with you and your brother in a short while," Vladi said as he gave Marco a knowing look. "But for now, please, let us enjoy our breakfast."

Marco couldn't enjoy his breakfast. He distractedly stirred it around his plate as he tried to sneak glances at "Señor Moisés," who seemed to have retained his appetite. *How could this even be possible?* he wondered over and over.

"What's the matter with you?" Julio asked his brother. "You have an odd look on your face. Why do you look at Señor Moisés like he's a ghost?"

"I know him," Marco replied, "but I'm not sure that he isn't a ghost." He didn't offer any other explanation, and Julio, knowing Marco, thought it best to wait until they were alone to press for more details.

Marco didn't say anymore until he saw Vladi get up and thank the handlers for breakfast as he headed out the door. Not even trying to disguise his haste, Marco's chair scraped across the floor as he pushed back to follow Vladi.

"Vladi, it is you, isn't it?" Marco launched his question at the man's back.

Vladi turned around, and Marco got a better look at his face. Although he'd aged into his mid-forties, Vladi looked healthy and vigorous. He looked like a man who lived well.

"Of course it is me. Have you ever seen another such ruggedly handsome Russian in your whole life?" Vladi smiled and laughed. There was no doubt it was him. "Can we not embrace after all these years?" Vladi asked. "It is the Latin way, is it not?"

Julio walked out the door to see his brother in a bear hug with Señor Moisés, both men vigorously slapping each other's back in friendship.

Marco beckoned his brother over. "Vladi, this is my brother, Julio. You made it possible for us to leave together."

The men exchanged pleasantries before Vladi again turned to Marco. "Please, when others are around, address me as Señor Moisés. I prefer my real name and background to be known to as few people as possible — for security purposes."

"I understand," Marco nodded. "I just can't believe that you are Señor Moisés. I would never have guessed this in a million years. Even more so, I can't believe that you are still alive. We heard that your plane vanished. When I first saw you, I thought you were some ghost returning from the Triángulo del Diablo," Marco half laughed. Julio gave a slight shake of his head and looked at his brother as if that were nothing to joke about.

"When I woke up in the ocean, to tell the truth, I wondered if I could be a dead man too." Vladi stopped for a moment in thought. "Come," he continued, "let us go back to my home where I will tell you the story in comfort and with no prying ears."

17

THE CAPITALIST PARADISE

When Vladi had used the word "comfort," Marco had not imagined what he meant by it. In addition to the air conditioned American pickup truck they rode in, a far cry from the jalopies in Cuba, the house they drove up to made Marco's jaw drop with awe. He did his best to stifle an audible gasp as they approached the sprawling and luxurious house. He didn't want to look like a peasant who had never seen wealth before. After all, he and his family had been well off in Cuba. In fact, he had been far better off than Vladi had been as a Soviet soldier. The most remarkable aspect wasn't the property's grandeur, but the fact that this place belonged to Vladi.

"This house is yours?" Marco couldn't help but ask. He needed to hear the confirmation.

"Yes, it is mine. Please come in," Vladi said with an unassuming air as he opened the ornate, gilded front door and guided the men inside.

The interior of the residence was just as regal as its exterior. They were escorted into a vast living room with floor-to-ceiling windows that looked out over an expansive lawn and tasteful garden. Marco and Julio's heads were swiveling trying to take it all in.

"This is unbelievable. But how?" Marco maffled. Julio was too captivated to give attention to Marco's remarks.

As they sat down, a stocky and smiling Cuban woman appeared and offered the men refreshments.

"You have a Cuban servant?" Marco asked with a note of distaste.

"I do not think of her as a servant, but she is an employee — and yes, she works for me in this house, as do several more," Vladi clarified. He endeavored to assuage any ill notions the men might have had. "All are here just as you are, but I have given them jobs and a place to live."

Marco could not wrap his mind around it all. "I can't wait any longer. I need to know how you went from a Russian soldier, near dead in the sea, to . . . this." He gestured around the room.

Vladi sat back and told the men his decade-long story of survival, hard work, and rise to affluence. He also told how he came to be the mastermind behind this large "underground railroad" from Cuba to the United States.

When he concluded his story, Marco leaned forward and pondered his words for a moment. "Even after hearing your story, I cannot reconcile this. You were a man who looked down on our people as superstitious peasants while you were in Cuba. And here you are helping us escape? And to a country that is a sworn enemy? To the domain of capitalism? How is this possible?" Marco asked. His voice intensified with each question.

Julio put a hand on his shoulder, an indication that Marco needed to calm down.

"I'm sure you can understand his . . . incredulity, Señor Moisés. It feels like such a fantastic story, even to my ears," Julio tried to smooth things over.

"What can I say? It is the truth. Maybe being near to death changed something in my head," Vladi said. "Maybe in part it was my gratitude for the Cubans who took me into their homes and showed me the way to a job and other help when I first became stranded. But what better way to use capitalists' wealth than to slip Cuban immigrants into the country right under their noses?" Vladi's lips turned up in a mischievous half-smile.

"That is —" Marco searched for the words. "You seem to have developed a more — let's say — generous disposition while here. Don't mistake me, I don't want to seem ungrateful for what you have done for me and Julio and all the others. I'm just trying to make sense of it all. It is all so . . . unexpected."

"It is true — while in Cuba, doing this kind of work would never have crossed my mind in a million years. Beyond our assignment, I only cared about returning home to my family." Vladi paused, reflecting. "And to this day, it is still my foremost hope."

"I think the thing that perplexes me most is the life you live here. You, so against the greed of the capitalist system, appear to live now as part of that same system. You've swallowed it. How have your ideals changed so much?" Marco wondered aloud. The man speaking to him didn't sound much like the old Vladi.

"Ideals?" Vladi smirked. "They went away when I crashed with no way home. Communist, capitalist — what did it matter? Come now, survival was my ideal — it was the one thing that mattered. I did what I needed to do. I saw opportunities, and I took them. I must admit that I do like American convenience, abundance, and courtesy. The food . . . is good too. Such things are not always bad. Today, I would not deny that I have considerable means at my disposal, but I have not 'swallowed' Yankee greed. Instead, I make it my point to use my wealth to also benefit others."

"But not without benefit to yourself first," Marco challenged in a condescending tone.

Why is he being like this? Vladi thought to himself. *Is he perhaps insecure that now we are not so much peers? Maybe he feels there is a wide gap in our status inside America? Marco had everything there was to have in Cuba. Now, he may need to rely on someone although he feels he is . . . above everyone. Hmm. That may be difficult for a man such as Marco.* Vladi's assessment was accurate. Marco was not content with this arrangement.

"To have my own land and business has benefits, yes. But should I be ashamed of it? I worked hard for all this. I was not handed anything because of family connections." Vladi took a dig at Marco's easy path to success in Cuba. "Which is why it is a surprise to find you of all people here. You had everything back in Cuba — connections, status, enough money and benefits. Why did you leave it all to come here and be reduced to . . . well, nothing?"

Marco winced at that last question. The acknowledgment of his current change in status rattled him.

But before he could reply, Vladi recalled, "Ah, it was that book on American democracy and economics that you read, was it not? Of course, I remember the debate we had when you were reading it in secret, right? It seems you are the one who swallowed the capitalist idea, whereas I took advantage out of necessity."

Marco seemed stricken by Vladi's judgment. Meanwhile, Julio sipped his tea as if no one else were in the room.

Marco replied with a quick recovery, "It's true that the book I read had some interesting ideas, but when we debated, I played the devil's advocate for no other reason than to goad you." Marco smiled. He didn't want to tell Vladi the whole truth behind the reason he left — that the coveted position he had once been so proud to hold in Castro's Cuba had progressively eroded his humanity.

Vladi smiled sincerely. "I have fond memories of those spirited debates between our younger selves."

Marco gave a small chuckle, "It seems like nothing has changed. We have picked up right where we left off."

"Well, we will have plenty of time to contemplate the merits and pitfalls of this American system, my friend, and I am sure you will have more to say on the subject once you see things with your own eyes."

Marco smiled, but his voice contained a note of sarcasm: "Yes, I can't wait to see these streets paved with gold and the capitalist paradise that you have brought us to with all its glorious democracy."

Vladi laughed sardonically. "Yes . . . 'capitalist paradise.' We will see how much paradise you find once you come to accept this as home."

EYES TO SEE

"**B**lessed are the eyes which see the things you see."

Julio thought of these words of Jesus whenever he slipped on his new eyeglasses, which he wore every waking moment. He looked in awe at the crisp, clear world around him.

He had saved a few dollars from his weekly earnings until he had enough to pay for an eye exam with an American optometrist. Julio finally got the prescription glasses he needed after waiting his entire life. The instant he put on his glasses, the world transformed into a crystal clear wonderland. He twirled around the office, admiring how everything looked through his new glasses — it was amazing!

But getting to this point had not been easy. He had struggled through medical school and his practice in Cuba with a donated pair of eyeglasses, a prescription meant for someone else. Still, it was better than nothing. Once, just before leaving Cuba with Marco, he came close to securing a pair of glasses for himself.

The people in Cuba always endured the same problems. Despite being a doctor, it still took a long time to secure an appointment for an eye exam at the polyclinic. First, he needed to find a day without obligations to visit his elderly and pregnant patients. Then he had to wake up at the crack of dawn to get to the clinic early, and even then, he couldn't be sure they'd see him.

Trying to get an eye exam in Cuba was an ordeal — the long lines, the waiting, and the uncertainty of whether or not the office had power that day or that the optometrist would even show up. After Julio finally got a prescription for his glasses, the optician didn't have frames or lenses available. When one was there, the other was not. As he thought back about the many obstacles he faced along the way, he couldn't help but laugh at the absurdity of it all.

He remembered visiting Óptica Domínguez, conveniently located on the Boulevard Varadero, back when he and Marco were still in Havana. A nice optician named Carmen told him, "You're lucky. We have lenses for this prescription." She bent behind the desk, took out a cardboard box, and rummaged through it, taking frames out and putting them back. Some were fine, and others were awfully unappealing.

Without losing her smile, she looked at Julio and said, "You're not in complete luck, but you should come back next week. We'll receive our shipment of merchandise on Tuesday, and it will probably include some frames that you can use. Try to come back on Wednesday. Customers shouldn't hear me say this," Carmen whispered, "but I don't want you to waste your time coming here for nothing." Being the good Cuban he was, Julio whispered his gratitude for her secret information.

The following Wednesday, Julio went to the opticians. When the doors finally opened, he was third in line. Waiting for his turn, he approached the desk. Carmen greeted him with a smile but informed him that once again, it wasn't his lucky day. They were doing inventory and had to categorize all the merchandise. "But don't give up. Come next Monday," she encouraged him.

As with all things in Cuba, patience was key. And Julio had plenty of it. He was the first in line on Monday, and he was lucky — they had frames, lenses, and electricity! The ever-pleasant Carmen handed him a receipt after he paid her $59.12 ordinary Cuban pesos (about two dollars in U.S. in currency), but instructed him to come back in three weeks to pick them up.

Never losing hope, Julio went back on the day Carmen told him to return. Despite the many setbacks and delays, she always greeted him with a smile and a kind word of encouragement. She pulled out a large book, politely flipped through it for a long time, and eventually found the page that coincided with his number, 379-R. She raised her eyes and, without losing her pleasant composure, told Julio to return in two weeks. There had been a delay at the workshop.

Why should something as basic as a pair of eyeglasses be so difficult to obtain? Julio couldn't help but think about all the people who had given up hope and were still struggling with poor vision. It was a harsh reminder of the systemic issues that plagued the country and the people who called it home.

He had seen this similar situation play out over and over again with his patients. When they went to a pharmacy to fill a prescription or when he had to refer them to a specialist, the same thing happened. They had to keep returning, no matter how urgent, because something was always wrong.

But all of that was now in the past. He finally had a pair of glasses fitted for his own eyes, and he felt grateful every time he put them on. Now he could see the world in all its glorious detail that he had missed for years. It was as if he'd been living in a hazy dream his entire life. Everything now was more vibrant — buildings, foliage, the faces of people — it was all so new and exciting. He even saw things he never knew existed — a ladybug on a leaf, a butterfly on a flower. And the best part? He could read without squinting and headaches. Most importantly, he could read the Word of the living God.

A new freedom that the refugees experienced was that of religion. Not only were they free to worship as they chose, but places of worship also made essential resources available for needy refugees. Local mission churches within the refugee community and Christian ministries from beyond their immediate area gave aid to anyone who needed assistance.

Most importantly, many people, including Julio, heard God's Word explained. By the illuminating work of God the Holy Spirit, they came to know and trust Christ Jesus alone. They were baptized publicly, able to openly declare their faith in Him. Something like this would have been unthinkable back in Cuba.

The Cuban refugees knew Pastor Gerardo Ortiz well. Even people who had never met him were familiar with him from a local Spanish radio ministry. He was a kind and unassuming man, loved and respected by all.

Gerardo had not always served as a minister. He had a formal education in metallurgical engineering. Details mattered to Gerardo. With the accuracy of a professional engineer, he had a comfortable, methodical approach to God's Word. Not to suggest he treated Scripture with cold precision — to the contrary, Gerardo was warm and genuine. When he taught the Bible in their community, people came from great distances because they perceived he spoke the truth.

For Julio, the opportunity to hear Pastor Gerardo explain the Bible satisfied a yearning he had felt much of his life. His knowledge of God and the Bible had been limited back in Cuba. Now he was keen to listen and learn.

Through the years in Cuba, Julio was told that God was "not allowed," but he never doubted God's existence. He knew the truth in his conscience, and the beauty and wonders of nature proved to him that God existed. Pastor Gerardo spoke to Julio and the other refugees about this same God as He is revealed in the text of their Bibles. It was this God who had been gently calling Julio to Himself over the years. This was the true God whom he had always wanted to know, so with rapt eagerness, Julio absorbed all that Pastor Gerardo taught in their little church.

Julio's faith went beyond just believing that God existed — he in fact believed God in every way. He trusted God, relied on Him, and took Him at His Word. His Christian faith bore fruit because it was real. He would ask the question, "What are we to be about?" Attending church was no mere religious formality. He participated as one who followed Christ in every respect as the Master of his life. Julio considered it joyful obedience to have the opportunity to worship alongside other believers.

Marco, on the other hand, in typical Marco fashion had no interest in what Gerardo had to say about his faith. He allowed Julio to drag him along to meetings from time to time, but he made no effort to listen to the Bible teaching except to be critical. When he did hear something that he didn't like, he spent the rest of the time thinking about how he could discredit and disprove the teaching and the teacher.

"What a joy it is to be among God's people and to sing praises to our great King!" Julio expressed one evening as they walked through the doorway into the meeting and looked around. His genuine contentment in the Lord overflowed. Julio eagerly looked forward to each church service and Bible study meeting in anticipation of what he might learn next. Whenever he spoke of it, Julio's speech turned to hushed tones that conveyed his delight. "You know when we've worked hard all day, and we are hungry and thirsty? I need God's truth in this same way!"

After three years as a believer, that enthusiasm had never waned. Having been denied access to a Bible and the Lord's church all those years in Cuba, Julio felt he had been transplanted from a barren place. He was now rooted where he drank from a plentiful stream of truth and understood how he depended on consistent discipleship in order to grow spiritually.

Julio told his brother, "In God's grace to His church, He surrounds us with mature people who have gone before us — who are able to teach and model what it is to follow Him. I always look forward to opportunities to hear Pastor Gerardo teach. When he preaches, we hear God's words, and they make their way into me and nourish my soul — that is so satisfying!"

Marco gave an eye roll that revealed his exasperation.

Indifferent to his brother's gesture, Julio proceeded, "Pastor Gerardo is an earnest man of God. I love what we learn from him."

"Of course you would," Marco replied with a cynical tone. "You seem so ready to trust anyone who comes to you under the pretense of Christianity. Don't you think that some of these characters are charlatans? They'll say whatever you hope to hear to gain followers for themselves. That should frighten you, my brother."

"Oh, you mean like Castro did?" Julio fired back with a half-smile. He knew

Marco would have no rebuttal. "Of course, I get what you're saying though," he added to soften the remark.

But it didn't matter to Marco, who had just become distracted. He tapped Julio's shoulder mid-sentence, not taking his eyes from the middle of the room. Marco recognized two of the faces at the gathering, although his mind refused to reconcile what he saw. Those faces would be etched into his memory for life. Unmistakably, it was them.

"Who are those men?" he asked Julio. "I mean . . . I know who they are, but why are they here?"

"Oh, you mean Rico and Jorge?" Julio casually acknowledged.

"Who?" asked Marco, still staring unabashed. "It's the priest and the boxer!" he exclaimed, perhaps a bit too loudly.

Julio gave him a hard look. "Yes, Rico and Jorge."

Marco watched, bewildered, as the boxer offered a flimsy folding chair to the erstwhile witch doctor, and the two distinct, bald men sat down beside one another and engaged in pleasant conversation.

Marco, his eyes wide in almost comic disbelief, turned to Julio. "What is going on? These can't be the same men from the boat. Not possible!"

Julio couldn't hide a snicker at his brother's reaction.

"God the Holy Spirit does marvelous work," answered Julio with a satisfied smile.

Santeria was a fringe practice in Cuba, a syncretistic blend of the polytheistic Yoruba religion of West Africa and Roman Catholicism. Followers of Santeria practiced many forms of spirit divination, which included animal sacrifices.

Julio explained, "Santero Ricardo, as he was called, heard Pastor Gerardo preaching truth. For the first time, he learned from the Bible instead of tradition. He could see in God's infallible Word that he took part in a great deception, he turned away from his past religion and superstitions to follow the way of Christ Jesus alone."

Marco's eyes made a slow, deliberate blink in response to his astonishment, as though he were trying to determine whether what he was seeing was real.

"He is a humble man — he just goes by Rico now," Julio continued, "We never bring up his past, although he does at times. He has immense gratitude for our Lord's mercy and deliverance from a false religion that was woven into the cultural fabric of many Cuban families. Now, he is most outspoken to tell anyone who will listen . . . and even those who don't," Julio chortled with a soft smile.

"Your reformed medicine man friend hasn't been among the orchard workers. What has he been doing? What does a retired voodoo priest do for work in America?" Marco asked with genuine curiosity, keeping his voice low so as not to be overheard.

"Rico has become a teacher in the little school for Cuban families. He also has a keen eye for eclectic items, which he buys and sells for extra income. He must have retained at least a little of his Santerían juju because it seems like everything he touches turns to gold," Julio chuckled.

Marco wasn't sure how to respond to that. He didn't want to admit his envy that this odd and diminutive man had become someone successful in his own right. He squinted in contempt. *He still looks like a weasel.*

Marco turned his attention to yet another curiosity. He nodded toward the jovial man who sat beside Rico. "And what's his story? I never pictured him as the religious type."

"Jorge, the boxer, first settled in Hialeah, Florida. He took an American moniker, 'Mad George,' and had a remarkable record in the amateur ring. He was a promising favorite, slated to debut as a professional fighter at a highly promoted event in Las Vegas. But sadly for him, a well-placed blow from an opponent left him with a career-ending injury."

"What a shame," Marco remarked sarcastically while he picked at a fingernail with feigned boredom. "That's no surprise he'd tried his luck at pro boxing in the States, nor that he ended up getting hurt." Marco still didn't think much of the boxer, considering the hassle he had caused everyone during their passage to freedom. The same inner workings that had resentment for Rico's success felt a touch of elation at the boxer's failure.

"Perhaps his misfortune was God's providence," Julio shrugged, always inclined to have a more gracious viewpoint. "Jorge used to be illiterate — living by the strength of his physical dominance. Rico, ever so compassionate and patient, instructed him how to read and write and do basic math. As Rico taught him these things, he shared with Jorge the Scriptures and prayed with him for the hope of knowing Christ Jesus."

Marco gave a short barking laugh that caused a few people in the circle to look their way. Responding with a slight grimace, he realized he needed to tone it down. *How those two ended up as friends is just too amusing, given their history.* He still found it unbelievable.

Julio surmised his brother's thoughts and smiled. "I know, it is rather remarkable. Rico would tell you that Jorge had a 'heart transplant' — God took his heart of stone and gave him a heart of flesh that's alive and filled with joy. He's living proof that people who were spiritually dead and blind are made new creations, transferred from the domain of darkness to that of Christ Jesus."

Marco rolled his eyes again, but Julio was passionate about this and didn't let it deter him. "Through the gospel, God the Holy Spirit changes a degenerate man and gives life when we were helpless in our depravity. He gives us faith and love for Himself that we didn't know before we were transformed by the work of Christ Jesus in salvation. What's more, He puts us in our right minds once and for all."

The din of voices quieted as the group prepared for Pastor Gerardo to preach.

Marco felt out of his element and voiced his thoughts before he could stop them. "What a comfort it must be to know some ghost looks out for you. Too bad He can't intervene before bad things happen."

A solemn look came into Julio's eyes. He moved closer and placed a hand on Marco's shoulder. "You're missing the point, brother," he all but whispered, also aware of the room getting quieter. "God is in control all along the way — no detail, good or bad from our limited perspective, falls outside of the Lord's control." Julio gestured toward the boxer. "It transformed Jorge's life when he came to know the Lord. He is a new man, altogether changed from the vile character we saw before. He put on the 'new man,' as the apostle Paul spoke about. Today, Jorge is as gentle as a kitten."

Marco scoffed again and shook off Julio's hand.

Julio continued, "Perhaps even more amazing evidence of how the Lord works when one submits to His truth is that they're now best friends. In fact, together they teach the Bible to our children. There's no more humble and engaged servant of our Lord than Jorge."

Marco had to admit he was awed by the transformation. He would never have believed it had he not seen it with his own fascinated eyes.

Julio gently tugged Marco into his seat as Pastor Gerardo began to speak.

The pastor taught from the ninth and tenth chapters of the book of Hebrews. This passage occupied a special place in Julio's heart, for it represented the foundation of how God had saved him. This was the good news of Christ Jesus alone. Being in a church now, Julio took particular delight in Hebrews 10:24-25, "And let us consider how to stimulate one another to love and good deeds, not forsaking our own assembling together, as is the habit of some, but encouraging one another, and all the more as you see the day drawing near."

Gerardo recounted how the ancient Israelites, enslaved by the Egyptians, knew about God but were hindered from practicing their worship. Then, as now, all of mankind had forfeited access to God as a consequence of sin. The only holy God could not be directly approached because of the sinfulness of every man. God forced the hand of the Pharaoh to release the Israelites from bondage so that they could worship Him and know His ways and follow Him.

Once the Israelites set up a tabernacle for worship, the high priest was the only person on the whole earth who could enter the Holy of Holies, into God's presence. Even then, such access was reserved for only one day a year, and the priest was required to bring the God-prescribed blood sacrifices of animals to atone for the sins of the people. There were many rituals and external washings, but they were not the ultimate solution — they pointed to another — a great High Priest — who was, Himself, the only acceptable sacrifice. Only Christ Jesus was sinless, perfectly righteous, and worthy of fellowship with the living God.

At the hands of government executioners, Christ Jesus offered His own blood as a ransom. His sacrifice obtained and guaranteed eternal redemption rather than a recurrent and transient reprieve, making it infinitely superior to the sacrifices of animals. The wages of sin is death, but there is one hope for doomed men. Pastor Gerardo showed them from God's Word how through this sacrifice, once and for all, by mercy and grace, the indelible stain of sin could be purified. Anyone who trusted Christ Jesus would receive a true pardon from Him — and this has always been the only way for fallen man to have access to God.

Julio knew himself to be among those who put faith in Christ Jesus' death as a ransom to secure his complete forgiveness. Not only could Julio know about God now, but Julio could also know his Lord. He had a right relationship with the trustworthy Creator of all the universe and all of history. Julio would be eternally grateful, and he couldn't help but ponder how the Lord had established his footsteps that brought him here. It was the Lord who guided him then and now.

Marco, of course, remained dubious about this crucial aspect of Julio's beliefs. *Why*, thought Marco, *would anyone have the notion that sins could be excused this way?* For Marco, the entire discussion of blood sacrifices seemed like the foolish talk of an ancient cult. Had he listened with ears that wanted to hear, he would have known the answer to his question.

Before they departed the gathering, Marco and Julio were greeted by Rico and Jorge. Marco, the ever-curious Inquisitor, couldn't resist the urge to question Rico, "What made you abandon your traditional religious beliefs for this church, so obsessed with reading the Bible back and forth, over and over again?"

Rico's answer was too basic to satisfy Marco's mind. "God made it clear in

His Word about the necessity to cure sin and the fact that my religion had no remedy. Once I understood, there was no turning back."

"That simple, eh?" Marco asked with a tone of derision, smiling and shaking his head condescendingly. "You're more gullible than my brother here." Julio frowned at Marco's rudeness. It was one thing for Marco to make those remarks to him privately, but another to go to a public meeting and mock others.

Rico, however, remained unperturbed. "Perhaps you cannot understand unless the Lord reveals His truth to you," he replied amiably, adding, "The Bible says we are like sheep. Left to our own devices, we will not choose what is right."

Marco huffed. "No one has ever mistaken me for a stupid sheep."

Despite the rhetoric, the unassailable reality was that Julio knew a joy in life that his brother did not experience now, nor had he ever. And although their convictions differed, neither of them was spared life's real problems. They both had to deal with serious difficulties. They still lived in a world of injustice and real hardship.

These days, Marco wanted to attribute his misery and all his problems to the burden of work they were doing for the ever-demanding Vladi. Marco had hoped for Vladi to save them from the misery on earth that Cuba had become, but as the years went by, he came to feel misled by the man he had once trusted.

BANEFUL ENVY

Once Cuban refugees set foot on American soil, they were met with numerous conundrums and new challenges. Señor Moisés had helped them get across to Florida, and they were free once they arrived, but many came to find that they had few prospects for finding a better job than working for Vladi. The citrus growers, including his own company, Red Star Citrus, provided the best option for gainful employment. This could be considered an opportunity or exploitative, depending on one's perspective.

Not that the refugee community didn't understand this arrangement — they knew the deal. They accepted that things had to be that way, as there were few better alternatives. In a pragmatic sense, it worked and provided what they needed to survive. Even government officials understood the value of the arrangement. They turned a blind eye to the undocumented status of immigrant workers who were indispensable to the citrus trade, which was essential to the state economy.

Vladi supposed he had a symbiotic arrangement that benefited everyone. Yes, he profited from the operation — no doubt about that. But he had no moral conflict about what he was doing, nor how he was going about it. It was the money from his own pockets that enabled him to continue aiding refugees. And who else would give the refugees much-needed jobs so that they could survive once they arrived in Florida? If Vladi didn't, perhaps someone else would, but they might not be as good to the Cuban refugees as he was.

But not everyone viewed what Vladi was doing through the same rosy lens of altruism. Some refugees, like the ego-bruised Marco, had a different outlook on their situation. Over the three years that he and Julio had labored in the citrus groves for Vladi, his perspective turned from gratitude to festering resentment that, in time, would boil over.

Like other refugees, Marco gratefully accepted Vladi's help at first, yet the hubris Marco had developed from his status in Cuba only allowed him to regard Vladi as an equal at most. And in his mind, he had no obligation to submit to this former peer who had turned into a sellout, the beneficiary of ill-gotten gain in a haven for filthy capitalism.

From Marco's perspective, Vladi had established what amounted to a human smuggling racket. He saw desperate Cuban refugees becoming workers in Vladi's "labor camps." Not only had Vladi become the capitalist he always loathed and fought against, but now he also exploited people in what Marco considered the worst way.

"He is preying on their desperation to escape the misery of Cuba under Castro," he told Julio on multiple occasions. At other times, he bemoaned his own perceived lack of success. "I cannot understand why, after three years, I have not amassed this capitalist wealth like our overlord, Vladi! I think he purposely keeps us poor so that his 'slaves' cannot leave."

"Well, then why don't you get out there and do something the way Vladi did?" Julio reasoned with him. "There's no one stopping you, except yourself. This is America. You have the freedom to choose your own course in life. Keep in mind that whatever you do, the responsibility is on you. This is the land of opportunity, not the land of guarantees. God has blessed you with good health and a keen mind, so do something with that."

When Marco remained silent, Julio continued, "People are willing to pay for help with whatever they can't provide for themselves and for things they're unwilling to do for themselves. If you know that and you're willing to do the work, it's really hard for you to go wrong. Whatever we do with our lives in America is bound to be an improvement over what we had in Cuba."

Marco wasn't interested in a pep talk — he wasn't looking for real solutions. He wanted someone to get on his emotional bandwagon. So when Julio mentioned that they were better off than before, Marco's thoughts went right back to reflecting on life back in Cuba and argued to the contrary. In his old life, he had been nearer to the top of the pecking order.

"Sure, Castro's economic policies had some problems — okay, a lot of problems — but in Cuba, I held some authority and had security in my position."

Marco had come to America with some presumptions about what it meant to be free and equal. But life in America was a jarring change in more ways than one. Marco couldn't wield the same influence upon people here, namely Vladi.

"I feel like I'm under that tyrant's boot!" he ranted to Julio as he paced the floor of their home. "I knew him before. And now he dares to make demands of me like I'm his slave? It's not right!"

Julio reclined in his chair and offered a calm reply, "Well, he is our employer. Therefore, he has the right to ask us to complete whatever work he requires."

Marco gritted his teeth, inhaled deeply, and pursed his lips at Julio. "Are you serious? Don't you even hear what I'm telling you? He's using us. And he's the one who thinks it's fine to elevate himself to become our taskmaster."

"Brother, your ego is not your *amigo*. I think you're taking it a little too far." By now, Julio had become as uninterested as he sounded. He picked up a newspaper in an attempt to end the conversation and practice his English reading skills. He had become weary of hearing these increasingly vitriolic rants.

Even beyond taking orders from Vladi, Marco found it difficult to adjust to the pace of life that accompanied American capitalism. To him, it felt like everyone moved in a frenzy of incessant wealth accumulation in order to spend more lavishly. The Cuban way of life didn't have the same pervasive sense of urgency. Life moved slower. People were less disposed to covet the next flashy car, bigger houses, or the newest fashion. Marco never quite felt at home in Florida — like he was an outsider in a strange land.

Marco's attitude toward the whole situation had deteriorated not long into his new life as a labor hand in the orange groves. Marco knew Vladi was the "big boss," but he had somewhat expected Vladi to sweat and get dirty down in the field alongside him and the other workers. He didn't understand that Vladi had multiple orchards and many workers to manage, along with the never-ending challenges that accompanied those responsibilities. Marco didn't even see him often. When he did, Vladi was driving around in the comfort of his air-conditioned pickup truck, only getting out long enough to bark orders to the field hands.

Marco made sure to glare in his direction whenever he saw Vladi sitting high and mighty in his truck passing along the narrow, dusty grove road. It was a futile gesture that Vladi could not even see from a distance. Even if he could, he wouldn't deign to notice. Yet it was Marco's sole means of expressing his contempt, at least for the moment. There eventually came a time when hot-headed Marco felt he had to speak up for himself and the other workers.

"If I don't do it, who will? Who else has the courage to question him?" he asked Julio.

The irony was that Marco already had one of the cushier jobs within the Red Star Citrus operations. His primary responsibility was quality control, checking and evaluating fruit. He helped monitor the timing of the harvest and yield. Since the quality of the fruit varied throughout the year, it was crucial to the growing operations that this be performed with accuracy. He was tasked with ensuring all field paperwork had been completed correctly, and any issues were reported to the growing coordinator-supervisor.

Marco was selected for this job because he was well-educated and he was precise. It wasn't as prestigious as the post he held in Cuba, but considering the various occupations available to orchard labor hands, quality control was among the more desirable jobs.

Still, Marco was paid the same as everyone else, and never once did he receive praise or special acknowledgment for his work. In the Red Star Citrus operations, he was just another labor hand, nothing more special. The trouble with Marco was that he didn't like that fact — it grated on his ego. When he later aired his resentment to his brother and other refugees, he did so with righteous indignation.

"Who does he think he is?" Marco complained to Julio. "How dare he sit in his fancy truck and live in the fancy house that he built on the backs of slave labor!"

Julio gave an eye roll to underscore that he was exasperated by the conversation. "We are paid labor hands, oh indignant one. He helps the community and us by giving us work to live. What did you think you would do here to survive? Did you expect a warm greeting from the United States government? Did you assume you'd be made a high-ranking intelligence agent? Complete with all the attendant benefits, of course!" Julio remarked with sarcasm. "Just what injustice do you feel is being committed against us? We were given everything we were promised — no more, no less."

Marco didn't answer. He instead let out an aggravated expression of dismissiveness mixed with annoyance and looked away.

"Pride and discontentment are at the root of all sorts of sin." Julio recently heard Pastor Gerardo teach the church about this. He added, "When we don't appreciate what our Lord provides, we're heading toward trouble."

Marco growled and continued with his work. The truth was that he had no real answer other than that he didn't like his new situation, and life had not turned out how he had imagined it would. That book about democracy in America that he had read years ago, the one that piqued his curiosity about the benefits of a capitalist society, had not painted in his mind the complete picture of reality. Some, like Marco, reached the new world and found it unforgiving. Others, like Vladi, thrived and developed businesses that contributed to the community.

What la basura that book turned out to be! It was misleading in its ideas about self-made men who have equal opportunities, Marco concluded.

Mostly, Marco was jealous. He despised Vladi because Vladi embodied all of Marco's preconceived notions of himself. So Vladi became the target of Marco's mercurial resentment.

"The next time I see that lizard, I'm going to tell him straight out what I think of him and his loathsome 'business'!" Marco vowed.

"Please don't," was Julio's irritated reply. He had no doubt that Marco would, indeed, speak his mind, and he had a dreadful sense that the outcome would be nothing less than disastrous.

A few weeks later, Marco came close to having his say. The Florida air was baking hot in the grove. Through eyes stinging with salty sweat, Marco saw Vladi get out of his truck. At last, the opportunity for which he had long been waiting presented itself. Marco put down what he was doing and almost gleefully walked toward the "big boss." Finally, he had his chance.

As he walked up to Vladi and planted his feet squarely in his path, Marco opened his mouth to speak. Before a complete word came out, Julio quickly sidled up to him and handed him a refreshing glass of water.

"You need this," was all Julio said.

Marco did need it. In the time it took a parched Marco to take a few gulps of water, another worker had grabbed Vladi's attention, and the two men walked off together.

Marco watched them walk away before he made an angry turn to face his brother. But he found that Julio, too, had shrewdly walked away in the other direction. Marco crushed the paper cup and threw it at his brother's back, missing him by inches.

Marco continued grumbling and swearing to his brother for a few more months before he found another opportunity to pounce on Vladi. He sighted the Russian in the orchard at some distance, talking to a group of workers.

Even better. Marco smiled to himself. *This time, I will have an audience — so much more effective than if he were confronted alone. Now, this is the perfect moment.*

Working a few trees away from his brother, Julio watched Marco stop and stare for a moment before striding off in haste. He saw Marco's target at a distance. Right away, Julio took off through the rows to try to catch him.

Before Marco was within speaking distance, Julio called out, still running, "Señor Moisés! Señor Moisés! Please come this way. It is urgent!"

There was nothing urgent, but Julio hoped he would quickly think of something or make up a story that he could later prove to have been "mistaken" about to excuse away the lack of any actual emergency.

With his attention diverted, Vladi wrapped up his conversation, turned away from Marco, and started walking toward Julio. Marco stopped in his tracks, deflated and snorting with anger through his flared nostrils.

"Why?" Marco shouted later that night as he burst through the door of the shanty home he shared with his brother. Marco knew that Julio had betrayed him on purpose this time.

"What do you mean 'why'?" Julio asked with innocence, not even glancing up from his meal. Julio always adopted a cautious approach when Marco was upset.

"Acckkkk," Marco hissed, "don't even pretend — you know exactly what I mean! You know how I've been waiting months for an opportunity to talk to him face-to-face about our situation!" he yelled.

"Our situation? Yes, we are in the same situation, but you know I don't share your outlook, and I don't want to be drawn into a conflict," Julio said mildly, taking another bite.

"It doesn't matter. I'm doing this for you too!" Marco pointed out, his words still hot.

Julio sighed and put down his fork. No use pretending he didn't know what Marco had been trying to do earlier and what he had done to stop it. "And I'm doing this for you. You need to change your outlook before you make a big mistake, brother. This is the life you have chosen — this is the life you made me choose along with you, and I am not complaining. I accept it, and I don't understand why you refuse to."

Marco paced, trying to rein in his temper, although not too effectively. He was still raging inside. *How can Julio be so relaxed about this? Why does he seem unaffected by this inequity? Does he not care? He would rather accommodate adversity than do something about it. Well, I can't!*

Marco, of course, considered himself exceptional because he wasn't willing to just overlook things — to forgive humiliation or to pardon an affront. He would make a stand for justice as he saw it. Indeed, he was on an altogether different track from Julio.

Julio met Marco with resolute eyes of his own. "Marco," he said firmly, "there's nothing wrong with you wanting to improve your situation. But the way you're talking about Vladi, all the resentment, it's not the way to do it. Call it what it is, 'sin' — and it only brings trouble.

"Christ Jesus told us to 'love your enemies' — pray for them and do good to them. I've learned there's safety in obedience and submission to our Lord. And Vladi is not my enemy, he's my boss, and I want the best for him.

"Look, whenever I deviate from the truth, I've found that trouble inevitably follows. And I won't envy Vladi's earthly circumstances — they're temporary. It's not to suggest we have a life without hardship or suffering, but it does mean that I choose to live in agreement with what pleases God."

"Don't start preaching again!" Marco bristled. He couldn't take his brother's complacent attitude toward their situation and his religious pretense for passivity. If his God could alleviate misery, why hadn't He done so? After all, Julio supposedly loved Him so much. And Marco had seen too much to sense that for himself — indeed, he had even caused much suffering, but God never stopped him.

Unruffled, Julio took a moment to think before he answered. "No one can force you to take my faith as your own, although you know I desire with all my heart that you would. No doubt, doing so would relieve much of your anguish."

Marco stopped pacing, his eyes wide with frustration. "But Julio, how can you be so content with our situation? I feel like a prisoner in my own life."

"Marco, I trust in God's sovereignty and wisdom — that we're here for a reason, whatever that may be. I may not understand it, but I'm okay with that because I trust Him. You, instead, question His plan for your life and refuse to submit to His will. You're playing with fire, Marco, but then you wonder why you're getting burned."

Julio continued, "God gave us the Bible to know Him and His will. Through His Word, He guides us and teaches us how to live a life that pleases Him. And when we submit to His will, we can rest assured that we are on the safest ground, protected by His love and grace.

"I would obey God's Word even if I thought it objectionable to myself because my Creator knows what's best for me. That remains true wherever I am and in whatever circumstances. For those who listen, He's a shield and protector. That's why I agreed to leave Cuba with you. I trusted Him." Julio gave his brother a poignant look.

Marco sighed and sat down across from his brother. He had indeed been the one to decide to leave, but unbeknownst to Julio, he had deep regrets about the decision. Almost from the moment that Marco fled Cuba, he had second-guessed the decision to go. Before he had even lost sight of Cuba's coast, he wondered if he'd made the wrong move.

Marco's selective memory had created an idealized version of life back on his island home as soon as the rotten character of Castro's Cuba was no longer right in front of his eyes. But at this point, Marco had gambled his position, connections, and prominence for the chance of a better life in America, a chance to be a better man. Now, he felt betrayed that destiny hadn't rolled in his favor.

Marco looked somewhat hurt by Julio's words, feeling slighted because Julio was too dismissive of his complaints. *He just doesn't understand why I can't accept this life. He hasn't listened to one thing I've been saying. For someone so righteous, I would think he would have more compassion for the plight of our people here — above all, for me, his own brother.*

Julio, knowing his brother well, could read his face. "I'm sorry, brother." He attempted to offer genuine empathy. "I don't mean to step on your feelings. I do understand you to an extent. To be honest, this wasn't quite what I expected either. But try to dwell on what we do have instead of whatever we left behind. We have freedoms now that we could have only dreamed about before."

"Yes, I know. I have the freedom to be dragged along to your Bible meetings," Marco remarked sourly. "I think you are enjoying these so-called freedoms more than I am."

"You mean I'm taking more advantage of them? Something that you're also free to do," Julio pointed out.

"Who has the time or energy for these supposed freedoms? It feels like all we do is work for meager wages and never get to enjoy any so-called liberty. You talk about obedience and submission, but all I see is slavery," Marco spat back. "Being forced to accept my lot in life and make the most of it, like some kind of slave with no rights or choices of my own."

After an awkward moment, Julio cleared his throat. He wondered how well this would go over, but he thought a clarification could be helpful for Marco. "Brother, I think you have slavery confused with servitude."

Marco gave a bewildered look. He had no idea where Julio was going with this, so he didn't respond right away. Julio took advantage of his hesitation.

"You bemoan your plight as though you were a slave — someone else's property without rights to your own life. But you do have some rights, Marco. You're more like a servant."

"How is that any better?"

"A servant would be like a labor hand — someone who is paid. The man who owns the orchard hires him. A fair day's pay for an honest day's work," Julio explained. "He goes home at the end of the day to his own home and family. If he wants to work, he can return the next day. He still has his own life to live, largely on his own terms. He could show up if he wanted or not show up. He has choices."

Julio looked Marco in the eye and placed a hand on his shoulder. "You have choices, brother. You have a choice to accept your lot in life and make the most of it or continue to be miserable. But you are not a slave."

Julio paused, looking deep into Marco's eyes, "The greater question is, are you content with the life you have? You say you're not. Or are you willing to give it all up and submit to God's will, even though that means abandoning your own desires and ways of thinking? It may feel like a hard pill to swallow, but true freedom lies in surrendering to Christ Jesus — that means losing our false sense of autonomy."

"You act as though your Bible is the only truth, and that anyone who deviates from it is inviting trouble," Marco contended. "But since we're talking about slavery, I refuse to be a slave to your narrow-minded beliefs. I'll make my own choices and live my life on my own terms."

Despite all of Julio's reasoning, Marco's ears were stuffed with his own pride, and he refused to back down now. "Well, I've spoken to several of the other workers. They agree with me, and they'll back up what I say. If they stand with me, I'm sure others will have the courage to speak up against their own oppression as well," Marco reasoned.

Julio raised his eyebrow in an "are you sure about that?" gesture.

"It's not much different from Cuba for most people — you just never lived that life," Julio reminded him. "Most in the community understand and appreciate how much more they have here. Don't imagine that your rants will garner much support," he cautioned.

Julio had a more attuned sense of the community and understood their real and nuanced feelings on the matter. His blustery brother was so consumed with his own feelings that he assumed everyone would feel the same as he did. But in the end, Julio reasoned that the easygoing Cuban refugees wouldn't want to make waves and compromise the meager life they had risked so much to find in America.

"What do you expect to achieve?" The question was genuine, but Julio also tried to guide the conversation. "You know Vladi better than I do, and from what you used to tell me, Vladi's not one to back down. I have scant confidence that your complaints will cow him into changing the way he runs things."

Ughhh! Why does Julio have to be so logical? But no matter how sound Julio's reasoning was, Marco's aggravation overrode his brother's good sense.

"He can't ignore all of us. If we stand together, he has to listen. Isn't this the 'American way'? I'm exercising my American freedom of speech. It's my right!"

"You are no more American than he is," Julio pointed out, not swayed by his brother's attempt to turn his own argument against him. "You are no more American than the rest of our community. We don't have the protections of citizens — it's not the same. If you anger this man, he's capable of retaliating in a way you may regret."

"Well, you may stay right here in this little shack of a house and cower, but I won't, and neither will the others. You'll see. I'll gather support until the day someone stands up for us all!"

As Marco left, he slammed the door so hard that it bounced back open.

Julio got up to close the door, abandoning his now cold dinner, but not before he peered out into the darkness. He watched his brother approach their co-workers, some of whom he considered friends. They stood around and drank their cervezas, as was their custom after the workday. He closed the door and sighed. He hoped that maybe a few of them could talk some sense into Marco before his impetuous brother lead them all into a bad situation.

The occasion came sooner than Julio thought it would. Less than a week later, Julio was among the last to leave the groves that day. As he came within viewing distance of their residences, he could see a group of men sitting around, partaking in their usual after-work sundown ritual. But this time, he caught sight of a large man among them and a smaller man standing squared up to his husky frame.

"Oh no," Julio whispered as he started to run. But by the time he got there, it was too late. Marco had already opened his mouth.

THE CONFRONTATION

"Señor Moisés!" Marco scoffed. "They should have labeled you Señor Rameses, like the pharaoh himself." Marco alluded to one of the few Bible accounts that he had paid attention to at the meetings Julio coerced him to attend. At least it had come in handy for something. "You are no hero deliverer! You have subjugated our people for your selfish gain!"

Vladi bristled. He had no idea what Marco was referring to or who this "pharaoh" was, but what he did know was that he didn't like Marco's tone. He was accustomed to being addressed with the respect accorded to a Lieutenant Colonel. He had also been used to at least receiving the deference accorded to a man who had acted charitably toward the labor hands and their families.

"Who are you to speak to me in that manner?" Vladi bellowed. Vladi's hard stare bored into Marco like two heat-seeking missiles. "You should show more regard for the hand that feeds you."

"You run your orchards like Fidel Castro runs Cuba!" Marco retorted. "You led us to believe that you were saving us from the hardships of life back in Cuba, yet you treat us like your own slaves."

Marco had gone too far with the Castro comparison. The shocked looks on the faces of the other labor hands, and even on the face of Marco's own brother, were not what he expected to see. Julio's warning whispered in the back of his mind. But he couldn't back down now. Marco had to commit to what he was saying, and he assumed that if he maintained confidence in his stance, the others would follow.

Vladi was offended that his integrity was being questioned by this "little man." He erupted with anger and struck Marco across the face. Marco reeled backward, holding a hand to his stinging cheek. Vladi was a warrior, and Marco was no match for his power and dominance.

Despite his anger, Vladi's face remained stoic. He didn't agree with one word of the nonsense that ingrate Marco spouted, but it had struck a nerve. Vladi was stern but fair. He took good care of those who pleased him, and he still took good care of those who did not. If somehow his management style could be likened to a dictator, at least he believed he was a benevolent one — nothing that approached the cruelty of Castro. After all, there had been no firing squads in Vladi's orchards.

"What did you suppose you would find here?" Vladi demanded. "Perhaps you assumed life in America is like Disneyland every day? Welcome to the capitalist paradise." Vladi opened his arms wide and gestured around himself. "Now you think it is all hard work for many and fortune only for a select few?"

To Vladi's way of thinking, Marco and any other hands who might have agreed with him were ungrateful. They uttered such words from a place of ignorance. Not only did Marco's contempt anger him, but also how Marco portrayed him to the others. He had, with much effort, helped them out from under the heavy burden of communism. They came with nothing. He gave them food, shelter, and clothing. They lacked none of the necessities, and he gave fair pay for a fair day's work.

Furthermore, Vladi was the one who accepted the risk and invested significant capital for equipment, land, materials, and supplies — everything required for their operation to work. And he had done it all with the true intention and desire to help the people he had spent time with on their little Caribbean island.

Part of what drove him was wanting to give back to the families of those who were there for him when he landed on America's shore with nothing at all.

And this man has the impudent brazenness to liken me to a dictator whose cruel oppression is known to all? Vladi would never betray his feelings, but Marco's words hurt.

The Cuban refugees Vladi aided weren't forced to work for him. They could do as they pleased. What did Marco expect of Vladi? It was not his fault that they had so few other options in this land of opportunity. They arrived with almost no marketable skills — practical skills they would need to succeed in a capitalist economy. Could Marco not see this himself? He couldn't, because those who were unfamiliar with the mechanisms of capitalism or operating a business couldn't comprehend it. Few knew what it took to buy land, buildings, equipment, and supplies. Most had little or no concept of managing resources — there was always too much or too little of something. They couldn't relate to the ongoing responsibility of making payroll. Ensuring his workers got paid was always on Vladi's mind. All they had to do was show up and do their job. He bore a heavier burden than Marco could ever realize.

"Nothing in this world is free!" Vladi told Marco as a man who had experienced the raw truth of that statement. "Are you angry that you have to get your hands dirty to feed yourself? I have news for you, *amigo* — your hands were dirty long before you left Cuba. But now, instead of being dirty with blood, they are dirty with a little orange juice! Is that not far better?"

Marco clenched his teeth, and his ears grew red with hot indignation at the mention of the former deeds that had indeed pricked his calloused conscience.

"I ensure that you have everything you need, yet you come here and complain," Vladi retorted. "How ungrateful can you be?"

"What is there to be grateful for?" Marco fired back. "We had a life of our own in Cuba. We may have been under the communist thumb, but we could live our lives."

Deep inside, Marco knew that what he said was skewed through a "grass is greener" prism. His selective memory idealized life back in Cuba.

I would rather just be in Cuba! Marco stewed. He was giving serious thought to leaving now. If he were going to be stuck in a hot, humid citrus orchard, he might as well be back in Cuba. At least that was home.

Vladi, with a sly expression, raised an eyebrow and fired back at what he considered Marco's pathetic whining. "Why not go back to Cuba, then? In Cuba, is it not those with resources and prominent ties who prosecute others and drag them into sham court trials?" His tone was both accusatory and mocking, but it left no doubt in anyone's mind that he had taken direct aim at Marco.

It was Vladi's turn to be the *Inquisitor*, and his remarks were direct and cut deep. "Power in life tends to make one corrupt. Your comrades in Cuba who are handed privileges in their positions endorse the virtues of sacrifice for the common good. Yet they are like a womanizing pope who advocates to the world the merits of celibacy." He knew Marco's own life back in Cuba made him the hypocrite now, and he didn't hesitate to point it out to everyone.

Vladi verbalized what Marco knew to be true and had reason to dread. "One who does not show mercy should not expect to receive mercy. Go back to Cuba? You can never return." Vladi punctuated each of those last words so they were left ringing heavily in Marco's ears.

Though his sharp words stung, Marco had never backed down during one of their arguments before, and he wasn't about to start now. He shot back, "At least in Cuba, I had a home and a position of dignity — not that of your hired servant." He turned to his fellow workers and raised his voice. "We all did! But look at us now, toiling for a man who is worse than Castro. He lied to us to give the impression that life would be better here, but is it really?"

The other workers mumbled among themselves. Marco took this as a sign that they agreed with him, encouraging him to go on with his self-righteous rant. If only he had looked at Julio's face, he might have paused. But he continued with passion as if trying to rally soldiers to a cause. "We are better off going back to Cuba than living as slaves in another country!"

At the mention of returning to Cuba, the energy disappeared from the air — any momentum Marco had gained fell flat. He had misread his audience, but that was because Marco rarely considered anyone's thoughts other than his own.

In an instant, the workers turned their heads and dispersed back to their modest homes. They had already lost far too much to Cuba. Their situation in America may have been less than they had hoped, but they all knew what would happen if they ever returned to Cuba. No one wanted anything to do with it, not even those few who may have agreed with Marco.

Marco had either deluded himself or conveniently forgotten the life that regular people lived back in Cuba, a life that he himself was often tasked to turn into a small taste of hell on earth. Sure, things were somewhat decent in Cuba, at least for him and those like him. His self-centered perspective assumed everyone would feel as he did, that what they had left behind was far better than how they were living in the present.

Vladi was fed up with Marco's impertinent behavior and grabbed him by the shirt. Pulling him close, he hissed, "If you do that again, you will regret ever knowing me!"

Julio looked on, humiliated, horrified, and helpless. There was nothing he could do for Marco. *Perhaps he had it coming,* Julio thought. *Well, yes, he brought it on himself. He might learn his lesson, but it's doubtful.* Still, Julio didn't want him to be harmed.

Vladi wasn't finished. Everyone knew he didn't usually display his emotions like this. If nothing else, Vladi was steady and firm. He may not have been overly friendly or sensitive with the labor hands when he made his rounds in the groves, but they'd never seen him lose his temper this way either.

Stunned silence permeated the orchard. The few workers who dared to stay in the vicinity looked on, shaken by the frightening scene they were witnessing. The veins in Vladi's temples bulged. Perspiration beaded on his nose, and he bared his clenched teeth. He took on the ferocious appearance of one of those thick, muscular Caucasian Shepherd dogs facing a bear in the mountains of Georgia back in the Soviet Union. This time, he would have the last word. He pointed his finger at Marco and boomed, "You do not like working in my business? Fine, you are fired! Pack up your things and leave my sight."

The cold look in Vladi's eyes was enough to stop Marco from answering back. They had argued in a lighthearted way back in their days in Cuba, but Marco had never seen this reaction from the strapping Russian.

Marco's fear and uncertainty, however, lasted only a little while before it was replaced by blind anger and hatred. The ignorance of those around him — especially that greedy "has been" soldier who had fallen from the sky into wealth — made him burn with contempt. He spat at Vladi's boot, then turned on his heel and stormed off. Marco swore to himself that he would find a way to somehow exact revenge on Vladi. As long as he remained alive, Marco would never forget this indignity.

THE APPEAL

Julio realized he needed to act quickly before Marco, or Vladi for that matter, did something else rash. He made a sudden decision to approach Vladi, who stood with his arms crossed and a murderous expression on his face.

"Señor Moisés," Julio approached with trepidation, "I know Marco has shown great disrespect, but please reconsider. He needs this job."

Vladi peered down his nose at Julio and huffed. "You actually expect me to tolerate such insolence? After everything I have done to help him? I will not hear of it. If he needed his job so much, he should have controlled his tongue for his own good. Who does he think he is? He is not a big bad Cuban prosecutor anymore. He is — was — one labor hand entirely through my goodwill. But now, he had better never set foot in my orchards again!" Vladi then turned and strode away, his displeasure evident in every step.

Confronted with the impossibility of the situation, Julio prayed in silence before he ran to catch up with Vladi. "Señor Moisés, please," he pleaded as he tried to keep up with Vladi's angry pace, "let us at least discuss this. I only ask for five minutes of your time, and then I will let you be."

Vladi turned and considered the man before him. Julio had never given him trouble since he arrived with Marco. He'd been a diligent worker — a decent human being who reminded him much of his sister, Olga. For that reason alone, he decided to hear the man out.

"Come to my truck. Let us talk in private and turn on the air conditioning while we both cool off."

They hurried back to Vladi's truck as the sun continued to set. Julio prayed he could persuade the determined Vladi to change his mind. Climbing into the cab, Vladi started the truck and got the air conditioner running, then gestured to Julio.

"What have you to say about Marco's outburst? I had every right to fire him for such contempt. I have worked many years to make a safe and peaceful refuge for anyone who wishes to leave Cuba, at my own considerable expense, no less. He had the audacity to question that in front of my men. They watch to see that they can depend on me to lead. They need to have that assurance. I had no choice. You cannot let that conduct go unchecked."

Julio nodded in acknowledgment. *He may no longer lead troops, but Vladi approaches the management of his business the same way.* He could perceive how Vladi's military discipline conditioned his steel-souled personality — respect for authority was paramount.

Julio nodded again and removed his glasses to wipe the sweat from the bridge of his nose while he mulled over what would be the best approach. After a moment's pause, he said, "I understand."

This is not what Vladi had been expecting. "What did you say?"

"I understand. I have lived with Marco for many years. We are brothers, after all. Don't think I'm unfamiliar with his temper, his self-serving personality, and his muddled views of his new life here in America. Oh, we've had conversations, and he's debated these things many times since our arrival."

Vladi leaned back against his door, his eyes boring into Julio, intrigued.

"I don't propose that Marco's conduct go unpunished. His attitude and behavior were unacceptable." Julio looked straight into Vladi's eyes, despite his nerves. "I simply request that you take some measure other than firing him."

Vladi snorted. "And why should I do that? He publicly and purposefully sub-verted my authority. That is grounds for expulsion. I cannot have my other work-ers supposing such blatant disrespect is tolerable. That bordered on mutiny!"

"That is why I ask for your grace. Though Marco may be undeserving of it, if you grant him a second chance, you will show your workers that you are a benev-olent leader, not a dictator, as Marco accused."

Julio paused to gauge how well his message was being received. He hoped to appeal to the man's pragmatic sense of how the other labor hands perceived his image in his operation.

"And why should I care what my workers think of me? So long as I provide them employment and pay them, they are obligated to demonstrate respect," Vladi countered. Though he wasn't fully convinced of his own remarks, he was curious to hear more of Julio's reasoning.

"If I may, what kind of leader do you prefer to be, Vladi?" Julio took a chance using the man's given name, something only Marco had done. "What kind of image do you wish the men to see? Do you want the name Señor Moisés to be whispered in fear among your workers as they wonder if their heads will be next on the chopping block?" Vladi opened his mouth to reply, but Julio pressed on. "Or do you wish your name to be revered here and even as far as Cuba, where men respect the ground you walk on, not because they fear you, but because you show mercy, grace, and love for your workers?"

"Love?" Vladi scoffed. "Is it not more effective to be feared than loved by one's subordinates, Julio? Love has no place in business. You are sounding like a priest."

Julio let the "priest" remark go but went on with the thought anyway. "Love has a place in every aspect of life, but none more so than God's love. If you know God as your Father, His love seeps into every aspect of your life and every person you interact with, because we cannot contain the Lord's love."

"If your reasoning is on religious grounds, you can leave right now," Vladi responded sharply. "I will not base my decisions on the premise of something that does not exist."

Julio was treading on thin ice. While Vladi was tolerant of the labor hands worshipping the one true God, the man himself was a scientific atheist. Julio recognized he would have to proceed with discretion.

"Okay, but what of your own name, Señor Moisés? Do you know why the Cubans continue to call you by that name? You do know about Moisés of the Bible, do you not? Your own name gives people hope. He was a servant of God, and because of that, he was a great leader who will be remembered throughout history.

"Like you, there were occasions when he was treated with disdain by the same ungrateful people he helped with passage to freedom. And do you know what God said of Moisés? God said he was humble, more than any man who was on the face of the earth. Would it not then be wise to manage your people with both the humility and the honor of one who is also called Moisés?"

Vladi was silent. He did not have a rebuttal to that.

"People do respect you, Vladi, and not because they fear you, though you are disciplined and exacting and you expect the same of others. They — we — appreciate you because you understand our plight and give us hope for a better life when we have no other. That is gracious — indeed, it's a kind of love."

Now Julio leaned forward, resolved to make his point. "Your name is spoken with hope in the streets of Havana. I know because I've heard it. People wish to know you. You have already earned their respect. You don't need to control it with fear — that would prove harmful to your good name."

Vladi pondered Julio's comments. He had to admit that Julio produced compelling arguments. Again, he couldn't help but associate Julio with memories of his sister, Olga. Both were so assured of their faith, something he both despised and admired in his private thoughts. To believe in something so purely — what comfort and joy that seemed to bring them. But Vladi still couldn't help but pity such individuals as willfully naïve. Well intentioned, yes, but naïve. In that regard, Julio was indeed much like Olga.

But Julio was also accurate in his observations. Vladi did desire to be a benevolent leader, one people respected out of loyalty, not fear. He was human and, at least on some level, he naturally cared about how others thought of him. Like most people, he wanted to be liked and respected. Not that he would admit as much to Julio. And that still didn't answer the question of what he should do about Marco.

"And your brother?" Vladi asked, now that he had time to regain his composure. "I respect your points, Julio, for your assertions are fair. But that does not change my judgment. I cannot let Marco's provocation go unpunished. What would you have me do with him?"

Julio took a few seconds to collect his thoughts. This was his chance. He had to express this just right if he hoped to keep Marco employed.

"I agree that Marco's behavior was improper, disrespectful, and unacceptable. I've tried to prevent such an episode for a while now, but he is stubborn. The truth is, he's jealous of you, Vladi."

This revelation stunned Vladi. He hadn't considered the possibility. "Me?" he asked in a somewhat humorous tone. It was surprising, but not unflattering.

"Yes. You know he held a position of privilege in our old life. When we first arrived here from Cuba and Marco learned of your success, he assumed he would find the same degree of success in America." Julio sighed. "As we know, that has not been the case. Marco refuses to adjust his way of thinking. Instead, he is caustic, self-pitying, interminably cynical, obsessed with being better than other people, and consumed with envy. To top it off, he carries a sense of entitlement.

"He really does feel regret and frustration. It's painful for him, and you see it in his rage toward himself and others. None of this excuses him, but I understand how these things can naturally make a man irrational.

"I pray the Lord will change his heart, because I sure can't. With genuine respect for you, I'm just appealing to your mercy toward him — please bear with us."

"What do you suggest?" Vladi asked.

"Perhaps you could give him a different position, a demotion, as punishment for his behavior, but please don't fire him," Julio implored. "He is too proud to admit that he needs this employment, but I am not. I'm humbled before God and see in you the benevolent leader you strive to be. I have confidence in your goodness, Señor Moisés, even if Marco has lost his way."

Julio leaned back against the passenger door. He knew there was nothing else he could say. He had either convinced Vladi or he had not.

Marco was responsible for quality control in the Red Star Citrus operation. It was one of the more desirable jobs, and it was clear to Vladi that Marco took it for granted. In contrast, perhaps the least desirable duty in the operation was working on one of the packing lines. The work required repetitive stooping, lifting, bending, and standing all day long, and they were indeed long days. It was boring and hard on the body. The rare breaks in the monotony were for sanitation — wiping off the packing line gates, belts, and rollers, and cleaning out produce bins. That was unpleasant too, and no one liked doing the work.

Even if he disagreed with Julio's faith, Vladi was persuaded by his perseverance. Perhaps firing Marco had been a reaction to a bruised ego. It wouldn't do to show his employees that a mere worker menaced him so much. Julio was right, demoting Marco would be the best move. Vladi thought about suspending him but then decided that reassigning Marco to the packing line, away from the workers who had witnessed his outburst, would send a stronger message. It would isolate Marco to an area of the operation where he could do no more harm to the workers' morale. That would help prevent future dissent without sowing fear among his workers.

"Very well, Julio. You have convinced me. Starting tomorrow, Marco will work on the packing line. You may go tell him."

Julio exhaled in relief, grabbing the truck door handle and stepping out. "Thank you, Señor Moisés. I will not forget your mercy."

BEING WRONG
ABOUT BEING RIGHT

hen Vladi finally left, Julio headed home, where he found Marco sitting at the kitchen table and watching a small TV. As soon as he closed the door, Julio launched into a hushed admonition to his seething brother.

"Marco, you are too impetuous. You attacked the man with your words, and did it produce the result you wanted?"

Marco made an irritated huffing sound, averting his gaze. Julio continued.

"Yes, you have a right to speak, but you must think through what you will say and how you will say it, and listen to the other person. What have I always told you? Be quick to hear, slow to speak, slow to anger — for the anger of man does not produce the righteousness of God."

Marco responded with a furious glare now, clearly resenting Julio's injection of religion into everything, particularly this.

Julio sighed, exasperated. "Marco, I saved your skin back there — not that you deserved it, though," he divulged. "Vladi had every right to fire you. Instead, he was gracious enough to let you stay on, although you're going to be doing penance on the packing line for the foreseeable future."

"Gracious nothing!" Marco stood up and protested. "The emperor has issued his edict to banish his foe to detention — exiled to hard labor in his loathsome stockade. Is that how it goes, brother? Well, so be it. He gets the last word . . . at least for now."

"Hush, Marco," Julio replied in a milder tone than Marco had invited. "You still need work, and you had it coming."

Marco pursed his lips and narrowed his eyes in annoyance. He didn't feel like listening to another of Julio's moralizing speeches. He couldn't disagree with Julio more strongly, and it was infuriating. Julio is naïve, he thought.

Julio maintained that they had no right to return evil for evil. In contrast, Marco thought the exact opposite. His heart was hardened and becoming more so.

"I don't understand why you aren't bothered by this," Marco reiterated to Julio. "Is it that your church brainwashes you so much that you can no longer evaluate our situation realistically? Does your church teach you that you should be a slave in the private kingdom of a greedy Russian prince?"

Julio thought carefully about his response before answering. "Marco, I understand your frustration. But please, don't mistake my words for apathy. The situation is difficult — I just view it and deal with it in a different way. When the Lord saved me, He produced in me a heart capable of humility and love. It's who I am, and those Christ-like qualities guide me in how I handle life. That includes difficult situations."

"You can't tell me that God wouldn't want you to stand up and fight against injustices against yourself and the people you care about — that He just wants you to be taken advantage of," Marco countered.

"Of course, speaking up for what's right is important, but can it not be done with kindness and gentleness?" Julio asked. "I may not fight with fists and harsh words, but that doesn't mean I'm weak. I can rely on the strength and direction of God the Holy Spirit through faith in His revealed Word to navigate even the toughest situations. That is divine guidance to help me subdue a bitter spirit even when I face injustices — real injustices, or those I just imagine."

"Don't start preaching again, Julio. I'm not in the mood," Marco grumbled, pacing the room in agitation.

Julio took a seat at the table and massaged his forehead. However earnestly he sought to be a peacekeeper for Marco and Vladi, mediating between both stubborn men was exasperating.

"Marco, whether or not we convince others of what we believe, my goal is to conduct myself in a way that promotes the welfare of others' souls and upholds the truth. If we fail to consider the spiritual consequences of our words and actions, we risk doing more harm than good," Julio said, pouring himself a much-needed glass of water. "I know it may be hard to understand, but approaching others with genuine kindness may open the door for God to work in their hearts."

Julio's assertion didn't sway Marco. "Why would you be kind to someone who does you wrong?" he asked. "That strikes me as weak and illogical. It just invites more mistreatment."

"It is natural to feel contempt for people who disagree with us, but by God's grace, it's possible to be about something more significant than the dispute," Julio replied.

Julio took a drink of his water as a flustered Marco continued to move around the room, vibrating with restless energy.

"Going on what you say, you believe yourself to be some kind of savior — fighting for what's right and true — vanquishing injustice in the world. But the reality is, you're being a bully, aggressively trying to silence whoever disagrees with you.

"Think about Vladi and all who are watching you in this situation," Julio reminded him. "How much more effective would your efforts have been if you'd approached him with humility instead of haughtiness? And would that also invite similar humility in others? Your confrontational approach has only pushed him further away.

"Julio paused to ensure he had eye contact with Marco. "You try to play the victim here, but the truth is, you're the instigator."

Marco bristled at the comment and stopped pacing for a moment, but Julio maintained his gaze and asked, "Think about how you talk to others, Marco — how's that working for you? Are your abrasiveness and defiant behavior making your life any better?"

But before Marco could reply, Julio answered for him, "It's not. Your approach isn't working, Marco. It's not making your life any better, and it's not making anyone else's life better either. You need to think about how your actions and words are impacting others.

"You may feel that you have a valid complaint this time, but you often speak out against issues and controversies, even when they don't directly involve you or affect you. Maybe you think more highly of yourself than you ought, or something. Maybe you're just feeding an aggressive, confrontational attitude — I don't know. Sometimes I feel — no, I know — you're looking for a fight, brother! That kind of behavior is *loco*."

Julio set his glass down with a thump that displayed the aggravation he felt. Surprised by the fervor of Julio's statements, Marco came to a stop and leaned against the table, watching his brother with a wary eye. Julio was usually calm and easygoing, but he was clearly growing frustrated.

"You're so obsessed with winning arguments and proving yourself right that you've lost sight of what truly matters — the well-being of those around you and the impact your words and actions have on others. You've ignored more vital concerns, like your own spiritual welfare, and instead you focus on relatively unimportant issues that don't matter in the context of eternity. It's not only ineffective, but it's also harmful . . . for you."

Julio's voice softened, and he looked at his brother with a mixture of sadness and frustration. "Think about it, Marco. Is this the kind of person you want to be? Is this the kind of life you want to lead? Constantly searching for a fight, always looking to prove yourself right at the expense of others? It's not strength, it's weakness. And it's not what Christ Jesus taught."

Marco reflected on what his brother had said, and a smug look crept upon his face. "But you haven't answered my question, brother. Are you saying that being a Christian means that you should ignore the injustices in the world and let evil men prevail against the good?"

Julio rubbed his temples again. Marco was being deliberately obtuse, but he answered nonetheless. "Being a Christian certainly doesn't mean ignoring or condoning evil — it means actively working to combat it. And yet, you seem to think that hurling angry words and arguing with people will change them for the better. That's not how it works.

"You can't change people unless you reach their hearts. It's not about defeating others or proving our point. The Bible is the instrument that accomplishes that change of heart. God the Holy Spirit applies His truth to make the changes, starting right there. No darkness of this world can prevent His light from breaking through." He gestured for Marco to join him at the table.

Marco hesitated before sliding into the chair across from his brother. He maintained his recalcitrant demeanor, but Marco could tell he was straining Julio's composure. It gave him slight pause.

"One true test of a man's character is how he responds to injustice and oppression. I know it's hard to witness the evil around us, and it's easy to get caught up in the trap of anger and a desire for revenge. But if I have reason to think someone has done me wrong, it gives me an opportunity to show myself to be a follower of Christ Jesus.

"He endured tremendous injustices, yet when He suffered, He didn't retaliate. When He was humiliated and mistreated, He didn't do the same in return. The sinless Son of God lived as a man with love for His Father and others — and we know that His life was perfect."

"Yes, and by doing nothing, the men who perpetrated those acts got away with it," Marco pointed out. "And Jesus ended up dead. So in the end, who won?"

Marco's contention added to Julio's frustration, mainly because Marco didn't understand the significance of the crucifixion and resurrection of Christ Jesus as he did. He perceived Marco's question as just a red herring that Marco tossed out to seize control of the discussion, which, of course, Marco preferred to debate on his terms. Julio knew better than to take the bait and, instead, stayed on point.

"Assuming you prevail and subdue your opponent, you still haven't truly won. Not in the ultimate sense. The character you've displayed isn't one that pleases our Lord, and one day — sooner than you realize — you'll have to give an account for your sinful attitudes and behavior.

"Marco," Julio's voice quivered with emotion. "Marco, I fear for your soul. The Lord is just and holy, and He can't turn a blind eye to sin. He has said in His Word that the wages of sin is death. That's an eternal death — forever knowing the fury of God's wrath. Men and women with hardened, unrepentant hearts will be swallowed into the unquenchable fires of hell, without mercy and without appeal. It's what we all deserve. Only those who are robed in the perfect righteousness of Christ Jesus will be accepted into eternal fellowship with Him."

Marco opened his mouth in protest, but his brother knew him well enough to anticipate what he was about to say. Julio put up a hand, gesturing to him not to speak. "I know you don't care about what God has said in His Word, but for my sake, and the sake of your own soul, would you please stop to consider where you're headed. Don't you see how much it matters?"

"No, brother. I don't see it." Marco obstinately persisted. "As far as I'm concerned, Vladi is wrong, and no one should get away with wrongdoing, especially taking advantage of others. We shouldn't stand by and take that abuse in silence, and it shouldn't go unpunished!" Marco crossed his arms.

Julio sighed. Marco had entirely missed the point. And this conversation was feeling similar to the one he had just had with Vladi. He needed a different approach.

"We may want to believe that we're fighting for what's right, but we have to also be mindful of our own motives. Satan is always looking for ways to deceive us, to make us believe our actions are justified when they're not. That means we have to constantly check our hearts and make sure that we're acting out of love and humility — not pride and envy. Even if we begin with the proper intentions, we still have a tendency to make things about ourselves. And what's the outcome? It just robs your peace of mind."

Julio refilled his water and took another long sip while Marco remained silent, thinking about his brother's words. It was a rare moment when Marco didn't have anything to say.

"I'm saying you're off course, brother, and it's time to turn around. I care about you, and I love you more than anyone.

"God calls His people to be peacemakers, not warriors. We're called to be humble, not boastful. We're called to be compassionate, not divisive. As a follower of Christ Jesus, this is what I'm to be about. And it would serve you well, too. I say this to you because I want to see you succeed not just in this moment, but for eternity."

At this, Marco scoffed, "No, brother, that's your calling. I still hold that you're a fool if you believe that absurdity. It's naïve and not the way the world works."

"What exactly is your problem with Vladi?" Julio demanded, trying to get back to the specific issue at hand.

Marco glared at him. "Where do you want me to begin? For starters, we do all the dirty work out in the sun — he gets the profit. He treats us like we're his worker ants. He takes off anytime he wants to go fishing, take a nap in his fancy house, or drive around in that cool truck of his."

"Is that really what you think he does? Marco, for such a smart person, sometimes you don't show it. Keeping a business running is hard!" Julio pointed out, adding, "Has Vladi ever missed payday to his workers? Has there ever been a Friday afternoon that he failed to show up and deliver your wages? Did anyone in the field ever ask about his cash flow that week? Did you ask how long it might have been since he got paid? How many paydays for himself did he miss? There's a lot more to ensuring you get paid than you realize . . . or that you're just not willing to acknowledge."

"Oh, poor Vladi! Yeah, he's the victim in all this? How ridiculous, brother. I've had enough of this," Marco declared. He pushed back hard on his chair and stepped away from the table. "This whole conversation is absurd. Vladi has made his stance apparent, and you expect me to act as you would. Well, I'm not you." Marco leaned across the table toward Julio's face, his temper flaring again. "And how I conduct myself is my business. If I want to be angry with Vladi, I have every right to be."

Marco turned to leave the room, but Julio abruptly rose and dropped his voice in a way he hadn't done in many years. "Marco, sit down!"

Marco stopped mid-stride and turned towards Julio, eyes full of bewilderment. It was uncharacteristic for Julio to use that tone, especially with him.

"You may speak the truth, but with the wrong spirit, you've lost the exchange — the whole thing crumbles." Julio threw his hands up dramatically. "You've made a fool of yourself all week," he continued. "You've rolled your eyes at every attempt I've made to relate to you and help you. Now it's your turn to listen, brother, as I've listened to your tirade and all your fuming."

Julio's voice wasn't unkind, but he was firm, and his eyes were steely. Marco knew he was sincere, and his face softened with a hint of remorse as his eyes were now locked with Julio's. He slumped back into his chair and, with resignation, gestured for Julio to continue.

Julio paused and took a breath. He spoke once more, this time with a more measured and direct tone.

"It is the way of Satan to accuse, so I want to believe you have better motives, my brother. But there is a competitive tendency in our flesh that too often gets our thinking twisted. You may believe that by winning every argument, by dominating and belittling others, you're proving yourself to be right, but that's not how it works. Nothing could be further from the truth.

"That's the way of the world, not the way of Christ Jesus. When we engage in strife, we play right into the hands of the twin depravities that have vexed all men from the beginning of time. You're only proving yourself to be a slave indeed . . . shackled by your own pride and envy. And for what? To win a temporary victory over a matter that will mean nothing in the blink of an eye?"

Julio leaned forward, catching his brother's eye and holding it.

"There is eternity ahead of us. Please, think beyond the moment. Think beyond your feelings. Think beyond this life."

Marco looked down, still scowling.

"I've told you all you needed to hear," Julio said gently, settling back into his chair. "So what are you going to do about it?"

THE OPPORTUNITY

Marco continued to stew about how unjust the affairs of his life felt, despite his brother's reasoning. Regret over leaving Cuba constantly gnawed at him.

At least there I had a respectable life. Sure, there were many things wrong in Cuba, he reasoned to himself, *but is this better?* Here, he was just another labor hand in the Red Star Citrus groves who enriched Vladi. *And to think, at one time I might have thought of him as a friend.*

At this point, though, he didn't know if Julio would go back to Cuba. Julio seemed to be handling life in the orchards better than he was. His brother was more accepting of their circumstances because he believed God had brought him into his new life.

Adding to Marco's irritation, Julio persisted in talking about a recent study of the Bible where Gerardo taught about how God is sovereign over all things, even painful experiences at the hands of others, and that God's love can help them endure. Julio would say that it was his grounding in the Scripture that enabled him to avoid the bitter spirit that Marco had. He recited Romans 12:14 as though it were always at the forefront of his mind: "Bless those who persecute you; bless, and do not curse." Marco, as usual, didn't find it as helpful as his brother did.

Julio realized his counsel had fallen on deaf ears, except that at least Marco didn't renew his efforts to confront Vladi and stir up trouble. Instead, Marco was privately preparing to choose what was perhaps an even riskier option — to flee.

Marco could bear no more. By allowing himself to dwell on the negative things in his life, festering resentment became a black hole that swallowed his mind. His thoughts became more twisted and irrational until eventually there was no light to see anything with clarity.

Marco recalled the long speeches Fidel used to make, rhapsodizing about American arrogance. Before he had seen what Vladi had become, Marco had dismissed such assertions as blustery rhetoric. But not so much now. *Now I can see what El Comandante spoke about in living color, right before my eyes! He was right all along.*

Marco's hopes were deflated when it became evident to him that not everyone enjoyed the so-called "American Dream." *This is a fantasy promoted by American capitalists for their own benefit!*

Those who didn't experience the privileged life were compelled to lick the boots of someone like Vladi. Marco missed Cuba and the life he knew there — he could identify with that way of life. Sure, Cuba had its problems, but he had held a position of authority, and he could work the system. *If I could return to Cuba, perhaps I could use my position there to effect changes for the better,* he rationalized, trying hard to shoehorn an element of selflessness into the decision.

However, this decision raised a whole new set of questions. *How would we get back? Even if we had the money for airline tickets, we can't just board a plane from anywhere in the United States bound for Havana.*

Unusual as it was, Marco was not the first-ever homesick Cuban. Others who wanted to return to their country had sometimes even hijacked commercial airliners, but Marco never considered resorting to such an extreme approach. *Even if I could carry out such an audacious feat, my welcoming party in Cuba would be the political police.* He knew brute force wouldn't work.

There was yet a much bigger question and the most dangerous one of all. *How can Julio or I return without being punished for defection?* When most Cubans left the country, they never looked back. There was little precedent for going back to Cuba — to leave was a one-way journey — there was no return.

Marco had an expert understanding of Cuban law. He knew the consequences for anyone caught could be a fate worse than death — life in a Cuban prison. In many cases, dissidents would face a firing squad, El Paredón. For the crime of defecting, they paid with their lives. Either way, if Marco were discovered they would make an example of him, and that possibility was terrifying.

As Marco worked at his monotonous job on the packing line throughout the long days, he had what felt like endless hours to think about the questions. *What conceivable explanation could I give for leaving Cuba? How could I account for a three-year absence and then a sudden reappearance out of nowhere?*

This is where his training as a lawyer would have to benefit him. He had bent and twisted the truth many times to conform to his arguments — couldn't he do the same if he went back? Could he maneuver through the labyrinth of Cuba's convoluted Byzantine bureaucracy laden with corruption and disarray to explain away his own absence?

Marco began to formulate a plan. *I'll need to put together some forged legal documents — something to present as evidence that I've been away for an extended time on official business on behalf of Cuba. I could draft contracts to make it appear as though I've been in Jamaica on a diplomatic mission. It is plausible that I was covertly dispatched to consult with former Prime Minister Michael Manley on our economic cooperation.*

Marco had been able to follow the news enough to know that Manley was preparing to stage a comeback, and it made sense for collaboration with Cuba to be part of his strategy. Cooperative exploits in bauxite mining and various light manufacturing industries would be proactive initiatives that could help absorb Jamaica's growing workforce and fuel Cuba's flagging economy, which had long since languished in the doldrums. Of course, that type of work would require a lawyer to formulate legal documentation between the countries. *Well, I am a lawyer so . . .* he thought, laughing to himself.

Yes, each day, the answers became clearer to Marco. However, Marco's contrived story had one enormous problem — it didn't provide any cover for Julio, should he also choose to return.

Marco also needed to find transportation back to Cuba, and a boat seemed the most likely option. *But I can't just walk up to an American captain and ask if I can hitch a ride to Cuba. I will need to do some scouting for just the right situation.*

Marco thought up a possible solution for that too. He began volunteering to deliver produce to the port. Besides enabling him to scout the activity around the area, it got him out of the drudgery of work on the packing line for a while. There he could observe the vessels as they came in and out.

Besides commercial fishing boats and freight vessels, which were unlikely to go anywhere near Cuba, there were recreational yachts as well. Many harbored along the east coast of Florida on their way down to the Bahamas or hop-scotching to other Caribbean ports, ideally Jamaica.

On most delivery runs, Marco would take extra time to walk around the docks, looking and listening for information that might be useful. The opportunity came one day when he overheard an exchange that caused him to stop and pay attention.

A booming voice, amplified by the water, carried over to his ears. "Just bring me the dang rope, woman! If we don't get tied off, we're going to float right back out to sea, and neither of us will get any more of that good John Barleycorn!"

Marco turned to see the irritable skipper of one of the smaller recreational yachts shouting at a woman dressed for the beach with her hair done perfectly and bright red manicured nails shining.

"You don't need any more rum, you drunken salt dog!" she yelled back. "This rope is heavy and disgusting! I didn't sign up for this. I came because you promised me nothing but sun and fun when I already told you I don't do manual labor. You're the captain, so do the captain-y things yourself." She spoke in a whiny, condescending tone. They seemed like quite an interesting pair.

"Accckkk," the sun- and rum-soaked skipper hollered in disgust. "Did you think this boat would sail itself? It takes work! While you're on deck sunning yourself all day, I'm making sure we stay afloat and on course. When do I get to take off and play? I asked you to help with one thing."

"Yesterday it was one thing, and the day before that it was another thing, and now today this. It's too much for me!" she complained. "I'm glad you never married me. I'll just go find myself a rich captain to marry, and we'll sail around on his yacht with his servants to do everything," she told him petulantly.

"They aren't servants, you snob! They're crew members," he corrected her.

"Well, I'm not one of your crew members — I'm supposed to be your girl-friend. And if you knew how to drive this thing, you wouldn't need help."

Marco could see that the man did indeed need help — and Marco might be just the man to offer it. He approached the boat christened the *Knotty Buoy* and called up, "Looking for rum, Captain?"

The skipper looked down, startled. A broad smile overtook his surprise. "Now, this is a man who understands me," he said. The woman rolled her eyes in disgust.

"I can get you the best rum and anything else you might need," Marco of-fered. He wanted to ingratiate himself. If he could make friends with the skip-per, questions about where they were going wouldn't seem so strange.

"I'd heartily appreciate it, good sir," the skipper told Marco. He reached into his pocket, showing Marco a wad of slightly damp money. "Go for the good stuff — I'm never cheap when it comes to my drink. Have yourself one too, on me."

When Marco returned to the *Knotty Buoy* with the skipper's package in hand, all was quiet. He walked around toward the bow to find the skipper lying on some cushions, soaking up the warmth in pleasant relaxation. Marco ap-proached the man, who sensed his shadow and opened his eyes. He sat up and took the package from Marco.

"Thank you kindly. Kill Devil Rum from Hampton Estate — buddy, you are a man after my own heart. Sit, sit. Relax and have a drink with me . . . " the skip-per paused, the inflection in his voice indicating that he was waiting for Marco to identify himself.

"My name is Marco," he said as he took a seat, politely turning down the rotgut but giving the skipper an audience, which is what he wanted anyway.

"Pleasure to meet you, Marco. I'm Buford, but call me Jack. So, Marco, are you a deckhand?"

"Yes," Marco lied without hesitation, "yes, I am. And right now I'm looking for work." *This might be easier than I thought.*

"Well, you're in luck, pal. I sorely need a first mate. My old lady is more of a bow ornament than anything else. We started out from North Carolina, and when she told me she'd been sailing before, I imagined she'd at least done the basics. But what she meant was she had tanned herself on her rich father's sailboat as they cruised around the Bahamas. I set off on the boat to relax and get away from life for a while, but how can I do that with no one else to help me mind things? I'm doing everything myself!"

"Where are you headed?" Marco asked. The situation seemed perfect, but their destination was perhaps the most crucial detail. What were the chances he could get near Cuba with these two?

"Jamaica. Finest rum in the Caribbean there."

Jackpot! Marco was elated. That was the best he could hope for. If they got him to Jamaica, he could formulate a plan to slip away and head north back home to his island.

"I hear it's nice, but I've never been," Marco replied with all the nonchalance he could conjure. "If you're serious about needing some help, I'd be glad to join you," he added, trying not to sound desperate, but holding his breath with hope.

"That would be great, Marcus!" the skipper exclaimed.

"Marco," he corrected him.

"Right. Marcos," Jack stated wrongly, but with rum-induced confidence.

Marco let it go. It was perhaps better if the skipper got his name wrong anyway.

"Welcome aboard," Jack said, reaching over to give Marco an amiable slap on the back. "I hope you have your gear, because we leave as soon as Mindy gets back from the grocery store."

At those words, a pang pierced Marco's heart — he should have seen it coming. They'd be leaving at most in maybe an hour or two. He wouldn't even have time to go back to the groves. But did it really matter? Any diversion could jeopardize his one chance to return to Cuba. How long would it be before another such ideal opportunity presented itself, if ever?

He was still thinking when a taxi pulled up to the docks. A furious Mindy got out, stomped onto the deck with a grocery bag, dropped it with an unspoken point, and stalked inside. Marco saw the taxi driver struggling with the rest of the bags and ran to help him.

Marco grabbed a few essentials he had brought with him. From the Red Star truck, he picked out three blood oranges that were almost ripe and tied them into a bandana handkerchief. It wasn't much, but along with Jack's provisions, it would do until they got to Jamaica. He couldn't take much more than the clothes on his back anyway.

As Marco boarded the yacht, Jack told Mindy, "This is my new first mate, Mark. He's coming with us to Jamaica."

Mindy could hardly look less interested and made a small *harrumph!* sound.

"He's here to help out so both of us can do less and spend more time relaxing," Jack added. Those must have been the magic words because Mindy whirled around, her mood lifting as swiftly as she turned.

"So nice to meet you, Mart," she smiled. "You can start by putting all that away," she said, pointing to the groceries. It was obvious that giving people orders came naturally to her.

As Marco helped Jack get ready for departure, he struggled to get thoughts of Julio away from his mind. If he didn't, he might lose his resolve. But it was impossible not to think of his brother, whom he was abandoning.

What will happen to Julio? Will he grow frantic when I don't come home? Maybe he'll think I died without any identification. His grief . . . No, I can't worry about those things, he told himself, shaking his head as if to loosen the thoughts.

But the thoughts clung on with a firm grip. Sad questions needed to turn into rationalizations. *Julio will be fine — he has everything he needs. He doesn't want to leave, anyway. He accepts life in the U.S., and he'll have his Bible and his church. That's all he cares about anyway.*

Julio had a life that revolved around new relationships in their little church, and Marco resented the other men Julio now referred to as his "brothers." Besides, it was dangerous to bring Julio back — he had no cover story. Maybe once Marco re-established himself at home, he could find a way to get Julio back home to Cuba should he ever want to return.

But when rationalizing didn't work to calm Marco's mind, rationalization turned to anger. *Julio would never have agreed to leave even if I could arrange it, and it would just hold me back! If he prefers to stay as a slave, then that is his choice.*

Marco resented that after trying to help Julio understand all the injustices that affected their lives, in turn Julio had only lectured him about what a bad person he was. *Well, now at least I don't have to endure any more of his moralizing speeches. His self-righteousness can stay in the orchards!*

But as the *Knotty Buoy* set off and the sight of land faded, Marco couldn't help but look back. His eyes squinted as he scanned the docks. Something inside him yearned for a goodbye, a heartfelt hug, even one more impossible glimpse of his brother — perhaps the last one he may ever get.

But Julio would never appear. *Obviously, there is no possibility he would be there because he isn't even aware of what is going on,* Marco lamented. He took a breath, turned around, put his back towards land, and set his eyes on the vast sea ahead.

PART III

A CARIBBEAN ODYSSEY

OVER THE REEF

Jack sailed the *Knotty Buoy* down through the Bahamas. They threaded the strait of about fifty nautical miles' width between the western tip of Cuba and the island of Hispaniola that links the Atlantic Ocean to the Caribbean Sea and Panama.

"Ladies and gentlemen, this is your skipper. We're now transiting what's known as the Windward Passage," Jack announced through cupped hands in his most commanding captain's voice.

"How nice, darling! They named this place just for you! Ha-ha!" Mindy fired back without missing a beat.

Marco found himself giving a half smile. He was almost beginning to enjoy their banter.

The island of Tortuga, the historic haven for buccaneers during the 1600s, lay far to the east. Ahead, the divided island of Hispaniola rose like an emerald from the crystalline Caribbean waters. Despite its beauty, Marco had a feeling of unease in the pit of his stomach that would last until they sailed beyond this territory.

He advised Jack to swing wide and veer to the east and hug the coast, staying just close enough to keep the lush green mountains of Haiti in their sight. Along that course, mariners might encounter Haitian fishing boats, but they were in-nocuous. He cautioned Jack, however.

"The *Tropas Guardafronteras* patrol these waters — that is, the Cuban coast guard. They are notorious and will be on the lookout for American vessels. If they intercept us, they'll be hungry for a shakedown. It will be a very unpleas-ant experience." He didn't say it aloud, but Marco knew that if the coast guard discovered him, his return to Cuba in their custody would be indefensible and bring fatal consequences.

Jack prompted Marco to navigate for a while. "Sounds like you know these waters as well as anyone. It's time you earned your sails, mate." Marco gave him a questioning look and opened his mouth to speak, but Jack interrupted. "I want you to take the wheel and steer the boat," Jack enunciated with deliberate slowness.

Marco held his hands up, trying to demur. "Oh, I don't know how —"

"Never mind that. Isn't much to it. And, you already know who to watch out for out there. Here." He turned the wheel over to Marco and gave him only cur-sory instructions. He wrapped up the hurried lesson with, "Steer the boat and don't let us sink," then walked away to join Mindy on the deck for sun, booze, and whatever.

As Jack headed off, Marco could hear him say, "Mindy! You've been baking in the sun too long. You're going to be a wrinkly old crow's foot!"

Half-offended, Mindy fired back a snarky reply, "Oh, there you are, waiter. Glad you're finally here to refill my drink!"

Jack and Mindy's partying and razzing had them distracted throughout the voyage. That had provided Marco with opportunities to look around the *Knotty Buoy* to see what he could use to make his getaway. When not snooping, Marco rehearsed the details of his risky plan in his mind. He intended to use Jamaica as a stepping stone to get back into Cuba.

I could just quietly walk off the boat when we dock at the harbor. He pondered the idea but decided against it. *Better to avoid customs and immigration agents. They* were almost certainly going to be around to check passports and IDs, inspect vessels, and ask probing questions. Even if they had no reason to suspect anything about him, the thought of that process made Marco uncomfortable. He preferred to altogether avoid being seen by authorities.

Marco soon discovered his chance at avoidance neatly tucked against the gunnel. In the event of an emergency, the *Knotty Buoy* had a rubber dinghy stowed there that could be used as a life raft. Marco assumed that when they drew close to Jamaica, they would anchor along the coast for the evening before attempting to navigate into the harbor the next morning with the benefit of daylight. He planned to lower the raft stealthily in the dark of night. That would be his best opportunity to slip away. From there he could choose a place to land undetected somewhere along the Jamaican shoreline and minimize the odds of encountering trouble.

After the better part of a week on the open water, the *Knotty Buoy* anchored in the tranquil aquamarine water of Oracabessa Bay on the northern coast of Jamaica about ten nautical miles east of Ocho Rios. They were not far from the harbor but, fortunately for Marco, close enough to what looked like a solitary stretch of beach across the reef. It was the same coast Christopher Columbus sailed along on his second voyage to the New World in 1494, when he claimed Jamaica for Spain.

Jack pointed to the lights of a villa on the brow of a cliff that overlooked a strip of linen white sand beach.

"That is 'Goldeneye,'" he said meaningfully. "It was once the home of the late British novelist Ian Fleming."

Marco didn't comprehend the significance, and apparently, neither did Mindy.

"How am I supposed to know who that is? I don't bother reading books with more pages than *Cosmo*."

To listen to her, one could come away with the impression that Jack was the most tiresome man in the world.

Jack sighed as though the feelings were mutual. "You watch movies though. Ever hear of James Bond?" he asked with condescension.

"Of course I have. I don't live under a rock. Very handsome."

Jack rolled his eyes and gave a slow blink. "Well, before movies, they were books. This is where the man who created secret agent 007 wrote all the stories."

"Oh, delightful! Why didn't you just say he wrote movies?" Mindy asked.

Jack shook his head in disbelief and turned to Marco as if asking to help him out here. Marco just shrugged. Taking a deep breath, Jack walked away, mumbling something about "rum dumb," "rum time," or "time for rum."

Later in the night, after confirming that Jack and Mindy were amply inebriated, Marco moved quietly off the yacht with the raft. He stuffed the handkerchief with his blood oranges into his shirt, then grabbed a nearby life vest just to be safe. Cat-like, he slipped into the life raft and shoved off with hardly a lap of a wave.

As he drifted away, he looked back at the *Knotty Buoy*. For a brief moment, he felt like he'd miss the bickering couple just a little. Then he put his paddle in the water and started to make his way over the reef.

It was a splendid moonlit night. Marco kept his eyes locked on the point he paddled toward. For several minutes, Marco's paddle moved through the water with ease. Then, as he pulled it through the water, he hit something with a jarring thump. Whatever it was didn't give way — instead, it rocked the raft, nearly capsizing Marco.

Caught off guard as he was, fear coursed through his tense body as Marco threw the paddle into the raft, splayed his legs, and grabbed onto the high side with both of his arms. His weight shift caused the high side of the raft to splash back down to the water, and he instinctively pulled his arms back into the raft. Repositioning himself, he cautiously looked over the side of the boat, hoping he might just be in a shallow area over the reef.

A black fin disappeared beneath the raft, confirming his worst fears. Marco could feel the rounded point pushing against the underside, moving across the width of his tiny boat, grazing the bottoms of both feet as it passed. Marco stared at the bottom of the raft, wondering if it would come back. *I'm getting away from here!* he thought and put his paddle back into the water.

Marco's head whipped around when he heard thrashing in the water nearby. In the moonlight, he could make out the dark fins of sharks swimming in circles, looking for smaller fish that lived around the reef.

That shark isn't alone. Marco's heart was pounding out of his chest. *This is a shark fiesta, and I'm right in the middle of their primo hunting territory.*

Curious and attracted by the splashes of his paddle, the sharks approached the raft. Marco felt one give it a bump, perhaps trying to identify food. Marco sensed his vulnerability as the buffeting caused his tiny rubber dinghy to rock back and forth. Another shark swam under and pitched against the inflated raft as it surfaced along the edge. The motion tossed Marco against the side, and he almost fell headlong into the water. Marco regained his balance, but his fear became a near-paralyzing force.

I have no idea how to evade these monsters! They're becoming more aggressive. But doing nothing isn't an option either. Splashes from his paddle drew them closer. Panic rose in Marco's chest — he couldn't fend off all of them at once.

Suddenly, the decision was made for him. One curious shark surfaced close enough to take a nibble on the raft, quickly realizing it wasn't dinner. Marco saw bubbles where it had taken a nip. A faint but distinct hissing sound could be heard as the rubber dinghy began to deflate.

With no other options other than to get out of the water as fast as possible, Marco paddled with renewed fervor, hoping that if he could make it to the beach side of the reef, it would be safer. With every few strokes of his paddle, he sank lower and lower into the water as the air left his tiny raft. About a hundred feet from the shore, the raft was flat and useless, and he was almost completely submerged in the water. Still at a depth over his head, it was only because of his life vest that Marco was able to stay afloat.

Marco wasn't a swimmer. Frantic, he moved his arms and feet and did his best to make his way toward the silhouetted shoreline. Creatures unseen bumped his legs as their paths crossed. Adrenaline surged through his body and propelled him toward dry land, flailing and splashing all the way. About thirty feet from the edge of the water, Marco's feet finally touched the bottom.

Marco hauled himself onto a quiet beach before daybreak, hunched over with exhaustion. He collapsed face down, gripping handfuls of sand in his fists. There he lay, with just the clothes he wore, the bandana handkerchief with his three blood oranges, and just over thirty soggy greenbacks in his pocket.

Oh, I've never been so happy to be covered in gritty sand in my entire life. Even my nostrils are caked with it. I don't care.

He turned over onto his back and scanned the beach. There wasn't another human in sight. A light breeze glided over, the wind licking the top of the water, thrusting up gentle glassy waves. He heard the soothing whisper of palm trees nearby over the mesmeric sounds of cicadas. Nearby, a giant banyan tree festooned with pendulous roots stood against a backdrop of lush jungle tufted with palms and tropical plants. He found himself enveloped in the heady scents of lush plants and flowers that surrounded the area.

Soaked to the bone, Marco lay on the sand, perfectly warm, and let the sunrise wash over his drenched frame. He slept there until the morning sun dried him completely.

JAMAICA — IT'S NO PLACE LIKE HOME

L ying on the beach, Marco may well have thought he was still dreaming if not for the nuisance of blood-feeding sand fleas biting holes in his skin.

With a grunt, Marco dragged himself to his feet, brushed off as best he could, and allowed himself a moment to take in the spectacle of sky and sea. He shook his head vigorously, more sand flying out of his hair and off his clothes, before taking the first few steps into an unfamiliar land.

He walked along the beach until he located a trail up to the road pointing to the A3 thoroughfare. Marco deduced from other signage that he must have made landfall on the outskirts of the sleepy coastal town of Oracabessa. He could see from the booths lining the one street through town that this was a popular fruit and vegetable market, but there were no vendors out that early in the morning.

Guess I won't be finding breakfast here.

Signs along the A3 indicated he was heading in the direction of Ocho Rios. There was almost no traffic at that early hour, so when he set off, Marco found he had the whole road to himself — sort of. He became captivated by the spectacular beauty and variety of the island's flora and fauna along the way. He watched a group of pelicans that fished at the mouth of a nearby lagoon. The morning dew glistened on the foliage, and Marco marveled at the variety of vibrant flowers. He bent for a closer look at an industrious beetle that bustled around foraging on a flower's parts. Blue-green lizards that sported a splash of red kept him entertained as he set out on the long walk along the coast toward Ocho Rios.

Marco hadn't gone far before his stomach let him know it was time to find something for breakfast. Without other options, he pulled open his handkerchief and took out one of the blood oranges he had brought along for just such an occasion. The tranquil island morning along Jamaica's north coast made for a pleasant walk as everything and everyone awakened for a new day.

So many sights and sounds along the oceanside remind me of my walks on the Malecón seawall back in Havana, he thought back with fond memories.

Although it took Marco over four hours to reach Ocho Rios on foot, he enjoyed the scenery along much of the way. He walked into town while it was still morning.

Ocho Rios was a tourist area, so currency exchange would be no problem, if necessary at all. The best exchange rates were found at a bank or travel agency, but local merchants and street vendors were glad to make transactions at street rates. Marco sighted a street vendor setting up for the day.

"A Coca-Cola, please," he requested of the vendor. The man handed him a warm bottle, and in exchange Marco gave him some of his sodden American cash. He received a small bit of change back in Jamaican coinage, but he kept the rest in U.S. dollars.

While drinking his Coke, Marco thought through his approach again. The plan hinged almost entirely on locating a certain Cuban dissident named Francisco "Frank" Díaz in the Jamaican capital of Kingston. When Marco had been a budding prosecutor, the Cuban government had tasked him with investigating the movements of Díaz, a former representative of the Revolutionary Council, an anti-Castro organization. Marco had gathered so much detail about this fugitive that he could write a book. He was confident he could recognize Díaz anywhere, and Marco had some ideas about where to begin looking.

Díaz was known to cruise the streets of Kingston in a closed car with dark-tinted windows. His preferred hunting ground was in front of the Cuban embassy. When he identified a Cuban alone, Díaz offered a ride. He would inform the potential defector that he could provide food, a plane ticket to Miami, and shelter in a secure hiding place until departure time. Once they arranged an escape, Díaz furnished a car that whisked the defector to a hideaway. The escapee would be flown to Miami in a day or so, where U.S. immigration officials had a program to process Cuban refugees.

Marco intended to take advantage of Díaz's assistance to the point where he would be at the airport to board a flight to Miami. If all went as planned, Marco would exchange his plane ticket at the Kingston airport for the fare to Havana. But there was still one huge obstacle.

I'm going to need to find a way to forge documents for myself before I get to the airport.

"Ugh," he muttered to himself, "I have so much left to do."

The first step to implementing his plan required Marco to travel down to Kingston, which, after going back to ask the vendor, he was vexed to discover was located on the far side of the island. That meant he had to somehow make a fifty-mile overland trek from Ocho Rios through the country's hilly interior along the western edge of the Blue Mountain range.

Driving in Jamaica was not for the faint of heart. It was precarious for residents and almost impossible for visitors. Although only about a two-hour ride, sparse road signage made it easy to get lost. Even if Marco had access to a car, for anyone not accustomed to Jamaica's roads and aggressive Jamaican drivers, it would have been recklessly foolish to attempt to drive himself across the island.

With the little cash he had on hand, about thirty dollars, Marco had to figure out a way to find a driver who would take him to Kingston. Any driver would want all he had, if not more. Then what? *First things first — I'll have to figure it out later. I might even need to get a bit . . . creative,* he told himself.

Marco headed for the main tourist strip of Ocho Rios, which was lined with hotels. *I'm sure I'll find drivers there,* he reasoned. It turned out he was right. As he approached the hotels, several cars with taxi signs on their roofs idly waited for passengers to pick up. He approached the first driver, who was already awaiting a fare.

Going to the next vehicle, Marco asked about the price in halting English, "How much for a ride to Kingston?"

The driver eyed him up and down. "More dan you can afford to be sure, mon," he told Marco as he took in his dirty and disheveled appearance.

"Well, that was rude!" Marco huffed under his breath and went to the next taxi. Trying a different approach, Marco offered the next driver everything he had to take him in the hope the driver would accept. "If you can take this now, I can get you more when we arrive in Kingston. I'll double your fare," Marco falsely promised, applying what he considered "creativity." He anticipated having to make a run for it when they got to where he was going.

The driver dismissed Marco's offer with a wave of his hand. He got no better response from the third and fourth drivers.

With the fifth driver, Marco switched up tactics yet again. "Please, my wife is in labor, and it's been a difficult pregnancy. This is all I have, but I need to get to her at the hospital right away. Can you help me?" he pleaded, hoping sympathy would win out.

It didn't. "Listen," he told the man, leaning against his window and feeling more than a little annoyed, "you could sit here all day and not earn any money, or you can at least get something if you take me."

The driver just laughed and looked at Marco. "I can tell you, mon, people wit much more money coming out of dis hotel today. No worries here."

Marco stood up and walked a few steps. Discouraged, he put his head back and placed his hands on his hips with a deep sigh.

"Psst, mon," Marco looked around to see if one of the drivers had changed his mind. Across the street stood a thin, six-foot-tall man in his mid-twenties. He wore a green tank top and faded blue jeans that hung low. Marco eyed the driver with some suspicion. Marco was in no position to criticize anyone else's attire at the moment, but he couldn't ignore the contrast between this guy and the neater appearance of the other drivers, who were wearing polo shirts.

The young fellow stood beside his car and waved him over.

Marco approached warily. He noticed the car lacked a taxi sign on top.

"You lookin' to get to Kingston, mon?" The man had overheard his conversation with the other drivers.

"Yeeees," Marco answered cautiously, "are you a . . . taxi driver?"

"Of course, I'm a driver, mon. You tink I'm just hangin' out here for my health?"

"Your car doesn't have a taxi sign on it," Marco pointed out. He thought to himself, *This doesn't look like the type of guy you'd want your mother or sister to ride with.*

"Listen, mon, doze odda drivers wit di fancy signs, they have to charge you what their company tell dem to. Dey gonna drive you all over to run up di meter and den rip you off. Me, I'm a private driver. I can do what I want. I can charge what I want. I can see you are in need, so I willing to help you out," he said. When the stranger slipped a chummy arm around his shoulders, Marco instinctively recoiled.

"How much to take me to Kingston?" Marco inquired. "I have U.S. dollars." He hoped the offer of American dollars would sweeten the deal with this driver.

"Fifty U.S.," the driver replied without a moment's hesitation. He was suddenly all business.

Marco had already figured out that it was a fair rate to take him across the island. The problem was that he didn't have that much money.

"Twenty-five," Marco countered, but with poor grasp of how to haggle. The driver, on the other hand, routinely negotiated for better rates as part of his everyday work. Haggling was an art.

"Forty U.S." the driver bargained, unbothered.

"Thirty," Marco countered. He had no choice but to hope the driver would accept as much money as he had.

"Thirty-five," the driver replied, to make certain he squeezed as much as possible out of the deal.

Marco shook his head, then went back to his search for another driver. But then, with a long, drawn-out pause and a kind of slow clucking sound, the driver agreed to Marco's last offer.

"Soooo, you'll take me to Kingston for thirty U.S. dollars?" Marco asked him with a certain amount of disbelief. Many thoughts sped through his head. *Why would this guy take so little? I mean, I need him to, but this seems almost too good. Is he just being nice? Nah, I doubt he actually cares about helping me. He could be desperate for a fare, too, I suppose. It might be hard to compete with those other, more polished drivers.* Marco reasoned, *This guy takes what he can get.* Marco tried to convince himself that the uneasiness that nagged him was all in his head.

"Sure, sure, mon. No problem," the driver reassured him as he opened the door.

Marco handed the man the money and got in the back seat.

If he tries to pull anything funny, I could take him in a fight, Marco convinced himself.

The man got in and started to drive.

Maybe it's just my lucky day after all, Marco thought as the hotels disappeared behind them.

The mechanical integrity of the vehicle was questionable. The engine knocked and clattered, other unknown parts of the car rattled, and black exhaust streamed from the tailpipe. Heat came up through the metal around rusted-out holes in the floorboard and burned the soles of Marco's shoes. Marco looked down through the holes where he could see the rush of the ground beneath them. But Marco was not in a position to be particular.

It was then that the thought struck him. *I should never have handed over the entire fare upfront — what was I thinking?* Marco castigated himself. Marco knew that hustlers worked Jamaica's tourist areas, but he was tired from last night's excursion and couldn't think straight.

In retrospect, he should have withheld half until he arrived safely at his destination, but Marco feared the driver would renege on the sweet deal. He felt fortunate enough to find a driver, any driver, and he hadn't wanted to do anything to scare him away. *Maybe it works out okay this time,* Marco reconciled, *but if I continue to make stupid mistakes, my luck will run out.*

The driver departed east out of Ocho Rios. At first, Marco recognized some of the landmarks from his earlier walk from Oracabessa. Then, several miles out of the way, they turned south onto a winding road. Not knowing the area, Marco assumed everything was fine and that he was well on his way to Kingston.

I'm paying a flat fee, so he can drive the longest route possible for all I care. Just as long as we get there. Then paranoid thoughts seeped into his mind. *If we get there.*

Outside of town, Marco felt himself pushed back into his grimy, slightly damp seat as the driver accelerated. They were traveling at an absurdly reckless speed, especially for such a twisted, pothole-filled road.

No wonder his car is falling apart, Marco thought. Every hole they hit sent Marco half-flying out of his seat. It reminded him of being bounced around in that Cigarette boat driven by smugglers over the waves as they raced away from Cuba. He held onto the door handle and tried to keep himself from being jostled around the backseat of the car.

Marco could only look out through the windshield, helpless to do anything else. Ahead, a gaping crater in the road looked big enough to swallow a small elephant. Marco gripped the door handle even tighter as they continued to speed toward the crater.

Marco's eyes surveyed the dense jungle forest on either side of the road. *How in the world is he going to get around that thing, especially at this speed?* It soon became apparent that the driver had no intention of skirting the obstacle.

"Wait! Slow dow—" Marco yelled. The car dropped into the hole and jounced back out. Marco's head smacked into the headliner before he landed back on his seat with a bone-jarring thud.

Marco rubbed the bump on his head and leaned forward. "Can you slow down? I'm not in a hurry, and this is unsafe."

"It's fine, no worries, mon. I drive dis road all di time. Jus hol' on tight."

They rounded a sharp curve. Now, Marco could see they were coming up fast on the taillights of a vehicle that appeared to be either braking or completely stopped. To Marco's consternation, his pleas for safety seemed to have the opposite effect, making the driver behave more dangerously — he didn't seem to be inclined to reduce his speed in the slightest.

Marco looked out the window to his left and saw that they had come out to a section of mountain road with a steep drop-off into the valley. On the right side of the road, the headlights of another vehicle approached from the opposite direction.

Marco gasped as he envisioned the two other options if the driver didn't stop. As they rushed toward the red taillights, the driver honked his horn furiously. The driver on the opposite side of the road answered with his own blaring chorus.

"I don't think that's working!" Marco shouted over the cacophony. A few yards from impact, Marco ducked and braced for the collision.

Instead of a head-on impact, Marco was thrown against the right side door as the driver swerved at the last second. Horns blared on all sides. Marco looked up to see them pass the car on the left while it forced the oncoming car up the mountainside to the right to avoid a collision.

I was wrong — I don't think I'm going to survive this. Marco put his hand on his chest, out of breath with anxious fright.

"Hey, man, that was a little too close for my comfort. Can we please slow it down?" Marco pleaded with the driver again.

This guy might be a little loco en la cabeza, so let's not do anything to make his crazy head worse, Marco reasoned with himself to restrain his own anger at the driver.

After a steep descent, the car entered an unpaved, forested part of the road. The dense canopy swallowed everything beneath it in shadows. For the first time since he cast his eyes away from the Florida coast, Marco was visited with a sense of loneliness.

Without warning, the driver stopped.

Marco's nervousness had gotten the better of him by this time. He leaned closer and tapped the driver on the shoulder. "Is something wrong? Is there a problem with the car?" Marco asked in such a way as to give the driver the benefit of the doubt.

The driver didn't answer.

Marco worried that the man had enough of his nervous criticism and would make him get out. *I should have just kept my mouth shut.*

"Hey, I'm sorry, I won't say another word about your driving, alright? Look, I'll just sit here nice and quiet for the rest of the way," he said in an attempt to appease the driver.

A blur of movement to his left caught Marco's attention. When he turned to look, what he saw startled him. There in his window were two wild-eyed, scabrous men with machetes standing in the road.

Machete-slinging farmers are not altogether unusual in an area where bananas are harvested year-round, Marco tried reassuring himself. Nonetheless, it was unsettling, and Marco's stomach sank.

Marco's attention was fixated on the two men. One wore tattered trousers and a black tank top that showed arms bulging with muscles. The faint red glow of a cigarette hung from his lips. The other man had a gleaming bald head and wore a gray shirt with frayed cut-off sleeves. He sported reflective sunglasses.

Why would he wear those in the jungle shade? Marco wondered with curiosity at something so insignificant. He knew he was in danger, and the terror was causing him to feel disjointed from reality, like he was floating above the scene and watching this all unfold.

The men continued to stare at him through the window as though they were sizing him up. The gray-shirted man tapped the window with his machete to get Marco's attention. Before Marco could even think about how to respond, the man yanked open the car door and growled, "Get out!"

He pulled Marco out onto the road by his shirt.

"Whaa-?!" Marco couldn't even get a complete word out before he rolled onto the ground, his bandana of oranges clutched in one hand. The attackers kicked sand into his face, blinding him for a moment. Marco sat up, spitting grit out of his mouth and trying to wipe the sand out of his stinging eyes.

One of the men quickly searched Marco's pockets, cursed when he didn't find anything, and then they both jumped into the car. Marco watched in astonishment as it sped away and a cloud of dust and exhaust blew back in his face.

Coughing, Marco reeled. Powerless, he couldn't hold back his anger. He raised his fist at the savages and screamed, "You flea bite!" But they couldn't even hear him over the crunch of tires spinning down the unpaved road.

Marco knew it was a lame insult, even if they had been able to hear it. In the chaos of the moment, they were the only English words Marco could muster to let them know just what he thought of them. He slapped the ground and grabbed a fistful of gravel, then threw it toward the car whose taillights were almost out of sight.

Exhausted, Marco lay back down on the dirt road and cursed himself. *I should have listened to my gut about that guy!*

"What am I supposed to do now?" Marco shouted up at the dense canopy with all he had. Now he was stranded somewhere along a dangerous jungle road . . . no money, no ride, no map. "Well, I guess I can't stay here," he grunted as he pushed himself up off the ground.

He had been so distracted by the crazy driver that he hadn't paid attention to what direction they were headed. *Ahh,* he tried to remember. The last road signs he noticed were for Whitehall, but that was quite a ways back.

Where am I? Marco turned back and forth, standing in the middle of the road. He wasn't sure if he should head south toward Kingston or try to double back north toward the coast and Ocho Rios. He looked south and grimaced — it would lead him deeper into unmarked roads and impenetrable jungle thicket.

Even if I make it back to Ocho Rios, he reasoned, *I'm right back where I started. Worse, because without money I'll have no way to hire another driver.* And he knew he had no chance of finding Díaz unless he could get to Kingston, so he had to keep going.

Lacking better options, Marco gathered up his two remaining oranges and proceeded on foot into the jungle. He tried to navigate from what he could see of the position of the sun that occasionally glimmered through breaks in the dense jungle canopy. However, the way the roads switched back, winding around mountains frustrated any sense of direction.

About an hour passed, and the steamy heat of the day began to take its toll on Marco. He was sinking deeper into jungle terrain.

26

LAW OF THE JUNGLE

The tropical jungle was rich in palms, silk cotton trees, and hardwoods. There were deep-cut gullies of ferns, cathedrals of bamboo, and limestone outcroppings grown over with blood-red orchids. The air was alive with the forest aromas.

Interspersed throughout the canopy of green was a virtual zoo of unusual wildlife. The exotic flora and fauna captivated Marco. He caught sight of electric blue butterflies and innumerable bee-like hummingbirds that flitted back and forth between the trees. The most striking birds were the red-billed streamertails, also known as "doctor birds," with their iridescent plumage and long swallowtail. Other birds were announcing their presence and staking out territorial claims. Black-billed parrots cawed as they flew through the trees overhead. Below, animals were stirring, digging, investigating — releasing the muted, earthy aromas of new life. Small lizards and brightly-colored poison dart frogs clung to the vegetation, eyes rotating around in their sockets as they watched this giant interloper wander through their domain.

The scene was draped and bejeweled with the boundless ingenuity found in creation. Streams of run-off that followed the same course day-in and day-out had eroded mud channels between the established vegetation. The tiny streams at the bottoms of these deep channels, which were little wider than a few inches, had formed waterfalls and rapids. There were islands in the streams where grass tendrils and roots clung to the mud and to each other. Ornate arbor-like structures of greenery emerged as one plant grew atop another.

This must be the most fantastic landscape for the small creatures that live here, Marco thought.

Marco spotted a pair of slender, weasel-like creatures that scurried around the base of the trees. They were cute at a distance. Marco recognized these fierce little animals as Jamaica's notorious mongooses. These weren't indigenous to the island. In the late 1800s, a sugar planter introduced nine mongooses from India to contend with snakes and rats in the sugarcane fields, which the mongooses did. However, after their purpose had been fulfilled, packs of mongooses flourished and propagated. They turned into an invasive species themselves, and soon the fields of the Jamaican farmers were overrun by these aggressive creatures.

Not normally one to take much interest in animal activity, Marco felt compelled to watch. Danger lurked in the midst of the splendor — in that aromatic and delicate stirring of new life, death waited. At first glance, Marco saw what appeared to be a thick vine dangling from a tree. But when the "vine" moved and flicked its forked tongue, Marco stopped in his tracks.

The Jamaican boa hung not far above the smaller of the two mongooses, which were preoccupied with a ground snake that warmed itself on a mossy log among the toadstools. The snake was lazing about in a small patch of sun that breached the undergrowth. Both mongooses approached the coiled ground snake from opposite sides. The larger mongoose struck first, taking a nip at it and jumping back.

The distraction was just what the big boa needed. The serpent dropped its full body onto the head of the smaller mongoose and wrapped itself around its prey. The doomed mongoose struggled in vain while the larger one bared its sharp teeth and summoned all the ferocity within its four-pound body to fend off the giant boa from its companion. With its lower body wrapped firmly around the smaller mongoose, the snake's head was free to face off with the other one. The boa reared its head and hissed. The mongoose responded in kind.

The boa watched with hypnotic patience. Its swaying head gave evidence that it was keeping rapt attention on the frantic little animal. The mongoose made quick movements in fits and starts. It feigned attack and backed away. With lightning speed, the boa struck at it — but the mongoose, agile and menacing, darted around to bite the snake from behind.

The two creatures twirled around each other, one calm and confident, the other impatient and angry. Evenly matched in the fight, both combatants made swift maneuvers and landed sharp strikes at each other.

The boa loosened its grip on the lifeless smaller mongoose, which enabled the serpent to move around once again. The other mongoose ventured closer to its motionless companion. The snake struck at it again, sinking rows of needle-like teeth into the soft body of the intrepid mammal. Although nonvenomous, the boa's formidable bite was enough to injure the mongoose and send it fleeing, leaving its dead companion to the snake.

Marco continued to watch with fascination as the snake turned its attention to its kill. The boa unhinged its jaw over the limp head of the mongoose and slowly swallowed its victim whole. Marco observed the boa's quarry form a moving bulge in the body of the reptile. It was both gruesome and remarkable to watch.

It must be the way of the jungle — kill or be killed — eat or be eaten, Marco thought to himself before moving onward.

Lush mango trees rustled as the wind picked up, and the floppy leaves of banana trees waved wildly like swarms of raving zombies. Then the rain started — at first not a torrential downpour, but heaving drops. Marco could almost hear them pelting one at a time, splashing into the foliage. Then it fell in rods.

The tropical afternoon deluge, though brief, was enough to soak him through. The rain did nothing to cool things down. Rather, it compounded the infernal tropical humidity and made the trek even more miserable. Marco kept going, slogging along the steamy mud road.

The sun returned as instantaneously as it had gone. Drenched head to toe in sweat, humidity, and rainwater, Marco wandered upon a small cottage a while later. Laundry that should have been thrown away fifty washings ago dangled from a frayed clothesline. Marco cased the area — there seemed to be no one around. From the line, he plucked off someone's work trousers, permanently stained with red bauxite clay. Looking at the discolored pants, he thought, At least it's something drier to wear. This will do.

Now hungry again, Marco savored another sweet blood orange, one of his two remaining. The sweetness of the orange contrasted with the bitter emotions that sprang up — the fruit evoked memories of time shared with Julio in the citrus groves. Among the few things he and Julio could agree on was how much they both liked this special strain of citrus.

Marco was already lamenting his loss, feeling the pangs of remorse for leaving his brother. *Laboring in Vladi's groves had felt unbearable, but had it really been that bad?* he second-guessed himself again. As each of his remaining oranges was consumed, Julio felt farther and farther away. Paradoxically, Marco couldn't settle on whether he should be feeling sadness or relief.

Evening shadows appeared on the shaded slope as the sun retreated behind the mountains. The setting sun filled Marco's mind with ominous thoughts. He reflected on everything that happened to him since leaving Cuba, and he was nearing his breaking point. Now he faced the prospect of spending the night stranded alone on a jungle mountain road.

The last straw came in the receding light of dusk when nocturnal creatures began to emerge. Fireflies started to twinkle here and there, then a cacophony of crickets and croaking frogs filled the air. The woods started to come to life. Giant, foot-long centipedes appeared and crawled about, and it only got harder to see them. Marco dodged out of the way a few times as the creepers got close to his feet, heedless of his presence. Then the undergrowth came alive with rustling rat-like creatures that sprinted around him. Marco had never seen a Jamaican coney — as far as he was concerned, they were giant rats.

I need to get out of the jungle . . . and fast!

MARCO'S WILD RIDE

Marco stood at the roadside, thinking. The last rays of daylight were fading and, after seeing the creepy crawlers of the jungle, he had decided to keep close to the road and take his chances with catching another ride. *Better than giant centipedes and jungle rats!* he reasoned.

As though out of nowhere, the sound of reggae music blared a high-pitched throb from tinny speakers. Marco saw headlights rounding the bend. It had been hours since he'd encountered a motorized vehicle of any kind. After the harrowing experience of the previous ride and his terrifying ordeal with those men, Marco was on edge and suddenly grew tense. He had no notion what to expect or prepare for.

What were his options? Back in Cuba, hitchhiking was common. Marco had experience. Few people had cars, and public transportation wasn't the greatest, so ride sharing was a common practice in Cuba — they called it *botella*. The key was always to keep it simple — don't ask a driver to ride too far or out of the way. Not all drivers were into picking up passengers, but if someone persevered, sooner or later he could get a ride.

Marco held out his thumb, hoping to flag down the car, although at this point, he couldn't afford to be patient. The car proved to be a compact truck, and its driver didn't appear to be slowing down. Feeling desperate, Marco threw caution to the wind and stepped out into the middle of the road. This forced the driver to brake hard, kicking up a cloud of dust. The Jamaicans who were in the truck were not amused with Marco's tactic, and they expressed as much. They cursed at him and insisted he get off the road.

Marco sized up the situation. In the back of the truck were numerous bunches of bananas piled one on top of the other. The sudden stop had caused several of the bunches to shift, revealing old woven sugar bags that bore what Marco surmised to be farm-cultivated ganja. He'd been a prosecutor back in Cuba, so Marco knew about the bootleg profits from drug trafficking.

Oh, great, Marco thought wryly. It figures that I'd go from robbers to stoners. Imagine me, a prosecutor, riding around with illegal growers. It would be the ultimate irony for me to get arrested for their crimes.

Marco moved a couple of steps toward the truck and squinted at the headlights, trying to catch sight of who was behind the windshield. When he got a look at the men up close, what he saw startled him.

These men sure have a wild and fierce look about them. They could be like the other ones who threw me out of the car and left me on the side of the road.

Indeed, these men were Rastafarians with long streamers of hair in dreadlocks that reached almost to their waists and hadn't been cut nor combed for years. The tangles fell in long, matted strands. Marco thought it gave each man the appearance of a male Medusa. Their curious features were accentuated in Marco's eyes by heavy, untrimmed beards that were just as matted. To him, they looked terrifying.

Should I try to get a ride with these rough characters or take my chances on this mountain jungle road at night? Marco weighed which was more perilous.

Of course, given their unlawful enterprise, the Rastas also had every reason to be leery of picking up a hitchhiker on a back road in the evening shadows. All these factors were a recipe for mutual distrust, fear, and tension. The driver in particular was wary of taking a roadside passenger and was more than eager to speed off unceremoniously.   But his Gorgon-like companion appealed to him. A brief exchange ensued.

"Look, di I pretty sure dat is 'Cheeko.' Ya know, *Cheeko and Payaso*."

"Di I look like di I care? He know how fi call police jus' like anybody else."

"Him look like Cheeko. Believe me, him will be A-okay wid what we haulin'. Besides, him noh got time fi bodda wid us nobodies."

The duo of comedian-entertainers had a lot of notoriety in Jamaica. Sightings of luminaries — royalty, statesmen, millionaires, musicians, and movie stars — were anything but rare around the island.

The driver countered, "But him have time fi be standin' out in di road inna di middle o' nowhere? If him a Cheeko, wey him driver?"

"Maybe him filmin' a movie an' get himself lost. Tink 'bout it — ef wi fine di real Cheeko. Den wi come rescue dis star, 'specially one who love ganja — we gonna score wiself all kinda rich connection.'

That logic gave the driver pause to reconsider his stance — this could be good for business. Both Rastas looked the stranger over closely.

"Ya Cheeko?" the passenger finally asked, then cracked up with laughter.

Marco gave him a quizzical look. He understood English fine, but he struggled with this strange dialect. He had trouble deciphering what they were talking about, but the passenger rubbed his upper lip and pointed at Marco, which made him think it had something to do with his mustache.

The driver gave Marco a long, suspicious look, then conceded. He mumbled something unintelligible, then motioned with his hand for Marco to climb in. The passenger opened his door and stepped out, allowing Marco to climb into the tiny truck cab and wedge himself between them.

Marco's face twisted as the odors from the truck hit his nostrils. *Ewww, these dudes smell like a skunk — just awful!*

"Small up yuself!" ordered the driver.

What's he saying now? Marco had a bewildered look.

The passenger could tell by his face that the message didn't translate for Marco. "Make room, he tellin' you."

"Oh, okay." Marco attempted to comply as best he could. "Er, so where are you guys headed?" *Perhaps I should have asked that before getting into the truck,* Marco chided himself.

"Wi on our way to Kingston to make a Rose Town delivery."

"Perfect." Marco was relieved to finally have good fortune on his side for once — or so he hoped. If truth be told, he would have been willing to go any-where if it meant avoiding a night on that jungle road.

The ride was hot and cramped, but Marco refrained from complaining this time. Precarious, badly-maintained roads alongside the mountains were just wide enough for one vehicle — a zigzagging track with endless hairpin turns. There were no guardrails to prevent driving over the brink. Marco looked down at the wreckage of a bus that had rolled over into the gorge only days earlier. It all made for a white-knuckle ride with the e'er stoned Rastas.

Throughout the ride, the pair kept addressing Marco as "Cheeko." He just went along with it. Apparently, they trusted this "Cheeko" fellow, which worked out well for Marco. He could play along.

Through the lush jungle between Castleton and Toms River, they came across villages of shabbily clothed islanders who resided in huts and squalor. The driver rousted chickens as they passed through the tiny settlements, laugh-ing at the squawking fowl. Places like these off the beaten path were without electricity or running water. Although the locals of these mountain villages were winding down for the evening, but they invariably greeted visitors with a hospitable wave and warm, wide smiles as they passed by.

At intervals, the islanders set up rusty, corrugated metal stalls along the roadside with an array of handicrafts for passers-by to peruse: pottery, straw hats, woodcarvings, inlaid boxes, Jamaican dolls, colorful baskets, and shell-crafted items with vivid tropical designs painted on them.

The proprietors of these makeshift roadside markets also sold locally-grown fruits and vegetables of all kinds: mangoes, papaya, soursops, limes, pineapples, yams, plantains, turnips, pumpkins, star apples, melons, rose apples, tangerines, green and ripe bananas, breadfruit, cocoa, beetroot, naseberries, and sweetsops.

As they passed, Marco looked hungrily at all sorts of tropical deliciousness. This made him even more keenly aware of the angry rumbling in his stomach.

While they bounced along the country roads of Jamaica, the driver confided in Marco. "Di rainy season been good fer growin' di ganja dis year. We get a beeg crop, but so does da udda fahms. Da ganja plentiful now, so di mahket too full."

"Wi love di plenty," the passenger explained. "But dat mean everybody compete an' it much too stiff, an' den wi don' sell fer so much. Moh ganja, less money — dat is crazy, eh?"

Having gained some understanding of supply and demand during his brief time working in Vladi's citrus groves, Marco was impressed by his companions' grasp of the concept.

These uneducated ganja growers out here in the highlands of Jamaica understand capitalism better than the socialist ideologues of Cuba.

"I know a little about the growing business," he informed them. "I was the right-hand man to a very wealthy American businessman."

The two farmers sat up straighter, their interest piqued.

"Wi listenin', mon . . . "

"He is a certain Señor Moisés in Florida. I bet — no — I know he would be willing to take the excess off your hands — all you can send — and at a good price too." It was a flat-out lie that Marco had improvised on the spot. Of course, he knew that Vladi would never partake of Russian vodka or even cerveza, let alone marijuana.

The guys just looked at each other, smiling, and kept repeating with approval, "Ya, mon."

By this time, they were engulfed in a hazy cloud of ganja smoke filling the cab. Not impervious to second-hand effects, Marco's mind wandered.

What was I thinking? What a preposterous fib, hah? Got to watch myself — that stuff must be scrambling my brain too. It could have had something to do with it, but even under normal conditions Marco sometimes just carelessly let his mouth outrun his good sense. He was trying to contribute to the conversation and ingratiate himself with his hosts rather than keeping his mouth under control. It was just the first idea that popped into his head.

The wasted Rastas were feeling content and more relaxed with their passenger. They were also excitedly proud of the quality of their freshly processed harvest. They passed a joint to their new friend and "business associate." Marco went along to keep them from being suspicious, but he merely feigned taking a hit. He held his breath and nodded his head as though it were good.

How much more of this can I take? I can't get out, but I've got to keep my head on straight. Marco already knew that he couldn't walk from the mountains down to Kingston. Uncertain as to whether he was experiencing a contact high, he tried to wrap his head around the awkwardness of his uncomfortable situation. Paranoia swept over him like a Caribbean hurricane.

I wonder if smoking marijuana is a sin? It probably is, he assumed, knowing Julio would think it was unwise. His doctor brother would not approve even if it had been legal. *According to Julio, the Bible plainly condemns intoxication — that was all he needed to know. These guys are among society's lowlifes. After all, I'm an educated lawyer — a man of the law, committed to what's right. What's more, I don't need any made-up religion telling me what constitutes right or wrong.*

Marco felt sure in his heart that he was doing his best to live life the right way, true to himself — his own reasoning told him so. In the end, he felt he did more right than wrong. For all Julio's talk of God, Marco felt it was unnecessary confusion.

You have to follow your own values, he consoled himself. *Look at these Rastas — they're all about "religion." They supposedly believe in God too, right? And look how wasted they are!* He almost wished Julio were along for a ride so he could make his point and find some satisfaction in seeing his "good" brother's embarrassment at these cretins claiming they have a connection to his God.

Well, at least I'm not like these degenerates. It's hard to make sense of what these guys are saying — they can barely talk. It's likely the cumulative effect of all that ganja has caused some form of madness.

But he had to keep acting cordially with these guys — otherwise, they might flip on him. *All I've got to do is get down out of these mountains,* he reminded himself, knowing that a momentary lapse of judgment could turn the situation from congenial to dangerous.

He struggled to keep his wits about him. They, in turn, thought Marco was funny for some reason — who knew why. They just kept laughing at whatever he said, even when he was being earnest. Having never looked at dreadlocks up close, Marco slowly reached out a tentative finger, curious to the textural feel, and asked, "Does your hair naturally grow that way?" The question sent them into hilarious fits.

"Mi a dead wid laugh, Cheeko!" exclaimed the driver as though enjoying a joke that Marco hadn't told.

Marco looked at the passenger for a clue.

"He's dying with laughter," the passenger translated.

"I don't understa-," Marco started to say, confounded by their amusement.

"We be all-natural, boy," the driver guffawed, his eyes tearing up with laughter.

"Shut yu blabba mout!" replied the passenger to the driver. "I say he talk too much," he translated for Marco.

As the trio descended into St. Andrew parish toward Kingston, the munchies were getting the better of Marco. He unwrapped the one remaining blood orange he'd brought along all the way from the Florida orchards. It was his last tangible reminder of Julio. He looked down at it for a while with sadness. In a moment he would have consumed the last thing he could touch connected to their life together.

Marco slowly peeled the orange as he continued to stare at it vacantly. "Were yu plannin' to marry dat orange, mon? Yu lookin' at it like yu lost yu true love," the passenger commented, noticing his peculiar expression and the reluctance with which he treated the orange. Marco gave a sniff and half smiled. With a side glance to his Rastafarian companions, he mustered up the graciousness to share what he had left with them.

They arrived in Kingston under the evening darkness, and Marco guessed they had timed it that way on purpose. The driver stopped the truck at the intersection of Port Royal and Church Streets, near the downtown market. Marco patted both men on the shoulder and expressed his thanks for the ride into the city before getting out on the passenger's side.

"Irie, Cheeko," replied the driver with a contented smile. "Inna di morrows."

Without being prompted this time, the passenger translated, "He say everything is alright and fine. See yu tomorrow."

Marco hadn't made plans to see them tomorrow, but he was relieved they left on good terms and didn't ask him anymore about that deal with Señor Moisés. He let them believe whatever they thought and hoped by morning they'd forget that they'd ever seen him.

INVENTADO

The piercing crow of a rooster claiming credit for the new day broke the morning stillness and roused Marco from a deep sleep. Still disoriented, he needed a few seconds to remember where he was and why he was there. With nowhere to stay the previous night, Marco had slipped into the courtyard of what looked to be a vacant home. At least he had found a relatively safe place to sleep that was off the streets of Kingston.

Marco's first groggy step landed his foot on an apple-like fruit that had fallen from a heavily laden tree in the courtyard. He had started to feel hungry again, so perhaps it was fortuitous that he had literally stumbled upon breakfast. He gathered up a couple of the fruits in his bandana handkerchief and hastily got out of the courtyard before anyone spotted him at the house.

Within walking distance, he observed a couple of homeless men bathing from a water hose. Sticky and dirty from a couple of days of traveling across the island, Marco welcomed an opportunity to wash up with some fresh water. He waited until they were done and then approached the area, doing his best to wash up in the muddy patch that surrounded the water spigot.

Refreshed and more awake, Marco found a seat under a nearby bus shelter and untied his bandana handkerchief to reveal the fruit he had collected earlier.

One of the homeless men nearby gave him an intense stare. Marco shifted with discomfort.

This fellow seems interested in my fruit, he thought. His first inclination was to hide it back under the handkerchief.

After a brief moment, he had a change of heart. *Perhaps I should offer to share breakfast with the others here. They look to be in some unfortunate circumstances.* But the charitable thought left as quickly as it had come. *Well, they can find their own fruit, can't they? If they weren't being so lazy, they could go pick it up in the courtyard just like I did.*

Marco began to work at peeling the inviting fruit, opening a surprisingly hard shell and exposing three separate yellow segments, each with a large black seed that had the appearance of a polished river stone.

The homeless man who had been so fixated on Marco's breakfast hollered at him abruptly, "Ackee!"

Marco looked up at the man. He accepted that he had difficulty understanding the Jamaicans, but the man's tone was rude. He frowned, indicating that he didn't want to be interrupted.

"Hey man, I'm just trying to eat some breakfast."

"Ackee!" the homeless man repeated, pointing at the fruit. Marco, somewhat annoyed, assumed the man suffered from mental illness.

It's best if I just ignore him. Maybe he'll lose interest and go away. Marco pretended to not notice the man and resumed peeling the fruit, then raised a bite of its almond-colored pulp toward his mouth.

"Ackee!" shouted the homeless man with alarm. He rushed toward Marco and knocked what was supposed to be breakfast out of his hand. "Ackee!" he looked directly into Marco's eyes and repeated scoldingly.

What's with these crazy Jamaicans?! Marco thought, exasperated.

Another homeless man in tattered clothing approached as though anticipating to be the spectator of an impending brawl. Instead, to Marco's surprise, the second man interjected with unexpected wisdom. "He say ackee kill yu!" the man reiterated the warning in a stern tone. "Ef yu eat it di right time in di right way den be right. Ackee an saltfish — den is a delicacy. Eat it di wrong time, it wi' kill yu!"

Prepared properly, the ackee fruit was an ingredient in many Jamaican recipes. Eating the wrong parts, or even the right ones when only partially ripened, could be lethal. Marco didn't know what he didn't know. He never would have expected a couple of homeless guys to save his life as they just had.

Marco mumbled his thanks and tossed the fruit into the grass. But that still left him hungry and without breakfast. After his hike in the mountains and having eaten only a few oranges the previous day, his energy waned. Without money, Marco had no prospects of buying food, and there was no other fruit to be picked from trees on the city streets.

Marco watched as a street vendor brought out his pushcart and organized his produce. A few ripe bananas fell from the pile onto the ground. Marco sat up a little straighter. He reasoned, *Anything on the ground is fair game, right?*

Marco stood and strolled over to the fallen fruit. He tried to remain as casual as possible, as though he were merely taking pleasure in the morning. The vendor saw him and smiled sociably. Marco reciprocated to avoid suspicion. When the man turned to tend to his other fruit, Marco saw his chance. He took a couple of rapid steps and reached for the bananas. He snatched up one in each hand and slipped them into his pockets. As Marco turned to face the vendor, he realized that he hadn't been as slick as he supposed.

"Hey, mon, ya gonna pay me for dat fruit?" the merchant asked. Marco stared at him for a moment before instinct kicked in and he sprinted.

The man chased after him a short way yelling, "Tief!! Tief!! Gimme back mi fruit, yu dutty tief!" But it was chancier for the vendor to leave his other fruit unattended than it was worthwhile to chase after two bananas, and Marco easily slipped away down a side street.

When he believed he had reached a safe distance, Marco stopped running. He leaned against a wall, wheezing, before sliding down and sitting on the ground. He took the bananas from his pocket, but as he looked at them, the vendor's words kept playing in his head.

I'm not a "tief." *That's ridiculous,* Marco rationalized to himself. As a prosecutor, Marco had his dealings with real "thieves," and he knew about the really bad people.

I'm not a criminal. I'm just a hungry man who picked up a couple of bananas from the ground. How much could they have cost the vendor anyway — no more than a few centavos, *if anything?* It wouldn't make much difference in his business, but the food would mean everything to Marco.

There were many in Cuba who felt just as Marco did at that moment. Circumstances back in Cuba sometimes made it necessary to just take what they needed. As delays plagued every facet of the supply chain, shortages swept the island. Marco had many times laid the blame for these factors on the hardships of contending with U.S. sanctions rather than the failures of Cuba's Soviet-style centralized economy. Yet, in reality, scarcity stemmed from economic dysfunction, mismanagement, and graft.

In hardship, people improvised. They found new uses for old things, and they worked out creative solutions to get what they needed. Cuba, it seemed, wasn't all communist after all. Government officials tacitly accepted black market trade, which helped fill consumer gaps. There were interdependent networks of people who knew people who could resolve a need. One often relied upon friends who knew how to obtain things.

Black market trade wasn't just a better option — often, it was the only option. Everyone at some point had to buy that way. Therefore, nearly everyone engaged in "illegal" commerce at some level, which afforded authorities a lot of discretion about whom they prosecuted.

The idealistic fantasy of communism held that everyone shared everything. Consequently, when lacking other options, desperation sometimes called for taking what was needed from someone else. The norms of Cuban society were bent in such a way that theft might be excused as long as it was not committed against a neighbor.

Inventado became a euphemism to replace the word "stealing" in the Cuban vernacular. Theft spread to every corner of the Cuban economy, even though it usually happened in banal ways. As a result, out of necessity, almost every Cuban became an offender in one way or another.

By any other standard, the act of stealing anything from anyone was theft, and by definition, the one doing the taking was a "thief." Ironically, Marco the attorney completely missed the connection between those concepts now in his moment of desperation.

As he ate the pinched fruit, Marco realized his plan to leave for Cuba required immediate implementation. This couldn't drag out, because he didn't have any resources, and he didn't have time to pull them together by conventional means.

He considered finding work in Jamaica to earn money and save for a way out, but that seemed implausible. Too many people were looking for work, so wages for basic-level jobs were low. One couldn't get a job worth his time unless he was initiated within the middle and upper strata of society. An outsider without connections could only expect to earn enough to subsist below the poverty line. Meanwhile, many common people of the working class who didn't have enough money lived in terrible conditions — filthy housing with woefully inadequate running water and toilets. Unchecked violent crime made life at this level even more unsafe.

Marco had almost no chance of being able to live, work, and accumulate savings for passage to Cuba. So without money, local connections, or any means other than his own quick mind, Marco would have to be "creative" . . . *inventado*.

THE GLEANER

At night, the streets of Kingston were haunted by shouts and clamor as the capital's nomads roamed. In the heart of the city, in an area called Half Way Tree, Marco found a place where he could rest in a former dental clinic turned night shelter for the homeless. He tried to keep to himself, but invariably he would be approached by a wasted vagrant who wanted to talk about women or hoped to bum a smoke.

The place had its ups and downs, but at least he had somewhere to sleep at night, and he could wash up and get a meal. Marco could pick up a ready-to-eat breakfast at mid-morning, and they served an early dinner after 2:30 in the afternoon.

After sundown, around 150 people poured into the shelter. Marco guessed that at least three times that many remained on the streets. The refuge housed a variety of indigent people with different kinds of problems. Some were evicted because they couldn't pay rent and were without family support. Drug abuse had taken many people down into Kingston's dark alleys. Others were mentally ill, and even the madmen feared one another.

On his way out from a long, restless night at the shelter, Marco strode through Kingston's commercial district. He stopped short when something caught his eye. There it was in bold print — a familiar name and photo in a headline of *The Gleaner*, Jamaica's daily newspaper.

This might be just the break I've been hoping for.

Miguelito Cervera, better known as "Michael," was a Cuban national living in Jamaica. Michael was a true mover and shaker whose remarkable business acumen often made newspaper headlines in Jamaica and elsewhere. He reveled in the attention. And now there he was — his photo on the front page of *The Gleaner*.

I'd recognize that trademark pencil mustache anywhere. Got to give it to him, he's a snappy dresser.

Michael was a nefarious character, a rare vestige of the Batista era. He had gotten his start back in Cuba's "golden years." As a bagman for the island nation's former dictator, Fulgencio Batista, he made daily rounds to collect the ten percent skimmed from casino revenues for his boss.

Michael had moved abroad to study international law in New York City and, therefore, spoke perfect English. In time, his business interests spread like tentacles into Mexico, Panama, and a number of Caribbean island nations, including Jamaica.

Michael was so entrenched in the Cuban underground that he was essentially untouchable. That made him one of the few linked with the former regime to survive the Cuban Revolution. Michael never cared about the merits or shortcomings of socialist ideologies — it was all about business — that's all that mattered to him.

Michael was a fixer — he worked behind the scenes. He maintained ties to Cuba, perhaps in a more capitalistic sense than Castro would have ever been inclined to acknowledge. Cuban officials were willing to turn a blind eye to Michael because, frankly, he was valuable in pragmatic ways. The man capable of procuring oil during the Cuban embargo was not about to be harassed in the least. He knew how to get deals done, securing resources when needed — for a handsome price, of course.

Michael maintained an office in Kingston, where he made use of the advantages available through his connections, including his friendship with Jamaican prime minister Malik Sinclair. Sinclair and his sister owned a chain of travel agencies, including one in a prime venue within Kingston's central business district. Given the advantages of its location, Sinclair allowed Michael to keep a small office there.

Locating Michael's whereabouts was not difficult — he was hardly hiding. On the contrary, he was a recognizable figure in Kingston. Marco's experience in investigations made it a simple undertaking to learn what places Michael frequented and get an idea about his routines by asking around. The answers led him to a blue and white shop of cinderblock construction in the business district — the travel agency.

Michael's amiable personality belied the underside of his more odious dealings. Marco had no doubt that Michael could get him back to Cuba undetected — it just depended on what Michael thought he could get out of it in return. Marco thought about approaching him with a proposition. Marco, who knew Michael's file like the back of his hand, had plenty of dirt on him. Maybe they could work out some mutually beneficial arrangements.

But Marco concluded it wasn't worth the risk. At this point, no one in the world knew Marco was here. No one could identify him or explain his appearance. As long as no one knew, he wasn't compromised. Marco would be beholden for life if he made a deal with Michael. He could always be ratted out.

Furthermore, Marco had nothing to offer Michael that the man couldn't do for himself — he had far more clout than Marco at the moment. Why would Michael bother negotiating any deal with a prosecutor trying not to be exposed and charged with defection? That wasn't a chance worth taking. Instead, Marco came up with something much craftier than lopsided bargaining.

ALL THAT JAZZ

he next morning, Marco walked to the travel agency where Michael's office was located. *This could be the jackpot.*

Of course, he couldn't just walk in and buy a one-way ticket to Cuba without money. Marco knew there were travel agencies where a person might procure a fabricated passport of any origin for the right price. Not that he would be a paying client, but there was still a high probability that at Michael's office, he could get his hands on a Cuban passport and most of the other materials he needed to forge his documents. Most importantly, they might assist him with another crucial detail that was difficult to obtain, especially without money — a passport photo.

Instead of searching for everything in the dark in an unfamiliar building, Marco knew it would be useful to case the place in advance. Later he could come back under cover of darkness and snatch what he needed. Still, the sense that this was theft eluded Marco. He rationalized that since he had no other options, it was acceptable. *Inventado.*

Marco bounded up the cement steps leading to the travel agency. His countenance transformed instantly the moment his hand reached for the front door. *It's showtime!* He plastered on his most cordial smile and prepared to perform. Marco beamed when the front desk agent looked up.

"Hello Miss . . . uh?" Marco glanced at her nametag and furrowed his brow, wondering if it maybe had a typo: Jhas. Aiming to be polite, Marco hesitated rather than attempt to say her name. He held on to his bright smile, encouraging her to help him out.

The young travel agent gave him a furtive glance. In a split second, Marco detected her apprehension.

Uh oh. Of course, she might be a little uneasy — I'm a stranger who just emerged from the street. And look at me! I might be worried if I saw me too.

He realized that beyond being amiable, he should have made an effort to tidy up. His disheveled hair, ill-fitting bauxite-stained trousers, wrinkled dirt-caked shirt, and a tad of odor to go along with it, naturally caused her to feel a bit uncomfortable.

I must look like someone who doesn't have enough money for the bus, let alone a vacation. Well, it's true, he humored himself. Marco had taken on the appearance of a street-dweller, so much so that he resembled the deranged drug addicts whom she had been warned roamed that area of Kingston. Either way, he looked like a man in need of some kind of help.

Jhas had just started her new job. Inherently kind and eager to be professional, she chose to give him the benefit of any doubt. Most of the time people just mangled the pronunciation of her name without bothering to ask, so she did appreciate his polite demeanor. She didn't leave him feeling awkward but returned a bright smile.

"My name is Jhas, like the music, 'jazz.' My parents were wonderful people, but poor spellers. How can I help you today?"

"Oh, got it — Jhas. What a unique name!" Marco flattered as he continued to make small talk, "I happen to love jazz. How about you?" *Still got it,* he beamed inwardly.

A little bewildered by his manner, she raised an eyebrow. She didn't know what to think about this guy, whether she ought to be nervous or even fearful.

She thought it would be impolite not to answer, but was a bit at a loss about how to respond.

Determined to be courteous and just do her job, she went back to asking how she could help the man. "Yes, I listen to it sometimes. Is there something —"

He interrupted her attempt at a professional conversation. "I'm really 'jazzed' to hear that! Ha-ha!" Marco then shuffled his feet in a little dance move and fluttered his "jazz hands" in a flimsy effort to lighten things up. It can be awkward when a lawyer tries to be funny. It had the sort of vibe of an old-fashioned, carnival sideshow barker, but hardly trustworthy.

Jhas stared at him momentarily before she let out a little laugh and rolled her eyes. He was kind of silly but otherwise rather harmless, she concluded. "How can I help you today?"

She's still trying to be all "Miss Professional," but I heard that little laugh. He knew he was getting somewhere.

"Ha-ha, oh, I wish you could help me with a vacation or something fun, but I'm here for business reasons."

Here on 'business,' eh? Well, that sounds sort of flimsy, he thought. Here I show up looking like a homeless guy off the street. Score one on the skeptical side of the ledger. Sometimes I should think through these things better. Time to divert the conversation.

Marco squinted a little and paused for effect. "But hey, wait a minute. Where's your Jamaican accent? You can't be a local gal talking all plain like that." He delivered a mischievous smile. "Are you American?"

"Oh, *di Patois*." Jhas flavored her reply with a bit of the accent Marco asked about. "Truth be told, I was born in Texas — *yee haw*." She twirled her finger in the air like she was throwing a lasso. "My father was an American POW in Vietnam. Mom was Jamaican. As unlikely as it was, they met in a small town in northern Mississippi not long after he came home from the war. Dad worked as a sheriff. After his death from cancer, Mom brought my older brother and me back to Jamaica to live with her family here. Then I went to nursing school in North Carolina. At this point, I can turn it on or off at will."

"That's so interesting!" he said. He leaned against the high desk, pretending to be more interested than he was. "I thought I heard a bit of a southern American accent in there. So how did you go from nursing to travel agent?" Resting his chin on his hand, Marco appeared to be giving her his fascinated attention.

"Well, let's say being a travel agent in Kingston is more fun than giving shots and emptying bedpans," she chortled.

Marco let out a loud laugh that came across as more of a forced bark. *That may have been a little over the top*, he told himself, clearing his throat. *Better dial it back — don't want to overdo it.*

"I understand that," Marco replied in agreement, trying to sound more serious. "So then, you must be new around here?"

"Well, yes," Jhas admitted. "Not new to the island, but I've only worked here at the travel agency for three weeks."

Good guess, you lucky dog, Marco thought to himself. Satisfied he'd made the right call, he resisted the urge to flutter his jazz hands again. *This will be easy — new employee, eager to please, and easily manipulated.*

"Being new here won't keep me from helping you with whatever you need." She flashed a brilliant smile. "So what brings you in today?"

That smile was filled with such kindness that any decent man at that moment would have abandoned his nefarious plan and let her get on with her day. But Marco wasn't such a decent man.

He launched into his rehearsed explanation. "Well, Jhas — is it okay if I call you that?" He paused for a beat but didn't wait for a reply. "I've been in Jamaica on extended business, and I need to fly back to Miami as soon as possible. The problem is, my passport has expired since I've been here. The U.S. consulate insists on new passport photos to renew my travel docs. You know how annoying the administrative protocol can be," he said, trying to garner sympathy.

"Anyhow, is there any way you can help me with this?" He dipped his head and looked up with his best hopeful puppy dog eyes.

Marco hesitated for an instant, worried that she may be too inexperienced for the task. He had concerns that he might be handed off to a more seasoned staffer, but after a moment of consideration, she nodded with a confident "can-do" attitude.

"Of course, I'd love to help you with that!" came the cheerful reply that said she was all about service. He'd just walked in the door and, through blind chance, happened to meet the nicest travel agent in all of Jamaica. Marco hadn't caught on, but she was the type of person who would have helped him no matter what — no false charm or fake plays at sympathy necessary. Jhas helped everyone who came in the same way. It was more like he'd fallen into a pond and come out with his pockets full of fish.

Marco congratulated himself on how well his act was going. *Of course, she'll help me. All it takes is a few nice words and presto! And even if she has suspicions, she's not confident enough to confront anyone.*

"Passport photos are just sixty dollars" — Marco did a quick calculation in his head — that totaled fifteen U.S. dollars — "and we'll take your picture while you're here today. We can have those ready in three days," she said in a manner that suggested this was the usual procedure. "So have you gotten to see much of our beautiful island while you've been here? We travel agents know areas that are off the beaten path beyond the usual tourist spots," she said, being more than a little helpful.

"Oh, hey, that's so kind of you! But I've seen more of the Jamaican countryside than I ever intended. Not a tourist in sight." He gave a little chuckle with his reply. *If she only knew about the harrowing experience of getting here from across the island,* he thought, humoring himself.

Marco lowered his voice and shifted to a more urgent tone. "I wish I could stay in your beautiful country longer, but I need to get back to my mother's side. She's not doing well," he told her, bowing his head and shaking it with feigned sorrow. "Three days is too long to get those passport photos. I need them right away."

Marco's amoral abilities knew no bounds. What he loved most about this type of prevarication was that nobody ever discovered the deception until it was far too late.

Jhas narrowed her eyes a bit. Marco wasn't sure how to read her reaction. Had the travel agency trained her to be skeptical of sob stories? He had a natural tendency to lay it on thick.

He elaborated, "She's in the hospital, and I couldn't live with myself if my mother . . . " He injected a somber pause, pressing his lips together and putting his fist to his mouth as if to keep from crying. "... if she died before I got home to see her. Is there any possible way we can get the photos developed faster?" he asked, putting a little choke in his voice and peeking up at her with intent hope. For Marco, a smooth liar, the story just rolled off his tongue.

Jhas looked at him with kind concern and gave a small, pitying gasp. Her expression softened, memories of her own mother surfacing. "Oh no, I'm so sorry." She put her hand to her chest, revealing her sincere sympathetic concern. "Yes, you need to get moving and be at your mama's side right away." Bringing back her professional air, she continued, "I know that for an extra forty dollars, we can have them expedite the process and have your photos ready by the end of the day."

Even though that was only an additional ten U.S. dollars, Marco had no intention of paying any of it. "Oh, that would be wonderful! You're amazing! But wait," he said, patting his pockets. "I didn't expect it to be quite that much. I need to run over to the bank to get some cash," he said looking at her, hoping she wouldn't ask for payment right then.

Jhas dropped her smile. "I'm sorry. It's our policy to take payment upfront." It pained her to say so after hearing his sad story, but she was a rule follower.

Marco sighed. How could he get past this sticking point? He turned up the emotion in his expression, willing it to show in his eyes. "I understand," he said, infusing as much sincerity as he could muster into his words. "It's just —" he broke eye contact and fidgeted with the sleeve of his shirt, "when I first came into town, I tried to hire a car, and some thugs roughed me up." He glanced up to check her horrified expression and then looked away, feigning embarrassment. "It's not that bad. I'm okay." He rubbed his shoulder, as though he were still in pain. "But they took all my cash." Now his eyes met hers. "I have money, I promise. I'll just have to go to the bank."

Marco could sense that Jhas was moved, although she remained hesitant. "I'm sorry, I don't make the rules," she said haltingly, but with sympathy in her voice.

"Look," Marco negotiated, "we can still take the photos, right? And then while the film is being developed, I'll go get the money. It's not like I'd ask you to trust me with the photos without payment. Only a scammer would do that."

A *double bluff.* He savored a moment of pride. Marco could tell that Jhas was on the verge of giving in to his reasoning, but not quite there yet.

"I promise as soon as we're done, I'll run over to the bank and get some money. You just keep them until then."

In fact, Marco was counting on that.

Jhas was coming around to his proposal. "Oh, all right." She flashed an encouraging smile. "It's not company policy, but I'm happy to make an exception given the circumstances just to help you. We'll get your picture taken, then you can pay when you pick them up later."

Marco was a little surprised it had been this easy, but was nonetheless pleased. *Sometimes I impress myself,* he thought. He'd pulled it off.

"What can I say but thank you?" He took her hand and peered into her dark brown eyes. "This means everything to me. And if anyone tells you that you're not the best travel agent in this country, they're a liar!"

Jhas's dazzling smile reached the corners of her eyes.

What a nice person. She really has a brilliant smile, Marco thought as he released her hand. *And it's not a total lie. She's pretty too.* Marco felt instant self-consciousness about his own appearance again. *No time for that. It doesn't matter!* Marco brought himself back to the task at hand.

Jhas tried to put her best foot forward by making conversation with this good-humored gentleman while setting up for the photo. "Where have you been staying while you've been here?" she asked with cordial interest.

Thinking fast, Marco replied with the first place that came to mind, "Whitehall." It was the out-of-the-way town he remembered seeing on a sign while stranded on the side of the road trying to find his way from Ocho Rios down to Kingston.

Jhas turned to him with delight. "We're practically neighbors!" she said, gleeful at this new information. "I grew up in Trinity, not even ten miles north of there. But, of course, you know that."

What are the chances? Marco thought, rubbing his forehead.

"Yeah, we lived on Bailey's Vale Road," she continued, although Marco desperately wished she wouldn't. "You must have gone by our home many times! My family has the fruit stand at the corner of the A3 down from Port Maria. Everyone stops there because it's the biggest fruit stand in the area. They have everything, and they've been there forever. You must have bought from them at some point."

"Oh, um . . . ," Marco, now flustered by this twist, had no idea what she was talking about. He panicked, frantically trying to find a way out of his conversational predicament.

"Well, I don't like fruit and I, uh, don't eat it much so, um, probably not." He laughed nervously and turned to an airline travel poster on the wall, which he pretended to study with ridiculous intensity. Not dissuaded by his seeming lack of interest in her hometown, Jhas didn't give up on making conversation.

"So what kind of business are you in?" she asked, hoping to land on a topic he might be interested in talking about.

"Well, I'm in government work — a diplomat of sorts — but, I really can't talk about what I do. You know, confidential," he told her with a conspiratorial wink. He had recovered from her last question without being caught. *I hope she doesn't have a family member who's a diplomat too,* he thought to himself.

"Ohhh, a man of mystery. I love that." She winked back. No mention of diplomat family members to Marco's relief. He was a little surprised she had bought the story, since his vagrant appearance belied the likelihood he would be any kind of dignitary. What kind of diplomat went around in bauxite-stained pants? But Jhas didn't seem to have asked herself that question.

"Well, was it all business, or did you get to have any fun while you were here?" she asked.

Look at me, he thought, *I've been up to my neck in "fun."*

"How could I come to your beautiful island and not have fun?" he teased with a delighted tone. The fairground barker was back on his game. "Of course, I tried to learn a few traditional Jamaican dances, but I never could get the moves right. Some of those dancers have amazing talent — I found them more fun to watch. Now, salsa," he said and raised an eyebrow, "that's more my style — assuming, of course, there is some pretty lady like yourself who knows how to salsa." *Why am I doing this? She already agreed to help you, estúpido. Just stop!*

"I sensed by your accent that you were Latino," she laughed and nodded her head knowingly. "Where are you from originally?"

Why did I do this to myself? Marco was kicking himself now for overplaying his charming act. "Puerto Rico," slipped out of his mouth. It was the first Latin country that came to mind that wasn't Cuba. Good choice, too, because it kept his story straight. He didn't need to raise questions in anyone's mind as to why he told her he needed a U.S. passport.

"I've never been there, but I've always wanted to go. I've just been waiting for a nice Puerto Rican man to show me around," she said with a laugh that suggested she was only half-joking.

She's being a little forward, Marco thought. But you brought this on yourself. Why did you try to be so charming?

"Ha-ha!" Marco tried to laugh it off without offending her now. "That would be the dream, wouldn't it? But I'm afraid I won't be going back any time soon," he said, attempting to look sorry.

Did he detect a hint of disappointment on Jhas' face? Ughhh, he had to keep this going at least long enough to get her help and get out of there. "Well, if you ever make it to Florida, I'd love to show you around — incredible place!" he assured her with a grin that came easily, knowing she would never find him there.

I hope she's not about to tell me she has relatives who are fruit-selling diplomats in Florida. The way it's going, there's always the slightest of chances.

"I may take you up on that!" she considered. "Okay, handsome, we're ready for those photos."

Those were perhaps the most welcome words Marco had heard in his entire time on this island. He hoped it would end the ongoing plethora of questions, and he could extract himself from what felt like an escalating flirtation.

Marco combed his fingers through his disheveled hair after a quick glance into a tiny mirror that hung on the wall near the passport photo area. He looked at the camera with a big grin.

Jhas snapped a couple of pictures and then looked from behind the camera.

"Has anyone ever said you look kind of like Cheeko? You know, from *Cheeko and Payaso?*"

This time, Marco found the inquiry amusing. He tried not to roll his eyes. "Yes, in fact, I have heard that." He thought about making up a joke about having a brother named Cheeko who got the funny gene but decided to keep his mouth shut for once in this conversation.

As soon as they finished taking photos, the phone rang, and Jhas moved to an unoccupied desk across the room to answer it.

This gave Marco an opportunity to have a quick look around. He could see open files for their regular clients that included passports and other travel documents. In a casual way, he tried to check what would be locked and what he might need to be prepared to pick open later.

Jhas took a message and ended the call. She stayed at the desk another minute to write a note. Meanwhile, Marco spotted an open locker with office supplies and a set of cabinets. He glanced over and checked to ensure that Jhas had her back to him before he pinched the top of a folder and silently slipped it out. He opened it halfway and peered inside, all the while making somewhat distracted small talk.

"The weather has been so nice lately. I mean, a little warm but lovely and sunny." Marco continued to ramble while he tried to figure out where Michael's office would be. He wandered around the perimeter of the room and casually turned a few door knobs to see if they would open. "Makes me kind of want some fruit . . . or some juice . . . or maybe a salad. Something cool and refreshing . . . " he said absentmindedly.

Jhas was distracted. Being a new hire she couldn't focus on multiple tasks at once. She didn't catch the slip in his story with the sudden desire for fruit he had told her he didn't like.

How am I going to find his office later without losing time? Marco pondered. He couldn't ask, so it would need to wait until he returned. Right now, he wanted to get out of the travel agency and away from this crazy web he'd spun. He was far too close to becoming a fly in his own trap.

"So is that it?" he asked. "You'll take care of this for me, won't you? For my mother's sake," he reminded her, casting his eyes down.

"Don't you worry, sweetie. I'll see to it myself. We're open 'til five. And I'll be right here when you come back to pick up those photos," she assured him.

"That makes me so happy. Bless you," Marco said. He put his hands over his chest in a theatrical display and backed up toward the door. "Bless you. I'll be back."

Marco walked out the door. His phony smile dropped as quickly as he'd plastered it on, replaced with a self-satisfied sneer. Oh, indeed, he would be back.

THE BREAK-IN

Marco spent the day mulling over what he would need to do and what information he would need to include in his fabricated documents. His understanding of how Jamaica's history led up to its current economic situation would be a crucial component in ensuring his alibi would be unassailable.

The productive blend of sunlight, arable soil, and rain historically made the fertile land of Jamaica ideal for cultivation, including the once-dense fields of sugar cane. Turning fields of green stalks into the ubiquitous crystals that sweeten coffee, tea, and cakes everywhere had been backbreaking work from the time the first cane fields were harvested centuries earlier. Since before the days when privateers and pirates plied their trade and filled the taverns of Port Royal, the labor of slaves from sub-Saharan Africa had been exploited to work the fields.

By the early 1700s, Jamaica had become by far the richest and most important colony in the British Empire thanks to the slave-fueled sugar trade. Jamaica was so important in the later 1770s that its defense took precedence over efforts to put an end to the revolt in the thirteen American colonies. Located in the heart of the Caribbean at the confluence of trade routes, shiploads of slaves came into the West Indies by way of Jamaica while sugar, molasses, and logwood went out. Jamaica also had a reputation as the most brutal of all the British slave colonies.

While history is disinclined to remember more benevolent plantation masters, there were plenty who were cruel enough to leave an indelible stain on the pages of the past.

As the last vestiges of slavery died out by the mid-1800s, descendants of slaves who toiled on sugar plantations continued to make up the bulk of Jamaica's workers. Marco knew that even within his lifetime the labor force on the east end of Cuba had also been supplemented by Jamaicans. They were furtively transported as "human shipments" to the notorious quarantine station of Cayo Dun in Santiago de Cuba as though they were nothing more than objects or animals.

Jamaica's modern industrial advantage depended on its access to a robust and reliable labor force, which afforded the island nation an economic competitive edge by keeping wages low. Knowing all this, Marco developed a plausible explanation for his absence that would weave together Jamaica's history with current affairs. All these factors provided the elements for a cover story that would ostensibly serve the diplomatic interests of both Cuba and Jamaica.

When he was confident that Jhas and everyone else had gone home for the day, Marco returned to the travel agency. He loitered outside near the corner for several minutes to ensure there was nobody around and then approached, sidling up to the entrance. Even in the dark, it took him less than two minutes to pick the lock on the front door using a thin piece of metal he had spent much of the day hunting for specifically for this purpose. The evening humidity made the wooden front door swell, making it harder to open than it had been earlier in the day.

With a last glance over his shoulder to ensure nobody was watching, Marco slipped into the travel agency with ease. Now, he only had to locate the passport photos and what else he needed to forge a set of counterfeit documents. He went straight to the desk where Jhas had been working earlier. There it was — a small manila envelope right where he expected it to be.

Bingo! The passport photos, as promised. I knew she would come through for me. Well, off to a good start. Finding everything else he required could pose more challenges. Nerves started to kick in. Marco's hands trembled slightly as he rummaged through files and drawers in search of a passport he could alter.

"Come on, come on. I know they must have one somewhere," he whispered, as he shoved various papers and office supplies around.

In a moment of clarity, the thought struck him, *Of course, they wouldn't keep them out in the open. Not secure enough. I'm in the wrong place.* It seemed sensible that they might keep important documents like passports secured away from the front room.

As Marco straightened up and scanned the room, his eyes landed on the door to a smaller office, a glass-pane door that he had found earlier to be locked. *This could be Michael's office,* he thought. *Worth a look.* He picked the simple lock with ease, entered, and switched on a small desk lamp.

With nervous urgency, Marco rummaged around the top of the desk, along the shelves, and unlocked filing cabinets. Not finding anything, he had already begun to worry about being there too long or having to leave empty-handed. With his heart racing, he thought, *I'm about ready to pray to any deity Julio tells me exists if it will help me find a passport.*

He tried the desk drawers, but the small one on the top right was locked. *Why stop picking locks now?* he shrugged. *If it's secured, maybe there is something important in here I can use.*

Inside, among a lot of uninteresting office stuff, sat a small black metal box. *Ughhh, I don't have time for all this lock picking,* Marco growled under his breath as he worked it open. The lock wouldn't budge.

What is going on here? Marco thought with exasperation as he jiggled the thin piece of metal he had used to pick the other locks open. He tried to pull it back out, but it stuck.

He growled louder as he jerked the metal piece back and forth, up and down, but to no avail. With another forceful pull and twist, Marco felt it snap. He peered down at the broken piece of metal in his fingers and flung it across the room, where it clinked to the floor.

Now what do I do? Frustrated, he glared at the other piece of metal broken off in the lock. He almost abandoned the lockbox, but then reconsidered. *I've spent too much time on this. Hmmm. No, of all the places in this office, a locked box inside a locked drawer inside a locked office is most likely to hold something important.*

Marco looked around for a tool to force it open. On the corner of the desk rested a small, knife-like letter opener. He took it and hammered the lid of the lockbox with the ivory handle. *That didn't do much — only a little dent.*

Taking the letter opener in his fist, he brought his arm up and then tried to plunge it into the metal box as hard as he could. "Ahhhh!" he yelped in pain as the reverberation stung his hand. "Oop . . . " he clamped his hand over his own mouth, reminding himself to stay quiet. He cursed under his breath.

This isn't working. He looked around the office again and spotted a block of sulfur on the opposite corner of the desk, a core sample that Michael used as a paperweight. Marco grabbed it. He placed the lockbox on its end with the jammed lock toward the ceiling. He wedged the letter opener into a tiny gap left by the metal lodged in the lock mechanism. With the paperweight in his other hand, Marco held his breath and hoped his aim wouldn't smash his hand. He brought the paperweight down hard against the handle of the letter opener. This time, there was some give. Marco was encouraged.

He smashed the paperweight down several more times until the lock broke loose. As Marco picked up the lid, he let out a gleeful laugh. *Good thing I persisted,* he congratulated himself as he took the passport from beneath a handgun and looked at it.

The name on the passport was Shorty Benavidez, but Michael Cervera's photo was unmistakable. *Well, this must be his office. It figures that he would have a fake Cuban passport,* Marco thought. He closed it and tucked it into his back pocket. *His is just as good as any. I'll change it anyway,* he told himself as he sat at the desk with a typewriter off to one side. He pulled it closer.

Without time to waste, he went to work putting to paper a viable storyline in the form of fabricated letters and agreements. With shaky fingers, he hurriedly tried to type out the necessary documents that would support his account.

Tranquilo, aceré, tranquilo, he tried to calm his nerves. *This is no time to fall apart. Everything hinges on getting this done.*

Marco contrived the explanation that the Cuban government had deployed him on a multi-year transnational diplomatic mission to secure trade contracts for mining bauxite ore essential for manufacturing aluminum. Jamaica had some of the largest bauxite deposits in the world. The Soviets had been working to make this another communist satellite in the region and deprive U.S. enterprises of their ability to exploit Jamaica's resources for themselves.

In a quest for commercial gain, the surplus of Jamaican labor enabled the necessary work to be done competitively — faster and cheaper than they could use labor from other nations. Indeed, like a Trojan Horse, Moscow was making inroads in Jamaica as established communists working from Cuba were already infiltrating the Jamaican labor unions.

Marco rationalized the inclusion of human components in this international trade venture because Jamaica's pool of workers made conscious decisions regarding their own destinies and the well-being of their families. They had family allegiances that kept them in Jamaica, so they took what they could get. Of course, they fancied going abroad for an easier time and better wages elsewhere. They were aware of a world beyond their island, but they weighed the risks of remaining home or moving away. They considered what would bring them the most meaningful benefits and chose their life and career paths accordingly.

So intent on getting his story straight, Marco missed the broader picture and the hypocrisy it painted. Securing ties with Cuba would have been a viable cover for him. Their government could profit from access to the cheap labor and resources that Jamaica had to offer. But, in the process, Marco had to rationalize the same kind of alleged labor exploitation scheme about which he opposed and feuded with Vladi over.

Marco was so caught up in finalizing his documents, he didn't hear the sound of a car pulling up outside.

NO WAY OUT

ichael was entertaining business friends that week, nothing out of the ordinary for him. He had his driver bring him back to his office late that night to pick up a couple of ultra-premium pre-embargo Montecristo No. 2 cigars from his private stash as a treat for his distinguished guests.

Leaving his driver waiting, Michael made his way up a narrow staircase at the shop doorway. The evening humidity always caused the shop door to stick, so he needed to give it an extra nudge to push it open.

Marco heard the bells jingle on the front door as Michael worked it open. His head shot up from the typewriter, and he looked toward the office door. Adrenaline jolted through his body. Exactly what he had been dreading was playing out before his eyes. No time to kill the light. In an instinctive, split-second decision, Marco slid from the chair and ducked behind the desk, cornered in the small office — no way out.

Should I try to remain hidden and hope whoever is coming in will leave soon without seeing me? Or maybe I should wait for an opportunity to make a run for the door. Marco's mind raced as he considered his options.

While still in the main office entry, Michael stopped in his tracks. He immediately noticed that his desk lamp had been left on, something he never did. He was an obsessively tidy person and had a habit of neatly arranging everything on his desk and turning off the light before leaving.

His eyes scanned the darkened front office of the travel agency. He couldn't pinpoint it, but he knew something wasn't right. His body stiffened with alertness. He had a gut feeling that someone else was in the room with him. Sensing the presence of an intruder gave Michael legitimate cause to feel alarmed. Kingston's commercial district was known to be an unsafe area.

Michael looked toward his interior office door, which stood open. It was normally locked unless he was there. He reached down and felt the key, still in his pocket. He stretched his short neck to peer through the doorway towards the spot on the edge of his desk where he kept an ornate ivory-handled knife that he used as a letter opener. Right away, he recognized it wasn't in its place. Somehow it had been moved to the center of the desk and sat next to his paperweight, which was also out of place. Somebody had been in there.

With muted footsteps, Michael eased into his office and moved furtively around the desk and bent over to examine underneath. He could see no one there, yet his unease deepened further. He stretched around to look behind his chair and under his desk.

Marco could see a shadow cast by the lamp from someone lurking around the desk. Marco held his breath, but he realized that his foot had been sticking out enough as the shadow peeked around — someone could have caught a glimpse of him. He needed to move!

The choice is made for me now — I have to run for it!

In a sudden, forceful move, Marco shoved his hands out and flung the desk chair into Michael, hoping to give himself enough space and time to get out. But extracting himself from an awkward position behind the desk took a second longer than he expected. That critical moment gave Michael enough opportunity, and he had Marco firmly by the back of his shirt collar before he could scramble back to his feet.

Pulled backward, Marco was knocked off balance and pivoted back onto the floor. The two men caught one another's shocked gazes as they swung around to face each other with Marco's collar still bunched in Michael's fist. There was a fleeting pause as the two bewildered men looked at each other with wide eyes.

"Who are you?" Michael bellowed as he bent toward Marco, who was now in a vulnerable position on the floor.

Marco's instincts told him this wasn't the time to start answering questions — he needed to get out.

Marco's right hand shot out to grab Michael's belt while his left gripped the arm that held him by the collar. He tried to pull Michael down and to the side to give himself room to escape, but Michael ended up falling with his upper body on Marco's shoulder.

Marco struggled to shove him off, and Michael floundered to get himself into a more upright position. Marco remained on the floor in an awkward, disadvantaged position.

With his free hand, Michael grabbed Marco under the chin and shoved his head into the desk drawers. The metal handle imprinted itself into Marco's scalp with a solid thud. It felt like he had been cut, but he didn't have time to worry about bleeding. Nonetheless, the bolt of pain caused Marco to let go, giving Michael enough time to get back on his feet.

Seeing the opened lockbox atop the desk, Michael lunged toward the handgun. Everything went down in an instant, yet it felt like time slowed. Marco saw Michael's knees straighten and his right hand coming up in his direction.

Is he holding a gun? Marco panicked at the thought. If he was, and that gun had the chance to take aim, it would be over for Marco, and he knew it.

Marco's vision narrowed and his instincts took over. This was now brute survival — win or die. Marco recoiled both of his knees toward his chest and kicked out, landing a devastating blow to Michael's knees.

Michael tumbled backward and fell into the bookcases behind him, the crash of his rotund body followed by the thuds of falling books. As he fell backward, Michael tripped over the lamp cord, which pulled from the wall plug and plunged the small office into darkness. In his fall, Michael had dropped the gun onto the desk, but neither man could see it in the dark.

Does he have the gun? Where's the gun? Marco thought. In the instant it took Michael to get reoriented after his stumble, Marco frantically reached around the desk for anything to grab. His hand landed on something hard — the block of sulfur that Michael used as a paperweight.

Michael regained his footing and desperately groped around the desktop trying to locate the pistol in the dark. He found the ivory-handled knife instead. Michael picked it up in his fist and took a hard swipe at the intruder.

Marco barely dodged the blade but felt the waft of Michael's missed swing. Michael's body pivoted. In the same instant, Marco hurled his arm around and landed a forceful strike behind Michael's ear with the paperweight.

Marco couldn't see Michael, but he felt him collapse to the floor. Marco instinctively crouched in a defensive position, expecting the man to get up and resume the attack. Within moments, it became evident that he didn't need to. Michael had ceased to struggle.

Marco took a step, and the toe of his shoe slid on a slippery, wet spot. In the dark, he couldn't make out the blood that pooled on the floor. Michael moaned and after several labored breaths fell limp, then silent. When Michael had fallen forward from the blow to the head, he had collapsed onto his own knife blade, slain.

Marco could feel his heart beating in his ears. He was stunned, but he made no effort to feel for a pulse or try to help the man. If he were truly dead, there would be nothing he could do anyway, and staying around would put him in more danger.

Of course, in his own mind, Marco deflected the blame for Michael's death. *I didn't kill him. I mean, I only tried to protect myself.* Even if he rationalized that he had acted in self-defense, and regardless of whether it was premeditated or intentional, Marco was responsible for his death. He had a sinking feeling deep in his chest but pushed it aside. *It wasn't my fault — I didn't do this!* he repeated to himself as he stared down at the motionless body. He ran his hands through his hair and pulled, a motion that contradicted the words he tried to convince himself of.

Marco's attention snapped toward the front door, hearing someone else coming up the steps. He glanced out the window and realized it was Michael's driver, presumably coming to check on what was taking him so long. Marco grabbed the passport and his documents and ripped the last page from the typewriter. He raced out of the inner office and caught the driver off guard, knocking him over. In trying to rush toward the door, he dropped everything in the dark. He scrambled to scoop up his passport photos and forged documents from the floor.

Marco ran out of the building like a hounded desperado, zigzagging through alleys and streets, trying to put as much distance as he could between himself and the dead body in the office. He felt queasy and shaken from the incident. But even more so, he would be on edge from then on, not knowing if someone had seen him in Michael's office.

FINDING FRANK DÍAZ

Getting away from the travel agency, Marco hurried all the way back to the homeless shelter with the documents he needed stuffed inside his shirt. He struggled with sleep that night. Fitful tossing resulted as his mind swam and his body was awash with adrenaline from the struggle with Michael, now dead on his own office floor. More than ever, Marco realized he had to speed up his plan before any investigators picked up his trail.

Although many years had passed since his prosecutorial assignment, Marco was confident he could still recognize Frank Díaz, a pale, slender, intense man who wore horn-rimmed glasses. Díaz was a freelance defection specialist, notorious for political skullduggery and the risky work of luring Cubans to seek asylum in the United States. His quietness belied his formidable character. Marco's plan was to locate Díaz and make use of the conspirator's help for his own purposes.

Marco was an expert at subtle inquiries. As an *Inquisitor*, he had the experience and training of Havana's best investigators. He anticipated needing to do some real leg work to track down Frank Díaz. Unlike Michael Cervera, Díaz would be elusive, not out in the open and easy to find.

As much as Marco could be his blunt self, he could also change his skin to render himself as whomever he needed to be to get what information he wanted.

It stood to reason that to find Díaz, Marco should start by identifying Cubans interspersed in the community. However, the typically outgoing Cubans could be coy when it came to matters of self-preservation. To uncover what he needed, he would have to be a chameleon and take a delicate approach.

Navigating from Pilón or Santiago de Cuba to Jamaica was not much further than the distance between Havana and Florida. People from both island nations could find transportation by boat across the strait. Anyone leaving Cuba from the southern coast had the option of making his way to Jamaica as a jumping-off point — although many immigrants went northward from Jamaica to Cuba, as generations of descendants from slaves departed in search of a better life beyond Jamaica. Consequently, many people in Cuba were of Jamaican heritage, but not the other way around.

To leave the country lawfully, Cubans had to first secure an exit visa from the government. Limits on those were stringent. Few were ever authorized to venture away from the island, but even if they were permitted to leave, they couldn't take their spouse or children. This ensured Cuban citizens were disinclined to turn their back on the homeland by defecting or criticizing the Castro government on the international stage. If there were Cubans to be found in Jamaica, they would no doubt be exiles without an exit visa. At least some of them would know of Díaz's operation and safeguard his crusade for the benefit of other defectors.

Marco put some effort into locating the community's Cuban residents. There were few Latinos in Jamaica, and those were an amalgamation of people from other Hispanic locales: Mexico, Puerto Rico, and the Dominican Republic. Subtle accents and phrases were characteristic of various Latino subcultures, and most Jamaicans could not differentiate between the Spanish dialects. That made it easy for Cubans to hide in plain sight. Marco knew he could recognize his own people out of a crowd — he just needed to find the right crowd.

The old saying that "birds of a feather flock together" worked in Marco's favor. That is, people who shared a common language and ethnicity tended to congregate together in culturally distinct neighborhoods within the broader community. He knew this to be especially true regarding the social character of his fellow Cubans. If Marco could identify where they gathered, he would be well on his way to locating Frank Díaz.

Marco commenced his search by engaging a diverse array of Kingstonians in casual chat. He kept an eye out for any clues that perhaps would have seemed insignificant to someone not as keen in the art and science of investigation. His first break surfaced out of a conversation with a street vendor. Marco asked if he knew where anyone played dominoes. Games of dominoes were a universal pastime in Cuba. Cubans met in public places to play on any day of the week. They enjoyed the camaraderie and competition. The helpful vendor directed him to a nearby park where kids played baseball.

As he wandered into the park, the sharp crack of a baseball bat hitting a ball drew Marco's attention to his right. It was a group of about a dozen teenagers playing a game of pick-up baseball. Absorbed in the action, they were whistling and cheering as one ran the bases and an outfielder scrambled for the ball. Walking along the chain-link fence surrounding their improvised baseball diamond, Marco could hear the boys shouting encouraging words to the baserunner in Spanish.

Esto es bueno — I'm in the right place, he thought.

At the far end of the park, Marco spotted exactly what he had hoped to find. Just as the vendor had told him, a group of Latinos were playing dominoes at a few small tables arranged in the shade of a cluster of blue mahoe trees.

Marco approached the group of domino players as though curious about their game. He greeted them with a casual but distinctly Cuban salutation. "*Aceré, qué bolá?*" ("What's up, friends?")

The men raised their heads and noticed a new face they didn't recognize. Before they could say anything, he asked to join as a fourth player. They welcomed him into the game — a small move in the right direction for Marco.

There wasn't much conversation going on, so Marco felt a little awkward at first. He didn't want to come right out and ask who was Cuban or pry into specifics about their circumstances. Instead, he listened to them talk and tried to discern their nationality.

Across the table, the youngest fellow nudged the guy next to him and whispered something in his ear. His compadre nodded. Marco's face reddened in a flush of self-consciousness as they continued staring at him. Nervous guilt caused him to wonder if they were on to him somehow, but Marco tried to pretend he didn't notice.

Just play it cool. They can't possibly know why I'm here, he reasoned with himself.

The men whispered to each other again. Both looked at Marco from the corner of their eyes, but they were more obvious about it now.

Maybe they're poking fun at my lousy domino skills, he speculated. Eventually, one of the men asked his name. *Why are they asking? Simple courtesy, or could it be they're on to me?* Either way, Marco wasn't sure he wanted to say his real name. He hadn't planned to provide an alias, so he hadn't thought about it ahead of time.

"Oh, um, er, I'm, uh . . . " Caught off guard, Marco stumbled over his words as though he didn't know his own name.

The guys laughed in unison, like they were in on an inside joke that eluded Marco. One pointed his way. "We knew!"

Right away, Marco felt a panic tighten his chest. "Knew what?"

"You are Cheeko, eh? Who knew you played dominoes?"

Marco, overwhelmed with relief, rallied himself to play along. He held one finger to his lips and whispered, "Shhh." He pointed back and joined in their laughter as though they had figured things out and were all in on a secret.

Getting mistaken for this Cheeko guy has its benefits, Marco humored himself.

Over the course of the morning and afternoon, players came and left the domino table, allowing Marco to meet an array of Cubans and other ex-pats. Working his way over to a comfortable spot with the two men who had engaged him earlier, he struck up a friendly conversation with them. Marco tested the situation.

In his native Cuban dialect, he casually mentioned without looking up: "My brother back in Vedado — I miss him. He was the real domino player in the family."

Without lifting their heads, the men's eyes shot up to give him a guarded look, then quickly returned their attention to the table. They recognized Vedado as a neighborhood in central Havana. Marco wondered if they would catch on.

After a pause that felt like forever, one man replied. "That's obvious, *amigo*," laughing in jest at Marco's lack of dominoes talent.

Marco gave him a quizzical look.

"Always you throw fat," the man told him, pointing out his rookie mistake of always throwing out high numbers first.

Well, at least they're still on amicable terms with me, Marco thought, relieved.

After some silence, the youngest of the men spoke up with a soft, contemplative voice. "I miss my grandfather back in Cuba too." He studied his hand of dominoes after pulling one from the boneyard. "He taught me how to play."

Marco tried not to show it, but he was smiling on the inside now. He was in. He decided not to press his luck at the moment though. He felt he needed to work into a level of trust that required more than just swooping in and playing a few rounds of dominoes. He needed to play the long game, so for now he dropped the topic and conversed about other trivial matters before telling them, "*Adiós por la noche.*"

He returned to the park's domino tables for several days in a row. For the most part, each day the players and the spectators were the same. Some of the men were reluctant to talk — they were in a contemplative state of mind, focused on the game, and needing quiet time to think. Others started talking more freely in Marco's presence as they began to feel more comfortable chatting around him.

Hmph, he chuckled to himself, *if I were still working to sniff out dissenters, this would be so easy.*

A few of the players were angry about the situation in Cuba. Among the biggest gripes across the board was their housing situation. From the beginning of the revolution, Fidel pledged to wipe out overcrowded tenements and replace them with modern houses and apartment buildings. It had seemed like a promising proposition. But to accomplish this, the Castro government confiscated private houses and apartment buildings from investors and Cuban exiles. A few of the men had been relatively successful property owners before Castro's draconian housing plan took effect. They were left with nothing except their primary homestead and a drastic loss of income. The government seized and redistributed their real estate without compensating the property owners for anything.

Almost overnight, the real estate market collapsed. Under the government's scheme of reallocating homes and apartments that now belonged to the state, the occupants had to apply to exchange their property for another if needed.

So even if someone wanted to move to another part of the island or even across town to another borough, they would need to apply to the government for another home and relinquish their current residence. Newly married couples who were allocated small apartments had an even more difficult time. Growing families could only move up to more suitable accommodations through an inflexible, bureaucratic process. Sometimes this would take years — even then, people were often denied. It was inefficient and resulted in unnecessary hardships for almost everyone.

Marco listened to the men's stories and complaints and pretended to be sympathetic to what they had experienced, tsking at appropriate moments and shaking his head as though he cared about their plight. The things he heard were, in fact, disturbing. Then again, Marco understood the system better than most and had the contacts who could make things happen. Because he and his family ranked higher within the Communist Party of Cuba, Marco's life had not been so directly touched by this issue. In his mind, the criticisms were mostly the complaining of losers.

Having left Cuba when he did, Marco had also been away for some years when the negative repercussions of many of Castro's policies had become even more marked. Marco hadn't faced these same problems nor the degree of oppression they had. These men had left Cuba in the wake of the serious losses they suffered. Ironically, Marco wanted to return to Cuba as he remembered it, while they were trying to get away from it all.

Marco was already committed to returning to his old life, but if he listened to these fellows too much, he might lose his resolve. He did use their discontent to his advantage, though, spinning his own false tale of woe.

"I had no idea the neighbors we had been friends with for years would tell such diabolical lies about me to save themselves." Marco invented his own account of what happened. He stared at the domino in his hand with the most sorrowful look he could muster. "But when the political police broke open our door and pointed a gun to the head of my daughter — a child! — that was the turning point. They demanded I pledge loyalty to the Communist Party of Cuba. I know it was done to intimidate, but that's when I realized we had to get out of there."

He heard sympathetic sighs from the other men around the table, who had experienced similar levels of savagery from the Castro regime.

"We were in grave danger, and it was just a matter of time before an inquisitor came for me. They forced our compliance under threat we would be harassed until they had me in prison. Then what would become of my wife and daughter?"

The men nodded and agreed in low undertones. Their new companion clearly had no choice but to flee.

"I told my wife I would die swimming across the sea before I let them take any of us!" Marco amped up the drama, mustering a phony tear and slamming his domino down on the table for effect.

The other men shook their heads again in commiseration.

"My wife and daughter are safe for now. I hope to leave here and meet with them again soon. However, I have run into complications and don't know how to take care of those arrangements," he remarked in a tone that indicated he invited suggestions. Without moving his downcast head, he peeked through hooded eyes to see how the others were reacting.

The men continued to stare at their dominoes, all with sympathetic expressions. Fortunately for Marco, he had correctly surmised how his own "story" would win them over. He assumed they were inclined to feel rapport and help someone they perceived had suffered the same as they had. Plus, his story didn't focus on him but on his fictitious wife and child. It took some effort and patience, but Marco pressed on, this time with a bit more dangerous question.

"So, *mis amigos*, is this beautiful island home now, or are you only here for a while?"

Marco anticipated this could be a delicate point. He held his breath and hoped he hadn't pushed the conversation too far.

One gentleman chuckled with a nod back to Marco. "I'm hoping to head for greener pastures soon," he said, rubbing his two fingers and thumb together in a gesture that indicated money. This was typical Cuban code language. Marco caught the meaning right away — the man was on his way to America.

Marco gave a congenial laugh. "Me too. I'm trying to come up with a plan."

The men traded glances, then one spoke on behalf of the group. "We can't help you, but maybe we know where you might find someone who can."

What he learned next, Marco would never have guessed. They directed him to the Caribbean Sounds Recording Studio, only a few miles away, there in Kingston.

Jackpot! His patience had paid off. Though Marco didn't have a name, he had a location. The pieces of his plan were coming together.

THE RENDEZVOUS

The Caribbean Sounds Recording Studio might have been the best equipped studio in the West Indies. It was a favorite destination for local and international recording artists, including Reggae Caliente, Desmond "Lionheart" Johnson, Jahmane Irie, Ras Kingston, and, of course, Reggae Syndicate. For anyone hoping to find a significant person who didn't want to be found, this was a hub for some of the most well-connected people in Jamaica.

Marco followed his newfound Cuban friends' instructions and set off on the long, hot walk across Kingston city. Upon arriving at the recording studio, he was to request to see "Francisco" — it was the code signaling the purpose of the visit, and men there could then guide him onward.

As soon as Marco entered, a man he assumed to be an assistant sound engineer led him to a back room. He did a pat-down search of Marco before saying a word. Once he was satisfied that Marco was unarmed and unwired, the long interview commenced. There were lots of questions, more than Marco had anticipated.

These guys are really thorough — I'll give them that, he thought.

Despite all the rigorous procedures, the man came across as more compassionate than portentous or sinister, but cautious nonetheless. Marco had taken part in his share of covert operations — therefore, he had a professional appreciation for the organization and smoothness of this affair. If they intended to insulate Frank Díaz, they had devised a clever system.

Convinced that Marco wasn't duplicitous, the man gave him further instructions. The ultimate rendezvous with Díaz was orchestrated by way of a well-connected Kingston musician, Jellicoe Barclay. Marco was told to show up that night at the Sheraton Kingston Hotel on Knutsford Boulevard, where Barclay performed the regular evening entertainment.

The Sheraton Kingston was the first major resort hotel on the island. Those who could afford it considered this to be "the place" to stay in the city. Even if they ended up lodged in Montego Bay or elsewhere on the island, many visitors spent one or two nights there on their way in and out of Norman Manley International Airport.

"The cue will be simple," the assistant assured Marco. "When you hear Jellicoe's band play the song 'Jamaica Farewell,' that's your signal. You are to immediately proceed north across the thoroughfare through the Trafalgar Park area in the direction of Devon House on Hope Road. If you don't hear the song in the set, it means something has been compromised and the move is canceled. Just leave the hotel and return to the studio in a few days. If the song plays, it's a go. You got all that?"

Marco nodded, and the man continued, "Okay, so once you get to Devon House you will see a taxi waiting out front. The taxi driver will introduce himself as 'Tom,' so you know it's the right guy. You are to tell the driver that your name is 'Mr. Moro' to protect your anonymity. Do you have any questions?"

Marco did not. He was ready to get off this island.

As the evening approached, Marco tried to make his way onto the hotel grounds discreetly. Maybe it was just him being self-conscious, but given his disheveled appearance, he felt sure the staff had a wary eye on him as a probable vagrant. He could not even have been mistaken for one of the resort hotel's neatly dressed maintenance workers.

Jellicoe's band played through the night from a small open-air stage near the hotel bar. Marco stayed back around the swimming pool, away from the crowd, where tiki torches cast dim shadows and obscured his appearance — or at least he hoped they did. The calypso music calmed Marco's nerves. It had a different flavor from the Latin jazz sounds of Cuba but still reminded him of home. He gently swayed and tapped his foot to the beat without even realizing it. For a few relaxing moments, he almost forgot why he'd come.

Jellicoe and his band performed several tunes that were familiar to Marco — "Zombie Jamboree," "Mary Ann," and "Yellow Bird." Marco's back straightened when he heard them playing the song for which he had been waiting, "Jamaica Farewell."

That's my cue. It's go time!

Marco could feel the rapid beat of his heart, almost astonished at how things were falling into place. Without delay, he hurried on foot toward the rendezvous landmark. From a distance, Marco could see the black, green, and gold Jamaica flag fluttering from the flagpole at Devon House. His breathing became labored from the combined effect of exertion and anxiety as he approached the appointed meeting spot. At long last, the waiting taxi came into view . . . and so did another.

Marco stopped short. *Now what am I supposed to do? There wasn't supposed to be more than one taxi.* He looked back and forth at the vehicles, trying to determine which driver looked most like he would be "Tom." *Okay, no need to panic,* Marco reminded himself. *Simple, I can just call out for "Tom" and the right driver will answer.*

As he continued to walk, both drivers stood leaning against their taxis, intently watching him. Marco felt awkward, as the men were close enough to make eye contact but too far away to speak to without shouting. He quickened his pace and raised his hand.

"Hey, Tom," he called out ambiguously, to neither man in particular.

"Yea, mon!" he heard in reply, but he couldn't tell which one had said it. As he got closer, he looked back and forth between the men.

"Which of you is Tom?" he asked.

"I'm Tom," they both answered in stereo.

Marco stopped and squinted. *Well, that wasn't in the plan,* he thought as his mind raced to figure out what to do next, becoming frustrated. *This was supposed to be a simple arrangement!*

Marco kept his cool and didn't speak further, not wanting to give away that there could be a problem. He was still trying to assess the situation when one of the drivers took his arm and opened the door to escort him into the back seat of his taxi while the other driver protested.

The first driver's confident actions, along with the tinted windows, swayed Marco to go along with this option. Marco ignored the shouting rival, assuming he was a try-hard desperate for business.

But the other driver wasn't about to give up. As Marco got into the cab, the other driver continued waving his hands wildly and yelled, "No, mon, yu put yuself in de wrong taxi!"

Marco paused for a half-second. The last time he had ignored a Jamaican who shouted at him, a homeless guy saved him from a lethal breakfast of ackee fruit. But this time, it was like these guys were making a scene competing to get Marco to choose their taxi!

Marco continued ignoring the other driver. He confirmed the identity of his driver — "Thomas" was on the dashboard placard — then sank into the car seat with a sigh of relief. His respite lasted only a moment. He bolted upright as the other driver frantically tried to open his door, which fortunately the first driver had locked. The man's intense shaking of the handle alarmed Marco.

What's with all these crazy Jamaicans? Glad I didn't get into the taxi with that guy! Marco pulled himself away from the window.

Wondering how they would shake the other driver off, Marco and the first driver's eyes met in the rearview mirror. The driver just continued to stare at Marco. *Maybe he's waiting for me to introduce myself, so he knows I'm the right person in the taxi,* Marco assumed.

"I'm Mr. Moro, by the way," he said, breaking the silence in the car.

"Nice to meet you, Mista Moro," the driver responded pleasantly. "Where yu goin'?"

Marco knit his brows, confused. "I thought you were supposed to know where we're going." The driver turned around in his seat and gave Marco a hard look. "Mi look like a psychic, mon? How mi fi weh yu waan go?"

Oh no! Instantly, it clicked that something wasn't right. Through the car window, Marco could still hear the muffled pleas of the other driver. "Mista Moro! Mista Moro! Yu in de wrong car, mon!"

Marco turned his head to the driver outside, his eyes widening in alarm. *What?! . . . it's the wrong taxi!*

Without another word, Marco unlocked and flung open the door. Springing out into the street, he stumbled and rolled onto the pavement. He wasted no time recovering himself, scrambled to his feet and ran. He bolted to the other taxi and threw himself inside.

His new driver, visibly relieved, greeted him, "Mista Moro, I presume?"

"Yes!"

"Hi, a me name Tom," he replied with a big toothy smile. "Real Tom."

"You know where we are going, right?" Marco asked the driver, gasping between hard breaths.

"Af course, Mista Moro," the driver assured Marco, as he threw the shifter into drive and hit the gas. Flung backward into the seat, Marco didn't bother trying to right himself. On the fringe of a sweaty, panicky meltdown, he lacked the energy to move.

Marco needed a few minutes for his adrenaline to settle down, but as he recovered his senses from the ordeal, he sat up to look out the window. *I should pay attention to where we're going and make a mental note of landmarks, just in case.* As they drove away from Kingston's central district, he was still on edge, but at least he could think straight again.

Marco's uneasiness crept up again as they approached a vacant lot that served as a transfer point. He kept his senses vigilant. He knew why his transfer needed to be done in a dark, out-of-the-way location.

This isn't sitting well with me. If things go awry, there's no safety. But really, what are my choices now?

He was already committed to escaping what he regarded to be his "slavery" in Vladi's orchards. However risky, he had resolved to go back and resume his old life in Cuba.

But as he had plotted his "escape," he neglected to take into account one aspect. That was the possibility he would return to a new kind of enslavement — the enslavement to fear, to the corruption within himself that had found its way to the surface, and to a troubled conscience at risk of becoming seared altogether.

When they pulled into a lot, another car awaited him, parked in the shadows. The black sedan, sitting with its engine running and a back door ajar, blended almost seamlessly into the night.

Marco chewed his lip without realizing it and wiped his sweaty palms on his pants. However unnerving this cloak-and-dagger, car-in-the-shadows business may have been, there was no turning back. He took a deep breath and opened the taxi door. Once he stepped out of the cab, Marco knew there would be nothing between him and whoever awaited him in the sedan.

A man emerged from the black sedan. A momentary sense of panic gripped Marco's heart. Suddenly, the possibility of this being a trap overwhelmed him.

What possessed me to consent to this arrangement? Being taken to a remote and unrecognizable location by strangers I know almost nothing about!

Marco cursed himself again. He should have learned his lesson when he and Julio departed Cuba in a boat with sketchy smugglers. Then, the fact that a swindling taxi driver and his two desperado accomplices abandoned him on a lonely mountain road should have driven home the point. And now, he had no means of knowing for sure the identity or real motives of these men. Part of him wanted to get back in the taxi and holler at Tom to drive away as fast as possible. But then, where would he go? He may not get a second chance at this.

Besides the possibility of being snatched by unsavory characters, a much worse prospect suddenly struck him. Had Michael's driver maybe gotten a better look at him than he assumed when he had knocked him over while escaping the travel agency with his forged documents? Were the police on to him? Could this all have shifted to being an undercover operation to apprehend him?

If anything could be worse than subjugation to Vladi in his orchards, it would be spending the rest of his life sleeping on cold concrete in a dungeon-like Jamaican prison where no one would ever find him.

Marco took a deep breath. He wouldn't get answers standing in the lot. He approached the sedan, hoping he wasn't making the biggest mistake of his life.

RODNEY'S LOOKOUT

arco breathed an audible sigh of relief when he recognized the man who emerged from the car. Frank Díaz looked almost the same as Marco remembered, with perhaps a bit more gray in his dark sideburns. Díaz reached out and clasped Marco's hand. It was less of a friendly gesture and more of an impatient one. However remote the locale, none of them wanted to be out in the open any longer than necessary.

Díaz pulled Marco towards him and pushed him into the car, the surprise of the maneuver resulting in a less-than-graceful landing in the back seat. As Marco quickly resituated himself, Díaz's eyes swept their surroundings before he ducked back into the car. The tires spun as the driver stepped on the accelerator and they sped away in a swirl of dust.

The drive was not long, but uncomfortably silent. Marco wondered if he should say something to Díaz. Thank him? Maybe he should have asked more questions instead of allowing a known fugitive to take him somewhere. Marco wiped his nervous palms again on his pants. His dread of speaking and his fear of remaining silent were at odds in an anxious tug of war.

They made their way to the outskirts of Kingston and then turned south toward the Hellshire Hills on the west side of the bay. This part of Hellshire was a sparsely populated area along Jamaica's southern coast that was hardly developed because of its rugged limestone terrain. A hot furnace of a wilderness, it was overgrown with thorny arid scrub vegetation and was home to more wild hogs and iguanas than people. With few paved roads, most parts were only accessible by dirt trails.

Díaz's safehouse was an abandoned movie theater that had been renovated and brought back to its former splendor — a relic of a cinema chain owned by Desmond Morgan, another Jamaican businessman with close ties to Prime Minister Sinclair. This majestic edifice stood on a hill called Rodney's Lookout. The prominent spot had a spectacular view of Port Royal directly across the bay against a backdrop of Blue Mountain Peak — at 7,400 feet, the highest point in Jamaica. Still, given the area's rural character, the local population growth had failed to sustain the location as a commercially viable site.

Approaching the perimeter of Díaz's hideaway, they passed through a band of Cuban exiles-turned-security-guards armed with machetes, sticks, and shovels, ready to fend off any attempt to capture Díaz or Marco. Given the island's notorious history as the dominion of plundering pirates and desperados, it seemed less than a coincidence that Jamaica now served as Díaz's base of operations for smuggling Cubans. Díaz maintained his silence when they arrived, gesturing for Marco to exit the vehicle.

A guard showed Marco to the room where he would stay and informed him he would meet with Díaz for dinner later. Until then, Marco was free to do as he pleased. Marco had anticipated that Díaz would want to meet with him right away, but he would wait. *The man must know what he's doing,* he thought.

Marco learned from the guard that this part of the island had been a sanctuary for runaway slaves in the early 1800s. Marco felt that he had broken away from his own form of servitude, so he thought of himself as a man with a similar intrepid spirit, a brave soul who had slipped away and fled his oppressor. He just hoped that he wouldn't share the same fate as the slaves who took refuge in these Hellshire Hills only to be recaptured later and suffer unthinkable retribution.

Sequestered within Díaz's compound, Marco wandered up a trail to a lookout point as evening approached and temperatures cooled. From there, he looked eastward across the bay and imagined how one of the most populous trade centers in the Caribbean may have appeared three centuries earlier, with wooden tall ships that sailed in and out of the harbor. He tried to envision Port Royal's appearance before two-thirds of the city was swallowed into the sea. The historic Port Royal earthquake was well-known Caribbean lore.

In the mid- to late-1600s, Port Royal was the wealthiest British city in the New World. It was also a pirate haunt with a sordid underbelly. There was a notorious concentration of brothels and grog shops, with tankards of rum and ale to accommodate Port Royal's glut of drinking, whoring, and gambling. An unsavory mélange of privateers and pirates prowled the streets and alleyways in search of carnal pleasures. Many referred to Port Royal as the "most wicked city on earth" — a Sodom of the western hemisphere.

Situated at the end of a thin finger of land about ten miles long that stretched nearly across the mouth of Kingston Harbor, the deep, well-sheltered water seemed perfect for a harbor and anchorage on its landward side. Between eight hundred and two thousand buildings were crowded onto just sixty acres — much of that isthmus was water-saturated sand.

On a Sunday morning in 1692, the ground began to heave and tremble as an earthquake liquefied the soft sand base beneath the city and turned it to quicksand. Streets became rolling rivers of aqueous sand that sucked people down and then crushed them to death when the tremors ceased and the earth reconstituted around them. There were historical accounts of people left buried with only their heads above ground, which roving packs of dogs gnawed upon in the ensuing days.

Thirty-three acres sank into the bay. Brickwork houses and buildings collapsed upon their occupants. Entire forts disappeared as the ground opened beneath them. Structures either slid into the sea or were sucked straight down along with the people in them. Within three minutes, half the city was underwater. The second and third shocks followed closely behind.

But it wasn't over. After the mighty earthquake, a devastating tidal wave washed over the rubble as if to ensure the totality of destruction. One-fifth of the population of Port Royal, about two thousand people, were thought to have lost their lives in a single day.

The plagues upon Port Royal did not even end there. As dawn broke the next morning, a thousand bodies choked the harbor. In the days that followed, the remains of the deceased continued to float up and wash ashore. The stinking carcasses of men and beasts fouled the streets, where they decomposed under the sun and were devoured by scavengers and insects. Without shelter, medicine, or clean water, disease spread rampantly among the remaining survivors. In the ensuing weeks, another three thousand people perished.

In an instant, one of the most prominent and raucous ports on earth had its population cut in half. The debauchery and vile sin of every sort manifested in the inhabitants of Port Royal was common knowledge. Its utter annihilation as an "act of God" was not lost upon the survivors.

If God was so good, Marco pondered, then how could such a God let anything like that happen? There were no doubt some innocent individuals in the community. Marco judged that not everyone in Port Royal at that time deserved to be destroyed in that manner. *I wouldn't have a God like that!* Marco mocked God in his heart with the faulty rationale that if this was the hand of God, then He stood to be indicted for such reprehensible carnage.

But the empty rationalizations borne of Marco's self-righteousness were no more than a fig leaf behind which he tried to mask his own guilt. Deeper, in his heart of hearts, Marco made inferences between what he perceived to be divine wrath on the depravity of Port Royal and his own sinfulness. He knew he was corrupt and his heart was dark, and he was fearful.

Marco suffered the torment of his own devices. His life was full of secrets and riddled with inconsistencies and contradictions. He wasn't at peace with who he was, nor could he reconcile who he was ever to be. He had tied himself into a hundred knots. The mounting evidence of Marco's life testified to his instability. He was like a rudderless ship tossed about in stormy waters, without direction or the ability to hold a true course.

Marco claimed he didn't believe in Julio's God — but as much as Marco denied it outwardly, he couldn't escape that his conscience bore witness that he was answerable to God.

As Marco turned to leave, he came upon a stone monument placed atop Rodney's Lookout — a placard put there by someone who had stood in this spot before him. Not a historical marker, instead, this was one meant to catch visitors' attention and guide their thoughts during a meditative moment. Marco wasn't the first to hike up to this overlook for its vantage point. But beyond gazing outward at the distant, panoramic vista, those who came here invariably found themselves in self-examination. Inscribed was the following:

THE WAY OF THE RIGHTEOUS AND WICKED

Blessed is the man
who walks not in the counsel of the wicked,
nor stands in the way of sinners,
nor sits in the seat of scoffers;
but his delight is in the law of the LORD,
and on His law he meditates day and night.

He is like a tree
planted by streams of water
that yields its fruit in its season,
and its leaf does not wither.
In all that he does, he prospers.
The wicked are not so,
but are like chaff that the wind drives away.

Therefore the wicked will not stand in the judgment,
nor sinners in the congregation of the righteous;
for the LORD knows the way of the righteous,
but the way of the wicked will perish.

God's Holy Word — Psalm 1

REPATRIATION

Although under vigilant security, Marco suffered a restless night plagued with anxiety. He and Frank Díaz had a meal together earlier in the evening, during which Marco was briefed about what to expect at the airport and immigration checkpoints. Díaz told him there would be someone in Miami to meet him and provide essential assistance from there. Otherwise, the process at the Hellshire compound was unceremoniously efficient.

Díaz was a man of few words, tight-lipped with all but the most essential details about the operation. Marco attributed much of the success of Díaz's scheme to his team's ability to keep a low profile. Marco had participated in the takedown of similar pipelines that were uncovered because someone couldn't keep quiet about the specifics or leaked crucial information that compromised the operation.

The next day, it took less than an hour to drive back through Kingston to the Norman Manley International Airport on the opposite side of the bay, situated midway along the same thin isthmus that led to Port Royal.

Marco was on edge. In his mind, there were various possibilities as to why and how he could be watched or followed. He wasn't yet in the clear by any means. Over and over he reviewed in his head what still needed to happen once he got to the airport.

I need to exchange this airline ticket. That transaction is sure to raise suspicions. My brain hurts from trying to come up with a way to circumvent this scrutiny, and I still haven't come up with anything. Assuming I make it past that, I have to contend with immigration officials. A sheen of sweat formed on his forehead.

As he approached the airplane ticket counter, Marco's perspiration now saturated his back and under his arms despite his usual composure under pressure. With butterflies in his stomach, he found it difficult to keep the nervousness out of his voice. He felt stiff, and he couldn't hide the tremble in his fingers as he slid his documents over the counter. As anticipated, the last-minute exchange of Marco's ticket prompted questions.

Marco's unusual ticket swap aroused the curiosity of the Air Jamaica ticket agent, who asked whether or not he was traveling to Cuba under duress.

Her eyes narrowed as she asked in a pointed tone, "Sir, do you have any fear or apprehension about going to Cuba?" Perhaps the slight tremor in his words was a giveaway, seeing that she crossed her arms, unconvinced. She called her supervisor over to the counter.

The airline supervisor asked the same questions again, giving Marco another chance to request assistance if he needed it. Jamaican officials had set up a system at the Norman Manley International Airport so that any Cuban only needed to go straight to the immigration desk to petition for asylum.

The airline supervisor beckoned an immigration official to come over and speak with him. Marco politely but resolutely maintained his decision to board the aircraft headed for Havana, hoping to avoid creating a spectacle. The officer checked Marco's passport, took his photo, made a few keystrokes on a CRT terminal behind the counter, and waved him through. He was on his way!

At this point, Marco thought he had successfully run the gauntlet to get on his flight, but there remained one last unforeseen hurdle to overcome. Jamaican immigration officials positioned themselves, hidden in the jetway, to allow one last opportunity for defection.

"Do you want to defect?" The question was asked explicitly and directly to the boarding traveler, out of sight of anyone who might interfere with an honest answer. Had he declared, "Yes," a government van waited at the base of the jetway to spirit the passenger away to safety.

Marco assured the assiduous officials that he did not want to defect and was traveling to Cuba entirely of his own accord. He then boarded the aircraft, steadying himself with one hand as he took his seat midway to the back of the cabin. With a tremendous sigh of relief, he settled back into his seat for the ninety-minute Air Jamaica flight that would take him on the last leg home to Havana.

Well, it looks like I made it through at least the first pieces of my plan, Marco congratulated himself. As far as he could tell, his audacious scheme seemed to be working. Although he supposed he could relax now, he still felt tense. It was more than lingering nerves — he was also anxious about what would happen when he stepped off the plane in Cuba.

There are so many variables. It's possible I've overlooked something. That thought weighed on him like an elephant sitting on his chest. As a professional interrogator, he wondered if they would ask questions he hadn't anticipated and catch him in a lie. Had he left any suspicious holes in his story or overlooked even a single critical detail that would betray him?

Will my counterfeit documents get past Cuban immigration officers? Is my explanation airtight? How likely is it they will accept my fabricated alibi? What will I do if they don't? It only takes one misstep, one suspicious mind, to unravel the whole scheme.

All these thoughts contributed to his anxiety, but there was something more, some dark foreboding that lurked in his heart. Marco still couldn't shake the feeling that someone was watching him — a feeling that would remain with him even after he landed back in Cuba.

PART IV

· THE RECKONING ·

DARK WINTER

"Mr. Gorbachev, tear down this wall!" Vladi let out a terse, derisive laugh. *What makes this "cowboy," Ronald Reagan, think he understands the necessity of the Berlin Wall to protect this outpost of the Soviet bloc from foreign decay and subversion?*

But then again, Vladi had never trusted Mikhail Gorbachev, with whom he'd been acquainted decades earlier. They first met shortly after university. Comrade Mikhail's family was Russian and mixed Ukrainian. Vladi considered Mikhail an intelligent and engaging conversationalist, but even back then, Mikhail didn't hold firm to Stalin's ideals. This, too, made him more than a little suspect in Vladi's mind.

Gorbachev is too soft, he thought, shaking his head in disapproval. Vladi might have been jealous about how Mikhail had advanced to leadership within the Communist Party's ranks. Now, Mikhail held the prestigious position of General Secretary of the party. Vladi imagined this could have been himself, had it not been for the misfortune of a crash that made him a forgotten castaway within enemy territory.

Although the strains between the USSR and United States had begun to ease, the Cold War still colored the perceptions and judgments of many. Vladi could only guess how people back home in Russia thought about the whole ordeal based on what he saw on American television.

In America, most people were cordial to him on the surface, although some had reservations. Vladi's conspicuous accent occasionally caused social awkwardness. It might have just been his feeling too self-conscious, but Vladi thought he detected a hint of unease towards him among the Americans he met. Maybe it was only his imagination, but he was convinced he could see distrust in the faces of those who didn't already know him.

Some declined business deals with him, ostensibly for various financial reasons, but Vladi conjectured the actual reasons had more to do with his heritage than his finances. He felt sure that any hint of the Soviet Union raised a red flag to some people, both literally and figuratively.

To get around this complication, Vladi crafted a backstory that was much less remarkable than the truth. He noticed that it gave him a more favorable reception with sympathetic Americans. He portrayed himself as a pseudo-American immigrant who had come of his own volition to taste the freedom that had been their birthright. He made up a story of a perilous defection to the United States to pursue the "American dream" so he could have a better life than those who remained under the oppression of communism. Americans ate it up. Vladi knew the story wasn't true, but ever the pragmatist, he stuck with the façade that worked for him.

Vladi considered the gullibility of Americans to be especially evident in Hollywood movies. American films were obviously effective propaganda, despite Vladi's conclusions about the limited believability of Hollywood's conjured illusions.

Typical American bravado! he thought while watching *Top Gun*, shaking his head vigorously. *What an exhibition of reckless egos! If this represents U.S. naval aviators, they display an appalling lack of military discipline.*

He knew how his comrades had been taught in the USSR during their schooling as officers and felt confident that the real "Top Gun" pilots weren't the cocky rule-benders portrayed in the film. They certainly didn't exist in the Soviet military.

He found the premise of *Red Dawn*, a movie about adolescent amateurs evading and fending off Soviet paratroopers, to be an even greater absurdity. It would have been laughable were it not so insulting. *Wolverines? Come now, the notion of a group of high school students who could outwit a Spetsnaz unit or KGB is mere juvenile fantasy. Ha!*

However, while reading Tom Clancy's novel *The Hunt for Red October*, Vladi hit pause on his derision. *Captain Marko Ramius — now, apart from cleverly absconding with a Typhoon-class submarine, he represents the apotheosis of a brilliant Soviet officer!* Vladi mused with pride.

So realistic and well-written, the book struck Vladi with a sense of consternation. He couldn't help but marvel. *How did Clancy, an American insurance salesman-turned-author, know so many minutiae about classified Soviet tactics and military details?* It troubled Vladi to contemplate that Clancy could have obtained his insights from a Soviet mole who had provided him military intelligence — unless maybe the leaks came from within the CIA.

Now there were hints that the Cold War might be thawing, though. Vladi dared to hope that this could lead to opportunities to be reunited with his family. As blissful as the thought was, at this point it came with a paradox of unsettling emotions.

It has been a quarter of a century since I have seen them. My girls are young women now, perhaps with their own families. Even his lastborn child, whom Vladi had never known, would likewise be grown up by now.

And what has become of Irina? These thoughts were too dispiriting for him to dwell on. Vladi refocused his mind on his work and tried to avoid speculations that only further fomented the anguish he felt in his heart.

Season upon season, life settled into a predictable routine. It helped provide an emotional diversion for Vladi — it also enriched his pockets. Vladi seemed to have the Midas touch. Over the course of two decades in the business, he grew wealthier with each passing year.

Vladi had built a palatial home, drove the finest automobiles, dressed like the rich people he saw on American television, and lived almost without limits. From May through September and sometimes into October, Vladi spent every spare moment angling for sailfish and marlin. Fishing was another diversion that, at least for a moment, took his mind away from the cares of this world.

Then came the Christmas Day freeze of 1989. A large, deep, high-pressure system of cold arctic air bellowed south, reaching Florida on December 23, 1989. Extreme cold temperatures were felt throughout Florida and much of the United States. A trough of low pressure over the southeast United States and available moisture from the Atlantic Ocean produced wintry precipitation that fell across the Florida peninsula on Christmas eve. Shortly after midnight, they lost power.

The freeze made records that Vladi and everyone else in Florida's citrus belt would have hoped never to see. The mercury fell to 19°F in Titusville, and temperatures were recorded as low as 8° in the northern part of the state. Even the ever-balmy Miami dropped to 30°. Areas in northern Florida received up to three inches of snow, while one inch was reported as far south as Sarasota. Sustained sub-freezing temperatures, ice, and sleet — one of the harshest cold waves in recorded history — swept over Florida, blanketing the state.

County after county, power blackouts cascaded like dominoes — the outages were widespread over the state. There was nowhere to go to escape the freeze — nowhere to get warm. Ice accumulated rapidly, and roads were impassable. Life ground to a standstill.

Florida residents were unprepared for severe winter weather. Normal winters in the southern states were mild, and those were the seasonal conditions Floridians expected. Even on the rare nights when overnight temperatures fell below freezing, the sun rose, and by mid-morning everything was toasty again. In years past, Vladi had seen the people of Florida dressed in shorts as they played golf over their Christmas holiday.

Vladi, on the other hand, had grown up with long, dark winters. In his mind, the Russian people were a hardier stock than the Floridians. His people could live for months in sub-freezing temperatures without batting a frozen eyelash. No one stopped work, school, or most other regular activities because of a little winter weather.

Vladi's training in the military had made him prepared for almost anything, but a freak winter storm in Florida caught even him by surprise. He hated to admit that his blood had "thinned" a bit over the years, and the cold wave was a shock even to his rugged skin now. For the next fifty-five hours, Vladi underwent various trials — all of which were unexpected.

Vladi's home was not immune to the effects of the harsh freeze, and problems ensued. Without power, the inside of his house turned frigid, with the temperature even indoors falling into the low twenties.

Stately as it was, Vladi's home was a lonely place. Except for domestic help and a rare visitor, he lived alone. But this cold solitude made his cavernous living room and bedroom feel particularly isolating now.

Sounds were dampened in the light snow, so the freeze blanketed everything with eerie hush. Transportation had come to a halt. There was no noise from automobile traffic, nor the usual sounds of aircraft passing overhead due to flight cancellations. No dogs barked, and not even the birds sang. Every creature found shelter and quietly endured the cold temperatures.

It was Christmastime, so the labor hands remained home with their families. No work could be done in the freeze anyway. There were no sounds of machinery operating. Even the absence of white noise from a refrigerator hum made the house conspicuously silent.

Vladi watched the condensation from his breath while he sat alone and shivered under blankets, layered in his warmest winter clothing. Against a backdrop of complete silence, he could hear every snap and pop of the timber frame of his home as it contracted and frozen water pipes burst. Not only was he without power, but he also lacked water.

Being without power and water were conditions Vladi knew how to handle from his upbringing in Russia and military training — they weren't the issues that troubled him now. The things that disturbed him most were his own thoughts.

The stillness of the house put Vladi in a dark, reflective mood. To its solitary occupant, the sprawling house felt more like a prison tonight than a palace. Thoughts he had long held at bay reemerged. Up from the deep, dark recesses of his mind came the voices of remorse to sadden every bitter hour. There was no diversion of work or fishing to deflect them, and his looming emotions were breaching the dam that had kept them contained, threatening to burst through and drown him in an awful torrent of despair.

He clutched the old pocket watch his father had given him. He ran his fingers over the Soviet emblem. Thoughts of home, the *rodina*, surfaced from his well of memories. The hands had ceased to keep time when he and the old watch had plunged into the Atlantic together. The moment the watch had stopped was also the moment that, in many ways, his life had as well stopped. Both of them had ceased counting the minutes, adding up to days that added up to years.

What remains anymore? It is like I am no more than a relic of waning glory . . . like this old timepiece, he thought with bitter resentment.

Time alone in dark solitude drew inescapable reminders that he was apart from Irina. He had tried so hard to keep what she looked like in his head — her infectious smile, her hazel eyes, and her perfect little nose. With time, these details were gradually fading from his memory, and her face had become more like a blurred apparition that eluded his mind. He would think he could see the back of her head sometimes, but when she turned toward him the details of her face fluttered away like chaff in the wind.

Even harder was trying to picture his daughters. *I had not spent enough time with their sweet little faces,* came the regretful thought. *If only I had known — how could I have known?*

His military commitments had occupied so much of his younger days, even back in Russia. They had always wanted to pretend to "serve" him tea when he was home, and he would read to them before bed. But their time together had been so brief, and now only snapshots remained in his distant memory. When they were together, his daughters had softened his hard exterior. Now, his macho tendencies were unbalanced without the presence of Irina and the girls in his life.

Then there was the child whom Vladi had not seen. A boy? Another girl? He didn't know . . . might never know. He imagined a son for unknown reasons — perhaps only because he had so longed to have a son. And, if so, was he strong and courageous like his father? Did he watch over his mother and sisters? Was he a protector? Did he look more like Vladi or Irina? It was almost unbearable that there was no face to associate with this child.

In addition, he contemplated how he might never meet his future grandchildren and how they might never know him. He clenched his fists. The thought caught in his chest, and he felt his throat tightening. He put his hand to his neck as if he could push the emotion back down and keep it from erupting.

Here, he seemed to have everything except the family he loved. He often watched the happy Cuban households, who had almost nothing in the world except their families, with a bit of envy. *They came here with nothing and remained poor, but they have love, laughter, and warmth among them.*

He wanted for nothing in a material sense, but he couldn't use any of it to get back what he wanted most. *What is my purpose for existing, then?* The more Vladi contemplated these things, the more his will to live diminished. A momentary notion of suicide passed through his mind.

A cold mistiness formed in his eyes. He knew that if he didn't keep his thoughts in check, it would lead him down a perilous path. *This is why I do not think about these things,* he rebuked himself as he sniffled and wiped his nose. He made an effort to collect himself. *I have stared death in the face without fear, but sad thoughts make me give up?*

He worked to shake himself out of his sorrowful state. He held onto hopes that somehow he would be reunited with Irina and the children. Those hopes gave him the will to press on, especially after the storm.

The winter storm claimed at least twenty-six lives. All over, Florida sustained heavy losses in agricultural production. Before the 1980s, the citrus industry hadn't experienced killer freezes for almost a century. Then, in 1980, Vladi's groves had been affected by a freeze that wiped out most of Lake County's more than one hundred thousand acres of citrus groves, but the situation now was far grimmer. This was the second impact freeze of the decade, and growers had no time for recovery. The crop damage was extensive. Losses amounted to thirty percent of Florida's entire $1.4 billion citrus industry.

As the winter weather abated, Vladi faced the dreaded task of taking stock of his orchards. He took an arborist along to survey the damage, but any iota of hope soon faded. The losses were colossal.

As he and the arborist moved through row after row, Vladi put his hands on his head, anxiously raking his fingers through his graying hair. He didn't realize how hard he'd been clenching his teeth until his jaw began to throb. The arborist inspected the few trees that remained viable, but their crops were ruined too.

"It's not good. You'll need to replant. You need to clear everything out of the groves and plant new trees. I'm sorry, sir." The arborist hated to deliver the hard news. The cost would be tremendous.

While the arborist was still speaking, Antonio, one of Vladi's best foremen approached him. "*Jefe*, I finished inspecting the irrigation systems." He paused with arms folded — obviously he did not want to continue. Clearing his throat, he avoided eye contact as he reported, "I'm sorry, boss. It's pretty much all gone. Almost all of the pumps were ruined, hoses and valves were split, and the groves are littered with shards of ruptured pipes." Vladi just stared at him for a moment. More money lost.

"Hmm . . . thank you for the report." Vladi's response was polite, yet solemn. "This is very bad. We must consider what is needed to rebuild. And the workers? Ahh . . . " he sighed. "This is their work. They depend on this. Later, we must have a meeting — with everyone."

Despite his tremendous personal losses, Vladi's workers were at the forefront of his mind. *I brought them here, and they depend on me for their livelihoods.* It wasn't an overstatement. Entire families relied on him, Señor Moisés. There would be plenty of work in the groves over the next few years — clearing, replanting, fertilizing, and maintenance. But newly planted trees would require at least five years before they reached productive maturity.

Five years without revenue — how can I pay them? He racked his brain in anguish. After he depleted much of his savings to fix the irrigation systems and replant the groves, what would be left to pay the workers?

This was perhaps the most concerning aspect for Vladi. *I have enough savings to make it fine and to rebuild, but these families I helped escape from Cuba cannot do the same,* he rightly assessed.

Most lived week-to-week — the Cubans sent any excess money to family members who needed it more. This affected not just the laborers and their immediate families but also their extended family would suffer, including elderly relatives. The gravity of the situation was palpable. *I must find a way to take care of them — somehow,* Vladi vowed to himself.

For two decades, Vladi had experienced the benefits of American capitalism for which he had formerly held such contempt. It had served him well, better than he had ever expected. But now, for the first time since he had landed in America, Vladi was experiencing the harsh realities of capitalist economics. He was free to make money but not spared from a catastrophe of this magnitude. It came with the risk that he could lose it all, and that was becoming ever more likely.

Vladi usually had a plan for everything, but once again he faced circumstances for which he had neither precedent nor guidance. Even the comprehensive military manuals he once could nearly recite cover-to-cover from memory were of no help navigating this current set of problems. Yet if Vladi had learned anything from life experience, it was how to adapt and overcome.

HEALING TIME

When the day came that Marco failed to return from the port, Julio grew understandably concerned. *Have the immigration officers who work the docks apprehended him? It is also possible that Marco's antagonistic mouth has landed him in some sort of trouble*, he speculated. Julio's initial uncertainties did not take long to recede, as those disquieting thoughts settled down to what Julio realized in his heart had transpired.

Marco had told him he was looking for a path back to Cuba. *He must have found a way*, Julio thought to himself over and over. He guessed what had happened, but didn't expect it to be so sudden. Although it would grieve him for years to come, he never revealed to another soul his private speculations about what had happened to Marco.

Even after Marco abandoned him, Julio continued to work for Vladi for the better part of a decade. With the heart of a servant and a medical education, he also cared for the health needs of fellow Cuban refugees within the community. Naturally, he was the first person called upon to administer first aid to anyone who got hurt in the citrus fields or when someone was ill in the church.

Aside from just work, Julio made America his new home in every sense. Of course he missed his brother, but life continued to move forward nonetheless. About a year after Marco left, Julio found a new kind of love and married the daughter of Cuban refugees — a family he had grown to know in the church. Julio and his wife now had their own family, with two boys, and a girl sandwiched in between.

Julio appreciated the employment and income Vladi had provided him at Red Star, but he ultimately decided that it wasn't how he was meant to spend the rest of his life. Over the years this became clearer to Julio as he cared for the minor illnesses and injuries of the labor hands and their families. He yearned to return to work as a physician. Julio couldn't point to a Bible verse telling him definitively that it was God's will, but he sensed it was a calling — that much was undeniable.

Even though Julio had been a qualified and experienced doctor in Cuba, that education alone would not permit him to practice medicine in the States. He had also been away from the discipline so long that he recognized he was no longer up to date on current procedures. *It will be a long journey back to serving in the medical field, but it is one I need to make. It is the way I will be able to accomplish the most good,* he told himself with firm resolve.

Julio began by going through all the proper channels. He applied for amnesty and worked his way toward U.S. citizenship. He discovered the Educational Commission for Foreign Medical Graduates, which enabled him to complete the United States Medical Licensing Examination program. Over a period of fourteen months, he studied for a sequence of three board exams for medical professionals who had trained in other countries, allowing them to become licensed physicians in their adopted nation.

Julio had earned Vladi's respect over the years. Following Marco's altercation with him in front of the orchard workers, Vladi admired Julio's calm demeanor and his reasoned appeal. From that point forward, their relationship developed further. Julio told Vladi about his aspiration to return to medicine.

"When you understand your highest and best purpose in life, the tumblers in your heart click into place, and the future begins to make sense," Julio explained.

Vladi regretted that he would be losing Julio, such a devoted and trustworthy worker. Nonetheless, he was magnanimous in his support of Julio's endeavor.

When Julio needed to focus on his studies, Vladi allowed him a flexible work schedule and all the time off he needed to prepare for the rigorous board exams. Not only that, but when Julio burned through his savings, Vladi offered to sponsor him and helped to cover his expenses until he completed the program.

Julio passed his boards and proudly received his U.S. medical license issued by the Florida Board of Medicine in early 1990. It was time to say goodbye to his old life and start on a new course. Julio hugged Vladi for the first time as a genuine friend on the day he relocated his young family to Lakeland, Florida, where he had found work as a physician with an established hospital. He was now Dr. Rivera to all.

Vladi wasn't the only one sad to see Julio leave. Julio was beloved by the Cuban refugees of Vladi's orchards, many of whom he had taken care of as their impromptu physician. He had made an enduring impression on the hearts of the refugees, who held him in the highest esteem and had formed a lasting affection toward him.

Despite the move and his own change of lifestyle, Julio had not gone that far. He still lived close to the citrus groves and remained a significant person in the lives of those with whom he had worked side-by-side for many years. Julio continued to take care of their medical needs and never charged the orchard workers, because he knew their financial resources were meager. But they repaid Julio many times over with their love for him and his family — something their money could never have bought.

Things began to feel much like home in a good way, with the shadow of Cuba gently resting over him. He had done much for the community back there and forged strong relationships with his patients in Havana. Julio missed them and their interactions over the years. Their faces and names remained in his heart and mind, and he often wondered about each one and prayed for them. But now, as he worked with the Cuban refugees, Julio felt like a piece of his heart had been returned to him.

Julio also got to help return a small piece of Vladi's heart to him. It happened when Vladi invited Julio to his home after the great freeze. During their visit, Vladi brought out an old pocket watch and showed it to Julio. He sensed that Vladi was revealing a sacred part of his life. Indeed, Julio had never seen Vladi act so sentimental about anything.

Since he had been in America, Vladi had never shown the watch to anyone. Julio was the one person he felt he could trust.

He confided to Julio, "This heirloom watch has been handed down from my grandfather to my father and then to me. I always imagined passing it to a son in time, but life has not given me that opportunity."

Julio could hear the hollow sadness in Vladi's voice as he continued. "This watch stopped when I crashed into the Atlantic on the way home to my family. My own life seemed to stop keeping time that day," he expressed with uncharacteristic emotion. "I would like to have it repaired," he told Julio, "but I cannot take it to an American shop without the Soviet emblem drawing attention. Someone will hear my accent and report me to the government. I cannot take that risk." He looked up at Julio with a gentle appeal. "Will you take it for me?"

Naturally, Julio was more than willing to help Vladi. It was a small request, but he could tell this meant much to Vladi.

"I will pay for the repairs. When someone asks about its insignia, you can say it came from Cuba, like yourself. That is true. We do not have to say how it got here."

Vladi placed the watch in Julio's hand and looked him in the eyes as though he were entrusting his most treasured possession to him. In fact, he was.

Later that week, Julio took it to a repair shop called The Watch Doctor. The watchmaker examined the vintage pocket watch with great interest. Indeed, he was curious about how Julio had come into possession of such a unique timepiece. The watchmaker didn't challenge his explanation, although he continued to marvel at the watch itself.

"It could be expensive to restore this, but I am up for the challenge. Few watchmakers would touch this," mused the man. "There are many parts in the movement. Some may be obsolete or unobtainable. If so, I can machine custom parts: clock wheels, pinions, barrels, levers, springs, bridges, dials, everything. If I can't do it, I probably know someone who can. Just give me time."

Two months later, the watch was ready. The repairs were indeed costly — the bill totaled $379. Unflinching at the price, Vladi gave Julio cash to pay the bill. But when Julio returned to The Watch Doctor, instead of asking for payment, the watchmaker offered Julio $600 to buy the vintage timepiece.

Julio, of course, declined.

The watchmaker tried one more time. "Well, the offer always stands if you ever change your mind."

Had it been anyone else, Vladi might have lost his watch along with all the money. But Julio wasn't that type of man. He was honest and loyal to Vladi and would never compromise their relationship for anything.

The restored watch was cleaned up and more beautiful than ever. It may have been close to a hundred years old, but it looked like new. This was one of the few things that would make Vladi happy, and Julio knew it. He could have everything else America offered, but that old watch was the only material thing that held sentimental value to him.

When Julio brought the watch to him, Vladi was speechless and held the watch gently, as though it were a newborn child. Julio was treated to a sight that few would ever see — the glisten of mist in Vladi's eyes. But the stoic Russian did not cry openly. He didn't need to. Julio understood what it meant to him, and left his friend alone with his restored treasure.

RISING TENSION

The Cuban labor hands didn't quite know what to make of Vladi. Truth be told, they had mixed feelings about him. Although Vladi had helped so many of them with their passage from Cuba out of sincere benevolence, his personality didn't always come across as warm and welcoming.

Due to his commanding presence, tone, and direct manner of speaking, the refugees found it hard to recognize Vladi's genuine concern for their well-being. Some were put off by his manner, while others just kept to themselves and didn't talk to him. He was like royalty to them, which called for their respect. All the while, they felt that at times his generosity lacked genuine empathy and sensitivity. Others adopted a view similar to that of Marco, feeling as if they were almost Vladi's serfs.

These divided views among the labor hands stemmed from their fragmented understanding of Vladi — they didn't comprehend the whole man. In their perception, he loomed over them as an imposing figure.

In part, this was Vladi's own fault. He had buried aspects of himself that the Cubans back on the island had known long ago — a spirited debater, a disciplined officer, an above-average chess player. He even had a sense of humor that often spontaneously peeked through his stoic exterior. Except for a sense that Julio had about Vladi, none of the other Cubans knew him as a loving father or husband. Some of those parts of him were a shadow of another life, perhaps lost at sea the day his plane had plunged into the Atlantic years before.

Vladi's distance was also to some extent deliberate. This stemmed from his former military training. Officers were strictly forbidden to fraternize with enlisted soldiers. This protocol enforced some distance and ensured that lower-ranking troops maintained respect for authority. Now that he was a civilian, that same decorum carried over into Vladi's business endeavors. The sad trade-off was that, since those within the refugee community were the nearest thing to a family that Vladi had known there, keeping them at arm's length just added to his sense of solitude and loneliness.

Vladi felt entitled to his lifestyle. He had been astute and disciplined, sacrificing to make it happen. Even though he worked hard for his accomplishments and had earned his success, there were a few labor hands who envied him nonetheless.

Vladi had his critics among certain discontented laborers who resented the disparities in their standard of living. This was in no small part due to the discord Marco had stirred up and, over time, it began to fester.

Even before the freeze, tensions had been stiffening among a small faction of workers. Marco's previous remarks about Vladi had sown seeds of discontent in the hearts and minds of some of the workers, which in turn allowed resentment to simmer and escalate to the point that some workers mocked him behind his back as "Czar Vladi."

The latest eruption of resentment arrived in the wake of the great freeze. No one was spared from the hardships. Like everyone else, the Cuban refugees had water pipes that froze and burst. The modest homes of some were flooded. When the electricity went out, there was no warm place to take refuge. Some with short memories were bitter and grumbled that conditions were less harsh in Cuba and their lives had been better there.

Worse yet, the Florida citrus industry was in the midst of an operational catastrophe. Production was off, and most of the groves were being bulldozed and cleared, including Vladi's properties.

Many growers sold their land for residential development, something Vladi refused to do. Sure, selling out had crossed his mind. The enticement of a prospective windfall was there, and it would have been the easier course by far. But confronted with hardship, his tenacious nature gave him the determination to avoid letting everything he worked for just evaporate. More than that, Vladi had his reasons, and they were honorable. His decisions were primarily driven by his desire to protect the ongoing interests of the labor hands and their families. *If I sold out now, I would be abandoning all of them,* he truly believed.

Central Florida had been a sleepy locale when the citrus industry had taken root a century earlier, but the environment for producers was rapidly changing. Disney World had garnered the most attention around the surge in growth.

The inauguration of the Magic Kingdom in 1971 brought a huge increase in tourism to the Sunshine State. By the 1980s, the surrounding region was straining to catch up. Mickey Mouse's dominion grew even bigger when Epcot Center opened in 1982, and then Disney-MGM Studios followed in the summer of 1989. About thirteen million people visited the Disney Florida attractions annually. Within the next year, Disney's chief competitor Universal Studios would open its gates.

Other less noticeable factors aided expansion and brought jobs and people to the region. For instance, the Reagan administration invested heavily in America's military. In 1988, the Department of Defense gave Martin Marietta and the U.S. Naval Training Center in Orlando a total of over $3 billion.

Every day, nearly two hundred people moved into one of six central Florida counties: Orange, Brevard, Volusia, Seminole, Osceola, and Lake County. Florida's population increased by more than three million within a decade, propelling it to the fourth most populous state in the union.

The crop that once gave Orange County its name was fast diminishing. Fewer than one-third of the number of acres that used to grow citrus trees a decade earlier were still in production. Faced with long lead times to replant and cultivate trees and the possibility of being wiped out by more cold weather, many citrus growers had given up and turned the frozen groves into commercial and residential real estate projects. Developers were eager to build, and build they did: single-family homes, duplexes, apartments, condos, shopping centers, and office developments sprang up everywhere. Finding real estate buyers wasn't as difficult as coming up with catchy names for the countless new neighborhoods.

Once upon a time, Walt Disney paid an average of $185 an acre for their original twenty-seven thousand acres. These days, the land was no longer sold by the acre but by the square foot, and prices were attractive enough for citrus producers to move on.

Most of the Cuban refugees resided in small, rundown homes, which made matters worse from their perspective. Seeing nice, new housing projects being built on the ground where they once labored in the citrus groves was hard to watch.

Vladi felt genuine empathy for them and helped as much as he could. Had he not also had everything taken from him in an instant? He knew what it was like to be far away from home and unsure of what to do. Vladi would never wish for them to feel the same way, especially after the community of Cuban refugees welcomed him into their homes with generosity and kindness during his time of need.

During those early days back in Havana, Vladi had a negative first impression of Cubans as being "simple-minded" and "superstitious." With time, his perspective had reformed. Over the years, Vladi had seen what many Cubans had endured under Castro, having everything stripped away — homes, food, everyday necessities, even family — leaving them with few alternatives but to comply. He used to think that the communism he and his comrades helped usher into Cuba was a good idea and a step forward.

At the time, he had not envisioned the destructive consequences and the pain that would be inflicted upon ordinary families. Now, the thought of these Cuban families losing everything again was too much. Vladi didn't see that as an option. Their circumstances evoked his compassion. He couldn't abandon them now.

Those feelings translated into action for Vladi. He didn't always show his emotions, but he was a powerhouse when it came to initiative. One of his pragmatic guiding principles was almost a personal maxim: *Feelings do not help anyone, but taking action does!*

Like the handful of other diehard producers who chose to stay in the business, Vladi set about replanting. Many Cuban refugees who worked for other growers suddenly found themselves unemployed and with scarce options. The few who did have work were treated poorly by growers more concerned about their own interests, as the bosses thought refugees should have been grateful for any work under the circumstances. Tensions were high.

Vladi, on the other hand, remained resolute in his determination to let neither unemployment nor this kind of unfair management become the fate of his labor hands. He took stock of his resources and the cash he had saved and determined that he could ride out the next few years with what he had. Things would be tight, but if he remained smart, they could make it through.

After the initial days of assessing the damage to Red Star's properties, Vladi gathered all his workers to speak with them. He let them know the enormity of the situation they all faced.

"We cannot hide from the fact that we are confronted with a difficult period ahead. Rebuilding the Red Star operation and reestablishing our productive groves will be a long and difficult undertaking. What is more, we face a financial strain," he told them in his typical straightforward manner.

Vladi saw a look of dread on many of their faces, and some in the group started to shift with anxiety. "I want to reassure you, though," he continued, "I have a plan to rebuild. I hope you will all be part of it." He told them he would make the necessary adjustments to keep the citrus operations alive and their jobs secure over the next few years.

With those words, Vladi saw men put their hands over their chests, grateful he had not come to tell them the worst, as so many had anticipated. There was a palpable sense of relief among most of the labor hands, and a few even approached him to shake his hand and express their thanks. With that, everyone got to work.

THE SHADOW
OF DEATH

Dr. Rivera was accustomed to taking calls for medical emergencies at all hours, but the call he got that morning left him shaken. He hung up the phone and looked at it with a blank, almost dazed expression.

His wife noticed the look on his face and asked if everything was okay.

He didn't answer. Instead, he turned and ran out the door without saying a word.

He arrived at the hospital just in time to see four men struggling to carry a large, unconscious figure into the emergency room. The man's face was covered with blood, but Julio didn't need a better look — he would recognize the Russian anywhere.

As hospital staff rushed to help get Vladi on a gurney, the man who had called Julio pulled him aside.

"Some of the labor hands found Señor Vladi unconscious on one of the orchard properties. They said he looked like he had been beaten pretty bad. They picked him up and carried him out as carefully as they could since they couldn't tell how bad he was hurt. They laid him in the back of one of the produce trucks while two men rode alongside to keep him from being jostled around too much on the dirt roads," the foreman, Antonio, reported.

"Antonio, do the men who found him have any idea who did this?" Julio asked.

"They don't know any details. They only found him after it happened. But they did say they noticed that four workers went missing today. They think those workers are responsible for the attack, given their temperaments."

"But why?" Julio asked with a catch in his voice. "Why, after all he has done to help them? I hear all the growers are going through a difficult time, but what could he have done to bring on such violence? Others were without work. I know he met with everyone and kept them paid — none of Vladi's workers lost their jobs." Although Julio voiced his questions aloud, he was talking to himself.

Antonio answered, "Until we find the men who did this, we can't be sure. But I know that those missing men had been speaking badly of Señor Vladi for a long time. And then after the storm, they were always saying, 'Oh, look at him in his warm truck or his nice big house while we're his slaves out here sweating then freezing and working ourselves to death for him.' They had black envy in their hearts. I know that."

That sounds a lot like Marco's talk, Julio thought, though he didn't express it aloud. Julio thanked Antonio for the information and promised to keep the orchard workers updated about Vladi's condition. In turn, Antonio assured Julio that everyone would pray for Vladi, not just for his physical healing, but for his spiritual well-being as well.

Julio thanked Antonio again, then returned his attention to Vladi. Julio had Vladi admitted to the hospital where he could receive proper medical attention and Julio could look in on him.

When Julio later looked over the tests he ordered on Vladi, his heart dropped. The reports indicated that Vladi's condition was grave — he had a brain bleed, among other serious injuries. The first few days would be critical.

A few weeks passed, and Vladi's condition stabilized. He grew well enough to continue recuperating at home, on the condition that he would take it easy. Vladi would have rather had to swallow a hundred pills a day than stay still and convalesce — it was the hardest order to follow. He had always been an active, hands-on manager in his operation. Now, he felt compelled to get back right away because his orchards were being replanted and put back together. But he had physical limitations — it was the first time that he was conscious of the boundaries that his body imposed on him.

Though Vladi had left the hospital, Julio continued to check on him. Vladi had been his usual stoic and less-than-verbal self about the attack. Although he couldn't get Vladi to say much about it, Julio could tell that this second near-death incident had left a profound mark on Vladi. It had affected him differently than the plane crash.

To Julio's perceptive eyes, Vladi looked worn down and defeated. There was a noticeable difference in his demeanor, and his posture bore the telltale signs of a crestfallen man.

The change is distressing, but not surprising. Such events tend to alter a man's perspective, Julio observed.

He worried about what might be going on in Vladi's head. In fact, the more silent Vladi remained on the matter, the more Julio's concerns intensified. *Depression can kill.*

He and Vladi had known each other for many years, so they understood each other fairly well. Julio was a thoughtful and discerning friend. Vladi had never been one for heart-to-heart talks, but Julio wished that Vladi would use their time together to discuss what was on his mind.

As much as he could, Julio sought to keep things light-hearted. He made it a personal aim to get Vladi to laugh, a mission that could sometimes be challenging. He also tried to ask questions that would draw out Vladi's thoughts and feelings, but this proved to be much more difficult.

Julio had more concern for Vladi than just his physical and emotional recovery. He hoped that this unanticipated mortal danger would perhaps bring Vladi to reevaluate his beliefs and think about spiritual questions that needed answering. He knew Vladi's spiritual condition was more crucial.

On one of his many visits with Vladi, he thought it a proper moment to approach his friend about his spiritual well-being. It had been years since Vladi had rebuffed him for broaching the subject. He had refused to discuss the matter then. That prior response caused Julio to feel trepidation about bringing it up again now, but it was important enough to override his own fears and try to help Vladi with those needs. He hoped that the passage of time and the changing circumstances had made Vladi more ready to have this conversation.

To Vladi, who always enjoyed Julio's presence, it was just like any other visit. Vladi offered Julio a cup of coffee then asked as he sat down, "How have you been, my friend?"

"That's usually my line," Julio replied with a smile. "I'm fine," he added, but the fatigue in his voice revealed the truth. "They have me pulling some long shifts at the hospital, and I try my best to visit the other Cuban families. Injuries and illnesses never seem to happen when it's convenient, but that's all part of being a good steward of the work our Lord has entrusted to me."

Vladi nodded, without giving acknowledgment to the "our Lord" part. "I am glad you are well, and I am always grateful for the good care you provide to my workers. They need you, and you have continued to be there for them. It is hard to imagine what they would do without you."

Julio gave a modest smile. "Maybe like your sister back in Russia? But I think she works more selflessly in the orphanage than I do here." Julio gave a soft chuckle. From what Vladi had told him, Olga ostensibly exhibited none of the ambitions that characterized Vladi's life.

Vladi sighed then sat back in his chair with his coffee. His eyes softened as his memory focused back in time. "Yes, she is, or was, ever so sacrificing. She would give away the last bite of her *kasha* porridge to a stranger if she thought they were hungry. She was a good and kind sister to me," he recalled with fondness, his eyes fixed into the distance.

After a moment of reflection, Julio noticed a shift. Vladi sniffed with a slight laugh and met Julio's eyes. "And for all that goodness and sacrifice, she got to live in poverty. That could be you too, my friend, if you are not careful. You give away your medical services perhaps a bit too freely and miss many opportunities to allow yourself and your family some additional financial security. Not to mention additional comforts which, take it from me, are not so bad." At that, Vladi gave a lopsided grin.

Julio acknowledged Vladi with a smile, not revealing the awkwardness he felt. *This already is not the direction I hoped the conversation would take, but best to be patient and stay with it,* Julio reminded himself.

Of course, Vladi didn't make the connection that Julio hoped to infer by mentioning Olga. However, he really liked how Julio cared for the refugee families. He just didn't understand why Julio continued to provide medical services to them without charge, even at his own expense sometimes.

Vladi returned to his line of reasoning. "You and I both came up being taught the evils of capitalist society, but here we are right in the midst of it. I have taken advantage of their system to make a better life for myself. Is that so wrong? I have done what other people were not inclined to do for themselves — I have worked hard, been disciplined, and produced what is needed, not only to get by, but to prosper. Now you are here — why should you not do the same? What is the saying — 'When in Rome . . . '?"

Julio acknowledged that he already had a better life in almost every way. Then he went on to explain why he was caring for the refugee families. "Aside from my salary at the hospital, I accept payment from those who can afford to pay. This is how I support my family. But as for many of the refugees, God calls His followers to visit orphans and widows in their affliction. So we're not to dishonor the lowly among us. When a wealthy, well-dressed man comes to me for help, I attend to him without hesitation. And when a needy family comes, am I to turn them away and not care for them because they don't have much?"

After a brief pause, Julio reminded Vladi, "And what about you? I know you acknowledge your success since you've been in America, and you make it sound like you're one of those greedy Yankee capitalists that Fidel always railed against," Julio smiled to soften the words into a semi-humorous statement, "but

I've seen you take risks and use your own resources on behalf of the Cuban families. You have facilitated their passage, and have you not provided them a foundation for a better life? Maybe you're not as different from me and your sister as you think."

Julio's words prompted Vladi to reflect on the "whys" of what he did. It rarely crossed his mind, if ever. He did what he believed to be right, regardless of whether he considered his motives to be good or not. But what Julio said caused Vladi to reflect on his own situation — how he got to America after being the sole survivor of the crash at sea. He literally had nothing and knew no one who could have helped him. Yet Vladi remembered the American skipper who fished him out of his drink and his kindness without judgment. His mind also drifted back to how the Cuban families had given him aid in his desperate time of need.

Vladi couldn't help but wonder why the refugees, who had such meager resources themselves, were so gracious and helped a stranger to the extent that they did. It ran counter to Vladi's former preconceptions about the selfish society he associated with American capitalism.

Deep within himself, his own unfortunate experiences and the subsequent acts of kindness he received that helped him survive had fundamentally affected Vladi. And without his awareness, the cumulative effect of these factors gradually shaped his character and influenced his actions.

However, Vladi kept those thoughts in his heart and did not let them pass his lips, as though he preferred to close himself off from it — otherwise, it would be admitting that Julio might have a point.

Vladi was such a cold, logical thinker that he would never admit that feelings influenced his choices. He believed that anything people did stemmed from self-interest. He didn't think in terms of pure motives. *By nature, humans are selfish creatures — how could one transform the way he was born?*

Perhaps that's why Julio's pure-hearted do-goodism sometimes bothered Vladi. Sure, Vladi helped the refugees, but he viewed it as a form of gratitude or indebtedness for their kindness toward him. Julio seemed determined for Vladi to see things his way, making the contrarian in Vladi want to argue even more for the other side.

Julio might wish to think he has unselfish motives, but no human does, no matter how good they are. Not even "Saint Julio." He wanted to push Julio into an honest admission of what Vladi thought to be a more authentic perception of himself.

Vladi continued his reasoning. "You suggest that people could have pure motives — such as you and Olga. But in truth, do you not do good because you fear your God's wrath if you do not? That is not exactly selfless — you devote your whole life to doing good works to prove that you have favor with your supposed God."

Julio looked as if Vladi had smacked him across the face. "That's not true, Vladi," he responded softly. The hurt in his tone was palpable. Vladi was questioning the motives that underpinned his entire life.

Vladi could see that his remark had offended Julio, and he quickly tried to smooth it over. "Look, Julio, the fact is that the labor hands are not beggars and I am not a charity. They work and receive payment. It is a business. Likewise, Julio, you worked hard for what you have accomplished. For many years, while other men slacked off, drank, and had irresponsible lives — you applied yourself, studied, and sacrificed to become a doctor. Now you have a vital and marketable service. It is not good business to feel sorry for every pitiful soul to walk through your door. You deprive your own family because others do not manage their lives and finances," Vladi contended.

Julio winced at Vladi's rather harsh assessment. He knew that Vladi's last statement was true sometimes, but not in most cases. But he remained gentle, as usual, despite Vladi's rather caustic skepticism. He couldn't see what was inside of Vladi's mind — he could only speak to what he heard. So, mustering patience, Julio attempted a reply.

"Perhaps you question my motives, but I'll just tell you, so you don't need to wonder. Our Creator provides every good thing — that includes what you consider my talent. It would be ungrateful for me not to use the gift I've been given in the manner the Giver intended. He's given me the mind, the opportunity, the desire, and even the freedom to be a doctor. And for what purpose? It's to care for others, and it is not for me to decide whether or not those people deserve my concern."

Vladi was about to argue but Julio continued, "We're instructed in the Bible, 'You shall love your neighbor as yourself.' When the Master brings to me someone with inadequate clothing or food, how am I loving them if I send them away without seeing to their basic needs? What does it reveal about who I am in my soul? I am a physician, and my work is to help people, regardless of their status."

Vladi decided to keep his thoughts to himself. Once Julio got going, he had learned, it was no use trying to interrupt.

"A human body without a soul is dead. Words are useless without the actions to back them up. So what would it mean if someone like me claims he has faith, yet my works, the fruits of my life, tell a different and irreconcilable reality?"

Julio didn't expect Vladi to answer this rhetorical question. Instead, he continued, having found a good segue. "Here's the more crucial matter — you've come right to the precipice between life and death more than once already. For whatever reason — only God knows — He's spared your life. Has that affected the way you view things?"

He noticed Vladi knit his brows in confusion. Julio berated himself inside for dancing around the point too much. So far, Vladi had remained calm, but Julio feared the anger that might erupt as he was about to touch a nerve. Rather than wait for a reply, he went ahead and explained what he meant.

"You've told me before that you don't believe there is a God. In that case, you wouldn't be accountable for your actions to anyone but yourself. But Vladi," Julio spoke his name in earnestness, with hopes that his sincerity would reach the man, "God has always existed whether or not you believe Him. He doesn't need any of us — we need Him. Faith is for our benefit, not for God's. Think about that. Vladi, you almost died. What if you hadn't recovered? Are you prepared for when you will stand in our Creator's presence to account for this life?"

Although he never let it show on his face, Vladi squirmed with discomfort. He wouldn't admit even to himself that, in the depths of his heart, he didn't know whether he truly had to answer to some higher authority and what judgment that could mean he would eventually face. Those doubts manifested themselves as irritation bordering on hostility, the frustration of which was about to be taken out on Julio.

Vladi remained unwavering that he owed nothing to a nonexistent God. "I do not need to live my life to please a judgmental bogeyman up in the sky."

"Then who do you live your life to please?" Julio asked rhetorically. He could see Vladi open his mouth, but held up his hand. "Before you say 'myself,' let me ask you this. When you were back in Russia, did you live entirely for yourself? No. As a child, you were answerable to your parents. Why? As a husband and father, you were accountable to your family, presumably because you loved them. In the military, were you not answerable to your superiors? That was your duty. Did you balk at orders in the military?"

"Never!" Vladi stated proudly and emphatically.

"Why then do you struggle with the idea of listening and answering to your Creator, who loves you and has every right to demand your obedient submission to His commands?" Julio asked in a kind tone.

"I had responsibilities toward those people. They were also responsible to me — for my life, for love, for my country," Vladi replied. "It could go in both directions. I could see for myself that they were there for me, and they could see I looked after them, unlike some imaginary God," Vladi returned a biting retort with a tone turning venomous. He became visibly agitated. "You want to talk about accountability?"

Vladi hesitated, exhaling rapidly, his face darkening in anger. In obstinance, he turned to look away from Julio, but then suddenly snapped back to face him.

"Where was your God when my flight home to my family dove into the Atlantic in the middle of the night?" Vladi shouted, flushed with long-held resentment. "Did your God feel obligated to come from the sky and save me? No! I saved myself!" In his rage, he overlooked Dan's significant part in his rescue. "I survived in the ocean alone, and granted, the Cubans helped at first, but I turned things around for myself! I worked hard to become a self-made man in a hostile country. No God handed me what I have."

Julio recoiled inside at Vladi's remarks — nonetheless, he listened with empathy. He knew that Vladi found it difficult to believe or trust in anyone but himself. He could see that Vladi was completely convinced of the infallibility of his own self-reliance, even if it bordered on delusion.

Julio also understood how Vladi had come to think this way. Vladi had survived an ordeal that most would not have, but he failed to recognize God's merciful intervention that preserved his life. Julio sensed that Vladi's extensive self-reliance must be exhausting and untenable. It sure wasn't bringing Vladi more joy — even with all his worldly accomplishments, Vladi's sense of emptiness deepened.

Despite the hard pushback from Vladi, the matter of Vladi's soul was immensely serious, and Julio wasn't ready to give up. He cared about Vladi enough to stay with him on this. Julio felt like this conversation wasn't finished, but unsure of how to continue, he silently prayed, *Lord, let me know confidence in the sufficiency and power of Your gospel. Your salvation is mighty. Without grace, we would all prefer You to leave us alone. He doesn't understand. Let him hear Your voice call from death to life. Strengthen me, Lord, to be faithful with Your truth. Please receive my prayer in Christ Jesus. Amen.*

Julio regained his composure and thoughtfully resumed their talk. "Vladi, I follow what you're saying about why you believe what you do, and no doubt you've felt the strain of maintaining that outlook given the circumstances. With all my heart, I believe there's help for that. Could I . . . could I just impose on you a little longer?"

Julio's eyes were so hopeful, it softened Vladi's face. The fuming redness had receded some, but Vladi didn't speak. Julio felt that he could continue, but perhaps he needed to adjust his approach for Vladi. He discerned Vladi's doubts.

In all other respects, Vladi is a logical thinker — reason-driven in how he approaches almost everything. So, if evidence is what he considers meaningful, that might be helpful.

With new resolve, he continued, "Vladi, there's something in us that makes every man naturally inclined to want to control our own lives. We live as though there is no God until creation and conscience testify to God's existence and, therefore, our accountability to Him. At that point, we must contend with our flesh, which is resistant to submit to an authority we can neither see nor touch. But does that mean there's no proof of His existence?

"In the pages of the Bible, our Creator has given us His own words for us — from Himself, about Himself. The reality of God is established by the integrity and reliability of His Word, not just by my awareness of His presence. God means for us to be wary of ourselves, mindful of why we doubt Him and why we cannot find Him, and awake to the deceptions in our own hearts. Instead, we must hold to the truth of His Word with every fiber of our being, even when we can't see Him. Consider what evidence exists that has been seen and touched by others before us.

"History accounts for a man almost two thousand years ago, conceived of a virgin, who claimed to be God incarnate and lived with perfect righteousness among other men. He defied all mathematical probability because His life fulfilled hundreds of prophecies, some written many centuries before His birth. In His brief three-and-a-half years of ministry, Jesus performed public miracles that even His enemies couldn't deny. This was the divine authentication of His claims to be the Son of God."

Vladi internally sighed. But he let Julio continue, seeing him grow more passionate by the second.

"Despite their firsthand experience and evidence they could see with their own eyes, many still refused to believe Him. It begs the question of whether their faith in Christ Jesus ever depended on what they could see for themselves. It didn't. Many people still rejected God-in-flesh when they could see Him with their own eyes and even touch Him."

Julio was every bit as logical and persistent as Vladi's sister, Olga, had ever been. But instead of conceding to Julio's reasoning, Vladi returned fire, unable to hold back any longer.

"Yes, but in the end, Jesus was a man who couldn't save Himself from death. Come now, exactly what is so divine about that?"

"It is true, He was put to death for claiming to be the Son of God," Julio acknowledged, "but that accomplished His purpose to redeem a people for Himself, even among His executioners. But it didn't end there. Three days later, He was resurrected to life as promised — a fact witnessed by hundreds of people, believers and unbelievers alike. Throughout time, skeptics have relentlessly sought to extinguish His disciples and the Bible that testifies of Him, but God has always preserved His truth.

"Vladi, ask yourself then, is He the greatest fraud in history, or is He the Son of God as He claimed? Honestly, which is easier to believe? If we can know that the accounts of His life were real because of overwhelming evidence, then we must acknowledge that what He said was truth, including the words He spoke about His Father in heaven. We also must admit that the truth of His death and resurrection holds up as well. He was the perfectly righteous sacrificial Lamb, who satisfied the wrath of God as the only acceptable substitute for all who will trust Him. He opened the only way for sinners to receive forgiveness and the acceptance of God.

"What does our dogged insistence on our own imagined sovereignty over a short life in this fallen world really have to offer? What idolatrous delusions? What hollow substitutes? Nothing compared to the greatest gift ever put forth to men — hope. Hope in receiving God's loving acceptance despite ourselves. That is what is meant by eternal life in Christ Jesus alone."

Vladi said nothing. He had an indecipherable look on his face. Julio gently proceeded, "My friend, you have known accomplishments in so many ways in this world. There's a question that we're given to bear in mind: 'What does it profit a man to gain the whole world, and forfeit his soul?' What if you had everything this world has to offer, Vladi, and then lost it all — everything — your soul not spared?"

Vladi gave no answer. Despite Julio's sound logic, he didn't betray the least hint of a reaction because he had numbed himself to Julio's words. He could neither refute Julio's assertions, nor bring himself to agree.

What Julio couldn't see was the storm of emotions brewing in Vladi's mind. He grappled to sort it out without conceding that Julio was right, but that only led to further frustration.

With a mixture of discouragement and hopefulness, Julio chose to leave the conversation at that. No matter what, Vladi had heard the truth. Julio knew Vladi had taken in every word he said but didn't want to accept it. He could only show his friend the way, not force him to believe. He also knew that signs and evidence alone could not in themselves produce saving faith — it had to come from God. Vladi had a tough shell and the machismo of a battle-hardened warrior.

Julio could see that Vladi put up a tough façade. What he didn't know was that Vladi was keeping silent simply because he didn't want to admit that Julio was guiding him lovingly toward the greatest need of his life.

TACKLE AT ROY'S

The ocean was warm. Perfect conditions for the fish to come out and play. Though he never matched his younger brother's fishing prowess, Vladi had always shared Erik's enthusiasm for fishing and being outdoors.

Some months had passed since the assault in the orchard. Vladi continued to regain his strength and mobility, although, at age sixty, it took longer than he expected. Whenever he felt able, he headed to the coast for his favorite pastime.

His first stop was always Roy's Bait & Tackle Shop in Hobe Sound, Florida, just across the Intracoastal Waterway from Jupiter Island. Roy's was somewhat of a local institution, a meeting place for fishermen to get a cup of coffee and snacks as they gathered provisions for a day or night of fishing. It had been in the same spot for over fifty years, ever since Roy and his wife had opened it in the early days of their long marriage.

On their honeymoon in the 1930s, they came upon a secluded road lined with banyan trees leading to a fishing pier along a quiet stretch of beach. The sand was clean, and the water looked so pretty — they felt like that would be a romantic place to camp. The old pier had a distinctive spot where the fish swarmed that they named Marilyn's Corner. The couple easily caught everything they wanted and more in their special little spot and had fresh dinner over their campfire each night. It felt like their lucky place, so they stayed.

They grew their little dream from a small bait camp to a thriving business. As they outgrew the space, they would just add on more. Years later, the result was a unique and jangly shop built from a hodgepodge of materials, with mismatched rooflines because of its evolving design. It was hardly an architectural work that would garner appreciation for its aesthetic character, but it had withstood hurricanes and the harsh salt air over time. Its weathered appearance contributed to the nostalgic vibe that Roy's regular customers felt such a connection to.

On this day, Vladi was among the fishermen who were grabbing their coffee and snacks before a day out on the water. Although he didn't mingle with the others, he kept his ears alert to overhear conversations about what types of fish were biting, where they were running, and the "secrets" of what other fishermen were using to catch them.

Walking towards the entrance, customers were greeted with a larger-than-life blue marlin mounted on the weathered blue-gray exterior of the building. Vladi shared in the amusement of new customers overheard exclaiming, "Look at that GIANT fish!"

Two freezers full of packaged ice stood like sentinels on each end of the front boardwalk. A sign on the front door with bold, orange letters announced, YES WE'RE OPEN. A chain of tinkling bells sounded as Vladi opened the shop door. He walked into the store with another customer behind him, although Vladi hardly noticed. As always, Vladi was mesmerized by the dazzling fiesta of merchandise on display.

Anticipating a big catch ahead, hopeful anglers showed up with what they called their "grocery list" for the fish, and Vladi was no different. Roy's business prospered, since customers' tackle shop grocery lists tended to be more expensive than their real grocery lists.

Inside, mounted saltwater game fish lined the top of the walls — flounder, shark, snapper, redfish, trout, and more. No matter how many times Vladi saw them, he always began his shopping by gazing at the parade of finned species hanging about. In particular, his eyes lingered on the glorious mount on the back wall, a sailfish that teased every fisherman's imagination.

There were dozens of framed photos spanning decades of patronage. They showed the shop's beloved owners, Roy and Marilyn, with loyal customers memorializing proud moments and a trophy catch. Over the years, Vladi had taken the time to look at each one, and sometimes he even felt a bit envious of those who had made it onto the "walls of fame." Despite the improbability of his being recognized there, Vladi never could have risked having his picture displayed in such a public manner.

Instead of a shopping basket, the shop provided bait buckets near the front door for fishermen to collect merchandise while they walked through the store aisles. The large and low-hanging American flag that hung over the front counter near the cash register grazed Vladi's shoulder as he bent down to take his bucket.

A freezer with worn-off paint just inside the front door was stocked with a variety of bait options such as shrimp and mullet. Vladi took a moment to think about what he wanted today. There was a good selection of live bait — shrimp, blue crabs, fiddler crabs, and finger mullet for catching big redfish — so it was always a difficult decision.

What am I looking to catch today? Do I feel ambitious? Vladi stood with his finger to his lips. *Yes, I will go with ambitious. So then, I will need cigar minnows or Spanish sardines for catching sharks and big cobia.*

A cat nonchalantly meandered like a drunken sailor through the aisles, waiting for a handout from some generous fisherman. Molly Brown had once been a "ship's cat." She had never hit an iceberg like her unsinkable namesake, but she'd weathered a few storms at sea and was deemed somewhat of a good luck charm to the fishermen who passed through. Vladi bent down to give his old furry friend a gentle pat on the head as they crossed paths. Vladi beamed as Molly Brown purred with contentment. Few things brought Vladi any sense of joy, but visiting Roy's beachside shop was one of them.

Despite all the years of acclimating to life in America, Vladi was still always astonished by the abundant assortment of products available to anyone with money to buy them. Among the experiences he found most amazing in America was going to supermarkets. He could never get over seeing all the variety of options on the shelves. Want a can of tuna? There would be at least five different brands, each claiming to be the best and most popular. Most fruits and vegetables were available any time of year. He could always get fresh produce and delicious meats — beef, pork, turkey, chicken. And here, even in a small establishment like Roy's, Vladi found himself slowly perusing every aisle, thinking.

He took his time wandering through the shop. He browsed all sizes of fishing poles and nets and colorful spools of fishing line. Aisle racks were filled with every imaginable sort of rigs, weights, hooks, and shiny lures. The more expensive reels glistened under the lights in a glass display case. As much as he wanted to get to the water and start casting, he couldn't help being "reeled in" by all the fishing gadgets and accessories.

A virtual arsenal of fishing knives lined one back wall. Their various sizes, colors, and shapes always attracted extra attention from the former Russian soldier. He picked up one of them and examined the blade, the fluorescent lights glinting off the shiny metal. There were two things that came from America that even Russians liked — Zippo lighters and American knives.

As usual, Vladi saw something in the shop that made him think about his brother, Erik. *If Erik had all this gear, there would be no more fish left in the world. He would catch them all!*

An awareness of another customer's presence roused Vladi from his sentimental moment. Despite being a few aisles away, Vladi could hear a man humming to himself.

Vladi glanced over, looking toward the other customer out of natural curiosity. Even though Vladi's height enabled him to see over the shelves, the racks of fishing rods on top obscured his view and made it difficult to observe the man in much detail. But he could see enough, and what Vladi thought he saw snapped him to attention and set his senses on high alert.

No, it cannot be. Vladi thought to himself. It was hard to know for sure. *My mind must be playing tricks on me.* Vladi didn't realize that he was now staring at the man.

Having endured the trauma of the crash and the privation that ensued, Vladi had been out of his senses during the entirety of their interaction. He couldn't even remember all of it. His mind had only retained fragments of memories, and the passage of so many years further clouded his recollection.

What's more, they were both older now, which was reflected in their appearance. Still, there was something familiar about the man. Somewhere in the depths of Vladi's mind, his brain registered that he knew him, and it insisted this was the same man. *But how can I be sure?*

The man seemed to be taking it easy as he ambled through the shop, munching on an apple for breakfast. Vladi didn't want to attract the other man's attention by examining him conspicuously. He cast his eyes down as if he were engrossed in the gear before glancing up again.

This time, the men caught each other's eyes just as the fellow bit into his apple. Both sets of eyes darted away from each other so as not to appear to stare, but not before Vladi glimpsed a detail indelibly etched into his mind. *Those unmistakable teeth — they could only belong to that skipper!*

Vladi's heart rate picked up as anxious adrenaline surged through his system. He had no way of knowing what this man was thinking. *Did I see a hint of recognition in his eyes as well?* Vladi worried. He had never said one word to the man, but had the skipper recognized him as a Soviet officer that day on the boat? If it was the skipper, friend or foe, this was the one person who could expose him.

And to make matters worse, Vladi was at the back of the store. Checking his exit routes, he realized his path out was blocked by the man. *I am cornered,* was his assessment. *There is no way out except past this guy.* It was a fight-or-flight predicament.

Although the political climate between the United States and the Soviets had been gradually changing, Vladi's own thinking lagged behind. He had become nearly politically agnostic over time, but his mind was entrenched in some of his own perceptions of the Cold War that he had formed before crashing into the ocean — almost as if he'd been frozen in time. From his point of view, he would always be a Soviet officer, and the United States would always be the Soviet Union's adversary. He believed that if anyone discovered his former identity, he would still be regarded as the enemy.

Vladi swore under his breath as he imagined the gravity of his situation. *I should have taken the chance to leave when the man was on the other aisle,* he chastised himself. In his peripheral vision, Vladi detected that the man was now staring at him more intently. Head down, trying to appear casual, Vladi avoided looking directly at him as he plotted his escape. Pretending to shop and not notice the man's attention, he tried to buy himself a few precious moments to think.

His long-dormant military conditioning began to surface. As a former Soviet special forces officer, Vladi had training that prepared him for almost every conceivable scenario. He asked himself intuitively, *Does this situation call for strategy or force?*

The fundamentals of close-quarters combat had been drilled into his mind, although he was bound to be rusty should it come to executing those moves. *Violent action should not be the first option if it can be avoided, especially since it could attract more unwanted attention,* Vladi recited to himself. Instead, could he pretend that he didn't recognize the man? *It might be too late for that.* The man surely caught the surprise in his eyes. But perhaps Vladi could still pull off ignorance.

The man got closer, and Vladi tensed. *Time is running out. I must decide how to handle the situation!* Vladi tracked the man through quick, furtive glances.

Next aisle over — he was there. *Should I just try to leave? If I cannot, should I somehow approach him?* As he wondered what to do, the man changed from humming to singing a song he recognized.

The man sang in a low voice . . . "Back in the U.S.S.R.," the Beatles hit from 1968 — a song that told Vladi everything he needed to know. Vladi had always been miffed that the Beatles had never actually visited the Soviet Union. They sang of something they knew nothing about, yet they capitalized on it anyway. On the other hand, Vladi liked the song because American kids had grown up singing this contemporary patriotic anthem that extolled the glories of the *rodina*, his motherland, perhaps to the chagrin of their elders. But in this context, it meant peril to Vladi. The man did know who he was.

As soon as the man rounded the corner, Vladi's eyes followed him. He had a clear unobstructed look at Vladi — and, within a split second, Vladi could read the sureness in his eyes.

Vladi's military conditioning kicked in — it was second nature. He had no more time for contemplation.

The man started to speak. In one swift move Vladi dropped his bucket and snatched a nine-inch stainless steel filet knife hanging from the wall at eye level. He grabbed the man and whipped him around, pushing him up against the back wall where an aisle endcap could obscure an onlooker's view.

Before a word could leave the man's mouth, Vladi had the blade between the man's lips. Moving to within inches of the man's eyes, Vladi gritted his teeth and snarled under his breath, "I have stuck wild boars three times your size! If you say anything, I will cut you a new set of gills and filet you from ear to ear!"

The man looked up at the sign hanging above the knife display — it read, "One cut and you're through." The irony did not slip past him.

Vladi needed confirmation that the man would submit, so with a low menacing voice he asked, "Do you understand?" and backed off the pressure just enough to allow the man to respond.

The man held up his hands and yielded, and Vladi cautiously provided an opportunity for him to talk. "Man, was my singin' that bad?" The skipper was surprisingly even-keeled, considering Vladi's manner of greeting.

Vladi was as brave as any man. Seeing this fellow was unshaken won respect in Vladi's eyes, but he wasn't as taken with the skipper's sense of humor.

"You are pretty feisty for a mermaid, buddy." The man tested his humor a bit further. "First time, I thought you might be tryin' to take me out with my speargun."

Vladi just continued to stare stone-faced without the slightest change in expression.

The quirky skipper remained unflustered by Vladi's stern expression. He squinted one eye and leaned in towards Vladi's face. "Hey, where'd you go anyway?" he asked in a conspiratorial half-whisper.

Vladi remained silent. *Is this guy as crazy as he seems?* Vladi had to wonder. Whether the fellow was in his right mind or not, Vladi wasn't sure if or how he wanted to answer this question.

"Hmmm. You never were much of a talker, were ya?" he chuckled. Trying to defuse the tension, Dan let him off the hook without an answer. "I didn't realize you were a fisherman," Dan continued. "But then again, why should I be surprised to find a mermaid in a tackle shop?"

Vladi's mind was racing. Normally, he was quick to size people up and read the situation, but for once he didn't know what to think about the other man. The skipper was an enigma, unfazed by icy stares and stony silence. That kind of strength seemed in opposition to the light-hearted demeanor he portrayed. Vladi couldn't reconcile his incongruent comportment.

Although the skipper could pose a potential threat, Vladi didn't sense that about him so much now. Still wary, Vladi remained reluctant to trust that gut feeling. *This skipper might be a convincing actor — really, he could be anyone. He is not actually a captain of anyone, just a guy with a boat who likes fishing excursions. What he does the rest of the time is anyone's guess.* Hence Vladi remained guarded.

"Name's Dan, by the way," the skipper said as though he were introducing himself to a new friend, not someone who had a knife to his face. "What are ya' fishin' fer today?" Dan tried once more from another angle to get some conversation started.

This guy does not give up, Vladi thought to himself. *Why does he keep talking to me when I do not answer? Why is he so nice, knowing I could kill him any moment?*

As if oblivious to Vladi's guarded silence, Dan kept right on going, "Redfish are bitin'. I'm goin' fer the limit today. Hey, how'd you like to come with me?"

Dan asked with genuine amiableness, as if they had been old friends who had just happened to run into each other. Vladi could hardly conceal his perplexed look. It was the one thing Dan said that caught him off guard. Until he spoke his next question.

"You remember my boat, eh?" Dan leaned in again and asked with a smile and a wink.

What? Vladi's head was screaming, although he remained mute.

But there was something curious about this skipper, something that drew Vladi. Maybe it was his jovial demeanor, or maybe it was the fact that he wouldn't shut up despite Vladi's stubborn lack of response. *One does not encounter this type of tenacity every day,* Vladi thought, bemused.

This presented another dilemma for Vladi. The first consideration, and the one of most concern, was that this generous overture could lead to a trap.

I would be vulnerable aboard the boat with no place to run. On the other hand, if I accompany the skipper, I can keep an eye on him to ensure he does not leave and talk to the authorities or to another blabby fisherman. Vladi was still the skipper's largest catch to date, after all.

One more consideration — an offshore fishing excursion was an offer that appealed to Vladi. *Besides, I would actually like to go.* Dan hadn't done anything bad so far. If he had wanted to, Dan could have already compromised Vladi, but he hadn't.

Vladi lowered the knife and nodded. *Maybe he is okay, after all.*

REEL SECRETS

In the season following the great freeze, Vladi invested his resources back into his operations by replanting the Red Star Citrus groves. Now, they could only wait for the orchards to recover and get back to full production. Vladi wasn't the most patient person — he found waiting stressful in itself.

As hard as it was to wait for trees to grow, it did allow Vladi time to think about other things. His thoughts frequently returned to the political climate of his native country. Despite Vladi's personal reservations about General Secretary Mikhail Gorbachev, the Soviet leadership had become more receptive to Gorbachev's reform ideas about glasnost and perestroika. After six decades of oppression and secrecy, Gorbachev sought to steer the country on a course of greater openness as well as political and economic restructuring.

Vladi's idealism about government had faded with his age, especially after experiencing life in America. Frankly, he wasn't so committed to any system or particular national policies anymore. He didn't care. However, he saw the improving political relationship between the Soviet Union and the United States as a chance to be reunited with his family, and that was all that mattered. Vladi thought that the time had come for him to act.

If I could simply hold my daughters in my arms again, I would gladly give up everything I have here. I wish to meet our child — perhaps a son — I am not sure. Irina must have endured so much hardship alone for these many years. My dear Irina . . . What then? There must be a way to go to them or bring them to me. I have to put my mind to it and think about how. His brain never stopped strategizing about how to make this happen.

Brrrrrrrnnng! The phone ringing snapped Vladi's mind back to reality. It was Dan. Since the day Dan noticed him in Roy's and invited him fishing, Vladi's perception had changed. He'd realized Dan wasn't a threat and had even come to regard him as a friend. If Dan called, only one thing could be on his mind — going fishing. Vladi chuckled to himself, *Always with the fishing. I do not think he cares or even thinks about anything else.* It was probably not far from the truth.

"Hey, mate, the new gal is ready fer her maiden voyage. I'm gonna be headin' out soon. Care to join?" Dan's cheerful voice was a sweet and welcoming sound on the other end of the line. As always, Vladi couldn't help but smile — Dan was one of the few people in the world who never failed to coax a smile out of him. In a way, he envied Dan's happy-go-lucky outlook, because nothing ever dampened his friend's spirit — not even him.

"Of course, my friend. I have nothing better to do," Vladi answered. He meant to sound sarcastic, but Dan took it at face value and replied in his cheery-Dan fashion, "Great, I'll see you soon, mate!" Vladi hung up the phone, but his smile stayed with him even after the conversation ended.

Dan was a master angler. He had recently upgraded his faithful, old forty-foot fishing boat to a brand new fifty-foot Viking Sport Fisherman, christened the *Reel Secrets* II. Dan had the vessel customized with a Simrad autopilot, state-of-the-art Loran-C radar, and twin Detroit Diesel engines that generated 735 horsepower each. The 805-gallon long-range fuel tank enabled him to venture much farther than the 250-gallon tank on his old boat.

In a way, Dan felt nostalgic about the classic wooden hull on his old boat, but having a fiberglass hull now meant less maintenance and more time fishing. Dan spared no expense on the interior of the new boat, either. It had an enclosed, air-conditioned cabin with multiple staterooms, a spacious head with a shower, leather upholstery, and a full galley with an icemaker — luxury accommodations by fishing boat standards. Dan also had an FM VHF radio installed to communicate with other boats in the area in case of any unforeseen emergencies.

Best of all, it wasn't all for show, because Dan always knew where to find the fish. He often inspected the six stainless steel rod holders he had installed on the new boat. Four contained brand new Penn Senators, each loaded with sixty pound monofilament line. The other two held Penn Internationals with wide spools and eighty pound mono for those marlins he would soon be chasing. The black and purple skirted lures that he'd just bought at Roy's Bait & Tackle Shop were guaranteed to be irresistible to the marlins — at least Roy said so, and he would know. Dan always liked it when Vladi could come along, in part because Vladi would spring for fuel and supplies.

Dan's eyes, kind and weathered, reminded Vladi of his grandfather's. Sometimes they would spend days out at sea. As always, Dan did most of the talking, usually about business and life. But there were days they could go for hours without saying a word.

They usually fished the deep waters off the east coast of Florida, but now it was late in the season. The end of September into early October was almost late enough to avoid tropical storms but nearly too late for the best fishing.

"Heard the sailfish and marlin were running south in the gulf between Isla Mujeres and Cuba. It's a long way down there, but worth the trip. What'dya say?" Dan proposed as he readied the vessel, knowing Vladi wouldn't object.

"Sure, why not. I have plenty of time on my hands these days," Vladi said with a casual shrug. In truth, he would be glad to put as much distance between him and life's cares as he could.

Klaus was the thirteenth tropical storm of the season. It had only briefly intensified into a hurricane during the first week of October 1990. Vladi and Dan waited until it passed before they set sail across the open water of the Gulf of Mexico.

Beyond surface conversation about the activities at hand, namely fishing, Dan and Vladi enjoyed swapping ideas about business. Both had keen minds about how to allocate resources and navigate the challenges of their commercial endeavors and investments. With enough time, they inevitably exhausted those topics, and their conversations turned deeper.

For the longest time, Vladi had avoided the subject of his family. Now, he finally felt like he could confide in Dan.

"I have a family in Russia," he let the words tumble out with no warning or fanfare. "I have a wife and three daughters and a child I have never met. My wife was pregnant when I left for Cuba. I do not know if I have a son or another daughter. But I miss them so much — every day."

If Dan was surprised, he didn't let it show. His face remained neutral, and he let Vladi talk, something he'd been hoping would happen for some time.

Vladi leaned his forearms on the side of the boat and stared into the sun-glinted sapphire waters. He continued without checking for Dan's reaction. "I want nothing more in this life than to be with them again. What does my business mean? What does money mean? It is nothing to me without them. Nothing." Vladi paused in an attempt to keep his voice from breaking. He cleared his throat. "I think that now the time is right to go back home. Political winds have changed. It is more favorable now. But . . . " Vladi was unsure if he could express his fears aloud.

"But?" Dan asked with sincerity. "What's keepin' ya? We can turn this gal around right now. Ain't nothin' to keep you from leavin'."

"I . . . I am . . . " Vladi lifted his head and pushed out a hard breath. "I am concerned about what I will find out about them after all this time," the words rushed out, louder and faster than he intended. Those thoughts had finally traveled from their confined place in his mind to the open air. Anguished questions followed. "Will my wife be married to another man? If so, do my children call him Papa? Will they know who I am? What have they been told about me? Have they been grieving all through these years, thinking I died? So many difficult questions. They torment me day and night. I am afraid to learn the answers, yet I need to know or I will never have peace."

Dan nodded slowly, understanding Vladi's predicament. He put a sympathetic hand on Vladi's shoulder. Vladi let his head hang once again — his blank stare didn't even register the pod of dolphins that passed beneath the boat.

"That is not all," Vladi continued. "I am not convinced it is safe for me to return to Russia. It is said that Gorbachev calls for better relations between the Soviet Union and the United States, but I am not sure if I can trust American news. How can I know they accurately represent the real sentiments within my country?"

His dreams of reuniting with his family were punctuated with nightmarish scenarios. The aggressive KGB he knew would intercept him the moment he stepped off the plane. They would never accept his story and would immediately peg him as a spy or collaborator. In fact, if they knew he was alive in America, they wouldn't stop short of sending agents after him here. There was no place to hide. Time had moved on, but in some ways, Vladi's anxieties remained trapped in another era.

Dan astutely wondered if Vladi had allowed this to be a bigger hindrance in his mind than it rightly needed to be. He probed Vladi's concerns in a kind-hearted manner that he hoped would gently nudge Vladi to follow through on his intentions.

"The political relationships have definitely changed for the better," Dan reassured him. "Maybe you're lettin' old concerns hinder ya more than they should?"

Vladi's lip curled in a sneer, and he huffed, "You do not understand the KGB, my friend."

That seemed like a fair assessment to Dan. He acknowledged as much to Vladi, "No doubt. I don't have firsthand experience livin' in such an overtly authoritarian society. I have to take your word for it. You would know better than anyone what perils ya might face."

Vladi mused aloud, more to himself than Dan, "I will need to make contact in a discreet way." Depending on how that went, he might try to bring his family to America, assuming they agreed and were allowed to leave the country. "I do not regret that I have come to know America. I would like for them to know this America. Here, people believe in life, liberty, and the pursuit of happiness. It is in your Declaration of Independence, no? Whether or not they realize those things is not guaranteed or perfect, but they live with that hope. That is the difference between here and the USSR and Cuba. Americans live with hope — hope that life can always be better. Who is to say otherwise?"

Dan nodded in acknowledgement. He chewed on the thought a while before he spoke up again.

"It's that part about 'the pursuit of happiness' that is so elusive," Dan reflected. "We may pursue it with everything we've got, but some of us never find it."

Vladi raised an eyebrow. It seemed like an odd reply coming from Dan. Given Dan's ever-cheery demeanor, Vladi assumed he had to be one of the happiest people in the world. Usually a wellspring of wit, Dan continued to open up in an uncharacteristic manner.

"Ya know, my friend, this new gal is a beauty, and she runs pretty well. She's all I've got, and I ain't complaining, but she can't fix things."

Vladi cocked his head and returned a curious look. "What things does she need to fix? A broken fishing reel?" Compared to Dan's, Vladi's comedic abilities fell short. "Russian humor," Vladi conceded.

"Did I ever tell ya how I came to name this gal, *Reel Secrets*?"

"Perhaps about fishing?" Vladi couldn't suppress a smile. "Well, I just thought that was a secret anyway." *More Russian humor*, Vladi thought.

"You're a sharp one, buddy. I suppose ya know all about keepin' secrets. Well, I ain't never told anyone, but since we're sharin' secrets, here goes . . . " It was Dan's turn to take a deep breath.

"Back in Jersey, I also had a family — my wife and I had a little boy. I'd been in real estate and doin' well. Always had a head for business — maybe too good, 'cause it took a lot of time to be that good."

Vladi nodded in understanding.

"You know what that's like. We needed money in the early days, but we reached a point when we had enough. When you're good at what you do, it's easy to get caught up in the game. My family was on the sidelines.

"When it got to be too much strain for her, my wife chastised me for neglectin' my family. She was right, and I knew it. My little buddy was six. That's a sweet age. Little boys think their dad is Superman — the best in the world — that ya know everythin' and do everythin' right. The next weekend, I took him fishing — ya know, fishing is good father-son time."

Vladi let a small smile tug at his lips. He would have loved to share his fishing experience with his own son — that was, if he had one.

"It's just . . . that . . . time . . . it wasn't enough time." Dan's words rasped as his throat seemed to close. Hands clasped together in a vise grip, arms parallel to Vladi's on the side of the boat. He also let his head drop to look into the deep blue. He paused for a few moments to pull himself together.

Vladi looked out over the water without a word. Dan was irrepressibly cheerful, even under the most trying circumstances, but right now, Vladi was genuinely concerned about what was going on with his friend. He had no idea what memories were finding their way to the surface. He said nothing, just listened.

"We were off the Jersey shore in an old 1950 Chris Craft Riviera, one of those mahogany beauties. It was a shallow bay boat, designed to be perfectly comfortable in protected waters. But a twenty-footer was too light to be out on the open water. I never should've left the bay. When you're young, sometimes ya don't have enough sense or life experience to know better.

"An early summer storm was brewin' off to the west. The cold water welled up from the deep, drivin' the warm water further out — just teemin' with all sorts of fish from the murky depths. The finnys were bitin' real good, and I got too comfortable, figured it wouldn't be too bad. What's a little wind, ya know? Not like a hurricane or nothin'. But let me tell ya, sometimes it's like the devil blew on the ocean! By the time I realized there was trouble, we were facin' a headwind and had to get back to shore fightin' it in that little Chris Craft. Its small engine was no match pushin' against that gale wind and strong current. I couldn't concentrate on anything else. Was all I could do to keep the bow of the boat facin' the oncoming waves. I knew if I could do that she wouldn't capsize, so I was focused — completely focused — on that."

Dan let out a breath. Clearly it had been many years since he had shared this story. Vladi could relate. He remained silent, just listening while Dan bared his soul.

"The rain started comin' harder and harder, the kind that hits your face like little stingin' pellets. The chop bounced us like it might splinter the hull every time it slammed back down on the water. It rattled every bone in my body. I can't imagine how it must have felt to a kid. He might have been scared. Maybe he thought it was fun. Maybe a little of both. I don't know, I was so preoccupied with gettin' us back. By the time I gave it a thought, it was too late to go fer our life jackets. Just minutes before we'd been fishin' comfortably without 'em. Who wants to fish wearin' one of them bulky life preservers, right? I had 'em neatly stowed where we could get 'em without much trouble. But trouble we had, 'cause it kept gettin' worse — the ocean churned real bad. I shouted over the wind to hang on with all his might and don't let go 'til we're home.

"Then in one careless moment . . . " Dan's voice broke. He took a deep breath, then he rasped out, "I let a wave catch us from the side. That little boat came out of the water nearly vertical. His tiny hands, those chubby little fingers, they just couldn't hold on. He went overboard. He didn't make a sound. I just saw the soles of his little sneakers as they disappeared over the side." Dan paused for a long while, his head all the way down. His voice faintly escaped from his lips. "We never found him."

There was silence. Vladi said nothing. There was nothing to say.

"My wife never forgave me. Can't say I blame her. Heck, I haven't ever been able to forgive myself. Sorrow broke her. She lost her mind and left. She couldn't be with me. I was a constant reminder to her of what had happened. Her child was gone forever, and it was my fault. I've been alone ever since."

Dan pulled off his cap and ran a hand through his hair. Vladi pretended not to notice when he wiped at his eyes.

"What's more, the police examinations made me relive it over and over . . . and over. They finally concluded it was accidental, but it felt like rippin' the scab off the wound every time we retraced what happened. "In my mind, those next few years were like livin' in a dark tunnel with no light at the end. Yeah, exactly like that. I don't know a better way to describe it.

"I gave her half of everything and then some. I took what was left, bought the old boat, invested enough to keep her runnin', and shoved off to Florida. Never looked back. I didn't want to think about the responsibilities of the life I left back on shore.

"You'd think I might have given up fishing. For some reason, it provides some temporary solace. Whenever I catch a good one, I like to think my boy is there along with me. Sometimes when I'm out on the water by myself, I talk to little Alex. That was his name — Alexander." Dan paused again. "But however much I wish, he never answers me back."

Dan straightened up and rolled his shoulders, as though shaking off the memories. Vladi remained leaning on the rail, looking out at the sea.

"I didn't mean to get all sappy," Dan said, turning to face Vladi. "Hearing you talk about goin' back to your family just got me thinkin' about it. If I were you, I'd go be with my family. It would be my life mission — whatever the risk, whatever it takes. I can never get my family back, but at least you have a chance. Don't lose it, buddy."

Touched by Dan's story, but not one to show his emotions, Vladi stepped closer to Dan and rested a firm hand on his shoulder. They were alike in many ways, and he wouldn't say it, but he hoped Dan knew how much he appreciated his listening to his own story. He also respected that Dan trusted him enough to tell him his own secrets.

Dan let out a long sigh that was more of an exclamation from the bottom of his soul. "Ya know, you can sometimes feel like you're all alone, and no one in the world can understand the pain you're feelin' inside. Thanks, buddy." He returned the gesture and put a comforting hand on Vladi's shoulder. "Now I know I'm not alone anymore."

MOST DANGEROUS CATCH

wo days into Dan and Vladi's fishing excursion, a new low-pressure area emerged over the Straits of Florida and, by October 10, quickly intensified into Tropical Storm Marco. Marco peaked with sixty-five mile-per-hour winds, but it remained just offshore of the western coast of Florida, cutting off any homeward retreat for the two men. They found themselves running the boat through a seam where black sea met charcoal sky. The calm and uneventful voyage they'd enjoyed so far gave way to a few tense hours until they cleared the weather system.

The lights of Cuba twinkled in the southern distance. Almost half a lifetime had passed since Vladi had last seen them, nearly three decades ago. His mind wandered back to memories of his time stationed there. Bittersweet as the feelings were that accompanied those reflections, there was just something about it. The island felt like a magnet drawing him back.

He was jolted back into the moment when Dan broke the silence. "Hope that's not what I'm thinking," Dan blurted, pointing to the lights of a fast-approaching craft advancing off the starboard. As it drew closer, Vladi identified the oncoming vessel. It was a Soviet Pauk-class corvette, a small patrol ship that belonged to the *Tropas Guardafronteras*, the Cuban coast guard.

"Looks like half the Cuban Navy there," Vladi quipped.

Dan checked his location to make sure he hadn't strayed into Cuban waters. His instruments showed he was still at least twenty miles outside of their territory. As much as Dan could determine, there had been no incursion. "They're hunting outside their jurisdiction," Dan muttered as the Cubans fired two shotgun flares about five seconds apart. Both men's heads followed as the flares arced past Dan's boat and landed in the water. The Cuban crew throttled their engines and closed in. Vladi and Dan turned to each other with trepidation splashed across their faces, both for different reasons.

Cuban authorities routinely kept a scrutinizing eye on their coastal waters. Even though they were well north of the maritime boundary line, this sort of dubious maneuver was all too common. The Cuban coast guard never let a few miles of open water stop them from intercepting vessels, hoping for a shakedown.

Unlicensed fishermen could face steep fines and have their boats and gear impounded if they were caught. The Cuban coast guard didn't need to look hard to find plenty of illegal activity in these waters. But just to make it worthwhile, they had refined their approach so they could sometimes intimidate others to extort bribes. Dan's nice boat was a prime candidate for such an exploratory stop.

Dan gave Vladi a quick summary of what he thought to be happening, and Vladi's countenance darkened. Vladi had been a lieutenant colonel in the Soviet military — he wasn't about to be intimidated by their ploys. He took a defensive stance on the deck — feet wide apart and arms crossed over his broad chest. He stared at the coast guard vessel, never taking his eyes away as it approached.

As the craft closed in on them, a thickly accented voice blared commands from a bullhorn, "*Guardacostas! Alto! . . . Parada para embarcar!*"

Although Dan didn't understand much Spanish, he'd been at sea enough to know when a coast guard was ordering him to stop.

The Cuban vessel pulled up alongside the *Reel Secrets II* and, without waiting for it to stop, an overeager coast guardsman attempted a grand, dramatic leap onto Dan's boat. However, between the forward movement and the wave chop, he misjudged the trajectory of his vault. He slipped a little as he launched himself from the boat and almost missed the side of Dan's craft. He hit his chest and chin on the side of the boat and clung to the edge with just his elbows, arms hooked over the side.

The fellow's shipmates gave exasperated shouts. "*Ay, tonto!*" said one, shaking his head as he prepared for a proper boarding.

No one moved to assist the coast guardsman struggling to pull himself over the side and onto the deck of Dan's boat. Least willing of all to come to his aid was Vladi, who loomed over the man like a stone monolith and glared at him as he wrestled to get on board. No longer able to watch the spectacle, Dan rolled his eyes and with an air of exasperation grabbed the back of the man's shirt, unceremoniously rolling him over the side and onto the boat like a flopping fish.

The coast guard officer jumped to his feet and mirrored Vladi's stance in a vain effort to recover his dignity. His colleagues joined him on Dan's deck. Several of the other coast guardsmen took positions around Dan and Vladi.

"What is this about, *señor*?" Dan courteously asked the officer who seemed to be in charge. He wanted to tell them that their boarding was illegal, but thought it would be better not to start out with a confrontational approach. Assuming that they didn't understand much English anyway, an angry tone could come across as antagonistic.

"*Inspección de seguridad,*" the man replied with a haughty air as he scanned the deck. Dan deduced from words that sounded familiar that they had boarded his boat under the pretense of a "safety inspection."

One of the coast guardsmen looked at Dan and asked, "*Armas?*"

"What? *No comprendo,*" Dan said. He didn't know many Spanish words beyond taco, burrito, enchilada. Oh yeah, and guacamole.

"*Armas?! Armas?!*" the officer repeated emphatically, pointing at his gun.

"He wants to know if you have any guns." Vladi whispered, turning his head down to translate.

"Oh! No, nothing in there but fishing stuff," Dan replied, mimicking the casting of a reel. But the officer had already stopped listening. Instead, he directed his crew to search the boat.

Though Dan hadn't moved, the officer held up an arm in front of Dan as if to block him. "*Por tu seguridad,*" he assured Dan. Reiterating that the inspection was for safety reasons, he intimated that this was conducted for Dan's own good. No matter how often he repeated it, Dan knew it was nothing but a ruse.

"*Ay, tonto!*" The words came hurling across the deck by a coastguardsman when a stray fishing rod got tossed into his face and jabbed him in the eye. Holding a hand over his wounded orb, he pushed the offender, who then pushed him back, and an impassioned exchange ended with the men grappling with each other on the floor of the deck. Dan couldn't understand what they were saying, but it was most assuredly full of heated curses. He shook his head, rolling his eyes again.

Are these guys actually Cuba's official coast guard? he wondered. *If so, how did they ever make it in? Such amateurs — it is embarrassing to even watch them.*

The crew radio squawked something unintelligible, and two more crew members boarded Dan's boat. Dan stiffened with greater unease about how this encounter might unfold.

One of the coast guardsmen, the second in command, pointed at Vladi and asked something in Spanish, although he spoke too fast for Vladi to understand. Speaking slower, he shortened his request, which he directed at Vladi. "*Identificación.*" Vladi knew what the officer was asking but acted as if he didn't understand. He shrugged his shoulders and tried to appear perplexed.

Vladi knew that the moment he opened his mouth, his Russian accent would be a dead giveaway. These coast guardsmen were goons, but the lead officer was sharper than the others. There was a chance he would question the incongruence between Vladi's native accent and his American ID. For this reason, Vladi remained resolutely silent.

The number two officer seemed annoyed that he needed to repeat himself, but this time tried to repeat the question in his best English.

"Your papers?"

Without protest, Dan and Vladi handed over their IDs. Vladi's fake ID as Moses Moskowitz had so far been convincing enough to get past officials in Florida — hopefully, it would pass with the Cubans too.

The coast guardsmen initially assumed from Vladi's dark features that he was Latino. The name on his identification was decidedly not of Latin origin, though, and the second officer looked between Vladi and his ID picture several times. He called the lead officer over, showed him the ID, and both men scrutinized Vladi with suspicion.

The officer in charge then pointed his finger, and Vladi could feel his heart drop. His tank top showed just the edge of the tattoo on his chest, but not enough for the Cubans to see the design. Even so, it piqued the curiosity of the already skeptical officer.

"*Ciudadanía?*" he asked Vladi. The officers didn't trust Vladi's identification and questioned him further. "Your country?!" he tried again in English, then muttered with irritation, "*Qué pasa con este hombre?*" Vladi knew the officer was wondering what was going on with him.

Dan noted Vladi's lack of response and the slight, anxious twitch of his eye. He saw Vladi's jaw tense. He could guess why Vladi remained silent. Vladi met his eyes, and Dan imagined a range of thoughts and scenarios running through Vladi's head at the moment. The men stared at each other knowingly. Dan held his breath and waited several seconds that felt like an eternity in anxious anticipation of what Vladi would do. He wracked his brain, thinking fast of something to get these jokers off the scent.

"Hey, you know what, I think you must have missed something inside the cabin," he said, making smoking gestures. But the officer ignored his ruse. Desperate, Dan pulled a wad of money out of his pocket. If these guys were just looking for a shakedown, maybe giving them what they wanted would get them to leave.

"Here, here. Dinero." He held out the money towards the officer. An imprudent junior officer leaped forward and took it. Without breaking eye contact with Dan, the lead officer swatted the cash out of the younger man's hands. The money swirled all about the breezy deck. The other goons shoved one another out of the way, distracted from the task at hand by trying to grab the fluttering bills.

Dan could discern from the slow blink and upward roll of the senior officer's eyes that his men were further exasperating him and worsening the situation. *"Cesen!"* he bellowed. *"O los mataré a todos!"*

Dan wasn't sure what the officer was saying but figured it was a threat. The offending coast guardsmen froze, slowly shoving the money into their pockets and sheepishly returning to the task at hand. One of the men mumbled petulantly as he looked down at his shoes, earning himself a disapproving look from his senior officer.

Already irritated, the lead officer was further enraged by Vladi's lack of response. *"Eres muy grosero. Ahorita, dame una repuesta. Cuál es su ciudadanía?"*

Vladi mentally translated the officer's words: *You are very rude. Now, give me an answer. What is your citizenship?*

When Vladi still didn't respond, the officer got right up in Vladi's face. "Your country, *chico?*" the officer said in English, dragging the words out in a slow, controlled way that denoted his mounting displeasure.

Vladi knew this guy was on a serious power trip, but he was caught in a bind. Back in his days in Cuba, he would have been confident and ready to take the coast guardsmen in a fight, no matter how risky the outcome. But now, years later, there was no doubt that he would be on the losing end of any aggression he started. More than just concerned for himself, he was also worried about the possibility that Dan would get caught up in a mess just for being with him, or even worse, end up hurt.

The lead officer's fuse was short, and Vladi's continued silence cemented his decision. Keeping his face close to Vladi's, he ordered his men, *"Ponlos en esposas."*

As two of his subordinates followed his instructions and reached for their handcuffs, it was clear he had decided Dan and Vladi's fate. They were being arrested.

The officers grabbed Dan by the arms first.

"Hey, wait a minute! You can't do this! We're Americans! *Americanos!* This is illegal — we're a flagged United States vessel! We aren't even in Cuban waters!" Dan yelled in desperation. He was never one to clam up under pressure, even if opening his mouth was his undoing.

Vladi saw this as his do-or-die moment. His arm lashed out and clutched onto the officer's wrist. Menacingly, he growled in perfect Spanish, "Let him go. If you hurt him, I will kill you."

Surprised by the threat delivered in Spanish, the man dropped his grip on Dan's arm. Every Cuban on board turned to stare at Vladi.

The lead officer grinned like a Cheshire cat. *"Entonces, hablas español."* Behind him, Vladi could hear the other goons speaking in hushed tones. He could only make out one word: *"Ruso."* They had easily picked up on his Russian accent.

Dan panicked and tried to turn the attention back to himself. "No, arrest me. I'm the captain. He had nothin' to do with anythin'. He's only a tourist client I took fishing. Leave him alone." Even if the Cubans could understand him, nothing he said would help. The men had their full attention on Vladi now. Dan could see the veins bulging in Vladi's neck.

"So much for going home to Russia," Vladi muttered within earshot of Dan. He had a sudden hollow feeling in the pit of his stomach. His life would be over if he were to be taken into custody by Cuban authorities. He knew about Cuban prisons, and he once knew a Cuban prosecutor with a seared moral conscience and a personal grudge against him. If he were to be sent there, he would have little hope of ever leaving the island alive. His forearms flexed as he clenched his fists.

The lead officer approached Vladi again. "*Eres Ruso?*" he demanded, his eyes darting up and down. Vladi refused to concede to being Russian. His military training dictated never to give the enemy information. Besides, any response he offered would be further betrayed by his discernible accent.

Under orders from the lead officer, the men attempted to restrain Vladi. Vladi hadn't wanted things to get physical, but he was now running out of options. With characteristic vigor, the stout Russian jerked away from the men — he wouldn't be put in handcuffs.

Trying to help his crewmates, one goon grabbed onto Vladi's tank top and tore open his shirt. If they had any doubts about his nationality, the hammer-and-sickle tattoo emblazoned across his heart removed them all. The ranking officer who had boarded their boat directed the others to hold Vladi still as he approached to inspect the tattoo more closely.

His lips curled in a sneer as the officer looked Vladi square in the eye and asked, "*Vy Russkiy?*" Vladi couldn't hide his surprise to hear the man speak Russian. The officer noticed he understood the language. "*Da, ya tozhe mogu govorit' na vashem yazyke,*" he told Vladi with a laugh. Yes, he spoke his language as well, appearing to delight in the fleeting expression of astonishment that crossed Vladi's face. He gestured for the other coast guardsmen to proceed with the arrest as ordered.

While the coast guardsmen were preoccupied with trying to restrain Vladi, Dan couldn't remain idle. He sprang toward the cabin and reached for Captain Hook, his trusty, rusty fishing harpoon. He knew there was an old saying that you never bring a knife to a gunfight, but he was out of options.

As the men worked to cuff Vladi, Dan's booming voice cut through the commotion. "Can I have your attention, gentlemen?"

The coast guardsmen froze and turned their attention to Dan, who stood with the harpoon facing them and sternly warned them to back off and leave his friend alone. "Let him go, or I'll run ya all right through!" He jabbed at the air with the harpoon to accentuate his threat.

His point was taken but not well received.

Two goons vaulted toward Dan from either side. He swung his harpoon from side to side, striking them both in the gut with the blunt end and dropping them to the deck.

Vladi didn't waste the opportunity. Breaking loose from the bumbling coast guardsmen who were attempting to restrain him, he sprang for the "hip loader" speargun that hung just inside the cabin door. He had one shot. It had to count.

With a quick aim at the second in command, he pulled the trigger. Vladi's weapon hit its mark. The arrow went straight through the officer's neck, the sharp, pointed end projecting out the other side. A small stream of blood trickled from the officer's neck as he stood in shock. For a second, everything seemed to stop, an eerie silence falling over the boat, then the officer collapsed face down onto the deck.

Dan bravely leaped between Vladi and the goons, Captain Hook still in hand, brandishing the harpoon's tip with an unspoken threat he was committed to keeping.

Dan's good-natured personality had suddenly transformed into something far more fearsome and primal. His ordinarily upbeat and chipper voice now transitioned to a deep growl. He let out a guttural sound, as fearsome as the most sea-hardened captain ever to traverse the Caribbean waters.

The chief officer's face turned dark with hostility. A cold, cruel thought was forming in his mind. He made eye contact and sneered at Dan with fiendish satisfaction as he slowly drew his handgun and leveled it at Dan's head.

Before Dan could register what was happening, it was too late.

In a chilling act of irreversible barbarism, he fired a bullet into the center of Dan's forehead at nearly point-blank range right in front of Vladi. The discharge of the gun was deafening. Dan felt no pain as the bullet burst through his skull.

Like a marionette with its strings cut, he sank to the ground. Blood bubbled from a round hole in his forehead and ran down into his open eyes, carrying with it his slowly uncoupling world.

Vladi was a military man, no stranger to death, yet the spectacle of Dan sprawled lifeless at his feet with his eyes still open as though staring back vacantly at Vladi felt surreal — almost as if time stood still. A torrent of dark thoughts rose within Vladi, all in mere seconds:

They deal in blood, do they? They killed my innocent friend, did they? These thugs must enjoy shedding innocent blood. These sailor boys were too young to remember actual battles — they missed the real blood-letting of the revolution their fathers knew. Maybe they need to be reminded. Have they no civility, no feeling? How cruelly they treat fellow human beings. They are not civilized — not human! Uniformed beasts. Vermin! Well, they will learn the error of their ways, and they will regret this day with their own blood!

The fury rising within Vladi's chest overrode his burning grief, strengthening him. The enraged tempest within Vladi burst forth like a thunderbolt. A roar erupted from the warrior as he kicked the gun out of the officer's still-outstretched hand. Before the officer could react, with one swift, lightning-fast motion, Vladi lunged forward and snatched a fishing knife that had been strewn on the deck, sliding it into the wretch's jugular vein with overwhelming force.

Vladi had grown up slaying wild boars in a similar fashion, and he felt no more sympathy for the low-life vermin who had just wantonly killed his loyal friend. With his face averted, Vladi drew back on the knife. He felt a momentary sense of satisfaction as the warm blood poured down his hand.

Vladi pulled the blade harder to the bone, exacting vindictive justice for Dan's murder. The officer's right carotid artery burst, and a jet of blood shot across the deck, splattering the face and uniform of another officer who was shouting in Spanish and scrambling to find his footing.

Vladi gave a menacing whisper in the officer's ear, "Da, ya govoryu po-Russki . . . *chiko!*" The last words the cretin heard before Vladi released him. "Yes, I speak Russian . . . *chico!*"

The officer flailed erratically, stumbling sideways on the deck in a circle. He kicked over tackle and knocked a bucket across the deck, all the while gurgling and bleeding from the mouth.

Without a shred of emotion, Vladi watched as the pathetic officer rolled around on the deck and bled out — no one could help him now. The officer's legs slowed and then stopped kicking. He lay jerking spasmodically for a few moments afterward. Then he stopped moving altogether.

Vladi stood, panting fiercely. The sickening reality of losing his friend hurt more than anything else the goons had done. One emotional moment, acted on in anger, had snuffed out the life of his friend for no reason. Vladi's aching heart strained to come to grips with the horrifying scene before him.

Darkening blood leaked from Dan's lifeless body and slowly pooled on the deck. Abruptly, Vladi pivoted and dropped to his knees in front of Dan as the warmth was leaving his body. In desperation, he searched to find a pulse with his blood-covered fingers — a move he knew was futile.

Two remaining coast guardsmen pointed their automatic weapons at Vladi's head. Physically and emotionally depleted, Vladi did not fight as they restrained him and took him into custody. They put their hands under his limp arms and hauled him to his feet.

Dan was gone. Their friendship was gone and could never be restored. The bonds of sorrow and joy they had shared were irretrievable. The friendship they enjoyed had been like a happy dream in Vladi's empty world, and now that dream had come to an end, and a jolting nightmare had begun.

It was a horrible day — the most horrible day of Vladi's life . . . so far.

COMBINADO DEL ESTE

"**V**ladislav Gavrilov, the Republic of Cuba has charged you with espionage, conspiracy to commit murder, murder with special circumstances, and smuggling, as an enemy of the state. By court order, you are to remain in custody in the Combinado del Este prison until a hearing is scheduled."

He and Dan had only gone out fishing. This was like a bad dream except Vladi couldn't shake himself out of it. Arrested and being tried for crimes he never committed — they had even pinned the all-encompassing charge of being an "enemy of the state" on him, which could be whatever they wanted it to mean and carry whatever sentence they desired. He found himself suddenly at the mercy of a tribunal that answered only to itself and operated by its own malleable rules.

Cuban officials didn't want to provoke their American neighbors over a seized vessel and the shooting of its U.S. captain under questionable pretenses, but Vladi was an altogether different subject. Extradition to Russia was being discussed. His "defection" from the Soviet military, from their perspective, could be high treason. Even if the Americans knew he was being held, it seemed improbable that anyone would rise to Vladi's defense. He was a man without a country.

Immediately following the reading of the charges, the guards grabbed Vladi's arms. He felt the cold, metal handcuffs click around his wrists before a guard kicked his legs out from under him. With brusque, jerking maneuvers, they repositioned his body to sit on the ground, his head shoved between his knees.

He could feel his own breath, hot and suffocating. His imagination reeled with what could lie ahead. He was familiar with the torture methods used by the Cubans — they were ghastly enough to make even the most stalwart Soviet officer queasy with terror.

The irony hit him hard. *The procedures for handling prisoners are presumably those we introduced to the communist revolutionaries nearly three decades ago. They will be used against me now.*

Upon being taken into custody by the Cuban authorities, Vladi was detained in the maximum-security Combinado del Este prison on the outskirts of Havana, awaiting what they euphemistically described as "further instruction." This too was ironic because Vladi had delivered the blueprints for this facility decades before. He might have been more nostalgic about visiting the site under different circumstances.

Combinado del Este was designed to be Cuba's newest model prison, but seeing it up close revealed the implementation of the concept was substandard. Beginning in the 1970s, the Cubans had constructed three- and four-story buildings upon foundations designed for two-floor buildings. As a result, the structural bases and underpinnings were crumbling and walls were pulling apart at the seams. Vladi saw things with an eye for precision, almost like an engineer. *It is a wonder that the upper floors have not collapsed . . . yet,* he thought. *This is Cuba, though. The inability of Castro's ham-fisted bureaucracy to carry out even the most ideal concepts would ensure it could never be done correctly.*

The facility looked innocuous on the outside. They had painted the buildings with bright colors, so the compound almost did not appear to be a prison. Inside was a different reality — it was a terrifying house of horrors.

First, two young prison guards wearing olive green fatigues stripped Vladi of his shoes and tossed them to other prisoners who fought over them, like throwing a bone to dogs. They then took Vladi to a side office. The room was dim, lit only by a couple of fluorescent strip lights hung in odd places across sizable gaps in the ceiling where the tiles had fallen and never been replaced. The failing ballast of one fixture made it flicker weakly. It was better that way — better not to see the roaches that scurried across the chipped concrete floor. Better not to see the flattened, once-beige cushions on a dilapidated couch covered in rodent droppings.

Vladi looked the room over and crinkled his nose in disgust. *How can any respectable human work in this environment?*

A corpulent man in uniform waddled out of the interrogation room, chomping a cigar. His eyes looked Vladi up and down, studying him for a couple of seconds before waving him over. Without looking at them, he stuck one arm out to the guards who brought Vladi, and they slapped the transfer documents into his hand. He signed the papers and gave them a receipt, and they removed Vladi's handcuffs. Then they exited the room without a word.

El Gordo, a byname Vladi had already mentally assigned to the fat man in front of him, coughed, scratched his belly, and picked his nose as if it were a casual night in his own living room.

"Empty your pockets," he instructed Vladi before he lapsed into graveled coughing.

Vladi reached into his trouser pocket and put a protective hand around his cherished watch. His heart stopped for a beat before restarting with a thud. *On no, not my watch,* Vladi thought, breathless with instant grief. He had anticipated confiscation, but there had been no place for him to stash the watch along the way. Vladi's eyes darted around the room, his mind frantic.

Is there anywhere or any way I can drop the watch and hide it away? Anything to keep it out of the hands of this awful man.

Reluctant to remove his hand from his pocket, Vladi let his fingers run over every tactile detail of the watch. Out of options and out of time, he pulled it from his pocket with slow reluctance. Real or imagined, he heard its ticking in thunderous slow motion — every second a heartbeat, every tick rushing through his ears. He cupped his hand around the body of the watch to conceal it from the man's view for as long as possible. Vladi looked down and studied the watch in his hand, trying to capture every beautiful detail in his mind.

I just need a few moments longer so this image is imprinted into my mind forever. He peered into the crystal face as if he were staring through a time portal. His mind drifted.

He could see his grandfather as he gave the watch to his father. His mind watched his father present it to him when he turned sixteen. The scene in his memory fast-forwarded to young Irina and their wedding, followed by the birth of each of their daughters. Then . . . then Vladi handed the watch to a young man — a son — whose face he could not see. A face he would never see.

His reddening eyes stung. Any other time he wouldn't dare show an emotion in front of a man like this, but there was no stopping the drip threatening to release itself from his nostrils.

This watch is the last link to my life — to my true self. Vladi sniffled lightly. *I will never hand you over to my son, no matter how many times I may dream of it now. It is as if our story, our legacy, ends here, old comrade. Even if he exists, I cannot see the face of my son. I cannot see his face, even in my imagination, because fortune will not allow our story to continue. Every time I try to see it, his face is blank — just like our future.*

El Gordo grew impatient and thrust out his short arm. "Vamos. *Muévete,* hand over whatever it is you have." His stubby, fat fingers made his palm look more like a paw than a dignified hand.

Vladi closed his eyes. His hand and arm felt leaden. His knuckles were white from clutching the watch.

He moved his fist over the waiting, outstretched hand and paused. *I am sorry, grandfather. I am so sorry, father. I am sorry, my son. I could not protect this. But I have no other option. Goodbye, old comrade.* Vladi released his fingers and let the watch drop from his hand. He watched it falling . . . falling . . . falling, each tick thundering as it plummeted. Then silence.

The watch hit its meaty target. El Gordo's eyes widened with interest as he examined Vladi's watch. Vladi felt a heave of disgust as he watched the man fondle his watch in his piggish hands. The Soviet insignia had caught his attention. He turned it over for a closer look. A hint of drool appeared in the corner of his mouth as he held a cigar in his teeth.

"Exquisite," he remarked lustily through his cigar-clenching teeth.

He signed a chit but retained both copies. Vladi never moved his eyes from the watch, knowing that this would be the last he'd ever see of it. He put his hand to his abdomen, aching pangs radiated through his gut.

The last meaningful thing in his life had been taken away. He had lost his only tangible connection to the life he knew before, and along with it, his hopes for the future — both gone forever.

The guards were called back in, and Vladi was led to a succession of dingy rooms to be photographed and fingerprinted for the Ministry of the Interior's records. They escorted him to another office where a young guard waited at a scratched-up metal desk.

Earnest yet nervous, he stumbled over his words, trying to explain that Vladi needed to fill out a form. The paper fluttered as the young officer passed it across the desk with shaky hands. *What kind of dangerous monster have they told him I am?*

Another man arrived, about the same age as Vladi — a handsome major who introduced himself in flawless American English. He spelled out the rules — they were fairly simple.

"From today on, you have no name," he explained. "You are 'Prisoner 379.'"

My lucky number, Vladi mused to himself sarcastically.

The major continued, "When you are out of the cell, you walk on the left side, head down, with hands behind your back. Never look at anyone. You will face the wall at each door or stairway until told to proceed. You will obey all officials. If you do not, you will be punished. You will be fed three times a day. Any questions?"

"Do I have a lawyer?" Vladi asked.

The major laughed. "These things take time. This is Cuba."

The next stop was a musty laundry room. The air was thick with warm humidity, intensifying the smell. The stale mildewy odor clung to everything. It was no wonder — rusty water stains marked the walls. Worse than that, black mold bloomed from the cracks where the floor met the walls and where the walls met the other walls, creating a fuzzy border around the room. Thick, mucus-like, brown mold decorated the various cracks in the middle of the walls and around pipes. Unidentified reddish-brown stains were also smeared here and there, but Vladi did not want to even think about where those had come from.

Vladi flinched as a drop hit the top of his head. He looked up to see water droplets forming from the middle of a brown, water-stained ceiling tile. Within a minute, Vladi's nose became stuffy, and his now watery eyes itched due to the mold spores that were rapidly finding their way into his sinuses.

He could hear intermittent plops of water around the room. He thought that must have been the only water that ever graced those floors. Nothing within the walls had even the slightest semblance of cleanliness.

"Strip off the rest of your clothing," the guard commanded.

Vladi knew exactly why they ordered him to do so. *When they strip a man's clothes, they aim to take his dignity.*

Although he comprehended their tactic, he couldn't quell the sense of hot humiliation that crept over his face and head, the exact feeling this exercise was intended to elicit. Once a successful businessman and, before that, a respected Soviet officer, he now stood bare and vulnerable. Nonetheless, Vladi held himself straight, shoulders back, with his head up, his bearing dignified.

I am not shedding my skin, he reminded himself. *I am the same man I was before I arrived.* They had done nothing to alter the core of who he was.

After the first of what would be many degrading strip searches, they issued him a second-hand, faded, slate-blue prison uniform.

Very me. His sarcasm had not dimmed.

He was also given rust-yellowed underwear, a pair of long trousers, and two shirts with a sour-smelling towel thrown in. Head down, Vladi shuffled along as instructed. They pushed him into another side room and told him to place all his things on a filthy foam mattress and roll it up so he could carry it. A pillow mottled with bloodstains was tossed on top. Vladi looked down at the blood. He had a more complete understanding than most of how grave his situation was.

After ordering Vladi to collect his nasty bundle, they prodded him along a long, narrow corridor with a low ceiling that made it feel subterranean. The walls on either side looked like they had been white at one time, but were now striped with dark filth. Sounds were just muffled vibrations, difficult to distinguish.

They went through a wide wooden door at the end that opened into a corridor lined with fortified cell doors on one side. The guard in front carried a chain and a rubber baton that thumped against the wall as he walked. Vladi counted thirty-nine doors. He was ordered to stand and face the wall while the guard fumbled with his keys.

With his nose six inches from the wall, Vladi examined the guards' crude graffiti, scrawled in childish pencil. The door clanged open with a foul rush of stale air to reveal a tiny cave. Vladi stepped into his dungeon. The guards unceremoniously closed the door behind him, leaving Vladi to his new "home."

To describe it as a cave was not a stretch. There were no windows in the entire building. During the summer, inmates suffered the stifling heat. This time of year, there was no reprieve from the cold. And the air seemed to be filled with plaster or cement dust.

From the ceiling dangled tiny stalactites formed by continuous drips of sewer water from the upper floors, so prolific that they could not be evaded. Everything was silent save for the splash of dripping water, the squeak of the guards' boots, and a man sobbing in a nearby cell.

In a corner of the chamber, there was a four-inch hole in the ground for an open latrine. It often backed up, covering the floor with urine and feces that filled the cell with the pungent odor of sewage. The walls behind it were alive with writhing maggots.

Home sweet home, Vladi thought with disgust. He did what he could to make the best of things, but the longer he was there, he came to learn just how deplorable his new circumstances were.

Flies were a plague that only let up at night, when their torment was taken over by swarming mosquitoes and legions of bloodsucking bedbugs and lice. Rats emerged from the latrine holes into the dark cells, silently stalking whatever they could devour — and human flesh was on their menu. The ravenous rats scuttled over the prisoners. It was unavoidable — a Cuban prison wouldn't have been complete without rats. Inmates swatted away rats and roaches as they struggled to sleep.

The abhorrent conditions were compounded by psychological games of interrogation that took place day and night. Vladi wondered if the authorities would ever give up trying to tease information from him. They tried to uncover details about bank accounts and money he had and how it could be accessed. They questioned him for hours, often about the details of his life in America, trying to elicit a confession of any kind, real or imaginary. Not that a plea bargain could have been negotiated — they wanted any desperate statement they could extract as more damning evidence in the impending trial.

There was a plethora of cruel psychological tortures: blindfolded immersion in pools — also known as waterboarding — intimidation by dogs, and firing squad simulations. This was all designed to coerce and elicit confessions, real or not, and to break the minds of prisoners. This was where they brought suspected CIA agents, where purged officials repented, and where all Cubans feared to tread.

Incarceration took its toll on both body and mind. The Cuban prison guards had a fearsome reputation for psychological torture, and they more than earned it. The guards' practices and interrogation techniques were thought to have been originally perfected by the KGB. But, in fact, they had become even more refined over the years as prison staff were sent to East Germany and Czechoslovakia for training. Their sadistic techniques became more scientific, more inhumane, and even more psychologically destructive as a result of these "upgrades."

Sleep deprivation was among their main devices. When prisoners began to nod off, guards would prod at them with long poles to ensure they got no rest. Other methods of sleep deprivation included placing inmates in solitary confinement in a barren room lit with fluorescent lights twenty-four hours a day, or locking them in refrigerated rooms where they would convulse with shivering until they cried from exhaustion.

Alternatively, prisoners could be confined for years in dungeons, blackout cells, with no light whatsoever, so that if and when they ever emerged alive, their eyesight would be destroyed.

And if that were not bad enough, Vladi knew of prisoners who had been placed in punishment cells that were another level of torment — the dreaded "drawer cells." These devilishly contrived units made South Vietnam's infamous tiger cages seem like homey quarters.

Besides constantly menacing prisoners with bayonets, guards often stripped inmates and beat them with thick, twisted electric cables, braided ropes, rubber hoses, pipes, and chains. Many prisoners had backs tattooed with scars from blows at the hands of overzealous guards.

Illness and disease were rampant. Malnutrition was exacerbated by the lack of medical attention. Damp cells caused respiratory problems. Many prisoners were infected with tuberculosis. To make it worse, the guards sometimes dumped pails of excrement onto the prisoners' heads. And fungi grew on prisoners because they were not allowed to wash off the filth.

Fortunately, Vladi hadn't endured the full extent of these torments. Not yet, anyway. Still, accommodations were atrocious, and the food was worse. They could say that prisoners got three meals a day, if it could be called that. Breakfast consisted of sugar water and a small piece of pasty bread crust. Lunch and dinner alternated between a couple of macaroni noodles floating in boiled tinned meat broth that looked and smelled like dog vomit, and watery cornmeal mush that was almost always garnished with a few maggots.

Vladi remained in custody, awaiting his trial. Discouragement and despair turned his emotions numb. *Who even knows I am here? It is laughable to think I would get a visit from an embassy. Even if so, which one?* Vladi remained a man without a country. There was no possibility of consulting with an attorney — there was no communication with anyone outside.

Even within the confinement of Combinado del Este, prisoners had limited personal contact except within the building where they were housed, and then only during meals or for ninety minutes three times a week in the prison yard. Vladi learned that his fellow inmates were a varied assortment of innocent men mixed with murderers, rapists, thieves, and drug smugglers.

A corrupt network of brutal guards who bullied the prisoners had complete control over Vladi's life. He was no longer a man to them — just "Prisionero 379." He spent almost every hour of the day confined in the small cell, staring at the walls . . . the ceiling . . . the floor. Vladi's worst torment was having too much time in his cell to reflect. He had nothing to do but let painful thoughts of his family play in an endless loop in his head. Images of Dan's bloody death frequently resurfaced before his mind's eye. The senseless slaughter of the one man with whom he'd genuinely confided was etched into his memory like the graffiti carved into the prison walls.

Many days into the ordeal, Vladi heard sounds coming from outside his cell, including a voice he recognized. He stood up and moved closer to the door, turning his ear in an attempt to hear more. The clang of a key rattled around the lock. *They are coming here.* Vladi took a couple of small steps back and bumped the wall. The door squealed as it swung open.

There between the guards stood a distinguished-looking man in his early fifties.

"Señor Vladi, it appears the table has turned."

Vladi was startled. Who here knew to call him Vladi? *This cannot possibly be a stranger.* Vladi craned his neck forward and narrowed his eyes.

"Marco?" Vladi didn't know whether to be concerned or relieved.

Marco's hair had begun to recede, and his face appeared fuller than Vladi remembered. The mustache that had given Marco such youthful character was gone, revealing jowls thickened with age and a type of cynicism that had molded his features into a sort of dour mask. His eyes were also heavier with the years. But, without question, the voice was that of Marco Rivera.

"It's Juez Rivera to you now," Marco corrected him without any apparent emotion.

Vladi could feel the chill in his words. The blood in his veins turned to ice as it ran from his fingers, up his arms, and to his chest. He knew this meant trouble for him.

Cuba's Ministry of the Interior had appointed Marco as the magistrate to preside over Vladi's trial. When the coast guard had learned of Vladi's identity, they notified the Intelligence Directorate, which maintained close ties with the Russian Federal Security Service.

"Imagine how delighted I was to receive news that my old compadre had been fished out by the coast guard."

Oh, I am certain he was delighted, Vladi thought. *He has the smile of a shark. And he has been waiting years to bite. Old comrade, indeed.* Vladi cursed this cruel, mocking fate.

Marco had never anticipated this day would come, but it was oh so sweet now that it had. He relished the prospects of justice being done at last and of this arrogant oaf receiving the humiliation he so richly deserved.

Who else could know how Marco felt betrayed by Vladi decades ago? Who else could know what a tyrant Vladi could be? Even worse, a capitalist oppressor, secure and cocky in his ill-gotten riches. As far as anyone would know in his court, Vladi defected to America for ideological reasons. He had colluded with the enemy for three decades. Who knew what secrets he could have revealed to imperialist Americans?

"I've been worried about you since you left, old comrade." Vladi's smile and tone dripped with sarcasm. "I thought perhaps you had disappeared forever. But now look at you! So important. And to think, just a short while ago you were just a dirt-caked labor hand in —" The slap whipped his head to the side, and all he could hear was the ringing in his smacked ear.

"Don't you dare," Marco hissed into his face. He couldn't allow the guards to hear what Vladi was about to say. He'd worked so hard to recreate his story and new life when he returned to the island. A few words from Vladi could undo it all.

Enraged, Vladi gave Marco a violent shove backward. The two guards caught Marco before he fell to the ground. Marco looked up at Vladi, a stunned expression replacing his smugness. Vladi knew that one impulsive move could bring extra trouble down on his head, but what did it matter now?

It does not matter. Marco's bitterness still grips him, and he will ensure I never leave here. I am a dead man one way or another.

"Always the tyrant," Marco stated as he got back on his feet, a wry smile crinkling the corners of his mouth.

"Was it a tyrant who came to your aid, who took care of you?" Vladi asked him earnestly. He knew he couldn't reason with Marco, but he felt compelled to defend himself.

Marco ignored the question. "We have enough evidence against you to have you convicted on at least four capital offenses. You can add assaulting an official to your list of charges." And Marco intended to extract every ounce of justice.

Vladi laughed. "You think you will get your justice now, amigo? Are you going to tell the court all you know about me? Shall I tell them how you know?"

"Watch what you say, comrade. I can have you executed at any moment or have your skin peeled off like an orange." Marco relished the last word as if he were rolling a fine cigar around in his jowly mouth, then continued. "I would have given the word just now, but I could never dream of a more glorious day than when I preside over your tribunal. You are a murderer. You were a tyrant back then, and you still are. It will come crashing down on your head. Then you will get what you have long deserved. And more. I'll see to it."

Vladi grimaced but didn't bother to respond. They both knew it would be nothing more than a public show. The outcome of this sham trial would only bring a death sentence for Vladi.

THE TRIBUNAL

Shortly after dawn less than two weeks after Vladi's arrest and detention, a fleet of unmarked Ladas drew up outside the Combinado del Este prison. They had finally come for him.

Guards handcuffed Vladi, and two soldiers armed with Polish RAK automatic submachine guns flanked him on each side. The procession of three cars departed the prison and headed west for the half-hour drive into Havana.

That morning, the sky was gray — everything was gray, including Vladi's disposition. A slow drizzle fell, streaking the glass of the Lada's back windows where Vladi was seated. As they neared central Havana, Vladi reflected on how many times he had walked along those same avenues as a free man. He never imagined that one day he would be driven through them as a prisoner.

Not much had changed since Vladi had last been there. As if no time had passed, the locals still congregated at some of the same little taverns and cafés where he once talked, laughed, and argued. He did notice how much the buildings had deteriorated over decades of neglect — stucco was chipped and their once vibrant colors had faded and peeled with age.

They passed through the Plaza de San Francisco where Vladi's eye caught the *Fuente de los Leones*, the Fountain of the Lions. *Marco bantered with me near there once about that book he was defiantly reading,* he vaguely recalled. Just a shadow of a memory, Vladi visualized the ghosts of their former selves, standing nearby conversing like two people who had somewhat enjoyed each other's company. The car turned the corner, vaporizing the ghosts as the memory vanished — the remnants of a long-dead life.

We used to get the best pork sandwiches there, Vladi remembered longingly as they passed a small cafe whose elderly owners he wondered about. *The stringy pork — it was so tender, and Cubanelle peppers made it a perfect tangy-sweet heat.* Vladi could still remember the taste. *It has been so long since I have enjoyed something so delicious and homecooked,* he sighed to himself. Especially after subsisting for weeks on rotten prison "food," if anyone could call it that. *I will probably never taste anything comparable again.*

Maybe that was a morbid thought, but sentiments drifted through Vladi's weary mind — a mere passing wistfulness that any normal person might have had on any normal day. Perhaps his brain was trying to shield him from the reality that today would be anything but normal.

Vladi's case was, indeed, something of an exceptional one in Havana. Many political detainees never had a trial in a formal setting. They were interrogated and then taken to prison for protracted and inhumane sentences that often turned out to be indefinite. Some were taken straight to a firing squad at "El Paredón," The Wall.

Mere suspicion of wrongdoing could be an ample pretext for execution in communist Cuba. One could be the innocent victim of overactive suspicion and negative assumptions, or of a denunciation from a neighbor or coworker, people they might have trusted most. Informants only had to point a finger at someone and charges could be brought against them. Conjecture was enough to support a guilty finding. Any real evidence that existed may have been useful, but rarely essential. It was decidedly injudicious and tragically immoral, but that's just how things were done — after all, *This is Cuba,* Vladi mused darkly.

In Vladi's case, he would get a trial, but it would be nothing more than theater, enabling the Cuban government to maintain an appearance before the international community that he had been "fairly" tried and convicted. The show trial aimed to make an example of Vladi. They would have executed him without the complication of a trial except that Fidel wanted a tribunal with all the fanfare. Fidel wanted the press to make a statement, sending a stern warning to anyone who would contemplate crossing the Castro government.

There was another driving force behind this charade — Marco. He'd been all too pleased to let Vladi know how much he delighted in his arrest. Marco exulted in the task of working up the charges against him. Revenge had practically fallen out of the sky or, in this case, been fished out of the sea. Marco was ready and waiting to have the final word in triumph. Not only would he have his private vengeance, but Marco would also get one up on Vladi.

The motorcade approached a large downtown building, the *Audiencia de Habana*. It surprised Vladi to see demonstrators assembled in the street, especially for an early morning trial. The agitators surrounded them and hurled objects at the car, shouting "El Paredón!" This didn't sit well with Vladi. Cries of *"Yanqui a la pared!"* which Vladi translated in his mind as "Yankee to the wall!" did little to ease his anxiety.

It was not a mere coincidence that demonstrators showed up in sloppy weather before most Havanans had downed their second cup of *cafecito*. These were Rapid Response Brigades, the latest contrivance of the Ministry of the Interior. They were paid operatives who could be called upon to stage demonstrations for purposes of intimidation or to frame whatever versions of stories the government wished to be reported by the news media. These paid protesters functioned on orders to instill terror in Cuban citizens by harassment, coercion, and doling out violence against suspected dissidents. They were a mechanism for social control, essentially criminal gangs — thugs granted power and perks to torment and act out with impunity.

Inside, the paneled courtroom had a wooden platform at the head of the room with a long table where the tribunal members were seated, all donning military uniforms. The Cuban judicial system didn't allow a trial by a jury of peers nor any crucial safeguards of due process for the criminally arraigned. The Communist Party of Cuba had contempt for what they considered the archaic principles of bourgeois law. Death sentences in Cuba were handed down by puppet tribunals that failed to abide by the most minimal standards of due process and penal law that existed in civilized countries. A token panel of judges appointed by the debased Cuban National Assembly, the CNA, would adjudicate Vladi's trial.

A typical Cuban tribunal consisted of only three members. One professional judge was "the chair," who presided over the trial. The other members of the tribunal could be "lay judges," who weren't even required to have legal credentials. To ensure this hearing would be as impressive and imposing as possible, they had an expanded panel of five members, including one who knew Vladi well.

Juez Marco Rivera officiated over the trial as chair of the tribunal. It was his moment in the spotlight to be recognized and to have the coveted attention of El Comandante Castro himself, who had taken a personal interest in the proceedings.

Seeing Vladi enter the chamber, Marco's face bore an expression of harsh satisfaction. Seated with his arms folded across his chest and smug with pride, Marco's persona dominated the proceeding. His whole demeanor was that of a man bent on revenge — and confident he would have it.

Vladi had no access to legal counsel — no defense attorney. He hadn't been allowed to contact anyone, and Cuban defense lawyers had been warned not to go near him. Vladi wasn't shown any evidence before the trial, so he had no chance to prepare a defense. Vladi knew it wouldn't matter even if he did. But he'd had lots of time to think, and he knew in his mind what needed to be said.

The tribunal began with a conjured up list of charges of the utmost gravity. Then the prosecutor laid out his purported crimes without giving Vladi much opportunity to defend himself.

The prosecution opened with a sensational lie delivered with flair by a young attorney with wire-rimmed glasses and perfectly coiffed black hair.

"The accused before you is a traitor to his country and ours — a traitor to the values that we hold for the good of all," the prosecutor began with a dramatic sweeping motion toward Vladi. "This man came to our country years ago as an officer of the USSR, formerly of their special forces, no less. While here, he sought out relationships and struck up friendships with high-level members of the Communist Party of Cuba with the intent of learning state secrets, knowing full well that he would later reveal his findings to our common enemy."

I never sought out friendship with that weasel, Marco, Vladi thought with an internal laugh. While it was the least worrisome of their condemning lies, it was indicative of worse to come.

"Once this slinking spy had enough information to be useful to the Americans, he deserted his post and defected to the United States. The circumstances call into question the events surrounding the crash of a Soviet Tupolev Tu-114 transport aircraft, costing the lives of the crew and dozens of his innocent comrades. By no coincidence, he was the only survivor, providing a pretext for extraction by an American agent. He spent decades there being further brainwashed and trained by the American CIA, only to return later as an operative of *El Imperio.*"

Vladi knew "El Imperio," the empire, was often used in Cuba to refer to America. *An operative for the United States? For the CIA? Could they get any more absurd?* Vladi displayed no outward emotion, but if he could, he would have put his head back and rolled his eyes. *I wonder if Marco dreamed up this preposterous tale alone or if they had to put all their puny intelligence together and rack their tiny brains to come up with this absurd story.*

"In the end, once his training was complete," the prosecutor continued, keeping eye contact with Marco, "the Americans sent him back to our paradise — as if we were stupid and could not see right through their weak plot. He has abandoned any communist ideals he once purported to have in an endeavor to subvert our government and assist in giving Americans what they have so craved for many decades. We will demonstrate to this honorable tribunal that he intended to perform acts of sabotage, and he is a treacherous hitman targeting the leaders of our glorious revolution. The accused to be tried before you was apprehended as he attempted to infiltrate Cuba to assassinate none other than El Comandante himself, our revered Fidel Castro."

Around the courtroom, there were hushed gasps and whispered conversation.

This performance is worthy of American courtroom dramas. This prosecutor should be in Hollywood, not Havana, Vladi thought, shaking his head. What a load of sensationalized, nonsensical dreck.

Beyond the bold accusations delivered in his opening, the prosecutor neglected to produce any substantive evidence against the accused. Of course, none existed, and they couldn't even be bothered to fabricate any. It didn't matter. This was merely a performance for El Comandante and the state media.

Instead, the prosecutor's arguments descended into a disjointed ramble. "While he was training to carry out his acts of treason, the defendant enriched himself. With eagerness and devotion, he took part in corrupt American profiteering. He siphoned off his own fortune through nefarious means and became a fat Yankee capitalist and an exploiter."

Well, that much is not entirely false. Vladi found a moment of private humor.

The more the prosecutor spoke, the more inflated his presentation grew. "What kind of vile traitor aligns himself with a nation as scandalous as America? He has allowed himself to be infected with American debauchery and has allied with their ruthless and corrupt regimes. As everyone knows, Americans murder each other at an appalling rate. He has chosen to live in a land with tens of millions of drug addicts. And he has preference for a system that winks at gambling establishments controlled by the home-grown mobsters. He has allowed himself to be seduced by the glitzy greed of Las Vegas and its dirty business that once corrupted our own Havana. And like New York, he too is obsessed with the frenzied pursuit of money. He forsook his noble role, advancing our inspired journey toward a utopian society for what? The likes of bleak and hopeless Chicago suburbs? To precipitate more drug addicts and poor victims of capitalism?"

What is he blathering about? At this point, Vladi wasn't sure which of them was more confused. *This sounds like one of Fidel's rants — meaningless rhetoric. I have never seen those places, much less been captivated by them. None of this makes sense!*

Oh, but the prosecutor wasn't done. "What kind of person would choose to align himself with a nation where prisons are filled with Latinos and Blacks pushed into a life of crime by an exploitative society that discriminates against them, systematically violating their rights, making them second-class citizens? His America is crime-ridden and in crisis because of their materialistic consumerism and the breakdown of the traditional families that our socialism supports. His America is the product of a society that has failed to establish a clear moral definition between right and wrong. And he wants to spread their poison here, in Cuba!"

Whispers and head nods rippled throughout the courtroom. The prosecutor paused for dramatic effect.

"They struggle, and they cannot bear to allow anyone else to do otherwise. They're afraid that we will be better. So they villainize our government and our people, and they send operatives like this man to undermine and destroy all that we have accomplished. His intent was clear — to assassinate Fidel so they can take down Cuba's civic framework and make it a microcosm of corrupt American culture with all its trashy comforts and degenerate insanity."

Another pause. Vladi couldn't help but be impressed by how the prosecutor had the courtroom hanging on his every word.

"I say to this honorable court that this man has played right into the hands of the imperial devils! He is a danger to our country, he has betrayed his own country, and he is a menace to all our communist allies worldwide!"

The prosecutor's caricature of American society, in which he held up Cuba as a moral exemplar, might have been more amusing if Vladi's predicament weren't so serious. After living in America, Vladi was no longer naïve. Cuba was about the farthest thing from a model society that could exist.

As sensational as the prosecutor tried to be, Vladi could not have defended against the prosecutor's half-truth assessment of American society, although he knew that didn't give the whole picture.

Vladi realized that the prosecutor was hoping he would counter by attempting to clarify the facts and present an opposing viewpoint that made it look like he was defending the United States. *Then they will point the finger and say, "See, he is an American sympathizer — a guilty collaborator!"* Vladi didn't take the bait.

Following his theatrics, the prosecutor dryly recited several laws that he said determined the appropriate level of punishment.

Vladi probably wouldn't have been allowed to testify in his own defense at all, except that Marco, exulting in the moment, wanted to hear what he had to say.

As usual, Marco had underestimated Vladi.

Instead of pleading or reacting by struggling through a clumsy defense, Vladi handled himself with the same strength and valor during the trial that had always characterized his life. What followed was a masterful oration as Vladi took the stand.

The prosecutor forged ahead with his examination. "Is it true that you were an officer in the special forces of the USSR before deserting to the United States?"

Vladi knew this was a leading question, and however he answered it, the prosecutor would spin it to suit the predetermined narrative. He wouldn't make it so easy for them.

"It seems you already know the answer, so why are you asking me?"

"Just answer the question," Marco interjected.

Vladi wasn't about to give him the satisfaction of the answer he was looking for. "You wanted to ensure the people of Cuba and the world could witness these proceedings today. Assuming anyone cares what you do in this ignoble trial, they will see an exhibition of Cuban justice at its finest." Vladi gave this a sarcastic emphasis, then added, "That is, the farcical character of Cuban justice!"

Vladi plowed forward before the prosecutor could interrupt. "Listen to me! Hear my voice? You hear the accent of an American? No? I was conceived and took my first breath in Kavkaz, Russia. Who else here has ever set eyes on the 'Land of Lenin'? . . . I did not think so. Well, I was raised there along with my family and guarded the soil of *rodina*, my motherland, before coming here to support yours!"

"Answer with a yes or no! Were you or were you not an officer of the USSR special forces?" Marco snapped, his brow glowing, flushed with frustration.

Vladi turned to Marco and looked him straight in the eyes. His manner was calm as he answered, "Yes, I served as a field grade officer in the USSR, and I arrived to your little paradise with an assignment to help secure a new and better government because a despot, the one before the oppressive tyrant you have now, abused his authority, to the harm of the decent citizens of Cuba."

"So you acknowledge that American imperialism caused Cuba's decline in the past? That U.S.-sponsored ventures during the Batista era exploited our glorious country and caused our people to suffer?" Marco gloated, a hint of a smile on his lips.

Vladi paused for a breath so he could answer in a calm and measured tone.

"Remember Fidel Castro at the dawn of the revolution? The one pledging to restore a constitutional government, to hold free elections, to respect human rights, and uphold freedom of expression?"

Marco put a hand on his head and growled, "I certainly do. And he did all of those things exactly as he said he would, prisoner."

"Is the accused criticizing El Comandante?" the prosecutor cut in, seeing an opportunity to affirm the charges that Vladi had come to kill the president. "You were sent here by the CIA to assassinate Fidel Castro!" he spat. "Even now you try to incite our people against our leader and our government!"

Vladi laughed at the prosecutor's allegations and answered, "If Cuba is such a utopia today, why are the imperialist devils not swimming to your shores? If the Communist Party of Cuba is everything your state-controlled news reports to anyone who cares to read or listen to its drivel, why are thousands upon thousands of refugees imperiling their lives to escape to the 'free world'? I know these families because they were once there for me. Indeed, I made sure that their loved ones would have safe passage and the means to support themselves for years to come. Meanwhile, El Comandante —"

"*Un momento!*" the prosecutor cut in. "Are you saying that you aided Cubans in defecting to the United States?"

Marco's panic was instantaneous. Out of self-preservation, he hadn't included allegations of aiding defection or human smuggling. He feared that it could lead to questions about Señor Moisés and a couple of brothers he once assisted in leaving the island. He needed to end this line of questioning, *pronto!*

"*Por favor*, prosecutor, we have already established that the defendant is being tried for multiple counts of espionage and murder. Given the charges that he was plotting an assassination, I am eager to hear what he has to say about El Comandante, and so you should be too. Will the defendant please proceed with his statement?" Marco held his breath.

Surprised by the interruption at first, Vladi surmised why Marco would be so anxious to brush over any questions about the topic of defections. The corner of his mouth inched into the tiniest smile as he resumed.

"Meanwhile, El Comandante reminds everyone about an imperialistic peril to the north. He exploits the threat of American interference as cover for every misstep, failed program, food shortage, your empty store shelves, power blackouts, and clinics without even the most basic medicine."

"You are the ones causing that. It is the American embargo, and we all know it!" shouted the prosecutor, practically foaming at the mouth.

Vladi held up a hand. "Cuba no more represents the true tenets of communism than America does. Instead, this place is one gigantic plantation that Fidel runs like a slave estate. Your entire system operates under the revolutionary phraseology with which he managed to dupe everyone. This Cuba is nothing like the ideals of communism we Soviets ever envisioned when we landed on your island three decades ago. I can only speak for myself, but I don't think any of us foresaw the pain that would be inflicted upon ordinary families. Today, the people of Cuba have a worse dictatorship than the one you deposed. You now have one with a badly organized, implacable bureaucracy — a new power class to erase all liberty."

The prosecutor kept looking at Marco as though confused about how to respond. Vladi was a more formidable defendant than he was accustomed to handling. The young prosecutor had never been confronted with a defendant who had the inclination or ability to turn his trial into a platform to debase their leader and the realities of Cuban life. This trial had Castro's attention, and now it was unraveling right before their eyes.

"You are nothing but parrots in green fatigues," Vladi continued, driving his point home while he held their attention. "Everything is a party recitation — empty slogans repeated by ideological slaves. I pity you when you learn how fruitless it was degrading yourself — that the price of advancement was to prostitute your mind and soul."

A hubbub arose among onlookers, and Marco slammed his gavel, calling for order. Things were not going as smoothly as Marco had envisioned, and he needed to do something before the news got back to El Comandante that the trial he was officiating had fallen apart. He had communicated assurances it would be a cinch.

Fidel was known to independently appeal settled cases while taking retributive measures against judges who failed to deliver the outcome he wanted. Marco couldn't risk this possibility. He was clever and far more capable than this prosecutor, so he interjected, trying to ensnare Vladi in testimony that the prosecution could twist.

"Señor Gavrilov, you admit you are a traitor, an operative of the CIA, a deserter from the USSR, and you have been aiding the enemies of Cuba?" It was more of a statement than a question, and Marco smirked at Vladi, daring him to get himself out of it.

"You denounce me as a traitor? Look at me!" Vladi pulled open his shirt, exposing the communist hammer-and-sickle tattooed over his heart. The room collectively gasped, followed by a restless rumble.

"I would carve this off my own chest before embracing the communism that Cuba represents!" Vladi growled. "Furthermore, if this tribunal is intent on purging a traitor in your midst, perhaps I can help." Vladi paused, leaving the thought hanging.

Vladi established eye contact with Marco and then gave him a wicked grin. The table had turned once again — Vladi had outmaneuvered Marco.

Marco stared back knowingly, and instantly his face turned ashen. How could the situation have unraveled like this? He'd made a fatal miscalculation by giving Vladi the stand, and he now realized it all too late. He quickly called the court to order as and announced an immediate recess to halt the testimony before Vladi played his trump card.

Should I shout it out right now? Vladi contemplated. *No one could stop me.* As long as Vladi was in the room, Marco was helpless to silence him. Once the truth about Marco's past defection left Vladi's mouth in the presence of these witnesses, the words could never be unheard.

Vladi almost gave in to the temptation that was on the tip of his tongue, but he thought better. With an uncharacteristic measure of mercy, Vladi sighed and held back, keeping Marco's secret to himself.

Perhaps it was for the better. Ever the rational thinker, Vladi had already considered the logical outcome of his options. If he used this opportunity to expose Marco, that vindictive move would not bring him leniency, only take down Marco down with him.

Before he had stepped into the room, Vladi had already figured out that whatever he said would not alter the trial's outcome. Whatever evidence he could have provided didn't matter, even if he had counsel. Whatever his lawyer could have argued would have been moot anyway. In fact, whatever the prosecutor had to say didn't really matter either. Nothing that was already said or left unsaid mattered. It was all for show.

The verdict and sentence to be imposed had already been determined by political hands before the proceedings had even commenced in whatever was

Cuba's tropical version of the Lubyanka. The puppet tribunal was a mere formality — it was to do nothing but read the sentence.

A fleeting expression on Marco's face suggested that he was momentarily bewildered as to why Vladi had chosen to maintain his silence. He took advantage of Vladi's hesitation and called the chamber to order. With deliberate movements, he opened the stout brown envelope that contained the dreaded document, sliding out the folded sheets of venom.

He had the honors of delivering the verdict, and he did so with relish.

"This tribunal, mindful of the obligation it bears to the revolution, to the people of Cuba, and to history, with full conviction of the nobility of its action, inspired by the same democratic precepts which honesty, love, fairness, and justice have aroused in the revolutionary movement, a worthy example for all the peoples of North and South America and the world, finds the accused, Vladislav Gavrilov, guilty on all counts as charged."

Naturally, Vladi's trial had played out as planned — Marco had obtained the conviction he sought, and the sentence was death. Vladi was to stand before a firing squad at the range he had personally supervised implementing as a military consultant to Che Guevara decades earlier.

Vladi's hands were bound behind his back, and they led him out of the courtroom to await his appointment at "El Paredón."

THE LETTER

One of Marco's office aides brought to him the translated copy of a letter delivered that morning via the courier, along with the original. The envelope bore quite a few stamps and labels along with a Russian postmark. By all appearances, this letter had been months finding its way to its intended recipient. Finally in Marco's hands, he studied the handwriting on the front. "Well, well," he said aloud to himself with a bit of a smirk before opening and reading the message within.

Greetings to Marco Rivera,

My name is Olga Gavrilova. My brother, Lt. Col. Vladislav Gavrilov, was assigned to service in Cuba many years ago. His plane was lost on its return home in October of 1961. Neither the wreckage nor remains of my brother were ever recovered.

As time went by and other members of his unit returned home to their families, naturally, we asked many questions concerning his fate. Some men said that you and Vladi, as we called him, were comrades. It is my hope that you can provide further insight to bring us closure with respect to his disappearance.

Being that you knew our dear Vladi well during his months with you, no doubt you have shared in our loss. We treasured our joyful times growing up together. He was a protective older brother — and genuinely caring. I felt proud of him. All these years later, it brings me pleasure to speak of him despite the sadness.

His wife, Irina, has remained with me to this day. I helped her care for their daughters, grown now, and one more child. Upon hearing the report that Vladi's plane vanished, his distraught wife went into labor, giving birth to a son — his name is Aleksander. The father he has never known is his hero. He is so much like Vladi, it is amazing to see how much they are alike. It is almost like we have Vladi with us in a way — although bittersweet.

It may seem peculiar to you to know that I still pray for Vladi — I pray for his life and more for his soul — and I will do so until we have confirmation that he did perish. He always disapproved of my faith, but I have confidence that God is with him as much as for us here. If you were to be separated from a brother you love as much as I love my brother, I am confident you would understand in the same way.

If you have knowledge of other details that can be shared with his family, even if it is to confirm his demise, please let us know.

Regards,

Olga Gavrilova

Marco leaned back in his chair. He read back through the letter and focused on one word — comrades. Giving it a snide chuckle, *Comrades? I don't know that I would ever say that,* he reflected sardonically. *Who would claim to be the comrade of a convicted traitor?*

Yet, upon a little more reflection, Marco's memory returned to their younger days when he and Vladi would meet and banter. *Those verbal spars never felt malicious. Mostly, things were amicable back then. Maybe our little debates were amusing in a way, because we both enjoyed needling each other.*

Marco laughed to himself and shook his head. *I did much prefer when at least our most fundamental ideologies lined up, even if we had different opinions about the details. But then he turned to the other side and became a greedy capitalist pig and worked his servants on his plantation, then called it "helping them."*

Marco's mood grew darker. *If Vladi loved his family so much, why wouldn't he have done everything he could to return to them?* He had a family who loved him back in Russia, *yet he carried on with his life as though they were not important.* No, he had been too busy *making himself rich in America to think about them anymore!*

Despite the venom inside of him, the letter caused Marco to feel conflicted. On the one hand, Marco despised Vladi. His conviction appeased Marco's pathological hatred for his former "friend." Marco resented that anyone cared about Vladi. In his mind, Vladi didn't deserve to be loved. *If only his dear sister knew what kind of man her brother had become,* he sneered — *what kind of traitor.*

On the other hand, something about Olga's plea caused a slight pang to gnaw at Marco. It might have even bothered him more if he had not closed off his conscience. This sister was to Vladi as Julio was to him. There was no denying that Marco missed Julio very much — it made his heart ache. How would he feel if someone had terrible things to reveal about his brother if he died? Would he want to know all about his brother's disgraceful offenses, or would Marco prefer to remember Julio with a halo around his righteous head?

Marco lamented that nothing he could do would bring Julio back to his side. Years of regret over his own stupid decision to leave Cuba in the first place consumed Marco. The whole ordeal was a mistake that had resulted in their separation, maybe forever.

Shaking his feelings aside, Marco consoled himself that he was a revealer of truths. *It is, after all, my job to uncover and expose the truth* — *is it not?*

With that thought, Vladi had a whole other side that Marco felt begged to be exposed, a lurid dark side he had a cruel itch to reveal to anyone who could have loved Vladi. *Perhaps this sister should know the truth about her brother rather than live revering a lie. Vladi will die as a convicted traitor, and I would rather he not die as an honorable Russian soldier in her mind.* Marco felt that was the "right thing" to do.

It wouldn't be kind to her to hide the truth about the sort of person Vladi has become, Marco continued in his twisted reasoning. *If she knows all the despicable things he has done, she may realize that he deserved to die. It might ease her pain.*

Marco took up his pen to write it all out for Olga, Irina, and Vladi's children to read, but when his pen hit the paper, he stopped. He straightened up and dropped his pen onto the desk, then he leaned back with his hands behind his head and reconsidered.

It is the truth that Vladi is alive — at least for now. Once his sentence is carried out, his life will be erased. So what obligation should I feel to respond to this letter? What information do I owe anyone? With that, he determined he would not act on Olga's plea and placed the letter in his desk, unanswered. As was the way in Cuba, many things were to remain in darkness.

47

GHOST FROM THE PAST

Along the Malecón seawall on the north side of Havana, Marco was on his customary walk home. This had been Marco's daily escape since the time he was a young man. Without thinking, he gently combed through his sideburns with his fingers. He sensed middle-age fading as his black hairs turned gray.

His walk this evening was later than usual, and it was a moonless night, but he could still make out the faded wash of pastel buildings that bordered the long, gray seawall. The rhythmic crash of the waves lulled his senses as they rolled onto the rocks. In this setting, his mind was free to drift, and it did — like a leaf upon the water, carried into deeper thought and reflection.

What a long day. The pressure of this heavy caseload from the provincial court of La Habana is such a strain. And the Gavrilov trial just adds a mountain of administrative work.

As Marco proceeded along his walk, the temperature fell considerably — much colder than usual, near 50° Fahrenheit. A stiff wind swept across the esplanade, scudding paper across the ground and raising great waves that leapt over the wall of the Malecón.

But justice is finally being served, Marco thought with satisfaction. He wouldn't have admitted, even to himself, that he hated Vladi — that he had settled a score. That he had the final word in a rivalry that had begun during their younger years.

No, Marco persisted in his icy rationalizations that he had just done what he needed to ensure justice. *Vladi was a capitalist oppressor who betrayed his people and his ideals. He enticed others to break the law and defect to America. His self-serving trafficking scheme didn't deliver the freedom and prosperity which defectors hoped for, but entrapped them in a form of indentured servitude in the least desirable conditions America offered. Everything is on his own head.*

In doing so, Cuban families were separated. It was this point that stung Marco most. He sorely missed Julio. From Marco's perspective, they were only separated as a direct consequence of Vladi's malfeasance.

"Would you wish to receive the kindness of Señor Moisés?" a calm voice called out from the shadows.

Marco jumped, startled. He swung around, searching for the source of the voice. Panic surged through his body like an electric jolt — he couldn't think! The question made his blood run cold. Was this some form of a rhetorical question to tease out a response, or did this unseen speaker somehow not know that Vladi had been sentenced to die?

Is it a trap? I can pretend I didn't hear. Marco struggled to determine how to react. If the confrontation was an ambush, should he challenge this person? *Should I run? But where?* His eyes darted about, searching for an escape route.

This was like déjà vu. The same type of encounter Marco had experienced decades before — the one that led to their odyssey. An unsettling eeriness washed over Marco. He felt transported back in time.

Was this the same deceiver from years ago? Marco wondered at such an astounding possibility. *This human trafficking racket is about to be shut down. Why would he still be soliciting on behalf of a traitorous kingpin, soon to be executed? Does he know who I am?*

Marco couldn't sort through the possibilities. It was impossible to analyze in the moment. His mind seized up.

With no time to weigh the optimal response, Marco fell to his intuition. He feigned ignorance.

"Who is this Señor Moisés?" The nervous timbre of his voice betrayed his brave act.

"I think you know him," a calm voice replied. Marco squinted and jutted his head forward, but the night was too black to determine from where the voice emanated.

Marco tried to buy time to determine how to handle the surprise confrontation. He had a sudden, disquieting thought. *If Vladi has agents who work for him in Cuba, they might have tracked me to corner me alone when I am most vulnerable. Could they know about Vladi's circumstances and seek to avenge him?* Marco feared the worst.

He gathered his wits enough to formulate another reply that would not expose his knowledge of Señor Moisés. "Why do you ask?"

There was no response.

The tables were turned on the former *Inquisitor*. Marco was accustomed to being the interrogator and the judge, not the subject of interrogation. Filled with angry frustration, Marco pivoted to an offensive angle. Summoning his most authoritative voice, he broke his silence.

"Your Señor Moisés is a convicted criminal. What is your association with him?"

No answer.

Marco's desperation heightened — he needed to make sense of the situation. Then it occurred to him, *It must have been the letter — someone must have found Olga's letter in my desk! If it were my superiors, they would have approached me directly.* Marco's eyes drifted to the left, and his head lowered a brief moment as he tried to work it out in his mind.

A list of alternative possibilities flashed before him: his office aide, the translator, the military courier. *Who is the treacherous mole in my office?* He pondered the question indignantly, with combined outrage and fear.

"Why does your conscience trouble you, Juez Rivera?"

Indeed, Marco felt as though a noose were tightening around his conscience. His nervousness escalated toward panic. It was clear that this person knew his identity and his status as a judge.

"Who are you?" Marco demanded sternly. "Step out and show me your face!"

The man answered without hesitation. "I am Acheros."

Marco's face fell at the mention of the name. *Him? Not possible!*

"And what exactly is your business with me, Acheros?" Marco probed, spitting out the name through clenched teeth.

Apparently, this stranger understood the connection that existed between Marco and Vladi.

"Have you and your Señor Moisés not taken enough from me?" Marco continued shouting into the shadows. "You may be fooled by him, but I am not. He is no deliverer. He betrays his people. He is condemned, and he will be punished under the law for his crimes. You too will be arrested and charged. You will be tried and face justice as his accomplice!"

"And what will be your defense, Juez Rivera?"

Marco's gut spasmed. He realized this person, calling himself Acheros, knew the situation. One way or another, this man had to be silenced, Marco resolved. Perhaps he could be bribed to keep quiet for now, at least until Marco could contrive a way of muting any possibility of him ever testifying.

"Perhaps we can come to an amicable proposition, Señor Acheros." Marco turned to a more respectful tone. "Let's have a talk. In consideration of your cooperation, I can ensure your safety, and perhaps even an improvement in your welfare."

Silence.

Marco's rage returned in a flash. He immediately reneged and withdrew his offer.

"I offered you lenience, and yet you dare to refuse it to your own detriment. Well, that is your choice then! Fool that you are, silence is its own answer!" Marco shouted into the night. "You will pay the price as well!"

Still, silence.

Unnerved by the eerie hush and overwhelmed with anxious dread, Marco fled into the dark.

BLOOD ORANGES

Mail service to Cuba was limited, to say the least. Due to the ongoing embargo and sanctions, no postal service existed between Cuba and the United States. However, mail routed through Canada or Mexico could occasionally find its way to the island.

If anything was to be delivered, it often showed up on Friday afternoon. But, this was Wednesday. In the middle of the week, one express parcel from Mexico was carried to the office of Juez Rivera.

Marco eyed the package on his desk, then proceeded to open it with caution. Ever since his encounter with Acheros, he had been on edge and paranoid about being watched. He suspected that Acheros, whoever he was, or someone close to this person had been keeping tabs on him since he ran off the other night, but he had no further encounters to confirm this. He had to be careful whom he trusted.

After gingerly opening the package, he moved aside the packing material and inspected the contents. What he found in the package caused him to grow quiet. This was most unexpected.

What is this about? he wondered. Staring back at him in all their brilliance and color were oranges — and not just any oranges, but the particular sweet strain of blood oranges he and Julio had cultivated in Vladi's citrus groves.

The fruit was not alone. The enclosed letter was from Dr. Julio Rivera of Lakeland, Florida. Marco's anxious hands trembled as he unfolded the note.

My dearest brother Marco,

I hope this letter finds you well.

My family now lives in Lakeland. My dear wife and I have three children —two boys and a girl. Our eldest favors his uncle. He is our little Marco. I so wish you were here with us to know them and share a part in their lives. Señor Vladi provided support through medical certification, so I am a physician once again here in Florida. Our Lord has been good to us.

For some years I have wanted you to know that while you are missed, I do not resent your decision to return without me. You can know that whatever sense of disappointment I felt, I have forgiven you.

One of my patients, a recent immigrant, told me that you are safe and even a magistrate in Cuba now. I am not surprised. You have always cared for the law and for what is right.

You have the aptitude to be a good judge. That is a greater responsibility than I would wish to bear. We know there is no perfect justice in this world. I only know on the authority of Scripture that mercy triumphs over judgment —it is the merciful who receive mercy from God, and people who know they need mercy are merciful themselves. It will only be in a New Heaven and a New Earth where Christ Jesus reigns supreme that we will know perfect justice.

A day never passes without wishing you were here to share a moment or a conversation. More so, there are thoughts on my mind that my own soul is compelled to tell you because I love you and care for your spiritual well-being above all else.

Christ Jesus alone has the authority to forgive sins. Not only does He have the authority, but He gave His life to legitimately secure forgiveness and God's perfect justice. The essential truth of God's Word is that His Son lived the righteous life that we cannot, however much we may try. This is grace. Our own good efforts are less than nothing in comparison, brother. To have God's forgiveness, you too must turn to Christ Jesus and follow Him as your

Lord and King.

If anyone should understand mercy, it is the one who has been shown mercy. I have hope now and forever because Christ Jesus is the Lamb without blemish, sacrificed in my place to satisfy the justice and wrath of God. Christ's mercy is for those who will trust Him. This is what I pray for you, even today, that you will come to know Him as I do.

Consider the Lord's promise . . .

"Blessed are those whose lawless deeds have been forgiven, and whose sins have been covered. Blessed is the man whose sin the Lord will not take into account."

Romans 4:7-8

Christ Jesus will not be ashamed of those He rescues, regardless of the darkness of our past. Even death for one who belongs to Christ Jesus is the doorway into His acceptance. He offers life to you. I implore you, dear brother, to lay your soul on His altar of mercy, have peace with God and know real forgiveness from the true King of Kings.

Your loving brother,
Julio

The moment Marco finished the letter, he acted on a vindictive compulsion to have a guard send one of the blood oranges to Vladi's cell. A firing squad would be assembling before dawn tomorrow morning. *This will be a fitting and proper final meal,* Marco thought, almost gleeful as he tossed one of the round fruits in his hand, like a diabolical juggler. *It's more than most convicted prisoners would receive.* He gave a subdued, cruel chuckle for his own satisfaction. *It's the least I can do for an "old comrade."* Marco knew it was another perverse jab, a reminder of Vladi's offenses against him.

Marco dispatched a courier to La Cabaña with the fruit, then he closed his office door for privacy. The contact with his brother was unexpected. He needed a moment to let it soak in. *Receiving this letter feels surreal.*

He went back and read Julio's letter again with more care, taking in every word and turning over every thought in his mind. When he finished reading, he remained upright, but all the bones seemed to melt within his body. This time he saw things in a different light.

Julio's kind words were heavy on his mind. *Julio always chose to see the best in me, even at my worst. He is such a good and kind person — so different from how I am or ever have been. I'm not worthy of his words,* Marco reflected. *If he only knew all I've done, the depth of injustices I've committed, he would never say this. He would never wish to recognize me as his brother again, much less tell me that his God loves me.*

There Marco sat, and despite his determination not to weep, the tears welled up in his eyes. His entire life, Marco had deceived himself into thinking his skewed senses had somehow ever sought justice, but it felt meaningless now — empty, even detestable. A wave of anguish and shame flooded through him.

Marco thought he was exacting justice by convicting Vladi. In reality, it was he who was condemned — found guilty by God the Holy Spirit. Marco could feel his conscience closing in on him. A question began to steal across Marco's arrogant soul, try as he might to repress what he sensed.

What if Julio is indeed right?

He had defected, then lied with forged documents to cover his crimes. This fact was irreconcilable. His past could not be rewritten. Marco was undone.

Even if no one else knew it, Marco recognized that he was guilty of the wrongdoings resulting in Vladi's conviction. What distinction was there between him and Vladi? Perhaps that was the real reason Vladi angered him so much — in him he saw his own warped reflection.

The Scripture in Julio's letter pierced his heart. Marco realized how he boasted in the law, all the while dishonoring God by breaking the law — not only the laws of mortal humanity, but God's Law.

Marco recalled a conversation years back when he was in Florida and Pastor Gerardo taught the Bible. Julio had returned with his characteristic enthusiasm, hoping Marco would take an interest in what the Bible had to say about justice. Marco pridefully feigned not paying attention. Yet when Julio read from the second chapter of Romans, the words had remained with Marco:

"Therefore you are without excuse, O man, everyone who passes judgment, for in that which you judge another, you condemn yourself; for you who judge practice the same things.

And we know that the judgment of God rightly falls upon those who practice such things.

But do you presume this, O man? — who passes judgment on those who practice such things and does the same? — that you will escape the judgment of God?

Or do you think lightly of the riches of His kindness and forbearance and patience, not knowing that the kindness of God leads you to repentance?"

Over all the years, those words had remained with Marco, walled up in the back of his mind, never allowed to break into his conscious thought. But when he read Julio's letter, the wall that cordoned off the truth crumbled.

Marco was undone — a broken man. He knew this was true. In this, he understood his hopeless state. He needed what no mortal being could offer.

Marco was gripped and overcome. Immediately, he fell to his knees and begged God for this forgiveness of which His Word spoke.

REDUCED TO NOTHING

After his trial, Vladi had been taken to a medieval-looking fortress perched atop a ridge near the mouth of the bay on the eastern side, opposite Havana. This was the Fort of Saint Charles, now known as La Cabaña.

Completed in 1774, the Spaniards built La Cabaña to defend the Port of Havana. After the revolution, it was turned into a political prison. Since Combinado del Este was operational, La Cabaña was to be decommissioned as a prison, but its deep, waterless moats were still Castro's favorite killing ground.

Vladi got out of the vehicle, hands bound, and looked up at the imposing stone fortress. He knew about its past — a history that would inspire fear in the most intrepid hearts. *Many times I've seen this place, yet I never imagined being here under these circumstances.*

He didn't get much time to look and reflect — his body was jerked forward, and he struggled to steady himself. Vladi's escorts hardly allowed him to walk uninterrupted. They pushed and shoved him, shouting insults and threats as they prodded him with the tips of their bayonets and beat him with the flat edges.

They mocked and laughed at him on his way to death row. "Traitor! So, you try to kill El Comandante. He will have the last word, fool!"

"We will show the Yankee bourgeois who is the Big Man!"

"Do your children know their father is such a loser?"

"Your wife probably has a real man at home, you coward."

Once inside the massive, ornate entry gate, they registered Vladi, whose identity had already been reduced to *Prisionero 379*. A higher-ranking officer, the man who would oversee Vladi's incarceration, joined his receiving party. To ensure he understood who was in charge, the guard flailed Vladi with a whip crafted from a dried stingray tail. Vladi sucked in his breath and winced as the tail bit into the flesh of his back.

Bloodied and in agony, Vladi was led through the complex along a cobbled street to the rear of a building. He let his mind turn away from his immediate surroundings and, instead, he thought only of Irina and the children. *Never again will I see them.* Vladi couldn't rid himself of that thought, and he could find no solace from his grief.

His feet shuffled clumsily over the gray stones, causing him to stumble on one that stuck up from the ground, surrounded by weeds. They stopped in front of a small dungeon-like block of cells. Vladi again became aware of surroundings that he recognized. Decades do not change a place like this. This was one of the enclosures designated for prisoners sentenced to death.

The guards removed Vladi's handcuffs and pushed him into the first chamber, one that adjoined a small chapel within the fortress. This place of confinement was supposed to have been part of the chapel at one time, but there was no hint of any divine connection now.

Hmph, if God exists, He must have forsaken this place and left it in the hands of the dark side.

This was where Vladi was to remain as he awaited his execution. There wasn't much of a view through the rusted bars across the stone window arches, although Vladi could see two masonry observation posts along the top of the three-foot-thick walls, where sentries with Kalashnikov PK machine guns kept continuous watch over the prison yard.

At night, the harsh, cold wind blew fiercely into those portal openings, through which Vladi watched owls as they hunted the rats that darted along the fringes of structures. The number of rodents astonished him.

After a long while on the first night, Vladi began to shiver — his nose grew numb with cold, and his ears hurt from the wind. He turned and slumped onto the hard, dirty floor of the cell. With nothing else to do, it was impossible to think of anything other than what lay ahead for him. He sat on the ground with his elbows on his bent knees, his bruised head in his hands, and contemplated his impending death. Unpleasant as it was, the activity of the trial and the subsequent transfer had provided a distraction. But now that he was sequestered in a dark cage, the grim reality of his predicament began to set in.

Over the following days, his perspective on everything started shifting. He strained to absorb the color and the last shafts of light from every sunset, unsure if it would be the final one his eyes would look upon. Within the confines of his cramped cell, he marveled at even the lowest of creatures, fascinated with the agile maneuvers of a fly and the blind but deft locomotion of an ignoble maggot.

Vladi restlessly grappled to come to terms with his powerlessness to change things beyond his control. *My life is to be extinguished, with little more thought than one might have given to blowing out a candle. One moment the flame is real, giving heat and light — to be seen and felt. The next moment it will be gone, as though I had never existed.*

His entire life, Vladi had been fearless. Nothing had changed. He faced the prospect of death with the same courage he exhibited in life. He did have regrets though. All hopes of ever seeing his lost family were crushed. This had always been the driving force behind his will to live, to carry on. It was the intense longing to be home, and somehow, to be reunited with them.

Not afraid to die, it was the finiteness of life that was so jarring. Vladi obviously understood that no one lives forever, yet he lived as though his own life might be the exception. Until now, death was something that only happened to other people.

He always thought of himself as a Soviet officer, a survivor, a fighter, a man. Surely death would spare him until the very last. But no. He understood clearly now — viscerally, with each breath in this squalid cell — that the earth on which he had spent his entire existence would continue spinning without him. It almost felt unfair that he had invested so much into this world, only now to leave everything behind. Nothing he could do would change that.

He could map the course of his life along a contentious clash between opposing beliefs — between those he was taught as a communist and those of capitalism and democracy that he learned to accept out of necessity. Now he understood the contrast between these ideologies was never so simple as a battle between what was entirely good versus absolute evil. Instead, it was an evil against a greater evil — both were the devices of corrupt men. There was a fracture in the fabric of the universe. Not every problem could be solved — not everything could be fixed.

There comes a time when old men develop doubts that rarely trouble younger men. Vladi reflected on how meaningless his ambitious military career felt now. *I was so focused on military achievement and the next promotion — absent from my family. What a waste of my life! Now, rank has no significance.*

When he thought about the surplus of wealth he had accumulated as the fruits of his business endeavors, he came to similar conclusions. What use was it to him now? His passions would soon grow cold and vanish and be forgotten. His prestige and what he'd accomplished didn't seem to amount to much. A hundred years from now, no one would remember him or even care that he'd ever lived.

Looking back, the days of hunting big Russian boars with his brother, Erik, seemed not so long ago. It was the same for his marriage to Irina and sweet moments with their once-young family before he deployed to Cuba. Then the plane crash, his business, and good times shared fishing with Dan. It all fell through his fingers like sand — everything that had ever mattered to him.

Most of all, Vladi wished he had taken the risk to reunite with his family when he had the chance. With everything else, he was a strategic thinker, but this had been a blind spot for him. Now he could see that he'd allowed a disproportionate sense of paranoia to govern the course of his life without giving thought to the consequences of those choices. A better day would come, he always reasoned, if he waited until tomorrow. But tomorrow was now today. And today might well be his last.

Now he wondered, *What if my family was always waiting there for me the whole time? I had been too careful, and the fate I tried to avoid happened anyway. Sure, there were risks, but they were risks I would have taken if I could have foreseen these circumstances. I would rather have come to this end fighting to be with my family, not living to remain safe!* In hindsight, there had been nothing to lose.

For his entire existence, Vladi had resilience on his side. Odd as it seemed, Vladi never expected he would die when their plane plunged into the Atlantic. He never gave up hope that he would live. An innate sense that he was a survivor flowed through him like the blood in his veins — at least it always had up till now.

When the great freeze devastated his citrus groves, it was a setback that could be offset by prospects of eventual recovery. Even when he was attacked in the orchard, death hardly felt imminent. Indeed, that had caught him off guard, but eventually he had been able to heal, and life had returned to its course. But this time . . . this time would be real. He felt it on an instinctual level, like the cold chill in his cell seeping into him. This was it.

The brevity of life surprised him. He didn't feel like he was done — there was more to see, to hear, and to do. *It has gone by so quickly — the end has come much sooner than I anticipated.* One day had followed another, and weeks had turned into months, and months into years. Now he wasn't sure of what, if anything, lay beyond.

For decades, Vladi had busied himself in futile efforts to mitigate the pain of separation from his family and as a diversion to avoid the ultimate questions about his mortality. There was no more avoiding the reality of personal death. The façade of scientific atheism, behind which he had hidden for so long, now looked ridiculous. So-called rational thinking was no longer enough for meeting death head-on. It was anything but assuring or even logical. His inner man was naked and exposed, and he knew it to be so.

For the first time in his life, he pondered questions like, *If there is a God, why did He preserve my life in the past, but not this time?*

Vladi's conscience tormented him. He felt compelled to question things he thought were settled matters.

If heaven and hell are real, how can I be sure about the outcome of any judgment?

Surely, if God is good, His justice is more trustworthy than a Cuban tribunal.

How good is good enough? How bad is too bad? How does He judge?

There were those conversations with Julio — Vladi now regretted his uncharitable disposition. Oh, how Vladi wished he had cared enough at the time to listen better. He also regretted being dismissive of his sister, Olga, when she spoke incessantly about the Bible and how she knew God guided her although she did not audibly hear His voice. Oh, how he yearned to hear from her God now.

A guard came by, disrupting his thoughts. The man surprised Vladi when he passed an orange through the bars of the cell.

Vladi tentatively took hold of it. "What is this?"

"Looks like an orange." The guard stated the obvious, missing the relevance of Vladi's question. Why had the guard given him an orange?

Vladi was in desperate need of food. As soon as the guard turned, he tore the peel off the fruit, revealing a deep red pulp. He had only once before savored anything so ordinary as an orange. More astonishing, the variety was a blood orange, exactly like those that were cultivated to supply his needs all those years.

Then he recalled the last thing Julio told him. "Vladi, you know in your heart of the sin in your own life — we all know this about ourselves. There is forgiveness available to you on account of the blood sacrifice of Christ Jesus alone. That is the only way to God."

Julio's words began to bore into his skull. It was the blood — not just any blood, but that of God's sacrifice for him, His own Son. Vladi understood, and he believed.

He heard no audible voice, yet he knew God had impressed something onto his heart as clearly as if God the Holy Spirit had actually called out to him, "Can you hear Me now, son?"

Vladi could now see the truth that Olga knew and that Julio spoke of. He had no doubt that it was all true. The God he'd denied was alive, and in Him was life itself. It was futile to think otherwise. This was the God who rightfully governed all of creation, and from Him all men must take their orders. If the world belonged to Him, it logically followed that Vladi did as well. Not just Olga or Julio's God, but also Vladi's. He had called Vladi to trust His Son who had been slain as a sacrifice in his place. But why? Vladi knew himself to be unworthy. He fell on his face, prostrate on the pitted floor of his squalid cell.

"Oh God. Oh God. You love me — why? The life You have given me is squandered. I would do whatever it takes to know You, but I have nothing. Nothing to offer. I am empty-handed. Please, oh please receive me. I will be the lowliest in Your Kingdom — even a slave — only do not cast me out. Forgive me . . . Oh God . . . forgive."

Vladi wept. Cleansed through and through by the blood of Christ Jesus, relief flooded his soul — beyond anything he'd ever understood. Thoughts of the God with whom Vladi was at peace filled his head. Despite the discomfort of the tiny cell with its cold stone floor pocked with holes, Vladi drifted off into a deep sleep.

50

THE DREAM

Vladi was sure he was dreaming, but it was all so real. He was flying on a Tupolev TU-204 airliner, Aeroflot 379, from Havana to Leningrad.

He couldn't recall the sequence of events that put him here. Everything was a muddy jumble that he couldn't quite decipher.

As the stewardess served breakfast with a garnish of sliced orange, Vladi questioned why she addressed him as "Gospodin Rivera," a formal Russian salutation for Mister Rivera.

"*Prostite*," she apologized. "I should have observed your title — Sud'ya. A judge. Do you prefer to be addressed as *Sud'ya Rivera?*"

Vladi did not answer. His face revealed his confusion.

"*Vse horosho?* Are you well?" she asked.

"*Prostite menya*," he spoke barely above his breath, "The name?"

The stewardess became more concerned that she had offended him. She attempted to clarify. "Our flight manifest indicates that you are 'Sud'ya Marco Rivera.' You may say how you prefer to be addressed."

"It does not matter," he replied in a weak voice uncharacteristic of the robust Russian.

Vladi was bewildered. He leaned back and closed his eyes, detached from the conversation, wondering if he was really on the plane.

People were conversing around him, but Vladi only heard muffled voices. He felt so disengaged. He touched his arm and then his face and wondered, *Am I even in my own body?* Yet his movements and thoughts were still wholly in his control.

Why does everything feel like a dream, though? I feel like I am not real — a dream when I am awake.

His rational mind was working completely fine. Thoughts like these shouldn't be in his head, but his emotions and physical sensations didn't match up — they felt removed — disconnected from his surroundings.

His perception of distance and time seemed to change — time was ephemeral, like in a time-lapse. There were gaps and distortions that jumped from one moment to another.

Am I dead? Am I going crazy? I feel like I am not real! His rational brain was desperately trying to find an explanation. *Am I in a coma? Am I dreaming, yet cannot wake up?* His mind could not produce the answer.

He knew he couldn't really be awake or perhaps even alive when, out of habit, he reached into his pocket for his watch and found cold metal. He wrapped his fingers around it and traced its familiar shape. He was almost afraid to pull it out in case it wasn't really there. But it was. He turned it over in his hand before opening it to find the familiar face. The ticking seemed louder than ever. His pocket watch.

How did this come to be in my pocket? He recalled the greedy delight on the face of the Cuban officer he only remembered as El Gordo as the man had closed his pudgy fingers around it. And yet here it was. *This has to be a dream!*

He searched through his ticket jacket for some clue as to his destination. There, he discovered a neatly folded note. Even more unexpected, it was from Marco Rivera:

> *I wish that I could be there so you can know my humble state without any doubt. And I would like to hear you say to me in person that you will forgive me. However impossible that may be, I will choose to think that someday you will find a way to do so.*
>
> *My name is on your documents. To transport you home in any other way would have been exceedingly difficult and would have taken months or years, if at all. We do not have another lifetime to wait. I would not expect the Soviet government to be understanding if you needed to explain how you got here and where you have been for the past three decades. I had a spare passport — picked it up in Jamaica a while back. It's a long story. Your passport photo came from a Ministry of the Interior file opened when you were taken into custody. Remember, your name is Marco Rivera until you make it to your destination.*
>
> *Did you find my little gift? The processing officer at Combinado del Este had been caught pilfering. After a few leading questions from an old Inquisitor, he confessed that it had belonged to "the Russian." I exercised my authority and claimed it for myself. I thought about keeping it as a memento of a formidable opponent, but this belongs to you. That is what is right.*
>
> *You are finally going home to Irina and your family. It is my hope that you find them well and that this part of your life is good together. There will surely be great joy in coming to know your son after so many years.*

Vladi gazed into the glass face of the precious timepiece, realizing that the true gift was not just the watch, but time itself.

Vladi let the note slowly slip from his hand. He stared forward in a daze. *Marco? No way. It is a dream. It is not possible.* He almost laughed, but then another thought suddenly registered like a bolt of lightning. He grabbed the paper from his leg and read it again closely.

"A son!" Vladi repeated to himself, breathing harder, his heart bursting. *A son! How could Marco know?* If this were a dream, Vladi hoped to remain in it. He wept tears of happiness.

EL PAREDÓN . . .
"THE WALL"

Vladi slept so restfully on the stone floor that the rattling keys of the guards unlocking his cell was the first thing he heard that morning.

"Looks like you were sound asleep," remarked one guard. "Usually, they're up all through the night before."

"What day is it?"

"November 22nd. Thursday. Must be your lucky day," the guard divulged with a sarcastic bite. "It looks like your appointment with the devil has been delayed."

"Do not sound so disappointed," retorted Vladi.

"And you don't get too comfortable. I hear it's just an administrative hold up," he informed Vladi with perverse delight. "The afternoon shift will probably come for you. Meanwhile, any last meal requests? Maybe some bacon and eggs? Steak? Some pie? I'll ask if the chef can fix you up something special."

When lunchtime came, the same guard reappeared. "I'm sorry," he said in a tone that didn't denote an ounce of remorse. "The chef reported they're all out of steak and pie. They only had 'sawdust soup' today. He felt awful, so he threw in an extra helping for you." The guard sneered, tossing the meal at Vladi's feet. The paltry cup clattered when it hit the ground.

Vladi was not disappointed, but the guard's cruel humor didn't escape him. However, he didn't allow himself to become angered. Vladi just considered it pitiful that this peon was so insensitive. *He must have a miserable life.*

The temptation to feel bitter was there, but Vladi never expected the guards to be more commiserative. *What should I expect? They give no award for common dignity or humane treatment in a Cuban prison.*

The guards came late in the day, motioning for him to get up. Without a word, Vladi was taken out of the cell, and his hands were bound with a thin rope. He grimaced as the guard pulled it cruelly tight so that it cut into his skin.

They marched him outside along a cobblestone route he hadn't seen since his arrival at La Cabaña. *Such a pity for this to be the last path my feet ever touch,* Vladi thought as he traversed the uneven terrain.

The distance wasn't a far walk — Vladi knew the way. His eyes captured the beauty of the moss and other greenery that grew through the sun-bleached stones of the high wall that rose up on one side. Guards' eyes and guns followed him from atop the wall.

They turned the corner. The cobblestones that led toward an ornamental archway leveled out. His feet were already aching from walking barefoot, and his hands were becoming numb from the tight ropes. Vladi stared straight ahead at the sculptured lion heads of sentinels atop stone columns. He studied the ornate oval seal they dutifully guarded at the apex of the arch between them. Vladi held his head high with dignity along the way, although the guards pushed his head back down. Each time, he lifted it back up in defiance to resume his posture.

What can they do, kill me? he reasoned, retaining a hint of his Russian wit.

They continued through the thick archway into a courtyard. Wide doorways lined one wall, a manifold of entryways that led to all manner of unspeakable horrors. The entrances were ornamented with medieval-style portcullises whose half-raised toothy bottoms looked like they were waiting to devour some poor soul.

Vladi knew the guards were making a point to guide him on a course that passed in front of portraits of Fidel and Raúl Castro, as though to get in one last jab. Vladi refused to turn his eyes to look upon them. He didn't want to give them even the smallest satisfaction.

A long, steep stairway of stone steps, worn and eroded by two centuries of tropical rainfall, led down into a dry moat. Stone walls two stories deep surrounded a grassy area at the bottom. La Cabaña's moats were never filled with water but were functional in the design of the original fort as a barrier against invasion. If any attacker breached one wall, they were confined to a kill box before they could complete an incursion.

They descended the worn steps toward the riddled wooden stake that stood a few meters from a wall of sandbags, where other prisoners waited. El Paredón . . . They had finally arrived. Vladi's eyes fixed on the stake. Dark stains of blood blotted the grain of the timber.

To be the subject of an execution was dreadful, but what made the ordeal worse was that prisoners were required to wait in line in view of the firing squad so that they had to witness each man before them being gunned down.

The protocol called for the convicted prisoner to be positioned downrange. The name and the number of the condemned were called out to confirm the identification of the correct prisoner before they blindfolded him.

Next, the death warrant was unsealed, and the charges were read aloud. Immediately following, the assembled marksmen were summoned to attention. Once they were positioned, "Ready — aim — fire!" signaled for the discharge of the executioners' fatal volley into the prisoner's heart.

When it came time to die, who would ever want to go first? Perhaps it would have been easier to be first, though, to avoid witnessing the horror before them. Today, Vladi was the second up.

Vladi stared at the filth-stained back of the prisoner ahead of him as the guards lined them up. He couldn't help but wonder, *Has this unfortunate soul committed crimes worthy of his fate, or has he too been a victim of similar malice? It is all . . . such a waste.*

The first man turned out to be a political prisoner, despite the fact that he had never been involved in the offense in question. As Vladi surmised, he had been the victim of a vindictive sentence intended to torment adversaries with the punishment of their family members. Sadly, this was a common tactic.

He had merely been the perpetrator's relative — hardly a crime, but in the eyes of Castro's justice, that made him an associate and co-conspirator. *"This is Cuba"* was a common remark among the locals when they were at a loss for any other rational explanation. Vladi listened to the reading of the man's death warrant, feeling compassion for the man and disgust for the rotten system that had brought him here. *This is justice, no? It is offensive to any reasonable human being.*

Of course, the man's indifference toward Castro had naturally turned to defiance as his unjust prosecution escalated toward this final ghastly act. But to his executioners, he may have just as well been any other incorrigible counter-revolutionary. Vladi figured they had perfected their rationalization.

Officers turned a deaf ear to the man's protests of innocence. "You must stop! I've done nothing!" Most of the guards had heard similar words so many times before — shrieks and howls of rage and sadness — that it didn't affect them anymore.

The man put up a struggle and had to be forcibly restrained by several guards. His pleas for mercy were frantic and pitiable, "Please! My wife! My children need me! Let an innocent man go back to his family!"

Vladi closed his eyes, finding it increasingly difficult to watch the pathetic scene unfolding before him, to listen to this. The man wailed in terror before they gagged him.

It had become a common practice to gag the condemned. The officers did so to prevent any last bold outcries, such as a declaration that Christ is King or "*Viva Cuba Libre!*" A final defiant shout against Castro and communism.

"Firing squad, attention!" the captain of the guard called out.

The marksmen raised their rifles. "Ready — aim — fire!"

The ragged crash of carbines produced a deafening thunder that echoed along the walls of the moat. And just like that, it was done.

The captain approached the limp prisoner and administered a *coup de grâce* — a bullet behind the ear, splattering brains and blood from his head.

The guards untied the prisoner's dead body from the stake, dripping in fresh blood, and transferred the corpse to a rough pine box. Blows from the hammers that nailed the lid on a wooden coffin echoed around the stone walls of the moat.

Vladi took in the nightmarish scene — intensely conscious of every sound and motion of everyone present in the moat. *This is Castro's slaughterhouse*, he thought. Now, the moment had arrived. This was it. Ever-courageous, he remained calm and cooperative. They would not need to gag him to keep him from wailing or begging for his life. He was resolved to go with dignity.

The guards jerked on his rope, pulling him to the stake to take the dead prisoner's place. At least a few of them seemed to have their own consciences troubled by this gruesome act. As their eyes met, Vladi could almost see it in the eyes of one of the officers who shoved him against the stake. The man quickly turned his head so as to avert his look. They pulled a rope tight around his waist.

"*Prisionero 379* — Vladislav Gavrilov," the commanding officer called. The last glimpse of light passed through Vladi's eyes, and the world went dark as an officer tied a blindfold around his head. He became acutely aware of the warm blood seeping between his toes as he stood in the same spot where a man had been ruthlessly put to death only moments before. Now his would be the same fate.

Everything felt unreal to Vladi. *This cannot be happening*, he thought, but he knew it was happening. Perhaps it was being blindfolded down in the moat, or perhaps it was his light-headedness, but his perception of sound was fading in and out — his sense of near and far becoming an auditory mishmash. The officers talked between themselves, but he couldn't discern their conversation.

One particular sound that came from a distance caught Vladi's attention. It was that of a UAZ-469, a Soviet-made military "jeep." He hadn't heard one in years, but it was so familiar that Vladi would have recognized it anywhere. He would never have anticipated that purring motor, which sounded like it was racing along the rim of the moat, would be one of the last sounds he would ever hear. It was a peculiar distraction under the circumstances, combined with the raised voice of a clamorous driver repeatedly blaring the horn and shouting for the *capitán*. Vladi supposed that an execution should be a more solemn moment.

The hardened captain of the guard grew annoyed at the distraction, but he was determined to proceed so they could all get this over and call it a day. He unsealed the death warrant to read the charges, then . . . nothing.

A breathless courier careened down the steep staircase into the moat and rolled onto the ground as he missed the last several steps.

The impatient captain grew more agitated. "State your name and your business!"

The wheezing courier could hardly get an answer out as he struggled to catch his breath. "I am Acheros, señor . . . " and then finished with a half-breath: "Open . . . dispatch, *capitán!*"

Vladi could hear a conversation up range, but the blindfold covered his ears, and he couldn't make out what was being said. He had never expected to feel eagerness to die, but this tortured the mind.

Vladi sensed the guards approaching him again. The captain of the guard gave an immediate order to remove the blindfold, unbind, and release the prisoner. Vladi blinked in the light as his eyes were uncovered. He tried to understand what was happening.

The captain called the guard to attention and read the dispatch aloud within the hearing of all present:

"Be it known that this day, the 22nd day of November 1990, this Revolutionary Court, having previously found that the initial sentence of death for Prisionero 379, also known as Vladislav Gavrilov, was both necessary and instructive to the formation of the people's respect for socialist legality and which would justly serve the interests of the Communist Party of Cuba, now decrees that this sentence is to be vacated.

"The Revolutionary Court grants this clemency for Prisionero 379, also known as Vladislav Gavrilov, not as an admission of any irregularity, compromise, or mistake on the part of the Revolutionary Court, whose initial sentence was appropriate, just, and without error, but solely as a matter of grace extended to the Prisionero, such grace consistent with the noble spirit of the Revolution and the Communist Party of Cuba.

"The Revolutionary Court, in accordance with the purposes of the Party and in the spirit of the Revolution, now grants a FULL PARDON to Prisionero 379, also known as Vladislav Gavrilov.

Signed this day,
Juez Marco Rivera, Magistrate
República de Cuba
Eres perdonado.
You are forgiven."

AUTHOR'S NOTE

THE PARDON followed the stories of Vladi and Marco over three decades. The courses of their lives turned in ways they hadn't planned, nor were they ultimately in control of what happened to them — their future, their fate. We observed the eroding effects of sin, and how pride wore away at their lives. We saw how Satan divides friends, and how God reconciles enemies. Most crucially, God reconciles those who were once His enemies to Himself.

While the tale is fixated on these two men, the true heroes were the bearers of truth and genuine faith — their siblings and a faithful shepherd of the Lord's sheep. Pastor Gerardo was committed to the sound preaching of the Bible. The seed of God's Word was then carried forward by Julio and Olga before taking root in the lives of Vladi and Marco.

Julio and Olga persistently loved Vladi and Marco although both men held to a worldview that was destructive to themselves and others. The eternal destinies of both were effectually redirected. In the face of hostility and even in their absence, Julio and Olga pressed on in prayer and their timely, uncompromising declaration of the gospel. These secondary characters behind the scenes were the means by which Vladi and Marco would encounter Christ Jesus and find redemption through Him. Often, that is the way it is in real life.

I hope you enjoyed reading the story as much as I enjoyed writing it. It was a story worth telling, and it is wholesome, which is better than being unwholesome. Even so, I want to leave you with a disclaimer.

Media like this is never a substitute for a faithful pastor's preaching from the pulpit of a healthy local church of which you are a member. Not a word of fiction ever saved anyone, although I've hoped to point readers to the ultimate nonfiction of the One who does save, that is Christ Jesus alone.

A novel, a movie, a clever illustration from the mind of any fallen man invariably comes up short. However good the story, the commentary, the song, or the poem, it's not where we meet our great Savior. He is always present in the Bible, the very words of God Himself. Unlike a fiction novel, God's Word is inspired, inerrant, and infallible. It is truth that is always trustworthy — more trustworthy than anything else we can know. Therein is everything He has told us of Himself. It's the only way we know Him in a saving way.

In closing, I encourage you to look to our sole source of hope, the Person and all-sufficient work of God the Son, as revealed in the pages of the sixty-six books of the Bible. It is a matter too weighty to neglect one's soul and those of our loved ones — it's either eternity in the accepting presence of God or an unthinkable eternity of His wrath without hope.

This is our time for humble submission to the Lord — now and forever. In doing so, we'll realize that our story has always been about Him. In Him, we have the trustworthy promise that when we reach the end of the story in Christ Jesus — all who belong to Him will assuredly receive . . . THE PARDON.

Rodney POWELL

THIS STORY CONTINUES IN . . .

THE

RANSOM

A PROFOUNDLY SATISFYING SEQUEL TO

THE PARDON